Rebuking The New World Order

Book & Newsletter Ordering Information

Individual copies of the book **Rebuking The New World Order** are **$15.00**. *For ten or more books, copies are just $7.00 each.* We encourage you to buy the books in quantities to pass them out to friends, relatives, and strangers! Please ask your bookstores to carry the books! Thanks.

At this time, you may also place orders for the book **In The Wake of Michael**, the **sequel** to the book **Rebuking The New World Order**. The pricing is the same for this book.

Yellowstone also publishes the *Newsletter* **Rebuking The New World Order** (6 times per year) and covers the approaching nefarious New World Order in light of Marian Prophecy. The cost is $25.00 per year. For each newsletter subscription, we will also ship you one free copy of the book.

Also, we publish The **Medjugorje Gazette** Newsletter (6x/year) for just $5.00 year.

Send your orders with check to:
Yellowstone Information Services, RD 2 Box 42 A, Bloomingdale, OH 43910 Phone: 740-944-1657 Fax: 944-1668
www.yellowstoneinfo.com e-mail: info@yellowstoneinfo.com

Yellowstone covers all shipping charges. *Ohio residents please add sales tax. Please visit our website for current news/events, and for additional ordering information.*

Rebuking The New World Order

Roger C. Thibault

Dedicated To Mary
<u>Coredemptrix Mediatrix Advocate</u>
Our Lady of All Nations, who once was Mary
Feast of Pentecost, May 31, 1998

Editorial Assistance provided by **Joseph Wilger, Marilyn Thibault, Thomas Thibault, Matthew Thibault**. Inspirational assistance provided by **Mary Grace Thibault**, and **Susanna Bernadette Thibault**. Additional corrections **by Mark Northrop**.

About The Author

Roger Thibault is a Purdue University graduate and former Dupont Engineer. He has been the president of Yellowstone Information Services since 1986. He is married, with four children - so far!

Yellowstone Information Services
RD 2 Box 42 A
Bloomingdale, OH 43910 Phone: 740-944-1657 Fax: 1668
www.yellowstoneinfo.com e-mail: info@yellowstoneinfo.com

Acknowledgements

A special thanks for feedback, comments, and assistance to my wife **Marilyn, Larry Romeo, Bill Langley, Dr. Brian J. Kopp, Ron Westernik & family, Matthew Cunningham, Anna Doyle, Vera Stepto, Brian & Vicki Scarnecchia.**

Thanks to my parents, **George & Annette Thibault**, for their love and the education they gave me. Thanks to **George & Mark Thibault** *(the world's <u>best</u> brothers)* and their wives. A special hello to my deceased sister **Mary!** To **Louis & Eleanor Windecker**, my wife's parents for their help in our lives. For all of my many website and e-mail contacts **(Jeana Davis, Rose Izzo, Nella Stevens...)** who have supported our site. For the **Medjugorje visionaries** – their many sacrifices. For our friends and relative who don't understand what this book is about. May they understand how very real it is...

For all of the *enemies* of **Our Lady of Medjugorje** who make me more determined to offer Her my support. I would be happy to die a martyr for **Our Lady of Medjugorje**.

A heartfelt thanks to **Our Lady of Medjugorje!**

Published by:
Yellowstone Information Services
RD 2 Box 42 A, Bloomingdale, OH 43910

Copyright 1998 by Roger C. Thibault

Printed In The United States of Jesus & Mary
Library of Congress Catalog Card Number: 97-091266
ISBN: 0-9661727-0-1

Rebuking The New World Order

The sun came up over Frenchman's Bay *just as if it was any other summer day*. That's exactly what Rick was thinking as he stood on the edge of the water across from the Exxon station on the outskirts of Bar Harbor, Maine. It was in fact July 2, 1998.

These people just don't get it. They have no idea what time it is, thought Rick as he bent down for a flat stone to skim it out into the bay. *They have no idea what the major worldwide events of the last few months have meant for them and their children. They read about them in the headlines and then went on to the stock quote pages. They just didn't register what they were reading. Who can blame them though, considering the doublespeak of the controlled media? The media passes on what it is told to pass on.* Rick's thoughts were on the "happy" campers rolling in from all over the country and world to Bar Harbor, Maine. They were coming in large numbers today, as in most days in July.

Rick turned around to check out his gear behind him. It was time to move his belongings back another few feet closer to the high tide mark, as the tide was heading his way. Just then a teenager threw an empty can of beer out of a car window that landed near Rick's feet. Rick couldn't believe it. He almost laughed as he looked at his watch and noticed that it was only 9 AM. He thought of Peter talking to the people at Pentecost "These people are not drunk, for it is not yet nine in the morning!" *Times have changed*, he thought. *If that kid tries that in Bar Harbor the locals won't let it pass. After all, Bar Harbor is the "save the everything" capital of the world. Of course, the environment came first, then whales, eagles, seals, and the list goes on. And then there's Gaia...*

Rick looked down at the T-shirt he was wearing that a friend had given him before he left for Bar Harbor - "Eat More Whales, Save The Baby Humans". Joe gave it to him in jail. They were cellmates. They swapped their sweaty shirts right there in jail! Joe had nothing against whales, he admired them as much as Francis of Assisi would have, but he was just trying to make a point in a world that had given new meaning to the word Pantheism.

Rick Tremont was soon to be AWOL from a meeting with a judge in Columbus, where he was just released with Joe Maclean and ten other men and women, young and old, for praying inside an abortuarium. Normally, he would have kept his date with Judge McCarthy (this was to be their third meeting), as he always kept his dates with judges, but he felt an inner call that beckoned him elsewhere.

One night, after he and Joe had just finished the Rosary in jail, he was lying down on his bunk when he heard a few words - "Bar Harbor", and "Con-teeki" – or something to that effect. Rick sat up and said "What?"

Joe raised up his head and said, "Are you talking to me?"

Rick said, "No, I thought I heard a voice."

"Great, now you're hearing voices. Don't tell the judge that! Well, what did you hear?" said Joe.

"I heard "Bar Harbor" and "Con-teeki" or something like that. And if you were Daniel you could tell me what it meant!" said Rick.

"It's obvious to me what it means," said Joe. "God is sending you on vacation to Bar Harbor, Maine. He knows you've been in jail for much of the last four years for His babies, and he's giving you some time off for good behavior!"

"Would you explain that to the judge for me Joe? Remember, by law, he's supposed to be sending us to another vacation site for a minimum of one year," said Rick.

"Well, be that as it may, I think you should talk to a priest," said Joe.

"About the voice or my vacation itinerary?" replied Rick.

"About both" said Joe.

Rick put his head back down on his pillow and in a few minutes was dreaming about moose, lobster, and the Maine coast. Seminaries, and beautiful blondes and brunettes also came in and out of focus in his mind. Rick was overcome by a burning desire to be back in the world, yet, not of the world as the saint speaks of. He was crying in his bunk now, unbeknownst to his cellmate. He didn't know how he could face another year in jail. Many of his former friends, relatives, co-workers, and associates were actually beginning to think that he was demented. On two occasions he was put in solitary confinement for such reasons. His jailers thought that his fasting and all night prayer vigils were signs of his dementia, and wanted him separated from the other prisoners. The world was now washing its hands clean of the life of the Rick Tremonts of the world. He was no Mother Teresa the world said. He was a lawbreaker. He was a nut by any other name. His own pastor had derided him from the pulpit in recent months, not by name but by description. The parish now "knew". Rick's mother told him. Rick was close to despair. *I can't stay in here any longer. Maybe it's true. Maybe I've lost it. Maybe I went too far. Maybe the judges are right...*

—Below Rick, Joe was quietly thanking God for having selected Rick Tremont to be his cellmate in the past year. The year, in prison time, was rapidly coming to a close and to perhaps blossom into another such year of prison life in recompense for similar charges and convictions relating to the first cause. Joe felt like he was in prison with Saint Anthony of Padua. In the four brief years that Joe had known Rick, in and out of prison, Rick had come to shed himself completely of the world as had Anthony. The conversions to Jesus Christ surrounding the last four years in the life of Rick Tremont were prodigious. Two doctors and two former clinic operators were amongst Rick's victims. They hated Rick at first contact. Rick had been a steel bar thrown wildly into the cogs, into the machinations that were their lives, livelihoods, and their pride. Rick caused them dreams and nightmares, through his actions and his prayers. These four had a new Master now, however. The blood on their hands and souls was washed clean by the Blood of the Lamb. All four were now evangelists for the Lamb. They owed their lives and souls to the Divine Mercy and the intercession of the young man who was now bemoaning what had become of his life.

A thousand people who had been in jail with Rick across the country were praying hard for him almost daily. He was on a fair percentage of prayer chains across the country, as one in desperate need of prayers. The saints of God know that the closer one walks with Jesus, the greater the fury of Hell that is unleashed against such pedestrians.

Joe Maclean fell off to sleep, halfway through his Chaplet of Divine Mercy.

Rick Tremont walked a tightrope beneath which was the abyss and in front of which was Heaven. The world was behind him. He felt himself tottering. Satan didn't actually have to throw Rick physically into any abyss. All he had to do was have him commit a grave sin, as the apostle to the gentiles speaks of. That would be enough, separation from God. Sin in Rick's mind, or through his actions or both. Death to the soul. Rick was perilously close to death. Yet, unknown to Rick, God had prepared a fail-safe safety net for Rick - *he would not be tested beyond his strength.* Yes, at that very moment there were many people praying for him in both the United States and Canada.

Bar Harbor? Con-teeki or whatever that word was? God, get me out of here. I'm afraid this ship is breaking up. God? Anybody home?

****

Father Charles Finnigan was not a happy camper. It was 10 PM and he had just received a call from someone at the downtown Columbus jail. The person on the other end of the phone wanted to come to confession at this hour. "Couldn't it wait for a decent hour?" said Father.

"I need help quickly Father. When do you normally hear confessions?" said the caller.

"I don't" said Father Charles.

"What?" said the caller. "Nothing" said Father Charles.

"Could I come over now Father?"

If the caller could see Father Charles's angry red face, the blood pumping through throbbing arteries like water gushing from a freshly opened fire hydrant, he would not have wanted to meet with the priest. A rush of angry phrases and thoughts passed through Father Charles' mind. He was about to slam down the phone and he burst out into the mouthpiece "absolutely..." He had fully intended to follow up with "not". In fact as the caller was thanking him, Father was wondering what had happened to the word "not". It was as if he knew he had said it, but in reality he also knew that it did not come out! The young man calling from the jail thanked Father and told him he would see him in about thirty-five to forty minutes. But Father was speechless, lost in the moment. He hung up the phone and sat down in a big recliner chair, and started gazing around the room and looking for some perhaps invisible force, like a guardian angel or something.

Father's brief respite from anger lasted about five minutes. He got up out of the recliner and headed for the rectory kitchen and put on a pot of coffee. His face was still red with anger. He was wondering why he was being treated like this. He was usually in bed by now and all of his parishioners at Saint Anthony's and everyone who knew Father Finnigan knew that he was not to receive calls after 9 PM. They just knew. Now there's a stranger that is going to be knocking on the door in a half an hour. Father Charles had a temper and he could just not control it right now. He unplugged the coffeepot and walked into the hall closet to get his windbreaker jacket. He was going to go take a ride in his Buick. He was going to make his getaway. Ten minutes had passed since the call. He was reaching for the door when there was a knock on it. He couldn't believe it as he opened the door. Twenty-eight year old Rick Tremont stood before him and continued to shock Father Charles even further.

"Hello Father, I'm Rick Tremont. I called you about fifteen minutes ago. I'm early because Officer Worrall was kind enough to give me a ride over. I thought I was going to be walking. This is Officer John Worrall of the Columbus Police Department", he said.

A man in a blue uniform stepped out from behind Rick on the narrow rectory steps and shook hands with Father Charles. "Pleased to meet you Father. I hope you don't mind me dropping by to say hello too. I heard Rick on the phone with you at the station, and I imagined what you might have been wondering about after your brief talk with him on the phone at this late hour. I just wanted to let you know that Rick was a good man, and that it was not a mass murderer freshly escaped from jail coming to visit you this evening!"

"Please come in," said Father Charles, forcing the words to his lips. He was wishing they would go away and just let him go to bed. That was not to be however.

Father Charles was about to undergo a major conversion. This Catholic priest was about to give his life and his heart to Jesus... and Mary for that matter, for the first time, forever. Before the hour was up, he would be ready for martyrdom if our Lord was to call him to it. His former life was over. No more New Age Sermons. No more pick and choose Catholicism. No more counseling that artificial birth control was O.K. for Catholics under certain circumstances. Father's ship had just come in. It was the same ship that Saint John Bosco saw in his vision. It was time to get on board.

****

Nathaniel Wellfleet once was dead. It was July 2, 1998, and he found his mind wandering back to his days before life began. He remembered the cabin on Rice Lake, owned by a religious group with their headquarters in a distant place. He had been there for over two months in 1997. He had come to them for help after a recent dark attack on his soul. He was never alone - they never left him alone, until the night of October 26, 1997. At times they had tied him to the bed. Sometimes it took five of them to do so. He fought with every fiber in his body, and then some. Yes, and then some, some unforeseen energy showed up. They and their kind had been the enemy once. He was once looking for his race to completely uproot theirs. Things had changed though, now. They finally left him alone. They were done with him. Not that he wanted them to go. They were finished with him now though, and he had taken up so much of their time. They were done with their rituals. They had others to attend to. They would drop in on him once or twice a day for a while though, to check on his progress. They had let him stay on, in the property that the group had owned. It was at his disposal. So there he found himself on the night of October 26, 1997...

He, this Nathaniel Wellfleet was from the same town as Melchisedech, at least the same town in namesake. It meant peace. Peace had finally come to Nathaniel. Nathaniel of Salem. Salem, Massachusetts. "You are a priest forever, according to the order of Melchisedech" - The words of scripture would often pass through his mind. Melchisedech was that mysterious priest of ancient times whose place in time spanned too many generations to be thought of as a mere man. It was believed by the ancients that Melchisedech was an angel of God. Such were the priest Melchisedech. For some reason, at this time in his life, Nathaniel had an affinity for this Melchisedech of Jeru-Salem. Perhaps it was that he Nathaniel, had been a priest of sorts.... Of sordid sorts... a sorcerer... a witch of ancient stock. A witch from Salem, Massachusetts. His exorcism had taken two months. He had nearly killed one priest, and injured another. Several seminarians were also injured in the process.

Yes, thirty-three year old Nathaniel Wellfleet had used up a considerable amount of the spiritual resources of the diocese of Peoria, Illinois, in the late summer and into the fall of 1997. Few knew of his exorcism, aside from the Bishop who had approved of it, the exorcist priest, five seminarians, two other priest assistants, and three groups of cloistered nuns that the Bishop had confided in for intercessory prayers for the soul of Nathaniel during the period of exorcism. It was a battle...

Nathaniel was again pondering that first night alone in the cabin last year. He remembered it clearly as if he was watching a movie in his mind. It had been a weekend to remember around the nation too. Nathaniel thought of the record snowstorm that had pelted Denver and the Great Plains. It was the fifth largest recorded snowfall in Denver. Denver was paralyzed in October! God had left his calling card on Wall Street the Monday after, too, with the largest single-day stock drop in history. It was only a test. Few had listened or passed the test. It was the first time in his life that Nathaniel realized that God was speaking. Not everyone had Nathaniel's opinion on this, however. Bill and Hillary, and their scientist bedmates had tried to blame it on El Nino. In recent weeks, Bill had been skirting around the globe pounding on doors holding up placards saying

"El Nino, Fear This!", and looking for signatures. That's all that was being spammed across newspapers, television, and Internet alike. *Fear This!* Bill and Hillary were running a flag pattern for the team - the ex-Patriots, heading for the traitorous flag of the United Nations and the One World Order, the New Age. *Fear This! Fear this collapse in the environment! In Mother Nature! We need to be one! We can't go it alone. It Takes A Village. We need signatures. We need the signatures of every leader of every former sovereign nation. We need to stop Global Warming. We need to save the world! Yes, we need to be one to fight this thing. Nature is going to initiate a great battle in the next few years! "Fear this!" taught Bill and Hillary. We need a world government to fight this, this, this thing! Fear This! Pollution is killing us! We need to penalize the wealthy west and send them back to the days of mass transportation. Too many cars for the proletariat! Too much freedom and free speech, freedom of religion. We're killing ourselves. We need the UN to impose higher tariffs on our fuel to save the world! We need to indoctrinate the kids, no immerse the kids in a sea of homosexuality - to eliminate homophobia, this disease that scientists have just discovered - taught Bill and Hillary and their ranks. We need to teach them that we have to recycle every aluminum can. We need to find every last one. The world depends on it. God, we need environmentalists today if ever we did! We need to teach the kids to hate the religion of their parents. We need to clarify their values. We need to get to them now even in pre-school. It's the New Age. We need to prepare. The world can no longer be run by homophobic politicians and dogmatic personalities. Out with the old. May the spirits protect us against El Nino!* "And can I have your signature Mr. Third World President?" *said Bill. It will help assure uninterrupted financial aid to your country, with a box of prophylactics and birth control pills in every box. You can't have the first if you don't take the latter. Did we tell you that already? Am I repeating myself? We need to be together on this. Let's get together to fight this thing. There are those above me who need this to come about. Don't think I'm here on my own. We need to fight this thing...*

El Nino - The Christ Child! Yes, Bill and Hillary, and most of us in the nation are trying to fight this El Nino, The *Christ Child thought Nathaniel. Has anybody heard of the word chastisements? Has anybody heard of the phrase 'repent and ye shall be saved'? Yes, fear of God, of El Nino, is the beginning of Wisdom. Anyone remember Nineveh? Yes, we need to fear El Nino. We need to fear offending El Nino, this Jesus Christ, with sin. Repent and ye shall be saved.* Such thoughts raced through Nathaniel's mind as he stood gazing out over Rice Lake at 2:30 in the morning. Even as a witch (Yes, in the 1990's it had become politically correct to call a warlock a witch. Warlock had such bad connotations that it was thought to be a degrading term. Unisex bewitchery was in!) Nathaniel had studied the Bible. It was good to know one's enemy. Yet, he had befriended this ancient Melchisedech, which led to his "downfall" in the eyes of ancient Salem, and led to his exorcism. God works in mysterious ways. *Thanks Mel...*

He could not sleep that night long ago, his first night as a free man - all alone! The winds that had just beaten down on the plains were rolling through Illinois on Sunday evening. The windows in the cabin were alive with creaks and wailing, droning and screeching. Something outside wanted to get in. All over Illinois and the Midwest there were winds bursting to 75 miles per hour or more in gusts. Lights were going out all over due to downed electrical wires. Well, if something wanted to get in, he would go out and meet it, armed with Jesus Christ, for the first time in his life. At two thirty AM he stepped out onto the porch. The spirits of Salem not related to Melchisedech dashed madly about wishing that they could hurl Nathaniel to his death in the near hurricane like winds, dashing him into the trees. Nathaniel was aware of the presence of Satan and his cohorts. He was not left with a spirit devoid of the knowledge of evil after his exorcism. Indeed, the exorcism brought about a keen awareness of such things for him, deep down in his soul. Another man might have fled for the covers, after turning all the lights on in the cabin. There was death everywhere about the place. Death and demons. Nathaniel smiled as he lit a cigarette, cupping his hands, and leaning back into the cabin doorway to get it lit in the raging winds. Father Davenport had tried to get him to quit smoking. Nathaniel explained to Father that it would perhaps be easier for him to have his "no-smoking" advice accepted if he himself would quit smoking...

For sure the evening sky is not pitch black everywhere in Illinois, land of Lincoln, but the skies around Rice lake, twenty five miles out into the country from Peoria were quite dark. Nathaniel was surrounded by miles of forests and sparsely spread out sprawling farms. He was surrounded by the lands of Rice Lake and Spring Lake Conservation Areas to the east, west, and north, and by Sand Ridge State Forest to the south. Between inhalations from his cigarette, Nathaniel was talking to Jesus, asking him for his protection this evening. He knew few lines of prayers, so he just conversed with Jesus Christ, his newfound Lord and Savior. He stepped off the porch and walked over to the shore of the lake. It looked like an ocean at battle. In the dark he could not see the other side of the lake, despite the mostly clear skies and starlit evening. The waves were pounding the shore. The white pines stood majestically all around him. He felt like he was home in Massachusetts, or in Maine, on one of those cold northern ponds surrounded by pines and balsam fir, void of all human presence, barring a few intrusions from seasonal hunters. The smell of the white pine was being forcibly driven into his nose by the strong winds. He felt good to be alive. His whole painful life had been worth it, if only to witness the beautiful power of God on this evening, all alone, deep in the Illinois woods. *Illinois woods? No, this must be Maine!*

All around him the winds rushed. They were fiercest closest to him. The demons continued hurling themselves at him in a tempest. They did what they could to harm him. In the end, all that they did accounted for naught. The man continued to pray. He took off his shoes and put them back up on the porch. He went back to the lake and sat down on the banks of the lake on three inches of pine needles, and stuck his feet in the lake. It reminded him of his youth in Salem, on the shore. It reminded him also of his many trips to Maine. The lake had the sound of the Atlantic surf this evening.

Nathaniel closed his eyes and thought of Jesus on the cross. He felt like he had put every one of those nails into Christ all by himself. Nathaniel was not unlike many men and women of today. If he had not recently been schooled in thought and faith otherwise in recent weeks, he would have been in despair - despairing in all hope for forgiveness from God. His despair was due to his past sins, which were prodigious, dark, and secretive. His sins had cost the lives of others. *The majority of the whitewashed, sanitized, politically correct world today is enamored with witchcraft. It is of great interest to the public at large. It needs the protection - the same protection from the dogmatic bigots that radical homosexuality, fornication, pornography, and the National Man Boy Love Association (child rapists) needs from the legal system - so thinks the wisdom of the world.* Nathaniel pondered such things as the waves crashed into his ankles.

The top of a pine tree twenty feet from Nathaniel snapped with a loud crash above him, and was blown for a hundred feet away from him, just missing the cabin. Nathaniel was startled by the incident. He was momentarily rattled. He began to talk aloud again to Jesus. He tossed his butt out into the air over the lake, where it threatened to come back into his face, with a fury of wind. He managed to somehow light another cigarette.

He began to consider all of the press that Salem, Massachusetts and its witches, past and present had been receiving in the last few days. Father Davenport had left Nathaniel with a computer and Internet connection in the cabin. Witches were everywhere on the Internet. No kidding. *The world loves a witch.* There was very little politically incorrect information about them. All of the stories were informational on what witches do and don't do, witch history, historical and present day stories about the "bigots" who don't appreciate witches, and how to become a witch. *Don't look for anything nice to be said about Christopher Columbus and the Franciscans he (Columbus) brought over in these articles. Nothing nice here about Bishop Fulton Sheen or Padre Pio. None of that bigotry here.*

Nathaniel thought of the USA EVENING national paper that Father had brought him on Friday, October 24, 1997. The headlines read "Witch Way Will Salem Go - Massachusetts city wrestles with demons - past and present". At first Nathaniel thought it was an article that exposed his former craft. No such thing. The witches of Salem, over 4,000 self-proclaimed witches were up in arms. *They were protesting the bad name that commercial witchcraftery was giving to their profession. Save the witches! "Foul!" they cried. A nation cried with them. Don't discriminate against our witches! The mayor cried! Let us have purity in our witchery! How can the city of witches stoop so low as to embrace unbridled commercialism! What tomfoolery!*

All of the articles, electronic and paper, proclaimed the glory of the occult, as if America had now come full circle to take it as its new religion. *Let us now gather to damn the judges of 1692. There, does that feel better Salem? Does that feel better America? Have we remedied the past? Let us gather in a circle and chant. There are others to damn...oh, to correct. Yes, history and people need to be corrected. Remember Salem!... Such was the media of the day!*

Yes, the media whitewashed Salem. The media whitewashed the occult. All witches were just wonderful kind people, shop owners and doctors - good working stock, every one of them. *"We're just religious people, more open and honest than the Christian bigots..."*

Nathaniel knew otherwise. *The media presented a false glamorous side of witchcraft. A better lesson would be to have everyone sit down and watch the exorcist again. THEN ask the audience whom they are going to serve. You gotta serve someone... Listen to the voice of the dark one in the Exorcist - the movie. Does the public, in love with darkness and the occult know that the voice - the wicked, cold, hot, demonic voice that came forth from the young girl was the actual voice of a real demon from Hell? Does the wayfaring public know that this voice was recorded in an actual famous exorcism? Does the country, does the world want to serve the master of the cold, frightening, darkened, shrieking voice that came forth from the young victim? Did the world really want to serve that being that scared the Hell out of the world, vomiting forth filth and treachery in this movie the Exorcist?* Nathaniel knew that not all that glitters is gold. He, Nathaniel, had come from an aristocracy of witches and warlocks. So many today had arrived at the dead end of the occult through other avenues – Ouija Boards, and other demonically inspired board and computer games. Almost every school system in the country now was encouraging the practice of the occult and witchcraft. *Sure,* thought the parents, *it was just imagination, these spirit guides and meditational games and exercises were just in the name of learning...*

The media left out the animal and human sacrifices. The masons left this out too, in their literature. Nathaniel remembered a Mason that he knew running for office. The 33rd degree Mason put down all of his Lodge affiliations right on his brochure! Nathaniel wondered if the public would have voted for him if they knew of all of the Satanic Masonic rituals and *sacrifices (including some that are best left unsaid),* that the lodge member had been a part of, and he, Nathaniel, too. There were close ties between witchcraft and Masonry, including the black Mass - the inversion of the Catholic Mass, with the desecration of the actual Eucharist. Witchcraft and Masonry had the same father, the Father of Lies.

Yes, Nathaniel knew otherwise. The witches interviewed had failed to speak of that which is only spoken of by the deeply initiated. The media failed to scour the evidence of sacrificed victims, literal dead mutilated victims, and to present a truthful view of the craft to the public. The media failed to show the connection of the occult to Masonry and politics and politicians. Ah, we would have few elected officials from their ranks, these Freemasons, if the world had known what they had done behind closed doors! But the public was not as innocent as it was sometimes made out to be. The man on the street knew the difference between good and evil. The public knew better than to believe that witches were benevolent benefactors in need of a better image. *But everyone has rights...*

Water was thrown out of Rice Lake dousing Nathaniel and putting his cigarette out. He lit another, successfully, after three minutes of doused attempts.

The winds howled. The midsection of the nation was paying dearly for the wind that evening. Thousands of homes, barns, and buildings were damaged before sunrise.

A line of witches had recently died out, sometime prior to that evening. The Wellfleet line of witches had been baptized. Nathaniel Wellfleet, last of generations of Wellfleet witches was now a Christian. He prayed and he prayed and he prayed to Jesus Christ. Should Nathaniel's story be known to men, it would give great hope to those who fear God can no longer love them because of what they have done or failed to do. Few would have the strength to hear the ghastly tales, all true, that Nathaniel Wellfleet would have to carry, locked away in his mind until Judgment Day. Yes, if men had known the secrets of Nathaniel, and believed in God's great love for him – Nathaniel, then men would never doubt God's love for every one of us, despite our most heinous crimes. All we have to do is say we're sorry, and just try. Just try.

Nathaniel prayed all throughout the morning until the break of dawn. Then he retired for a short morning nap. Father Davenport would be by this morning. Nathaniel was looking forward to his visit.

Nathaniel Wellfleet snapped back to the present – July of 1998. He was camping himself, alone on a mountain in Maine, not far from the summer resort of Bar Harbor. It had been nearly a year since his exorcism. He had lost all of his former friends in Salem, including relatives. They cursed him every night. Nathaniel battled back. Nathaniel performed his rituals and fought them. He was performing his rituals this very evening, around his campfire at 2 in the morning. He was reading his Bible. He had just finished the Chaplet of Divine Mercy. He was praying for the conversion of witches, and all those involved in the occult, especially the Masons. He prayed for those entrenched in the occult in politics that were attempting to bring about a Godless New World Order.

Yes, a long line of witches was dead. Nathaniel had just recently completed his first semester of seminary. He was on a retreat. He was told there was to be a religious conference in Acadia National Park this coming weekend. There was no place on earth where he would rather be. He was proceeding with three days of fasting and penance prior to the conference.

The flames shot up and danced before the face of Nathaniel Wellfleet as they had done a thousand times before in his former life. *To God be the glory...now, and forever, Amen,* thought Nathaniel. He was studying the book of Revelations, the Apocalypse, chapter 12 – *"And a great sign appeared in heaven: A woman clothed with the sun, and the moon under her feet, and on her head a crown of twelve stars: And being with child, she cried travailing in birth, and was in pain to be delivered..."* Nathaniel knew that the "people in darkness" had seen a great light. He knew that it was definitely not the end of the world that was approaching, as the errant tabloids and itinerant preachers had prophesied. No, the world was about to be delivered from darkness. Satan's time was running out. The world was about to see an era of peace foretold at Fatima so long ago. Yes, sin and destruction and pain abounded, as well as other minor chastisements, but there can be no resurrection without a crucifixion. Blessed days were ahead of the world. It was with great joy that Nathaniel had come to be a part of this approaching gathering. An Era of Peace was about to unfold within the next few years...

****

The *Seven Steps* pulled into The Bar Harbor dockside and dropped anchor just as Rick Tremont was dropping his bags on the grass on the knoll overlooking the public dock. By his reckoning, using the "soccer field method", Rick guessed that Seven Steps was just over a third the length of a soccer field, he put it at about 110 yards. The blue fiberglass hull and white upper decks were so glossy that it looked like the private motor yacht had not yet left the "showroom floor". In fact, the boat was completed in April of 1998. Its owner was the billionaire marketing genius from Utah, Sam Stillwater.

Sam was really Robert Smith at least until 1983 when he changed his name for marketing purposes. The product he sold was himself, or rather the seven step method for excellence that he had pioneered after reading his first book on New Age Spirituality back in 1976. He meshed that subject with bits and pieces of his Mormonism to come up with his 'business theology'. He and his current staff of over 80 "Seminar Initiator Executives" had brought the company up and over the 5 billion dollar mark in gross sales of seminars, tapes, books, pamphlets, and royalties for fiscal year 1997. Fiscal year 1998 was going to make '97 look like small potatoes.

Sam's company, Seven Steps Institute, had close ties to the world's elitist political, environmental, and financial leaders. Sam was doing everything he could to help such organizations bring about the New World Order. It was his passion. It was his paycheck. Sam regularly bought and sold, in a matter of speaking, his high ranking positions on the board of directors for large national and international companies, non-profit organizations, and political machines. Such groups included the United Nations organizations, Communications Companies, Computer Hardware and Software Companies, and other more nefarious groups like the Club of Rome and Planned Parenthood. In reality, they - these organizations and the few personages who really control things, bought Sam. Sam was expendable, a mannequin. Sam helped launder money for them. They paid their taxes to Sam, to the Seven Steps Institute, so to speak, instead of governments. Sam gave them the money back in donations. They gave him contracts to indoctrinate their employees into the club of Satan, step by step, through the 'me first, I can do anything, I AM who AM' method of tutorials. Most of the workers of the industrialized nations of the world have had such training, through the Seven Steps Institute, an affiliate, or an offshoot. You name it, time management, employee relations, contact management, account management, supervisory skills, communications skills, reorganizing and downsizing skills, international diversification training - all of the themes that the Seven Steps Institute covered were covertly laced with anti-God rationalism and even occultism. Most people would laugh at such a thought, but it was true enough.

Sam was in town for a meeting of the Environmental Worldwide Task Group (the EWTG). The EWTG had been given Burnt Porcupine Island in Frenchman's Bay by the United States in the latter part of 1997. Actually, the United Nations had taken it, but in the media the transition had all of the appearances of a generous benevolent donation on the part of the United States. Two thirds of the populace of Mount Desert Island was in an uproar over the usurping of this great jewel of Acadia National Park, this historical Burnt Porcupine Island. By summer the media had more than two thirds of the island bowing to the worldly wisdom of the EWTG and those who fed it. The environmentalists were in ecstasy to have the EWTG now claiming Bar Harbor as worldwide headquarters.

The EWTG was being positioned by the UN to oversee all environmental lawmaking and policing activity for the entire world. In some of the poorer third world countries the EWTG had already begun taking over all secular-policing activities. Such activity was not hidden from the world in several out-of-the-way places. Police station signs, police cars and uniforms were being replaced with EWTG signs and symbols, vehicles, and uniforms. To most, the EWTG was a godsend, with a small g. Salaries and overhead were now being bolstered by international money. How wonderful that the world would want to 'help our police force', thought the poor and downtrodden. The UN and the United States laughingly brushed aside the EWTG's reported involvement in detention camps and police bases that had been coming into the limelight through not the mainstream press, but the religious press in the last few years. The United States denied such facilities existed, and where it could not suppress such reports, claimed that the military was assisting in county airport developments and regional jails. Progress. That's all.

And so Sam came. He came to the dedication of the EWTG facilities.

The facilities constituted over 150,000 square feet of the most posh office space imaginable, all set up with state-of-the-art technology to help the over 200 employees (excluding maintenance and food service workers) of the EWTG now based there save the world. The press would never see two-thirds of the facilities that now housed the more secretive affairs of the organization. The sea kayakers would never return. It was stated in all park literature that the island was now off limits to park visitors. The island was now under armed surveillance due to what the UN said were many threats against the environmental policies of the UN by subversive groups throughout the world that were not environmentally friendly. It was rumored that the UN had put over a quarter of a billion dollars into the facilities on Burnt Porcupine Island. The shallow and deepwater docking facilities were capable of handling the largest of boats in the world. The salaries for the 'civilian workers' handling restaurant and maintenance duties were the best on Mount Desert Island.

Ambassadors from nearly every nation were in attendance, as well as presidents and Prime ministers of countries near and far. Sam Stillwater was to be the second speaker that evening, Thursday, the 2nd of July. Sam had signed a 100 million dollar *Seven Steps Institute* check for this, the UN's pet project, back in the fall of 1997. "My Dear fellow world citizens, friends of Mother Earth, and fellow environmentalists at arms, we have..."

****

A few months earlier, in Overlook Bluffs, Oklahoma, on the day after the major quake that rocked Los Angeles, Father Albert Green held a parish council meeting. Father began with an opening prayer, and then afterwards spoke on the reason for the meeting. "As you know, I will be in Maine for part of this summer on a working sabbatical in the Portland diocese. My initial reason for calling this meeting was to introduce you to the priest who will be with you for the summer, Father Bob Helmut. Father Bob was just called to the hospital, as his sick mother has just taken a turn for the worse. He is a native to our area. His introduction will be delayed until our next monthly meeting. He'll be joining us from the University of Dallas for a few months".

"And now", continued Father Green, "I wish that was the only reason that I had called this meeting. It was not, however. I have some grave news... there will soon be certain things that we will no longer be able to speak of openly in our church without fear of being closed down immediately. With the worldwide environmental catastrophes *(Russia, China, Northern Europe had also experience sever quakes in the same week)* that have taken place this week, there has been a hastening of what I can only now call a universal One World Government movement. Even until days ago I was scoffing at my conservative parishioners who brought me supposed news of this movement over the last few years. I thought they were uneducated idiots. I now wish I had believed. I could have used that time to prepare the parish and warn other priests. Not that we could have done much but pray. That is our most powerful weapon, however, even now. The directives that the Pope, all of our Bishops, priests, nuns and religious have received, however veiled at this time, are serious. I cannot show the directives to you at this time, for they have only been communicated to me verbally, by accident, I dare say. Let me say again that they are indeed serious".

Father continued, "As you know the quake in Los Angeles this week was a 100-year quake. The flooding in New York City this week and in much of New England as well has been specified as a 200-year flood. The world powers took immediate advantage of the weakened state of our country and our previously weakened U.S. Constitution. The United States will be long in recovering from these events, barring direct intervention from God."

All of the council members began talking in elevated voices to Father and each other. Some were yelling. Robert Davidson yelled louder than all the rest. "Father, be specific - what can't we talk about?"

"Soon we will no longer be able to mention unborn children or abortion, patriotism, or speak against divorce, contraception or birth control, and we'll no longer be able to speak against women priests and deacons - to give just a few examples. Apparently the enemy believes that there will be Judases in every parish to turn us in should we maintain orthodoxy. I have been told that in the coming months, no Mass will be said without at least one woman at the altar with the priest. Priestesses, or witches I should say, will soon be on our heels. If we do not follow these directives, we will be heavily taxed, jailed, or closed down due to violation of international treaties. Most of you know of Father Peter Jevic, who transferred over from Tulsa a half a year ago to help out our diocese. His church, Saint Margaret's in Milford, Nebraska is now closed. We do not know where Father Peter is. He was preparing for his large Friday evening prayer group when word of these events came to him from the Bishop via fax. He spoke against the New World Order/One World Government to the 700 or so people who were packed into Saint Margaret's. The authorities were ready for him - because he has been writing books on the subject and speaking against it since the day he was ordained 6 years ago. So, we've lost one parish so far, and we can't find the priest. Furthermore, from what I've been told, every Bishop in the country has received an unsigned notice of the trouble that the priest is in and why. The Bishop's are taking this as a shot across the bow. From the wording of this letter in question, I was told, any priest who speaks against current world events is game for arrest."

The noise level at the meeting was increasing. Everyone was talking as Father was trying to tell the story. Though it seemed that all 12 council members were shocked, it was not for the same reason in each case.

"I think it's about time that the Church has stopped its attack against women, contraception, and abortion. Frankly, I see all of this as a breath of fresh air. Furthermore, the Church has never really cared about our planet either, overpopulation, social justice, and the environment. Just look at Columbus and Cortez for example. Murderers, all of them. I am ecstatic to see that things are about to change," said Sherry McGivern, a council member. Patty Kurwalt and Harold Muncie agreed in moderately loud voices. Then there was chaos. Only 3 of the council members were speaking adamantly against the "new laws". Six members became surprisingly quiet after the initial shock. A line had been drawn. The apostasy was nearly at its perihelion. Judas was howling with a pained laughter that sent reverberations throughout the underworld.

****

Most of the world, that was not experiencing a direct frontal attack from nature and/or the politics and abuses of the New World Order was proceeding on its normal course. The kids were at soccer and baseball. Families splashed in the oceans at Key West, the Gulf of Mexico, and southern California. Tag sales, bake sales, and bingo raised money for football players and cheerleaders at Public and Parochial schools across the nation. Few parents wondered why the Catholic school cheerleaders and sometimes students looked like prostitutes in their skivvies, as did the rest of the cheerleading world. The kids were getting a good education, at least. Their parents, who often dressed for fornication themselves, were proud of them. The divorce rate for North America had just passed the marriage rate. Chrysler Corporation was having a boon year. High Tech was through the roof. These Tech stocks continued to make grandmothers and college students overnight millionaires. Some people were experiencing heart failure due to the tremendous up and down cycles of Wall Street. There was a handful of businesses going under, or being put under by order from the power brokers. Those who fought the mergers, the conglomerates, and the coming One World Government were targeted companies. They received unscheduled IRS audits. The market cycles were beginning to follow the patterns of nature, and sometimes staggered as a drunkard struck with blows. It was up, up, up, however, after each event in the great outdoors had passed. Only 29% of Catholics were attending Sunday Mass. That was up one percent from 1997. In areas that were hit hard by nature, or where the economic impacts from such events hit closer to home, Mass attendance was hovering at 50% or more. Some had heard the call. By and large though, it was business as usual. Television viewing was at an all time high. North Americans didn't know their scriptures, but they certainly were television literate...Elsewhere, many came in **His** name, *one* in particular. There were wars and seditions. Nations rose against nations. There were great earthquakes in diverse places, and pestilences, and famines, and terrors from heaven; and there were many great signs....

****

Not everyone living within driving distance of Franciscan University in Steubenville, Ohio was as of yet declared a Saint by the Church. Sometimes Paul and Barbara Bohatch thought that this was what their friends, relatives, and acquaintances thought when the topic came up when they were away on trips. The discussion usually went something like this - "Oh my God, you live in Steubenville. How lucky you are. We wish that we lived there, but we just can't move there because of money and the job situation. We'd give anything to live there though. I can't imagine living near Franciscan University. Have you met Father Crowe, the President? Do you know Professor Robbins or Professor Scmitt? We've given their conversion story tapes to hundreds of people. Have you met that holy Marian Professor, oh, God, what's his name? You know who I'm talking about." After a few more sentences such as the above, the questioner would take a breath and pause for an answer.

Indeed, Franciscan University was unquestionably the hub of Catholicism in the United States, at least in terms of per capita orthodoxy! Yet, like the prophet that Jesus told us of that would not be recognized in his own town, not everyone in Eastern Ohio felt the same way about the University – but the support was there. Yes, there were many Protestants who took offense at this branch of what they thought was the "Whore of Babylon". Surprisingly however, it seemed that a large part of the Protestant community was a supporter of Franciscan University. Indeed, the President of the University, Father Michael Crowe, had a tremendous following in the Protestant world - pastors and lay persons alike. This support however, did not come from compromising the Catholic Faith, interestingly enough! Perhaps it was in part because of Father Michael's unwavering orthodoxy and loyalty to Jesus Christ and His Vicar on earth Pope John Paul II that caused so many to love him. Certainly, the love, this charity that Father Michael possessed for everyone Christian and non-Christian alike was a major factor in the popularity of the priest. It was like having a mirror image of Pope John Paul II right there in eastern Ohio, in the person of Father Michael Crowe, TOR (Third Order Regular - Franciscans).

So indeed, Franciscan University, Steubenville, Ohio, and surrounding areas were a great font of holiness, pilgrimage, and promise, but the battle was there too. The same devil, the same demons that filled the Masonic Halls in Paris, Mexico City, Montreal, and Washington DC spent a good deal of time in Steubenville too. As Jesus had his Judas, the Church in this part of Ohio had theirs. Some were priests. Some were laypersons, Catholic and Protestant. Many were Freemasons or under their influence.

The worst however were the ones who would not recognize the proverbial prophet (in the form of a priest or the mission that he stood for) in their own hometown. These were the Sunday Catholics and Sunday Shepherds. They were the lukewarm, neither waxing nor waning, destined for cuspidor, barring conversion.

These are the thoughts that went through the minds of both Paul and Barbara Bohatch, when the Steubie U (Franciscan University) admirers drowned them in affection for their hometown. As husband and wife, and as faithful Catholics, they read and studied their Catechism and Bible daily with their children. More than that they prayed, and they prayed, and they prayed. The Rosary was their favorite prayer. All of this brought them to the realization that they were not in heaven yet, as close to it as some of their friends in far away places thought they might be. No, it was certainly not heaven this Steubenville area. Yet, it was where they chose to be. It was where they wanted to raise their six children and any more children that God might send them (as many as He (God) would like to send them, for this was and has always been true Catholicism). At least here, the Christian remnant, the Catholic remnant was strong. In truth, perhaps only one in twenty families took their faith seriously - seriously enough to pray together (at least a daily Rosary, perhaps the Chaplet of Divine Mercy too), and to attend faithfully not only Sunday Mass, but frequent daily Mass as well. But what is the percentage elsewhere? Yes, the remnant in Steubenville and surrounding communities is so strong that it was quite capable of shaking the very foundations of the earth - through prayer, and the power of God - the Father, Son, and Holy Spirit.

The Bohatch family did not choose Steubenville on their own. Just a few years ago they lived in South Carolina where Paul had an engineering job with Union Carbide in Charleston. In Paul's case if he had to prepare a list of states that he would like to live in descending order, by the time he would have come to 49 or 50 he would not have been able to remember the last one or two states "undesirable" to him. One of them would have been Ohio. The top five choices hands down would have been Alaska (where he had worked in college), Maine, Montana, Wyoming, and Idaho. When the Bohatch family was uprooted by God in the mid 90's, Paul and even Barbara to some degree wanted to move to Maine. Maine had won because of its beauty - ocean and wilderness, and proximity to relatives. Yes, they wanted to move to a quaint little town called Bar Harbor, Maine. Well, quaint for 8 months of the year anyhow, when the millions of visitors to Acadia National Park were not rolling through! Such was not to be however, for God then brought them to Steubenville in haste! He had prepared 7 acres for them there, and He was not about to be brushed aside. Whenever Paul talked about his misgivings in regards to not moving to

Maine, Barbara reminded him "But what about the Faith! You moved here for the Catholic Faith. Why don't you build a lighthouse in the field to remind you of Maine!" They still had their annual camping trip to Bar Harbor to look forward to. That was a great consolation to Paul, Barbara, Catherine, Luke, Peter, Mary, and Bernadette. Admittedly, Bernadette might have received the same consolation by having Mom or Dad stick her little baby feet in the kiddy pool in the back yard, but she would have fun to.

Maine had something for everyone. For Paul it was being able to stare out at God's great ocean under a starry sky late in the evening, and to breathe in the intoxicating aroma of a northern balsam fir and spruce forest mixed with a salt mist. For Barbara it was the same as well as the joy of not being a homeschool teacher for a few precious weeks. For the kids, it was the excitement of everything having to do with God's great outdoors! Ah, fishing!

It was June 30th, 1998. The Bohatch family had just loaded the last bag into the family van. Goodbye steel city! Goodbye smothering Steel City air! Hello Bar Harbor! The Chevy van, with canoes and pop-up trailer attached, was now in motion.

"You want to drive this van and trailer up that big hill with all those cars up there! Summer conferences are underway. You'll never even make it to the top. They'll have to call the National Guard to back us out of there" said Barbara Bohatch.

"Nemo problemo said Paul as he aimed the van for the top of the hill. I just want to run into the Portiuncula (small chapel at Franciscan University), and say hello and goodbye to Our Lord and Mary with a Hail Mary, and ask them to bless our trip. I need to get some holy water too. Don't leave home without it." Paul drove around the circle at the top of the hill, passing dorms and other college buildings, then made the mistake of turning right on a narrow road into a parking area to get closer to the Portiuncula. He squeezed the car into a tight spot in a gravel parking area and dashed off to the chapel as he yelled to Barbara and the kids "I'll be right back. We'll be out of here in a minute."

Fifteen minutes later Paul came running back to the van. He opened the door to the van and immediately sensed the mood. It was not vacation-like. It was 91 degrees outside and the van was even hotter. The baby was screaming, and Barbara was yelling at the boys for not helping the baby in the back with them. "Sorry", Paul said. "I felt like I was supposed to pray the Chaplet while I was in there."

"You felt wrong. You did it again - left us waiting. You always do this," said Barbara raising her voice.

"What do you mean - 'I always do this'?" said Paul, matching the decibel level in his wife's voice and then some.

The baby cried harder. The parents yelled louder. The oldest children, Catherine and Luke had tears coming out of their eyes. They were veterans to fights like this. Not so much in recent years, but in years gone by. These arguments hurt the children tremendously. The older ones hearts broke every time it had happened. Sometimes they thought the battles were over for good, but on rare occasions they resurfaced.

Sometimes in a weakened state, Paul wondered if all of their prayers were doing any good. People thought they were the model Steubenville Catholic Family. *If they only could see us now*, thought Paul. *Nobody would hang around with us.*

"Start the darn car", yelled Barbara.

Paul started the car and backed up dangerously fast.

"Stop", screamed Luke. "You're going to hit that blue car."

"Damn it", yelled Paul, "Where did they come from. How am I going to get out of there." In the meanest calm tone he could muster up, Paul said to Barbara "Would you get out and back me out of here, I need help."

"Oh, now you need me. You sure do need help Mr. Holy Roller. I wish your friends could see you," said Barbara as she stepped out of the car, slammed the door and walked to the back of the car to direct Paul's efforts in freeing the car from its tight spot. "You're stuck. If you move the van forward or backward 6 inches you're going to hit either this blue car or that white car. We have to wait now thanks to you. Thanks for the vacation", yelled Barbara as she approached Paul's window.

Barbara got back into the van. The baby was screaming now. Students and conference attendees passing by made strange faces as they looked into the van. One pious looking young student that looked as skinny as a toothpick (probably from fasting per Our Lady's requests from current apparitions) took out his Rosary and made the sign of the cross and began his silent prayers with his Rosary dangling in his hand as he walked by. Paul had seen him do this and knew that the young man was praying for him and his distressed family. Paul was full of anger and almost swore at the young man as he passed them. By now, four of the children were crying, the temperature in the van was 98 degrees, and the baby was screaming at peak decibel levels.

Two young ladies who were walking by praying on their way to the chapel heard and saw what was going on. One of the girls knocked on Barbara's partially opened window and asked if there was anything she could do. "Just leave me alone", Barbara yelled out, with her hands covering her reddened, tear covered face. The girls walked off, continuing their prayers.

When the temperature reached 99 degrees in this brief span of a few minutes, and when the old wounds that were thought to have been healed reopened, Paul couldn't take it any more. Not that Paul was an innocent victim of a wife lacking certain qualities in communications - he was taking shots with his words, tone of voice, and an unholy cleverness to win the war of words. He simply couldn't take the arguing anymore. He screamed out "You're a pain in the neck, you know it. I hope the kids don't grow up like you. I hat..." Barbara cried louder, hurt more than Paul could know, and came back with a few choice words herself. More praying students passed by. The baby screamed. The other children suffered.

A spark of light came into Paul's head during the heat of the battle, probably through the inspiration of his guardian angel. "What are you fighting for? What did you come here to Franciscan University for just a half an hour ago? Who wants you to fight?" He knew the answer to all of the questions. They were fighting over nothing; he came to the Portiuncula to ask God to give them a blessed, peaceful trip. And the devil and demons were spurring them on, notwithstanding of course, their own fallen nature. In that brief moment Paul had decided to apologize and to get a hold of himself and started to pray. Similar thoughts passed through Barbara's head.

The baby screamed louder, the children cried, and the blue car and the white car were not going anywhere. Neither was the Bohatch family. Life was not always a beach. With the best of intentions in the back of their mind, and wanting to really have peace right then and there, Paul and Barbara Bohatch resumed their yelling. Paul wished he had gotten the air conditioning fixed before they had left. The auto repair shop had wanted $700 for a new system, so Paul had deferred on the repair thinking they would not need the air conditioning in cool Maine.

A young man who owned a small blue car that parked next to Paul's van while Paul was in the Chapel came up to the van and knocked on Paul's window. "Sorry about my parking job, I didn't think I'd be long. I'm going now, so I'll be out of your way." "Have a great day! " the young man yelled to Paul as he was getting in his car.

With the red car now gone, Paul moved the van and trailer with ease, and in 20 seconds was coming off of Holy Hill, home of Franciscan University.

What did I do Paul thought? *What did I do to my wife and children? Oh God, I can't undo what I just did. How did I do it? It's like its not me, but it was just the same. It has happened to me before, but not so much in the last 3 years. Oh God. I can't believe I did this. I did it all about 120 feet away from the Blessed Sacrament, the exposed Eucharist in the Portiuncula. What am I? How can I live with myself?"* Inside he was remorseful and repenting. On the outside his face still looked full of rage. *What has become of me? What will become of me?* thought Paul, as he headed the van for Route 22 and Pittsburgh. He started to pray a silent Rosary.

Barbara really felt like having Paul stop the car and let her get out. She was angry. Yet, she too was full of remorse. It was tough to stop the train of anger. She wondered if any other family in the country was having problems like theirs right now. She began to pray a silent Chaplet. The older children were praying silent Saint Michael prayers to themselves at the whispering insistence of Catherine, the oldest. Their father had taught them to do this whenever the parents started to argue.

In millions of homes across America and the world, parents were yelling at each other and threatening divorce. Catholics were no exception, sadly. Padre Pio, the deceased Franciscan priest, who bore the stigmata of Christ, once told a confrere that if the demons that he was allowed by God to see could take on a visible form, the sky would be completely blackened, and the light of the sun would not be able to penetrate to the surface of the earth. These guys know where we live. They're all around us. Saint Paul told us that the real battle is against the principalities and princes of darkness. In a figurative sense they can make a mountain out of a molehill. They can take a bad parking job and turn it into a divorce - but only if we let them. We let them by not praying. We let them by walking away from Jesus and Mary.

Paul continued to pray and think. He seriously thought again that if any of his friends - the men he went to church with, or prayed with, or kicked a soccer ball with had seen him during the argument a few minutes ago that they would never want to be near him again. A lot of people had thought that he was a holy man. Wives had joked in front of their husbands that they wished that they were like Paul. He had been spoken of highly in recent weeks by good people. *What a mess-up I am. Yeah, if they knew what I was really like, I'd scare them all off. I wonder how Jesus puts up with me. I'm embarrassed to call on Him and His Holy Mother Mary. God, how can I even think of calling Mary? She wouldn't want to hang around me! I just scared her away. I'm the one who goes around like a lay Catholic evangelist. Who do I think I am?* Such were the thoughts of Paul Bohatch as he headed to Bar Harbor with his family, somewhat delayed during an intended brief stop at the Portiuncula to say hello to Jesus, Mary, and Saint Francis! He was on the fifth sorrowful mystery 20 miles out of Steubenville. *Yes, I know Lord; I helped to drive the nails into your hands and feet by arguing, no, screaming at my wife a little while ago. Help me Lord. Lord; let me ask you why. Why? You know I don't want to be like that, yet I am. Why? You know Lord, if someone had given me the script of what was going to happen today, I would have completely avoided all arguments with my wife. I would have done things differently - not just for the sake of being a good actor, but for your sake, and mine, just to be good. Why did I mess up?"* A scripture verse popped into Paul's head at that moment - *"If thou, O Lord, wilt mark iniquities: Lord, who shall stand it?*

Unknown and unseen by Paul, Barbara, and the children, a pack, or call them a herd of ghoulish black beasts were falling away from the Bohatch van, one by one, as the van headed towards its destination eastward on I-22. It was *that Rosary* again. Satan was furious. If it was within his power, he would have destroyed all of western Pennsylvania at that moment to stop that Lady's Rosary from being said. Satan and his myrmidons knew where that van was headed, and they were not happy campers.

After he finished his silent Rosary just west of Pittsburgh, Paul had the nerve to ask everyone to pray a Rosary for peace in the family. *He felt like a hypocrite and perhaps he was.* No one was real excited about it; they had just been through a war and were in a state of shock still. Praise the Lord however, the baby was taking a nap and had a beautiful smile on her face. Despite the lack of voter participation, Paul started the Rosary. They took turns with the decades praying almost angrily during the first few decades. Barbara didn't join in till the fourth decade. After the fifth decade and the Hail Holy Queen they were a new family. They bounced back. After all, that's what Christians are supposed to be - good bouncers. They own the Resurrection after all!

After the Rosary, the family began to talk again. Paul pulled off of I-79, which they had now been on for ten minutes, and aimed the van at a McDonalds for a much-needed pit stop. They ordered their meals and were on their way. "Thank you Lord", thought Paul as they were driving along again. He felt like he had been raised from the dead! He reached out with his right hand to his wife's left hand draped over the arm of the captain's chair. He put his hand in hers. There was no movement in her hand at first, but then her hand began to show signs of life. They were a family on vacation once again. In a few days sacramental confession would solidify this resurrected family.

****

In a rectory in Columbus, Ohio, Rick Tremont was finishing up his forty-five minute confession. Officer John Worrall was in the next room waiting on his friend. He was not Catholic, but he was beginning to understand things Catholic. He had heard all of the tales of this supposed Whore of

Babylon, this so-called nemesis of Christianity, this Roman Catholic Church. He, like the rest of America and the world, to be more precise, had heard it all - on television, radio, and in the press. The deluge of charges had come from fire and brimstone preachers, "Bible-only" preachers, and the man on the street. John Worrall had a larger view of things, however. Over eighty percent of the rescuers that he had arrested in the last six years were zealous Bible-thumping, Rosary praying Catholics. Yes, these Catholics toted the same Bible as their detractors, the Protestants and Bible-only crowd were using, with an additional seven books that Martin Luther, through his own arrogance had removed from the Bible. *Jesus had quoted from some of these books that Martin Luther had brushed aside, that were no longer found in Protestant Bibles! So, who was Bible-only* he thought? There were no Protestant Bibles five hundred years ago. The only ones around were the Bibles that were being painstakingly copied by the monks in dark cells in the 'lands of Christianity', which just happened to be Catholic, barring Eastern extraction. The turning point for John's understanding of Catholicism was when a fellow officer had signed him up for *THIS ROCK* magazine, a Catholic apologetics publication for the laity. John was reaching a point in his understanding of the Faith of Old where a decision would soon be needed regarding his own faith. While awaiting Rick Tremont, John Worrall had his nose in the Bible - in John 6:48-59. *"He that eateth my flesh, and drinketh my blood, hath everlasting life: and I will raise him up on the last day...For my flesh is meat indeed: and my blood is drink indeed...After this many of his disciples went back; and walked no more with him...Jesus said to the twelve: Will you also go away?* Officer John Worrall had heard all of the arguments that Jesus didn't really mean this. Strange, most of those arguments had come from the Fundamentalists - those who believed the Bible literally in all instances - *well, at least it seems, when it was convenient to do so.*

Rick Tremont's confession was initiated flippantly by Father Finnigan. Within minutes, however, the scales were falling rapidly off of the once darkened soul of Father Finnigan. God was melting Father Finnigan's heart as Rick was speaking to him.

He knew whom Rick was working for. He began to wonder who he, Father Finnigan was working for. The turning point had come when Rick had mentioned one of the doctors, the former Catholic abortionist who had converted his life through the inspiration of Rick Tremont. Father Finnigan knew the doctor. He was in his parish. In recent years Father Finnigan knew that a profound change had come over the doctor. *Now Father knew the rest of the story....*

That evening Father received his warning. He saw himself before the judgment throne of God. He found himself acknowledging that Hell was what he, Father had chosen for himself. A Lovely Lady dressed in blue appeared between Father and the throne of God. She begged for more time for the priest. God told her that this priest had served no one but himself for the last 20 years. The Lady interceded for the priest again and asked that he be given more time and another chance to serve Him. The Lady's wish was fulfilled.

Father did not sleep well that evening. He lay in bed praying his Rosary till almost sun-up. Some might think that Father's former devotion to Our Lady had saved his soul, had won him the friendship of a powerful intercessor. Yet, he had never been fond of Our Lady. *It was the many Rosaries of his mother that had brought him such a Fortune...*

****

Raphael Morales sat in his makeshift office at the Coliseum after the conclusion of the 1998 National Medjugorje Conference. Once again, just as they had done since 1989, just under 10,000 people were heading for the highways and airports leading away from San Francisco. Their spirits revived, with smiles on their faces, they were heading home to loved ones, to their jobs, to their communities with renewed vigor and energy to carry on with life in these trying times. Despite the overall success of the conference however, a seed of doubt had also been planted in the minds of many of the pilgrims. For some, without much prayer and discernment, the seed could mushroom into a fatal spiritual illness.

The Medjugorje conference held June 26, 27, and 27, 1998 was history. Raphael was sitting alone in the office. In the background was heard the sound of beeping fork trucks backing up, and police guards shouting orders. The coliseum crew attended to their duties along with the many conference volunteers going about their business with walkie-talkies in hand, and radio headsets in use - with boxes, bags, and tools in both hands.

Joan Hampton poked her head into Ralph's office. "You O.K. Ralph?"

"Yeah, thanks Joan. I think I'll be fine after a few weeks in the Bahamas. The only problem is I'm not going there! Just kidding Joan. I'm so tired that I can't even think right now. I was trying to put the picture of Our Lady of Guadalupe back in its case, and I went to take the 7/8-inch bolts off the case with a Phillips head screwdriver. It all seemed so reasonable to me. Mike saw me, and he told me to go take a nap. I'm glad that Jean is driving us home later, because I am not capable of driving."

"Well, let me know if you need anything, I'll be running by your door about a hundred times in the next 3 hours" said Joan.

"Thanks Joan. God bless you."

Raphael put his head down but he couldn't sleep. He and his staff had put together a lineup of 11 holy speakers from around the world to address the conference just now ended. The preparations for this year's conference had taken 11 months. Speakers were checked and cross-checked. Yet Jesus had his Judas, and Raphael had his. The first 9 talks had been tremendous. The conversions were numerous. The confession lines were impossibly long - with over 20 priests hearing confessions simultaneously at one point on Saturday night! Heaven felt so close. There were only two talks and a Mass left on Sunday just before 10 AM. The tenth speaker scheduled was Father Andrew Campbell, a Franciscan who had lived in Medjugorje for just over one year, several years ago. His theme was to be "Why Medjugorje?: Village of Tobacco and Grapes". He was to speak on the state of Medjugorje just before Our Lady appeared to 6 children on June 24, 1981, the town's transformation to holiness, it's continuing conversion, and how we can bring our own communities to the same conversion to Jesus Christ through Mary.

The first half-hour of Father Campbell's talk was wonderful. He brought many a pilgrim to tears, tears of remorse for sins, and tears of joy for hope - in Jesus through Mary. He led the pilgrims through fifteen minutes of the prayers of Saint Louis Marie de Montfort, including the consecration prayers to Jesus & Mary so often emphasized by Pope John Paul II. Father then told about the tremendous conversion story of Sister Anna Elizabeth Delgrado. The pilgrims were unable to control their tears. It was a story on par with the tremendous conversion of Wayne Weedle, Thomas Rutbensky, and many others. Yet, the miracles surrounding Sister Anna were even more phenomenal. Then, to the surprise of everyone, Father Campbell introduced Sister Anna to the audience. Sister thanked Father and then Our Lady of Fatima for her conversion, and then went back to her seat. Time was running short on Father's talk. He had ten minutes left. The word Medjugorje had not yet been mentioned. Raphael Morales sat in the back with a worried look on his face, and trouble in his heart. Bishop Eric Pastuszek had spoken privately with Raphael about an hour before the conference. He told him that it was his understanding that Father Campbell no longer believed in Medjugorje. He told him of an incident relayed to him by a priest in his diocese. Apparently Father Campbell had taken shots at Medjugorje right from the pulpit in Saint James Church in Medjugorje, Bosnia-Herzegovina. Father Campbell had been to Medjugorje 38 times, and had been the spiritual director for thousands of pilgrims with him on these trips. He was often the main celebrant of the Mass at Saint James. Raphael had invited him to speak at the conference just 6 days ago, to replace Father Harold Barker who would not be able to come because of illness. Father Campbell had heartily agreed.

Raphael looked at the itinerary for the conference. He stared at Sunday's schedule in the brochure. The 10 AM talk outline was specific: **Father Andrew Campbell: Why Medjugorje?: Village of Tobacco and Grapes.** Something was not right in Denmark. Something was not right in San Francisco. Something extraordinary was taking place in the coliseum. And then it happened. Father Andrew Mary Maximilian Campbell started to tear apart Medjugorje. He tore apart Garabandal, Betania, San Nicholas, Our Lady of The Americas, and the supposed mission of the Missionary Image of Our Lady of Guadalupe. The Image of Our Lady of Guadalupe was two feet from the podium. There was a polite rage in his voice as he pronounced the arsenal of names, dates, places, and reasons for his disbelief in these and many other so called apparitions of the Mother of God. He held Fatima up like a beacon in a storm, which it truly is, as he proceeded to level everything else bearing the prefix Marian since then.

Raphael stood up from his seat in the back of the darkened coliseum. His face was as red as a tomato. Tears and anger and fatigue were all over his face. He had not slept for 50 hours. He wanted to scream. *He wished that Father Campbell would drop dead right here and now. He hated him.* That is, thoughts of such hate and anger came into his mind. Raphael tried to push them out. He tried saying a Hail Mary silently. He got as far as "Hail Mary."... Raphael could not be contained. He walked towards the sound and video engineering section. He told Richard Williams who was at the controls, that Father Campbell was all done with a quick movement of his hand across his throat, fingers extended in knifelike fashion. Richard turned down Father Campbell's volume and started Michael O'Brian's "Mine Eyes Have Seen The Glory" on cassette tape. The audience started to stand and stretch. Father Campbell, taken aback briefly, checked his watch. He still had two more minutes. However, he had said enough. Though he could hardly be heard over the music, he thanked the audience for attending the conference, thanked Raphael Morales and Mary, Queen of Peace Ministries for inviting him, blessed the audience and said goodbye. His job was done. He thanked God that he was able to speak his mind. His new book would be out in 3 days. He had just introduced the theme to 10,000 people....

****

John T. Trudeau was having a less than perfect day. He just got off the phone with his lawyer. John was being sued by two groups, the Southern Poverty Legal Defense Fund, and the Jewish Protection League. John was less thrilled about the suit from the latter group in light of the fact that his great great grandfather was Jewish. The balance of his great great grandparents were Catholic. Since the great-great days, however, the family had become Bible believing fire and brimstone non-denominationalist Christians. John T. had lived in the mountains of Montana all of his life. His grandparents were some of the first pioneers to settle Northwest Montana. John T. was already in Heaven as far as he was concerned. How could Heaven get any better than the Bitterroot Range? Despite this however, he did wish to enter into Heavenly Glory after his life on earth was over, even if it meant not seeing Montana on a daily basis. He had a row to hoe yet though, he had these suits to make it through. He had a New World Order to fight...

John was being sued by the parties in question for a whole host of reasons, all false allegations. On the top of the list was slander. When you're fighting a New World Order, you're bound to make enemies...

John was fifty-five years old. From the way the government pursued him, you might have thought he was the world's greatest criminal. Yes, the government wanted him too. Yet, John was a good Christian man who started his day with prayers and a half an hour of Bible reading, and ended his day in the same fashion. Why did the government want him? Well, he belonged to one of those "M" groups. John was the leader of the Minutemen of Montana, the most well known militia in the United States. The government would have John's powerful voice and message stopped, somehow.

Despite threats, suits, and even more than we can say, John continued on in his battle against the powers that be – the wealthy family or two that controlled the world. The Clintons, the Gores, the Newts and company are just puppets. There is a plan to this wicked madness. John continued on...

John Trudeau was branded, not by name, but by classification, as a "kook", by Rush Limbaugh and the mainstream press. All this because John thought that the Devil had a plan, a conspiracy against God and man. Rush verbally abused men like John Trudeau daily. Some thought that Rush Limbaugh was the Red Herring being used by the establishment to control the fire, to control the minds of conservative men who would turn themselves over to him. *Mega dittos and all that. That means I'm with you Rush - what cliff do you want me to jump off of?* It was o.k. If Rush took millions of people with him to the god of Conservatism, as long as he kept them from seeing the conspiracy, and the unbottled True God. Yes, there was going to be a New World Order. It's not that Rush was all that bad. He would tell the world about the New World Order – the day after the United States had been reigned in. Then his job would be complete. On that day, millions of loyal Rush fans, Christians for the most part, would be allowed to take the wool off of their eyes. The damage would have already been done. Many would have permanent blindness, however, and follow the Antichrist, the big cheese, the long expected one. They would follow him all the way to Hell, to the conservative cheerleading section.

John's weeks were spent giving lectures at Universities such as Yale, Purdue, Notre Dame, UCLA, and large and small high schools, colleges, and even grammar schools throughout the country. To be sure, in regards to the political and military aspects, John was the most knowledgeable man alive regarding the coming New World Order/One World Government. He remembered most of what he read, and he'd read it all. He had friends on both sides of the fence. True friends who loved God, and loved their country.

John was the backbone of the American Militia Movement. He was a good Christian first! Yet, in the media, John was always portrayed as the demented one with an ax to grind against proper authorities. Because of this, John had only a few thousand people who honestly believed in the work he was doing. For sure, he helped inspire patriotic and Christian thoughts in the minds of tens of thousands of others, but these numbers too, drew the line at preparedness. Nobody would ever try to take away their freedom; after all, they were United States Citizens. John must be deluded…They had sympathy for him, however…

From the day John Trudeau was honorably discharged from the United States Army in 1968 to the present day in 1998, John had been working to preserve freedom in these United States. John knew that time was short, and that the battle lines were being drawn. He continued in his work. He would often quote the forefathers of the United States, who across the board, wholeheartedly agreed that the day the citizens of the United States of America were disarmed, freedom would be GONE! "Americans have the right and advantage of being armed – unlike citizens of other countries whose governments are afraid to trust the people with arms." – James Madison "Liberty and order will never be perfectly safe until a trespass on the Constitutional provisions for either, shall be felt with the same keenness that resents an invasion of the dearest rights." – Madison. "Before a standing army can rule, the people must be disarmed; as they are in almost every kingdom in Europe. The supreme power in America cannot enforce unjust laws by the sword, because the whole body of the people are armed, and constitute a force superior to any band of regular troops that can be, on any pretense, raised in the United States" – Noah

Webster. One could go on writing ten books full of such quotes from the founding fathers. True, the whole lot of them were Freemasons or Deists, but some of them had hearts of gold and tried to break away from the bonds of Satan's Masonic Lodges and false teachings. We do have the wonderful example of George Washington who warned this nation of the dangers of the Lodge – his own secret society. God rest his soul.

Whenever John spoke, the Bible was his main resource – the King James Version. In fact John nearly condemned all other Bibles. He warned the audiences of the "New Age" Bibles that were cropping up everywhere. And erringly, he warned the audiences about those so-called Catholic Bibles. God, he hated the Catholic Church – not the Catholics, he had a lot of Catholic friends - true friends – but he did hate that Church with a passion. It was the King James Version for John or nothing. The same was true amongst the ranks of most the militias in the United States. The same was true amongst most Bible thumping ministers. King James or death! Strange thoughts coming from these people who themselves condemn the revisionism of the Clintons and men and women of the same clubs and cloth. John T. Trudeau hated revisionism. He hated revisionism when it came to American History, the founding fathers, the Second Amendment, and the United States Constitution. Hypocritically, however, he would have nothing else BUT revisionism when it came to his Bible – he would have nothing but the KJV, revised, and revised, and revised.

John put a spin on Catholicism and Catholic Bibles that the Spin-Doctors of the Clinton Administration could not have matched were they put to the task. In John's mind it was as if Saint Michael came down from Heaven in 1600 bearing millions upon millions of "King James Version" Bibles, therefore eliminating the need of any historical Bibles of the "infidels", these Catholics. *That isn't the way it happened, John. We've got another case of revisionism here. Sure John, there have indeed been many bad Catholics John, but didn't Jesus have his Judas? Does that mean the message of the Apostles is invalid? Does that mean the gates of Hell have indeed prevailed against Christ's Church, this Catholic Church? Isn't that against scripture?*

Well, anyhow, that's the way it was. Occasionally John would get into a verbal hassle or two with a Catholic who knew his faith, and the Bible. The Catholic usually made the most sense, and had facts and history on his side, but John always won the argument. John often wondered if the Catholics involved in the militia were not behind most of the espionage dumped on the freedom fighters in this country. After all, he regularly was at odds with many Catholics regarding Christianity as it relates to these times, the times of the coming New World Order. He'll never forget that night in Cleveland when that Bible Thumping Catholic stood up and rebuked him for blaspheming Christ's Church at the end of his talk. The "infidel" began passing out Rosaries and tapes from the Mary Foundation regarding Marian Apparitions. That was proof enough for John as to just whose side that Catholic was on. John figured the guy was planted there by the ATF or the FBI.

The Catholic dishing out all those tapes and Rosaries that night had offered to send John Trudeau to Medjugorje, where the Blessed Virgin Mary had been appearing since 1981. John blew him off with a patriotic line and a Biblical quote about "demons appearing as angels of light". John never bothered to "test the spirits" as the Bible says. He never thought about Medjugorje again, until July 3, 1998, the day he was scheduled to speak on "preparedness" to a group of fired-up patriots living on Mount Desert Isle, home of Acadia National Park.

****

Victor Rushmiller's family had been on the family farm for over 110 years. The Claremont, New York State farm, once nearly 350 acres, was now reduced to just fewer than 50. The rest of it was no longer in the family. This fact never settled right with Victor. Some of the land had been taken by treachery, murder if it must be said - albeit many decades ago. This was his greatest cross in life, and he took it with him wherever he went. In the back of his mind he sometimes thought that he would one day get the land back somehow, new houses or not. It was his by rights. He was being consumed by the land.

In the *Poem of The Man God*, authored by Maria Valtorta, supposedly through the direct inspiration of Jesus and Mary, there is a story quite applicable for Victor's situation. Maria lived a life like Blessed Anne Catherine Emmerick and countless other suffering souls. Her life was full of pain and anguish, but her heart and soul were full of love and joy. Her life was a continuous crucifixion. There are those who are still trying to crucify her - the proud intelligent, the arrogant, and the misinformed. That is the norm however when dealing with saints. It seems we must test their veracity with blood. Victor could have benefited from having read this chapter in which this story in question remains waiting for landowners everywhere. However, things as they were, it is not likely that he would ever even hear of the book, barring a miracle. Victor is a Southern Baptist not given to reading Catholic "lies". His pastor would not have approved either.

The story that Jesus relays to Maria Valtorta goes something like this. Jesus was teaching the crowds one day. When he finished a man came up to him and said "Jesus, tell my neighbor to give me back my land. He has taken a corner of my property knowingly, and refuses to give it back. There he is over there."

"Tell me" Jesus said, "Can you still feed your family with the land you have left?"

"Well, uh, yes, I can, but..." said the man.

"Then forget about it," said Jesus. This is the part that would have been highly applicable to Victor. You see, he often wanted to shoot one of his neighbors over the land dispute that existed only in his mind. History had put a right-of-way and physical gate on Victor's property, adjacent a 40-acre section of the former family property that was sold off a few generations ago. That right-of-way went right through Victor's current farm. Since it was treachery that caused the family farm to be taken away three generations ago, Victor was not happy about someone else having a right-of-way through his land. After all, the whole tract was still his in his mind. He was the sole heir. Murder had put that right-of-way through his front yard over 100 years ago.

Victor didn't really have anything against his new neighbors. After all, they had just fallen into happenstance - they bought an available farm on the free market as far as they were concerned. In Victor's mind however, they had inherited the "original sin", the murder. They had nothing to do with it. They were however, reaping the rewards from it. Victor broke the new family in slowly. Tom and Martha Rutbensky had no idea what they were getting into. Neither the sellers nor the real estate agent gave them a clue as to what to look forward to in regards to their new neighbors. The house would not have sold if they had.

Tom Rutbensky was an award-winning cameraman with KDKY television in Buffalo. Martha was a marketing executive with Ruben Schottle Inc., a national land developer. They finally found the place in the country that they had been looking for years. It was their dream home. They had not been graced with children, but the farm would help them make up for it. Tom could work his hobby of farming till the cows came home. The 40 acres were prime corn land. He and his buddies could hunt, hike, and even fish on it. Martha was just looking at getting out of the city. To her, the two-year-old house was ideal also. There was a bit of country in her. She loved the kitchen.

Three weeks after Allied Van lines said goodbye, it started. Victor had tried to be patient with himself, but he could no longer wait. He was hoping that the situation that he wished to create could start through a direct confrontation with his neighbor through no fault of his own. He was hoping that Mr. Polock (Tom Rutbensky) would accidentally cut down some of his trees or mow one of his fields by mistake. Unfortunately, Tom did no such thing. Victor had to initiate the war himself. He gave it his best effort. He locked the gate at the head of the right-of-way. He would finally meet his new neighbor.

Tom Rutbensky was not a happy guy that evening. At 6 PM he rolled up into the head of his driveway - that same right-of-way, only to find the gate (an old gate that he hard hardly ever noticed before) locked. He knew that Victor Rushmiller and his wife owned that several hundred-foot stretch of right-of-way. He swore to himself, hit his dashboard so hard with his hand that it immediately swelled up, and almost backed up to then drive through the gate at a gallop. He didn't however. He parked the car and walked, rather jogged over to Victor's house 500 feet away. As he knocked on the door, Tom tried to put his anger away. *Maybe the kids locked it he thought. I'd better smile; this is our first meeting. God, I could punch this guy out.*

A man answered the door. "Are you Mr. Rushmiller?", Tom asked.

"Yes, that's me Can I help you?"

Tom wanted to deck him right there. He knew what Tom was doing there. "Yes, someone locked the gate on our driveway, and I was hoping you could open it for me."

"I locked it, the tall skinny man replied. It's my road, my gate, my lock, and as far as I'm concerned you're trespassing. You need to find another way to get to your house. That road has been ours since 1865 and nothing is going to change that. I'll unlock it this time" said Victor.

Tom's face reddened. He could not believe what he was hearing. In fact, he wanted Victor to repeat himself. Tom felt like he was in a dream, a nightmare. He felt detached from reality. He yelled out "What?".

Victor repeated everything he had just said. Tom was yelling obscenities at him as they walked out to the gate together. Victor unlocked the gate and walked back to his house as if Tom was not even there. He responded very little, and looked absolutely unperturbed. This fact sent Tom into an even more heightened state of rage. He would see this man in court, if he didn't kill him first.

This incident with the gate took place on June 1, 1985. Over the next several years, such events became a monthly, weekly, and sometimes daily occurrence, with sometimes greater and sometimes lesser degree of severity. Guns were sometimes involved. Though no bullets were ever fired, two grown men came close to dying several times. Guardian angels wept. Guardian angels prayed. Guardian angels prayers were heard before the throne of God. The demons also pleaded before their master. They promised their dark lord that Tom and Victor would both fall. He was not happy. The demons were years into their assignment and they were not playing horseshoes. A near miss does not count as a lost soul. Only damnation will do. Satan raged. From the increasing angelic activity surrounding the Rutbensky's - their home, their possessions, their beings, he had suspected that the battle would be greater than he had anticipated. He also suspected that something was afoot. What's so special about a Polock family that doesn't pray, doesn't go to church, doesn't read the Bible, and hasn't been to confession in 25 years? Satan was befuddled. With a searing glare from his eyes, he inflicted a terrible burning pain on the demons wavering before him, and sent them whimpering back to their place of assignment, promising them more of the same if they did not soon find success.

"Hey Tom", Tom's uncle Dan Wojens called out one Saturday morning as Tom was sitting on his 40 foot cabin cruiser at the Horse Trot Yacht Club one morning. "Permission to come aboard requested", Dan called out.

"Dan you old skunk, what are you doing up this early?", Tom said.

"I brought you something Tom. You remember that place we went in Portugal where the Virgin Mary was supposed to have appeared to those three kids? Fatima, I think?" said Dan.

"Well, it's happening again in a place called Mejoogorski or Medjugorjee, a little place in Yugoslavia. She's appearing to six kids giving them messages for the world," said Dan.

"You don't really believe that Dan, do you?" said Tom.

"I don't know," said Dan, "You ought to read this". Dan handed Tom a newspaper entitled "Apparitions at Medjugorje", by Wayne Weedle, from Charleston, South Carolina.

Tom laughed and put the paper down. His life was about over. Life as he knew it, as Martha Rutbensky knew it. Yes, this life of Tom Rutbensky to the extent that Victor Rushmiller knew about it was about over. Tom and Martha had only their guardian angels and their relatives in heaven praying for them. Satan had waged a war against them. God won. Tom was about to give his life over to Jesus & Mary, forever. Martha would follow in time.

That evening Tom read Wayne Weedle's newspaper - every word of it without putting it down. Prior to this, he had almost thrown out the paper once or twice. He used a section of it to clean up some coke he spilled on the deck. Then something made him pick it up later on in the afternoon. In the next few weeks he read several books on Medjugorje. Then he watched all the videos on the subject. He soon made his way to confession after his aforesaid 25-year absence. He was back in the Church. He was on fire, on fire with the light of God. Martha had a hard time of it all. After all, no one knew Tom as she did. This was not the Tom that she knew. For years she fought this change. Then one day she understood. She was right; this was not the Tom she had known. Tom had put on

Christ. Now she too, would follow. They were one now. One in Jesus & Mary.

Within a short time of his conversion, Tom had started Medjugorje Missions, a Catholic evangelical group using a newsletter, retreats, conferences, videos, and audio tapes to bring thousands into, and thousands back into the Catholic Faith. Tom had quit his job with KDKY television and was working full time for Jesus & Mary. Miracles followed Tom wherever he went, wherever he spoke. Yes, the conversions were numerous. Tom was also producing Bishop Whalen's weekly television show.

It's time to get back to Victor though. Victor was about to go on vacation in early July 1998. In Victor's mind he and his family had lousy neighbors. It would be good for him and his wife and two children to get away for a while. They needed a break from their situation. Over time, Tom Rutbensky did come by and apologize for acting the way he did. In Victor's mind it seemed like Tom was sincere, but there was something sneaky about it. It wasn't the Tom that he knew. He couldn't put his finger on it. He had actually heard Tom on the radio two times in the last few years talking about his conversion and a place called Medjugorje in Yugoslavia, but he didn't understand it, and wasn't buying it. He had also seen advertisements for Tom's speaking engagements several times in the early 1990's. As far as he was concerned Tom was the same trespasser that he had always known. Besides, his Southern Baptist preacher had warned about this stuff called New Age, false visionaries, and other demonically involved happenings that were taking place around the world at an alarmingly increasing rate. This stuff slid off Victor like grease. He never ventured to ask Tom about it. He tried not to talk to trespassers, even those he was beginning to warm up to. *Warm up to?* Yes, grace was operating at Victor's house too.

The car was loaded up. Victor's wife Marianne and their sons Paul and John got into the car. The UPS truck that had just come and gone from the Rutbensky's house had just left a cloud of dust hovering over Victor's front yard, engulfing his car, home, and orchard. Victor was being driven by the demons. They tormented him day and night. He counted acres in his sleep. In his dreams he walked the lands now in possession of the Smiths', Rutbensky's, and Rutherfords. He had done this ever since he was a boy and his father had relayed the sad family history and happenings at the farm. He walked up to the gate on the right-of-way and locked it for old time's sake. It felt good. It was comforting. He hoped Tom wouldn't have his key with him, when he came back from wherever he had gone off to this morning.

"Everybody ready? Bar Harbor he we come" said Victor Rushmiller to his family as he started the car. His family had not seen him this happy in years.

As they were heading out their long driveway, they passed Tom Rutbensky heading up the right-of-way. Tom had a tremendous smile for the Rushmiller's on this beautiful July morning that seemed straight from Heaven. The Rushmiller's waved to Tom, returning Tom's wave of his hand. Victor gave him a great big smile, a sneaky grinch smile.

The gate had not been locked for two years. Tom could not believe the gate was locked. He was about to smash his hand into the dashboard in reminiscence of times gone by, but just before his hand hit the car he stopped himself. He got out of the car and got down on his knees. He prayed 15 decades of the Rosary right then and there for the conversion of the Rushmillers. An hour and a quarter later he left his car and walked to his house to get his own key to the gate.

"Tom, you're late. Where have you been? The travel agent has been screaming at me on the phone. We've got to be at the airport in 70 minutes. Did you forget we're taking 124 pilgrims to Medjugorje today, including 3 priests, 2 nuns, and a Bishop?"

"You're not going to believe what just happened to me," said Tom.

****

Three hours into their trip, Victor told Marianne what he had done with the gate. His wife was upset. After all these years she was beginning to speak to Martha. Just a week ago Tom had asked him again how his garden was doing. Victor began to feel hate. *It was not that he wanted to give harbor to hate. He was just beginning to be aware of its presence inside him. He did not like the feeling.* Aside from the fact that Victor wanted to shoot him a few times in earlier years Tom Rutbensky had been a good neighbor. Tom was always throwing complements his way about his yard, garden, orchard and other things. Victor was feeling ill, and he knew why. He pulled off the highway and drove into Burger King. "Break time everybody. Get whatever you want, we're on vacation." The all walked into the restaurant and sat down while they thought of what to order. Tom put his State Farm briefcase on the table *(he was a State Farm Claims Adjuster)*. He opened up his case and took out a plain post-paid postcard. As Marianne walked up to the counter to order for everybody, he excused himself and walked towards the restroom. He pushed open the door, walked up to a stall, and pushed the stall door open. Five minutes later he emerged with an addressed post card in hand: *Dear Tom: Sorry about the gate. I don't suppose you know this but my great grandfather was murdered last century where your house now stands. The land was then stolen from our family. That's all I've thought about for 40 years... My pastor tells me that you're not a Christian - and that all Catholics are going to Hell. I've heard you on the radio a couple times. If you're not a Christian then I'm rather confused. Please put a word in for me upstairs. Your neighbor, Vic.*

****

Isaac Yoder unhitched the horse from the buggy. He was just returning from Lehman's Hardware store in Kidron, Ohio, which was about seven miles from his house. He was still half dazed from his adventure. Not that a typical trip to Lehman's left him in a daze. It was that stranger, that "Englishman" (non-Amish) that had rattled him. Isaac rarely spoke to the English unless it was necessary in a business transaction, or a polite greeting. He made the mistake, however, of saying "Top of the morning" to Ralph Piccarreta, who was up visiting from Wheeling, West Virginia. Ralph took that as a lead-in to talk to the Amish man about Our Lady's messages to Father Gobbi, Spiritual Director of the Marian Movement of priests. "Speaking of morning... have your heard about the Blessed Virgin Mary's messages to Father Gobbi, concerning the times we are living in... Ralph was really pushing it. He'd just outdone himself. The poor Amish man might just as well have mentioned the price of beans and Ralph would have found an angle...

Isaac continued checking out the non-electric grain mills, used for turning seeds like wheat and oats into flour. The mill that had been in their family for generations was finally giving out. "No, can't say I have said Isaac", looking around to make sure none of his Amish friends saw him talking to the "Englishman" about something that was surely a forbidden subject. Isaac turned the handles of some of the grain mills. They wouldn't do. It would take a half an hour to make enough flour for a loaf of bread with one of those new-fangled cheaper mills. He needed one of the more expensive ones behind the Plexiglas. He called out to an employee who came to help him. "Do you have any more of those green mills from Denmark", he said the Lehman's worker.

"I'm sorry, we're out of that one. We have more coming in eight weeks. We can reserve one for you with a deposit if you like."

"Yes, I think I'll do that please," said Isaac. Isaac's mind was racing. He knew more than most Amish about the coming changes to America. He had even heard of the coming New World Order. He was aware of the forthcoming "New World Religion", the blending of religions. He'd read a little about the dangers of New Age. Most Amish are not aware of the coming changes. Their secluded lives preclude such knowledge. Even as Isaac had agreed to put a down-payment on one of the mills, he was hoping that the economy would still be operating under somewhat normal conditions in two months so he could consummate the purchase of the expected mill. They would need that mill when times got tough. Yes, Isaac was aware that these United States were about to see some changes...

The Amish are a good, kind, and hardworking people. They had their Bible. Yet, in their dusky theology, Jesus Christ was not quite a Savior for them. He was not quite God for them. Jesus Christ was not quite a personal Lord and Savior for these good people. Yet, wait, Christ died for all men. Perhaps one day the Amish too will see the glorious aspect of the Savior, this Lord Jesus Christ. Perhaps a new dawn, a brighter, more colorful dawn was about to descend upon the grim pastel of the beliefs of the Amish and their Mennonite cousins of the world.

Even though Isaac made no motion that he wanted a conversation with Ralph, Ralph followed him and the Lehman's employee, Larry, to the cash register. In his heart, Isaac wanted to do nothing more than sit down and talk with Ralph for the next hour or two. Yet, Isaac completely ignored Ralph. Ralph followed him out the door to his buggy. A beautiful Morgan horse was attached to the cart. Yes, Isaac was bucking the system. The Amish don't use Morgans for carts, they use Standardbreds. More than one Amish Bishop questioned Isaac on his horses! Mostly in jest, of course.

Isaac was getting into his buggy, not even acknowledging Ralph. "So, would you like to hear a tape on Marian Apparitions?" said Ralph. "I'm Ralph Piccarreta, by the way" said Ralph.

"Isaac Yoder is mine," said Isaac. "I'm Amish, not Catholic", he said.

"So" said Ralph. "Jesus was Jewish. It's a big world out there. Lot's of people. God loves us all. Tell you what. I know you're allowed to travel with us "English" in our vehicles when needs arise. Can I take you somewhere? Do you need any buggy parts or anything else? We can listen to a cassette tape on the way."

"Mr. Piccarreta, I must say that I find you somewhat annoying. I like you however. Can you take me to a friend's farm? He breeds Morgan Horses. He has a mare of mine that is being bred to his stallion. He is twelve miles from here."

"Let's go," said Ralph, leading the way to his less than posh 1979 Ford Station wagon. They both got into the car, and Ralph continued babbling on... "My wife died seven years ago from cancer. God she was a Saint. We both started going back to Church when we hit sixty. Towards her death, my wife was praying the Rosary every waking moment. The whole last year of her life actually. We lost the kids though, for now. Six of 'em.

We never practiced our faith. Yeah, we went to Mass on occasion. That doesn't cut it with kids. For years I've cried over the poor example we set, Nancy and I. God, I wish we could have those years back." Ralph pulled out of the Lehman's lot and headed south for Winesburg, upon receiving directions from Isaac.

"Morgan Horses – you some kind of renegade?" said Ralph.

Isaac began to smile for the first time. In fact, he couldn't stop laughing. Isaac grabbed his bearded chin to try to help in controlling the laughter. He looked just like Abraham Lincoln. "You know a little about us Amish," said Isaac.

"More than I'll admit" said Ralph. "The Blessed Mother sent me to you… Oh, maybe not to you specifically, but I felt Our Lady wanted me to be here today. Well, yeah, I guess to meet you."

Isaac's face fell stern again. That wasn't any problem for Ralph…

"Yeah, the darn kids won't even step into a Catholic Church anymore. I guess I can't blame them. Our Lady says to just pray for them and she'll protect them – our kids. That's all I can do. And that's all I do since I retired from the steel mill. You know Isaac, as a matter of fact I was here to get a grain mill too. I'm actually trying to make a few preparations for these end times we're living in. Oh, I know the spiritual aspect is all that really matters, but, well, you know, the Antichrist and all that. Things are going to be tough for Christians…"

Isaac's ears perked up. "Ralph, you're not going to believe this, but, well, I believe most of what you are saying. I'm aware of this New World Order, even the Antichrist. I know the hour is late…"

Isaac never heard the tape that day. Ralph couldn't stop talking. He wound up giving the tape to Isaac as he dropped him off, later on in the day, back at Lehman's. Isaac didn't know how he'd ever hear the tape. He didn't have a cassette recorder. A week later, a neighbor friend gave him a ride back into Lehman's. The Baptist neighbor agreed to play the cassette for Isaac. When they arrived at Lehman's neither man wanted to get out of the Chevy Truck. The tape was called the "Thunder of Justice" by Ted Flynn. It was produced by The Mary Foundation. The Mary Foundation strikes again. Hank and his passenger Isaac didn't move until the tape was finished. Then they just sat there staring. Hank began flipping through his Bible, the Gospel of Luke. He wondered why Baptists never prayed the Hail Mary. He was reading most of the words of the Hail Mary prayer right there in the Gospel of Luke. A new day was dawning for Hank Harper. The new day had already dawned for Isaac the day he met Ralph. In a few weeks, the Baptist and the Amish fellow would be meeting in the woods adjoining their properties to pray the Rosary together. Hank had procured a couple of Rosaries from a Presbyterian minister he knew who had come to believe that God had indeed sent Christ's Mother Mary, here and there throughout the world in recent years, to bring man back to his senses, to bring mankind back to Jesus Christ. Hank told the minister he just wanted to "inspect" a couple of those bead things. The minister passed along a couple of booklets entitled "How To Pray The Rosary" too, for inspection purposes, of course. Hank had never been so embarrassed in his life.

Isaac saw nothing wrong with smoking his pipe during the Rosary. Rush Limbaugh would have been proud of Isaac. God didn't mind the pipe either... A Great Horned Owl shuffled out of the trees above the heads of Hank and Isaac. Perhaps he was bothered by the smoke. Isaac took the pipe out of his mouth and looked up with Hank. Then they got back to business. "Hail Mary, full of Grace,..." - *Frank's Bible was open to the Gospel of Luke, Chapter 1.*

****

Alyssa Palmer had been a United Nations fan since she was in cradle. Her parents had taken her there many times in her youth. She had been there with grammar school, high school, and college groups. Now it seems, her dreams were coming true. She had been invited to a meeting of the Population Council of the United Nations. Her many influential contacts and even her own business helped pave the way for her invitation. Soon she would be a paid advisor for the United Nations, regarding environmental and population matters. She was reminiscing of the old days and graduation from Purdue just after having received word from the UN that she was selected as an advisor to the world governing body.

Alyssa had grown up in Holden, Massachusetts, and went to Purdue University after high school. She graduated from Purdue with dual degrees in Communications and Environmental Sciences. With the exception of a C in drafting, Alyssa had straight A's across the board. She had a full four year scholarship to Purdue, and unlike most college graduates these days, she graduated with over twelve thousand dollars in the bank, a Chevy Blazer that she owned outright, and zero debt. She earned most of this herself. She had some support from her none-to-poor family, but she was a hard worker in her own right. She was in "all" of the extra curricular activities at Purdue. She worked for "all" of the causes. So many causes.

Alyssa had been through the boyfriends sure enough. She had lived with two of them. She and her friends at Purdue had shared excessively in the pleasures of alcohol, Marijuana, and then some. She was not a pothead like many of her comrades. She used it medicinally. She did, however, take her medicine on a regular basis. She kept her head about her though, unlike some overindulgent ones she had known. She was planning for the future, planning a career, perhaps her own business. She thought she might like to be a foreign ambassador for the United States, or work for the United Nations.

Upon graduation, her Mom & Dad, and brother Christian made the 1000 mile trip out from Holden to be there with her. They all spent a few days together at Purdue.

On Sunday Alyssa informed her family that she would not be going to the Methodist services with them because she had recanted Christianity. She told them that it was bad for women, the environment, and simply was not logical. They were greatly saddened, but took it in stride. Mr. and Mrs. Palmer went to the Methodist Church for a 10 AM service, and Alyssa and Christian hung out at the Purdue Memorial Building. They watched TV, caught up on old times, and talked about their plans for the future. When her parents returned, the family walked around the campus, past dorms, engineering buildings, pigeons, squirrels, an underground nuclear reactor, libraries, and fountains. When they came to Cary Quad (Quadrangle), a dorm across from Owen Hall, they all sat down on two wooden benches in a park-like setting across from the main hall entrance of the latter dorm building. It was a green that Mr. Palmer used to play football on when he attended Purdue. He had graduated with BS in civil engineering, then followed by master's degrees in civil and chemical engineering. He left Purdue in 1961. Every engineering and chemical company in the United States wanted him. He went to work for Metcalf & Eddy, then Dupont, then Exxon, and finally launched his own consulting business. Albert Palmer reminisced about his days at Purdue. His wife too. She had met him at Purdue. She was an English major. The Palmers were about to depart Purdue. Albert and Beth Palmer knew they had only a few minutes to talk to their daughter about her faith. They struggled to break into the topic.

"Alyssa, we spoke to the pastor at the Methodist Church on Crabb lane. He said he didn't even know who you were. You told us that you had gone there over the years," said Mr. Palmer.

"Yes, when you were home for Christmas break this past year you even told us something about the sermon he gave the week before you came home, something about how all religions are equal in certain ways. I remember that, because it bugged me when you said it," said Mrs. Palmer.

"I've been their fifteen times or so in the last four years," said Alyssa. I've also been to the Catholic Church Saint Thomas More, over that way about ten times. I've been to almost all of the Churches in the area at least a couple of times. I've made a study of it, a project out of it. I came to the conclusion that they had all lost whatever light they might have once had.

All the churches are hypocritical and unrealistic, and dead to the world. Don't do this, don't do that. No birth control, no abortion, no pre-marital sex, no sex education - while people are dying of AIDS and thousands of children are starving to death."

"Honey, the Methodist Church doesn't have firm guidelines on most of that" said Mrs. Palmer. It's really quite a liberal family. The Methodist Church is doing everything it can to bring about AIDS awareness and prevention. They understand the needs of different individuals. You know how your mother and I feel about these things, but the Methodist Church has not set up a lot of roadblocks based on ignorance of God like the Catholics. I think you've forgotten your faith and confused it with Catholicism. You say you've been to their church – why?" said Mrs. Palmer.

"Wait a minute Mom, back up, what faith? Did I ever know faith? Sunday school and sometimes Sunday services when you weren't busy. Is that faith? Where was faith in action?"

"Don't talk that way to your Mother Alyssa. We fed you, clothed you, and helped put you through Purdue. And now this" said Mr. Palmer.

"Look Mom, Dad, Christianity is going to kill the world. Unchecked population increases are going to do us in. You sent me here to learn. I learned science, history, math, computers, whatever. Use the science, or use the math, or use the history - the environment is approaching the point of no return. Yet, Christians say, *bring on the children, extend the life of the old - put God first.* What God?" said Alyssa.

"You know very well that the Methodist Church does not speak against population control or birth control Alyssa," said Mrs. Palmer. That's that Catholic nonsense that you've gotten into your head."

"That's part of it Mom, I don't know what the Methodist Church teaches, or the Presbyterians, or Baptists, or the Moonies for that matter. Pick and choose Christianity. What do you want Jesus to be for you? How do you interpret this reading or that reading? Sola Scriptura. Martin Luther was an idiot. And the Wesley's and Calvins of the world only took his ball and ran with it. It seems the only enemy is the Catholic Church, you're right."

Christian just sat there. In his heart he felt that Alyssa was right. She had set a fire under him. He knew that this discussion was not for him at this time, however. He knew his parents felt like they were losing their daughter in more than one way at this college graduation. Mom & Dad had to have their say with Alyssa, because from this day on she was out in the world on her own now.

"What do you mean we're right?" said Mr. Palmer.

"It's the Catholic Church that is the real roadblock. Mr. 'Better Than Thou Art' in the Vatican and all of his followers. Well not all of his followers, just a small percentage of them - the ones who actually follow the Pope" said Alyssa.

"Alyssa, I have no idea what you're talking about. Your Mother and I and Christian have to get going, we've got a long drive ahead of us. Just tell me though, what do you mean when you say we're right," said Mr. Palmer.

"I was just saying that Protestantism is better for the environment than Catholicism. You sent me here to get a degree in science. I got it. All of my classes, all of my books, and most of my professors have taught me that the world is in grave danger of annihilation right now, as we speak. There is an unseen battle going on in the world right now - overpopulation, food production, pollution, vanishing species, vanishing rain forests and on and on - all of this vs. the Pope. It's odd. I admire the Pope for taking a stand on things. He's got guts. The world seems wishy-washy compared to Pope John Paul II. I mean, what do we stand for as Methodists, Presbyterians, Baptists, or Mormons. Any fool with a Bible is free to interpret it however he wants to - there's the Reformation for you again. Everything is fine for us as long as we accept Jesus Christ as Lord and Savior, Mormons excepted. All talk no action. The Pope has chartered an exact course for one-fifth of the world, that is, the Catholics, to take. However, he has chosen poorly. He will turn us into cannibals soon with overpopulation. And he's got this thing against women. I hope the next Pope is a woman. Then maybe I'll become a Catholic."

"Don't talk that way Alyssa," said Mrs. Palmer. "Would you promise me you won't be going to anymore Catholic Churches Alyssa? I can't understand you anymore, and I think you've picked up some bad habits from doing so."

"Look Mom, I don't like the Catholic Church, don't worry. I'm just searching right now. I'll probably be back to the Methodist Church soon. They seem to care about old Mother Earth, as well as most of the churches in the World Council of Churches. There seems to be a general unity emerging in such groups now. I'm studying the situation now. I think religion is coming back full circle with this unity, oneness, or whatever you'd like to call it. I think that Christianity is on the brink of getting its act together. They're talking more about concern for the world now, about ending wars, poverty, pollution, and the helping the environment in general. Some of what is happening is really starting to get my interest as the walls of separatism are coming down. I'm sorry I didn't go to Church with you this morning, I should have."

"Call us when you get to Bar Harbor, Alyssa," said Mr. Palmer.

"Sure Dad" said Alyssa.

"Do you need any money to get you through your first few months?" said Mrs. Palmer?

"No thanks, I'll be O.K.," replied Alyssa.   Mrs. Palmer handed her daughter an envelope with one thousand dollars in it.

"We knew you'd say that. Take this to help you get started. Don't lose it. There's a thousand dollars in it. I should have gotten you travelers checks but we were in a hurry when we left."

****

Graduation and May of 1991 passed. Several more boyfriends passed. Alyssa was proud of herself. Upon graduation from Purdue, she set up a clothing store, a boutique of a certain nature in Bar Harbor, Maine. She had been there almost every summer of her life with her parents before her college days, and she was in love with the place. The quaint, small town of Bar Harbor was one of the busiest coastal towns in New England for three months of the year. It was the gateway to Acadia National Park - America's premier doorstep to the Atlantic.

Alyssa had set up shop in 2000 square feet of rented space in an old but remodeled building on the corner of Bar and Jordan streets, the busiest spot in town. She owned the 8000 square foot building within a year and could have retired on rental income. Her store, "One World Clothing" prospered, however. In some of her graduate studies in a joint program between the University of Maine and College of the Atlantic (the latter in Bar Harbor), she came across her old friend hemp. Hemp! Marijuana! It was used as a fuel in some countries! It was used as a clothing fiber in some countries! It was used as medicine the world over! They even made sneakers of it in Israel! It made the best ropes, was an ingredient in Eastern dishes, and was an excellent cash crop (not stateside, however, unless you were a fly by night gardener). More than that, if you read enough into the concocted reports from the pothead scientists and environmental wackos of the world you would find this baby just might save Mother Earth. You can make paper from this stuff - a renewable resource (smoke it when you were done, figuratively speaking)! How excellently Bohemian. Needless to say Alyssa's One World Clothing was a pioneering effort in hemp-mania. She did well. The brand name hemp sneakers sold well. The hemp T-shirts and informal dress shirts sold extremely well. There were hemp blankets, worry beads, teas, ropes, hemp paraphernalia, foods, and much more. The shop also carried a full line of other "Save The Earth" products, videos, tapes, and books.

Alyssa looked back on her accomplishments a long time. She was brought back to current time when a customer asked her "Do you happen to

know if the factory where these hemp sneakers are made uses fossil fuels?"
"No, I'm sorry", Alyssa replied, "I'm not sure."

****

The Bohatch family had chosen Bar Harbor Campground as their temporary residence for the next two weeks or so. They would soon be arriving. Though the campground did not go right to the shore, it was just two miles from the main entrance to Acadia National Park, offered many campsites with commanding views of Frenchman's Bay, and the blueberries were everywhere. They could have gone into the park to a more rustic setting on the ocean, but that would have meant no showers, hot water, and other facilities that are handy for a family with a baby and young children.

There were a few things that Paul couldn't get off his mind during their two-day trip, and even now as they were nearing the end of their trek to Bar Harbor. They had to do with the times, as Christians now know them. They had to do with Our Lady's messages from Medjugorje, and elsewhere - from Father Nairobi and the Marian Movement of Clergy, to Akita and Betania. The theme of the messages from these Marian sources and others were similar - *Pray hard, Jesus is not exactly ecstatic with the way things are going on down here now.* No, the world was not ending. In fact, the world was about to experience a glorious new beginning in God's time. The world was about to enter into the Reign of the Immaculate Heart of Mary and the Eucharistic Heart of Jesus - it doesn't get any better than this. First, however, the gold must be tested as if in fire. If man did not turn back to God through his own volition, then God would send the chastisements as in the days of Noah *(though never the great flood again!)*, as in the days of Sodom and Gomorrah. The Virgin Mary had told the world through several sources that the world today is in a much more sinful state than in the days of Noah. What punishments are we to expect if we do not turn back while we yet have time?

These birth pangs of the Reign of Peace foretold by Mary at Fatima, Portugal in 1917, and seen by numerous saints like Saint John Bosco would come on many fronts. They would come in the form of persecutions against Christians and the Church, particularly the Catholic Church, the Bark of Peter as Saint John Bosco saw. The attack would come on all sides until Christ's ship, the Church, was safely docked between the two pillars representing the Immaculate Heart of Mary and this Eucharistic Heart of Jesus. Yes, one day everyone everywhere in the world will universally accept Jesus as Lord and Savior, and Mary as Coredemptrix, Mediatrix, and Advocate. There will be no exceptions in the end. Until then, the attack on purity through contraception, sex education, abortion, homosexuality, and immodesty would continue. Until then we would apparently have our Rwandas and Bosnias. Until then, we will have public, private, and often even Christian (sometimes Catholic) schools paving the way toward immorality and impurity through the coercion and programs of Planned Parenthood, the National Education Association, the National Catholic Education Association, Freemasonry, and the governments at the local, state, and federal levels. Until we are converted it seems that life will not be considered sacred and abortion, the murdering of our unborn will rule the day. Until our conversion, it seems that we will have the need to indeed be chastised a little by God for our own good. For if a child is not punished for the wrong he does, the child will grow up unruly.

As Paul was considering these things to come, not in a morbid way, but in a factual and necessary way nevertheless, he could not help wondering about the series of faxes he received prior to stepping out the door on vacation. He had mentioned them to Barbara, but it was almost as if he did so in passing and not really with the intention of bringing the subject for discussion with her. The faxes were from three different Marian groups. Over the years, Paul had supported various Marian groups that were conveying Our Lady's messages from current or recent apparitions from around the world - only those that worked in full obedience the Magisterium and Pope John Paul II. From time to time some of the groups had asked if their supporters would like to be a part of a phone or fax tree - a group of people that could quickly convey Our Lady's messages in a hurry if need be. Such would be the case if a message was given for the world in which it might be likely that the world's media - the major networks, newspapers, television and radio stations, would intentionally not want to cover. Since the major networks are all controlled by unseen powers and movements, it is not likely that an urgent message from Our Lady would be covered in any event. Certainly, every word of hope that the Virgin Mary brings to the world is of urgent importance to all mankind. However, Mary has told us in various places, that specific warnings and/or chastisements would be foretold by her some days before they are to occur, and that the time from the alert to the incident(s) should be a time of prayer, fasting, penance, conversion. Of Course, Mary has told us not to wait! We should do these things today, this morning, tonight, every day! Christ told us to pray always! In the case of Medjugorje, for example, Mary has given the six visionaries ten secrets (four of the six have received all 10 secrets thus far) dealing with mankind in relation to God. The seventh secret was reportedly a warning, perhaps a lesser chastisement that was minimized or mitigated because of the prayers and penance of the faithful. The latter three secrets of Medjugorje have to do with warnings or chastisements of a serious nature. They have not yet been fulfilled. They will serve as last attempts by God to call mankind back to Him, through own will, through our own "yes" to God. We have been told that these three secrets cannot be eliminated - that they will occur. The date of each of the three warnings will be told to Marie Pavlich, one of the visionaries, ten days before each event happens. The foretold events could come back to back, or they could come spaced in time. Marie is to tell a Priest of her choosing (she has chosen Father Andrieu Stiz) of the particular event's imminence. Father Andrieu is to pray and fast for one week, and then, if he chooses, at the end of the week he may pass on the news of the foretold event these three days before it happens. Again, it is likely that the world press will not be on the edge of their seat waiting to relay the information. That is why some of the Marian groups of the world are preparing for such events. And that brings us back again to the faxes in Paul's machine.

Our Lady's monthly messages from Medjugorje had always been brief, and in a certain sense universally applicable. Such messages generally carried the theme of "Pray, Fast, Penance (Confession where applicable), Conversion of Hearts, and daily Mass (where applicable)". Generally the specifics were left to our hearts - to apply these rules, these characteristics to ourselves, and the world will then improve one by one, starting with each of us. Yes, there had been times, often, when these six visionaries had received certain information regarding an individual or event, but these messages were generally given by Our Lady as being private messages to help a particular situation or event in a person's life. Indeed all of Our Lady's messages are properly to be called "private messages" by the Church and laity and are never to be held as binding on anyone, even if they are one day approved by the Church. So, when a so-called "message for the world" is received by a visionary, this too, per definition, is a private message. Regardless, from the stating of the first message received by Paul's fax from Our Lady, Queen of The Americas group in Anaheim, California, it was evident, if authentic, that this was the 8th secret of Medjugorje - that a chastisement was about to befall the world! The message was:

Dear Friends of Jesus & Mary:

We have just received via fax a message from Medjugorje. We believe it concerns the 8th secret given to the visionaries, a chastisement of great proportions, and the first of the three warnings/chastisements spoken of at Medjugorje. The fax failed, and our copy is in part illegible. The phone lines to Medjugorje are out of order. We have contacted sources in Zagreb, Dubrovnik, and Split, but we cannot confirm the message. We do know that at this time all traffic to and from Medjugorje is being turned away. Please tell any pilgrim groups enroute or preparing to go to Medjugorje that they will be detained at airports in Croatia, Bosnia, and Slovenia. We were told that a young Bosnian who attempted to leave Medjugorje in an ultralight aircraft drew gunfire from snipers on local hillsides. Some believe that he made it all the way to Dubrovnik.

Until the report we received is confirmed, we will not release the partial fax that we have received, which could only confuse matters through speculation. If it does concern the 8th secret as we perceive, and if the news has been relayed by Father Andrieu after his specified period of prayer and fasting (7 days), then the world now has less than three days to prepare for the first of three wake-up calls from God. Of course, our only preparation is our daily preparation - prayer!

Lastly the word "America" was in the fax content. Also, as some of you may have heard, 15 minutes ago the West Coast began experiencing tremors centered in Seattle, but felt from Los Angeles to Juneau. Several cities began earthquake preparation less than ten minutes into the tremors. Also in the news this morning, the National Weather Service was surprised to wake up to a major storm development just north of Grand Turk Island in the Bahamas. The "little" thunder squall was upgraded to a Tropical Storm about 30 minutes ago, 8:32 EST. The storm has been dubbed "Michael".

Perhaps unrelated, but needing your prayers regardless, the United Nations has called for emergency closed door meetings for all ambassadors and top level agency personnel. There is some heavy action taking place in New York right now.

We will keep you posted by fax, and if necessary, by phone.

The Peace and joy of Jesus & Mary be always with you.

Sincerely,

Horace and Regina Nielsen
President & Vice President, Our Lady Queen of The Americas
Anaheim, California

The second fax Paul received was as follows:

Buffalo Marian Center
133 Amy Kriss Drive
Buffalo, NY 14203

7/30/98
9:02 AM EST (time of writing)

Dear Marian Centers:

We have received a letter of condemnation concerning the reported fax supposedly received by the Anaheim, California Marian Center (Our Lady, Queen of The Americas) regarding the 8th secret of Medjugorje being imminent.
The fax letter from Medjugorje (via Mostar) is reprinted below.

Saint John's Church
Rectory
Mostar, Bosnia-Herzegovina

7/30/98

We condemn the supposed fax received by the Anaheim, California Marian Center called "Our Lady, Queen of The Americas" supposedly regarding one of the secrets of Medjugorje being imminent. No such fax has been sent from Medjugorje. Please disregard all material and information that you may have received from this center.
At this time, we completely dissociate the happenings at Medjugorje from this California center. We also request that "Our Lady, Queen of The Americas" discontinue the use of the word "Medjugorje" and refrain from covering all news pertaining thereof.
Finally, as you know, Bishop Milesovic is said to be preparing a formal condemnation of the supposed happenings at Medjugorje.
Sincerely,

Father Michael Plaz/for Bishop Milesovic

The third letter that Paul received prior to leaving for Bar Harbor was also equally interesting:

Office Of The Sacred Congregation for the Doctrine of the Faith
Vatican City, Rome

7/30/98

Dear Marian Centers/Catholic Publishers:

In light of the apocalyptic letters (faxes) reportedly circulating through many Marian offices on this day of June 30th, 1998, we hereby declare that all such letters regarding the imminence of secrets concerning unapproved events in Medjugorje, Bosnia Herzegovina be ceased.

The Holy Father disapproves of all such threatening reports.

In Christ,

(unsigned but stamped)

The Sacred Congregation for the Doctrine of the Faith

Such faxes were not to be found only on the desk of Paul Bohatch on the morning of June 30, 1998, but on the computers, in the fax machines, and on the desks of thousands of other individuals and Marian centers by midday. These same messages were accessible to millions of others throughout the world who had access to the Internet. The mainline press carried no mention of the events on this day or in the days to come.

Aside from calling some friends and family to tell them about the faxes, Paul put the information temporarily in the back of his mind. He did however, send three faxes, and make three additional calls of his own. He faxed a display ad to the Bar Harbor Times, the Ellsworth American, and the Boston Globe. He paid for them with his already maxed-out American Express Card, while taking care of the details with his follow-up calls to each of the three newspapers. The ad read as follows:

First Annual Acadia Medjugorje Conference JULY 3,4,5
Acadia National Park
Mount Desert Isle, Maine
Speakers To Be Announced
Schedule:
Friday: 3 PM-7:30 PM Jordan Pond
Saturday: 10 AM-7:30 PM Sand Beach
Sunday: 10 AM-4 PM Cadillac Mountain (We hope to have a noon Mass)
Admission is FREE
For Additional Information Contact:
Paul Bohatch
Cellular Phone: 740-269-9999
Paul may also be contacted at Bar Harbor Campground 207-997-4488
(7/1-7/14/98)

Paul felt bad for several reasons. First, he did not know why he was doing this, other than the fact that he had missed the last several Notre Dame and Steel City (Pittsburgh) Medjugorje Conferences and would like to make up for it! Also, if there was any validity to the fax from Medjugorje (the first one from Anaheim), he would like to be together with as many prayerful people as possible. Perhaps, and more importantly, he had not mentioned anything about such a gathering to his poor wife. Perhaps some husbands would have discussed the matter! How was he going to tell her? She was looking forward to some R&R. Oh, and then there's the matter of the National Park Service! That's why Paul mixed up the meeting place - to keep the rangers guessing! And a Mass? You need a priest for a Mass. Paul packed away the necessary Mass items that would be needed just in case he ran into a traveling priest open to Our Lady's call. Call it impulsive if you will.

****

In an area surrounding a little hamlet in Bosnia Herzegovina, a town in which Pope John Paul II told Bishop Paolo Hnilica that the last battle of communism would be fought, this same Medjugorje, confusion reigned, at least on its borders. Inside its border, the people calmly prayed the Rosary, and went to Masses on end. UN trucks rolled everywhere at will, but that was about all of the vehicular movement, aside from an occasional fly-by from UN jets. Ah, this UN machine was so well lubricated by now, and was flexing more and more muscle everyday, in little towns like Medjugorje, and in big towns like Washington DC. If the world only knew how far into the skull of mankind the talons of Big Brother, call it Big Money or the New World Order had already pierced. And how rapid was its advance! And the president of the United States and his comrades were laughing at it, and at us, in their beer, and in their bestial brothels.

Yes, by early in the evening in Medjugorje, the phone lines were beginning to mysteriously fade in and out. Attempted short wave and other radio communications failed too, mysteriously, some thought at first. The UN roadblocks were not mysterious. They were just there.

Unseen vultures, black as death - no death themselves, were darting about the hills, streams, and other borders of the small Catholic town, trying to pierce the shroud protecting the town. But if the Serbian jets and tanks and mortars, and Muslim bombs and machine guns could not pierce Medjugorje's Heavenly protection, then neither would the red and yellow-eyed imps and specters from Hell. Our Lady was there, and her mantle was upon Medjugorje. Communications with the outside world, however, were severed on this Tuesday, June 30th, 1998. Now what would Hell have to fear from a lovely Lady dressed in blue?

****

"What are you thinking of honey" said Barbara Bohatch, getting a little annoyed at her husband's aloofness. "You're so quiet", she said.
"Oh, nothing honey. Nothing really..." His voice trailed off.
"I know you're up to something. What did you do?" she said.

****

Rick Tremont was sitting up against the wall of Don's Shop & Save in Bar Harbor, just before noon on Thursday, July 2, 1998. His backpack and duffel bag were beside him, accounting for everything he had taken with him from Ohio. He had purchased enough food to last him a few days, a week if need be. He had just finished praying over his milk and cheese when two ladies with French accents approached him. "Pardon me, can I ask you if you are here for the Medjugorje Conference?" asked a beautiful young lady about Rick's age.

Now Rick was not exactly looking and feeling his best after his cross country trek with Greyhound, sleep depravation, and lacking a shave, shower, and even that very intimate feeling of a mouth freshly brushed with Aquafresh. Rick stunk rather badly and he looked rather scary. God bless this young lady who still had the nerve to address Rick in his current state. Rick was taken aback at the young lady's beauty and did not really take in what she had said.

"I was wondering if you were here for the Medjugorje Conference?" she said again boldly looking into his eyes. "Oh, you mean someone else on this island has heard of Medjugorje? Praise the Lord", Rick said. "But what conference, what do you mean?" he said.

"The Bar Harbor times has a large ad in it for a Medjugorje Conference on July 3,4, and 5th", she said.

"Wow, I can't believe it", Rick replied. "Right here in the town of Bar Harbor?" said Rick.

"Actually it's in the park." She opened up the newspaper to a 3 column times 5-inch add for the conference. "By the way, my name is Therese, and this is my mother Anna" said Therese.

"I'm Rick Tremont. Pardon my looks, I'm fresh out of jail, just off a bus, and lacking in the use of certain amenities at this moment." Rick mentioned jail to peak the attention of his newfound friends. He thought for a moment that he had just stooped to bragging. In an instant he felt remorse for having mentioned it.   He knew that Therese and her mom would ask him about jail, and that he would come out smelling like a rose in their eyes.

"Babies?" said Therese.

"What?" said Rick.

"Babies.   You're a rescuer, aren't you?   There's one missing in Ohio." said Therese.

"What?" said Rick.   "I mean how did you know?   Am I the only Christian around here that's not a mystic?   How did you know?" said Rick with a perplexed smile on his face.

"You might want to change your shirt Rick," said Mrs. Pierpont.   "We saw a news clipping of the rescue you were last in on television last night. CNT ran it from their archived file of your last arrest. They also showed you and the others at your preliminary hearing a few days ago - you had that same shirt on.   The camera showed a close-up of you and your shirt. Therese and I almost died laughing - the reporter had the nerve to say that you were showing a great disrespect for 'life' - the irony of it - 'Eat More Whales, Save The Baby Humans'.   *The reporter was serious about your disrespect.*   They mentioned you were AWOL at another hearing yesterday, but they dropped your charges just the same as they did for the others. They told it all on national television, in a clipping that lasted less than 30 seconds.   Oh, the prosecutor was quite upset at that in your absence.   He wanted...."

"What!" said Rick.   "They dropped the charges?"

"You're a free man unless you've got some parking tickets you haven't paid," said Therese.   "You didn't know?"

"God!   Man, praise the Lord!   No, I was on a bus!..."

"Well, congratulations then Rick!" said Anna Pierpont.

"Thanks.   Oh God, I'm a free man..."

"Rick, you might be shot however, with that shirt on in this town" said Therese.   "You might consider changing it."

"Oh, yeah" said Rick.   "Oh, don't get me wrong.   I've been out on the whaleboats every time I've been here.   I love seeing them..."

"Sure you do.   You probably throw coke cans at them when you're out there", teased Therese, balancing herself on one foot as she gave Rick a mock kick to the ankle.

"Are you sure they dropped the charges?   Why?   They had an air tight case against us."

"You're a free man, to use the judges words verbatim.   We don't normally watch television, but they had one on at Rosalie's last night. Have you ever had pizza at Rosalie's?" said Therese.

"Yes, I have" said Rick, "I was here often with my family in my youth - the food is great there".

"Wait. Wait. Wait. Why? Why did they drop the charges?" said Rick again.

"Your arrest procedure was improper," said Anna.

"Oh my God" said Rick. "Officer Worrall planned it all I bet. He was crying when he had to arrest us. He'll lose his job…"

"God will bless him a hundred fold," said Anna Pierpont.

"You're from Quebec I would guess from your accents, aren't you?" said Rick.

"Nova Scotia. A small town called Gunning Cove, on the Southeast tip" said Therese.

"I'll go do our shopping Therese. I've got to get that ice for the cooler before we go," said Mrs. Pierpont. She nodded to Rick and went into Don's.

Rick's heart dropped like a bombshell out the trap door of a B-34. He thought the girl of his dreams was leaving momentarily, off to a foreign country, never to be seen by him again. He was standing now, as he had risen some few minutes ago. He had the great desire to reach out and hold this girl's hands and never let go. He became quite nervous, and even sad, despite his newfound joy, his new friends - Therese and her mother. He did not want to say goodbye….

"What brings a runaway rescuer to Bar Harbor?" said Therese.

"The ocean" said Rick with a smile on his face, trying to regroup himself.

"I wanted to stick my feet in the Atlantic", he said.

"A funny man" replied Therese. "And the real reason?"

"I don't know how to say this, but I think God brought me here. Strange as it may sound, I don't think our meeting was by chance either," said Rick.

"Well, if you can guess where I went to College, I'll take that as a confirmation that we were supposed to meet", Therese replied.

Rick thought for a moment. There was only one school that came to his mind. But she lived so far away from it. "Steubie U" said Rick without flinching.

"Ohhh my God! You said it. Oh my God - and I'm from Canada. Oh my God…." said Therese. "Oh my God. Another God incidence." "How did you know?" said Therese.

"Well, it really wasn't anything. Every time a meet a fired up young Catholic, and I've run with the best of them, I think of Franciscan University in Steubenville. Most of the friends I've made in the last four or five years went to Franciscan University. Aside from the holiest used car salesman I know - Randy Engels of the Rescue Movement, most of the rescuing activity in our country has had some connection to Franciscan University. It's incredible when you think about it. I hope I can talk with you about it sometime, but, oh, God, you're leaving...."

"Not today" said Therese.

"But you're mother said...."

"We're just going to visit relatives. We're going to be here for two weeks."

Heaven thought Rick. *Sorry God! "That's great*," said Rick.

"Before I propose a Rosalie's pizza to you and your mom, I better ask if you're married or engaged or anything like that. On top of that, since you're from Franciscan I might as well ask if you're off to the convent soon," said Rick.

"Neither of the above, but formerly close on several accounts," said Therese. "And you?"

"Neither of the above, but formerly close on several accounts, convent excluded" said Rick.

"You went to Franciscan too?" said Therese.

"Ohio state. I'm a chemical engineer" replied Rick.

"I'm a nurse," said Therese.

"How did you know I was a fired up Catholic?" said Therese.

"It's written all over your face," said Rick.

"You'd make a lousy poet", Rick.

"Thanks", was his reply.

Mrs. Pierpont came out of Don's with a half a carriage of groceries. "Honey, we need to get going. We've got to be in Boston in five hours. I think we're going to be late, even if we were to leave right now. We need to get this ice back to the cooler at the campground. We're off to visit a brother and sister of mine Rick. Most of our relatives live in New England."

"Mom, you won't believe the conversation that Rick and I just had" said Therese. "Well, I hope I can hear of it from Rick himself, tomorrow perhaps. Will you be here for a few days Rick?" said Mrs. Pierpont.

"I hope to be here a while, at least a few weeks" said Rick

"We'll be here about two weeks ourselves, Rick," said Mrs. Pierpont.

"Yes, Therese just told me," said Rick.

"I have a feeling that we'll, well, Therese will be seeing a lot of you" said Mrs. Pierpont again.

"You don't even know this jailbird!"

"I see you're not married. You're not divorced are you, or engaged?" said Mrs. Pierpont.

"What? I mean no," said Rick.

"Mom, what are you doing?" said Therese.

"Then aside from our immediate family, I would trust you with Therese more than anyone else in the world", she said.

"Oh, great mom" said Therese. "Do you already have a wedding present picked out for us", she said, playing along with the game. She knew however, that her mother was quite serious. She knew that her mother was right. It was enough for her mother to see Jesus Christ in Rick Tremont. When a young man is walking with Jesus & Mary, everything else amounts to a pile of straw. When a young man risks liberty for the unborn, in a holy and prayerful way, there is joy in heaven. Yes, Therese knew why her mother had spoken that way. And beneath his grubbiness, his bristles, his odor, dirty clothes, and apparent poverty, Therese herself was fairly sure, but not positive, that there was a handsome man indeed. *My God, what am I thinking*, thought Therese, as she was saying goodbye to Rick.

Rick was almost at a loss for words as he was saying goodbye to the Pierponts. As he was looking at surely the most beautiful girl in Nova Scotia, her long black hair, her tanned face, her commanding stature, and even her simplicity, he found himself hoping that her mother would start working on their wedding plans. *Oh God, I'm here for God, what am I thinking about marriage for?, thought Rick. Wait, He brought me here. Jesus introduced me. I'm going to marry that girl! Jesus, perhaps you don't want me to be a priest after all. You brought me here to meet Therese! How can I know for sure? Jesus! Let me know. Before this vacation is over, let me know!*

"Goodbye Therese, bye Mrs. Pierpont" said Rick, "I'll see you tomorrow."

"Goodbye Rick" said Mrs. Pierpont.

"Bye Rick. You owe me a Rosalie's pizza," said Therese.

"Wait," said Rick. "Where tomorrow?"

"The conference" said Therese.

"Are you sure about this? You can't have a God conference in a National Park these days. Do you think this is real? I mean the fellow left a campground for a contact address, and you said the campground didn't know anything about it. Besides, there aren't any facilities outside of restrooms at Sand Beach and Cadillac Mountain. To tell you the truth, I can't see them allowing this at Jordan Pond either - the restaurant there. This is the peak season for tourists" said Rick"

Mrs. Pierpont spoke up - "It will happen Rick. Trust in God. With God all things are possible. The more improbable for man, the more probable that it will be a holy success for God. I will grant you that this is all probably news for the Park Service. I have a feeling that they and/or others will try to put Our Lady out of business here. So we should all probably start praying for this conference and this mysterious Mr. Paul Bohatch, I think that's his name. Keep us and my brother and sister in your prayers too. We're on our way down there to try to drag them and their families up here to the conference. I'm not sure if I'll even tell my sister about the conference. I could mention it to my brother, but my sister, I don't know. She might put up a quick wall if I do. They both fell away from the Catholic Faith a long time ago. My sister thinks we're all going to hell, us Catholics, from her "Bible believing" perspective; and my brother the engineer got too smart to believe in God. Perhaps his hearing about you will inspire him to come, you being an engineer and all," said Mrs. Pierpont.

"I'll be praying for you. I'll be here with the whales, God bless them, each and every one. Oh, I've got to get this shirt off. Bye!" said Rick.

"Rick, one more thing, did you hear about the fax from Medjugorje?" said Therese, calling back to him from 10 feet away.

"What fax?" said Rick.

"I'll tell you about it tomorrow" said Therese.

****

At 4 PM on Tuesday, June 30th, 1998, several million high school students from across the nation were watching an Apache Attack Helicopter come speeding into their living room with no apparent concern for the safety of the inhabitants on the part of the pilots. *Well, it was a television commercial for the Army. It was one of those action packed 30-second commercials that make a man or woman of any age want to go out and do such exciting things as shown in the commercial.* Indeed, the Army Recruiting Center phones across the nation were ringing off the hook. "Introduction To The Army" brochures, booklets, CD-ROMS, and even videos were being sent out to hundreds of thousands of young prospects at alarming rates. Most of the students were caught off guard. Some of the students were not. The latter wondered at the wording of the commercials, brochures, and videos. What was lacking was the phrase United States or U.S. Whose Army was this? There were no U.S. flags to be seen in the ads. There was no mention of Uncle Sam or George Washington for that matter. None of the aircraft or ground vehicles were identified. Just a bunch of guys and ladies in green uniforms. Whose Army was this? Who are these people? So few people on the receiving end of these commercials asked themselves or others whose Army this was. Army, be all you can be. What army?

The other branches of the *Armed Services (whose?)* were not to be outdone. All across the United States similar ads from the Marines, Air Force, Navy, and Coast Guard raced across hundreds of millions of television and computer screens. Phones were ringing off the hook. None of the callers asked "Whose Marines?", "Whose Air Force?", "Whose Navy?", or "Whose Coast Guard?".

Similar ads were running in so-called democracies throughout the world at this time. Hard as it might be to believe, many of the international advertisements for "Armed Services" were actually running some of the same clippings for the military advertisements that were being used in the United States. They didn't even have to paint the trucks, planes, or jeeps to protect the innocent. That had been done long ago. UN blue, green or light brown were the favorite colors. Everybody liked them!

Thousands of young Christian men from around the country, the cream of the crop from God-fearing families across this once great nation of ours were being rounded up for arrest. They were being sent to jail for failing to register for the "Armed Services". **Whose Armed Services?** Many of the families of such young men sent their children into hiding. They and their children did not wish to be a part of the military arm of the coming One World Order. It is one thing to follow George Washington or Abraham Lincoln in defending one's country. It is another to go off to do the battles of George Bush, Satan, Bill Clinton, and Cecil Rhodes & Company. Stiff sentences were being handed out by the government for those who failed to register. Often the families of these youth were being attacked by the long arms of the IRS, state social service organizations (mobilized to "protect" the other children in these families - sometimes removing the younger children from the family) and other federal, state, and local agencies. The favorite book of these young men had become the life of Saint Edmond Campion. Indeed, some of these young men followed Edmond into underground Catholic Seminaries, and into the priesthood.

****

One might be tempted to have preconceived misconceptions about a man called John Wesley from the northwest woods of Alabama. As it is, one would be correct in this regards to assume that John was not a Saint Louis Marie Grignon de Montfort man. Furthermore, it would be a correct guess to assume that the man neither turns toward Mecca nor Rome daily nor annually, not even on special feast days unbeknownst to him. Yet, despite all of this, our John is not a Methodist. Our John finds himself in the shoes and person of a Baptist minister, in the heart of the Baptist Nation in the middle of the Bible belt. This is John Wesley, a 39-year-old Baptist minister, father of 5 children, principal of a Baptist grammar school and high school, and devoted husband.

John and Paulette Wesley live in Schuster Alabama, with their children John, Paul, Cindy, Elizabeth, and Robert. Their children's ages are from 1 to 15. Schuster is a town northwest of Birmingham that no one has ever heard of who hasn't lived there. You don't drive through Schuster by mistake. You just go there, but you can't get anywhere from there unless you leave there first, retreating on the roads you came in on, and then heading left or right to somewhere. Yet, Schuster was home to 2000 people. It might be best to call them pilgrims or patriots. Call them heroes. They said yes to life. One thousand one hundred of the "capitas" were under the age of 21. The families in Schuster averaged 5.1 children. When Mother Regina from Birmingham, Alabama, the very holy cloistered Catholic nun of cable television and short-wave radio fame heard of the town in 1993, she wanted to do a series on the town, to find out what makes them tick. Sadly, however, the town did not want to be a part of Catholic television. Almost all Baptist, with just three Baptist Churches and one Methodist Church, Catholicism had no roots here. The townspeople had what they thought was a proper and required measure of caution in regards to the Papists. Mother Regina and the nuns, priests, and brothers of her order prayed that someday the town would call them for the interview. Mother did not want to force the interview by just dropping in on the town and interviewing the man on the street. She would not come if she did not have the consent of at least a few of the pastors. So they prayed in Birmingham.

They were good people here, however. Everyone was welcome. Catholics were indeed welcome, but not the Catholic Faith. From what they were taught, including their ministers, Catholicism was a disease formerly related to Christianity. Theirs (the people of Schuster) was not necessary a bigoted approach, as much as it was an educated approach. The truth of history has not shown through in the textbooks of North America or Europe. The proliferators of the enlightenment have wreaked their havoc. Cortez, sent by God to end human sacrifice has been deemed a Hitler prototype. The early history of North America has been whitewashed free of Catholicism. From the simplest things like the children of America not being taught that Columbus' flagship, the Santa Maria was named after, dedicated to, and put under the protection of the Virgin Mary. Lacking also is the knowledge that when Columbus and his men stepped on the land of the strange New World they recited the "Hail Holy Queen, Mother of Mercy". In Schuster as elsewhere, the children and their parents did not know that the countries of Central and South America are 95% Catholic. Neither did they know why. It is because the Virgin Mary appeared to an Indian, Juan Diego, in 1531. Due to the many miracles and graces from God brought by Our Lady, the Indians were lovingly and happily swept into Christianity, into Catholicism, nine million of them within ten years. Have "we the people" been taught that Our Lady apparently appeared to George Washington at Valley Forge in 1777 as history would have it. Have we learned of President Washington's constant prayers to God during his days as General? Have we or the people of Schuster memorized Mary's words to him as reported in the National Tribune, Volume 4, #12, December 1880, as passed on by his friend Anthony Sherman? Do our children know that in 1796, the United States Supreme Court ruled in Runkel vs. Winemiller that: "By our form of government, the Christian religion is the established religion and all sects and denominations of Christians are placed upon the same equal footing." So much of America's Christian beginnings, particularly Catholic Christian beginnings have been erased from the books and minds of men. So many books lacking truth and wisdom have appeared to fill the void in not only American History, but in the history of Christianity and the world since Jesus Christ walked the earth as Man and God!

If our bookshelves are lopsided, then our minds will bear brunt of it. So many books have been written against the faith in modern times, and in the history of our country. The bookshelves in Schuster looked much like the bookshelves in most Protestant towns and homes. It is no wonder that the people of Schuster, or the people of Buffalo, or the people of Santa Clara sometimes have grave misunderstandings and biases against the Catholic Church - for it is often the logical thing to do, given the material at hand. Unfortunately, this too is further ingrained by a handing down from prior generations.

It still stands, however, that the holiness of this town is plainly evident, lacking only in certain amenities that would come with further prayer and study. In current times, the fabric of this town was held together by ten Baptist and two Methodist ministers manning the four aforesaid churches. All of the men were good men working for God with all of their hearts. Some of the men were saintly. John Wesley was at the head of all of them, not by his own doing but by the will of God. His holiness preceded him. His fasting had decimated his body to the thinness of a high school wrestler awaiting the sectional playoffs in February, long after regular season had passed. Yes, as a fundamentalist, John took Jesus at His word when He said, "This kind of demon can only be removed by much prayer and fasting." When Rev. Wesley called for a fast, for the sick, the injured, or some other good cause, the whole town heard about it within 48 hours, and sometimes 25% of the town, the total population included - would fast, sometimes for three days on bread and water. There are many a Baptist who would hesitate to call a miracle just that, but the word was often used by John Wesley when thanking God for hearing the prayers of the people when just such an incident occurred.   John was indeed the Rock that everyone in Schuster looked up to in good times and in bad. He had no enemies save the unseen forces that were always looking about for a foothold on him, his family, and Schuster itself. God permitted few breaches in the defense of Schuster by the forces of darkness - because of the long and continuous prayers of the people. For a time however, He, in his Wisdom, did allow a certain dark mist to mask the readings and meanings of John 6:48-70. All things however, work for the greater glory of God, as this would later on prove.

The town of Schuster owed much of its blessed state to a minister called Earl Potter.   Reverend Earl Potter was a fire and brimstone Baptist preacher who must have had an extreme case of high blood pressure as far as most folks gleaned. When birth control began to sweep our nation with a vengeance in the 50's and 60's, Earl Potter took it to task. He would demand to know of his congregation why they had resorted to the tricks of Satan to satisfy their lusts. He told them from the pulpit that their fate would be Hell, if they continued to follow the husband of the Old Testament who had spilled his seeds in order not to procreate. He asked them if they were reading new-fangled Bibles that had dropped this and other pertinent Bible stories that he would bring up with them to defend his stand. His was not the most theologically sound approach, but in the end, it worked. He demanded children from them. If he suspected that a couple was using birth control he would confront them - from the pulpit, at the door, whenever he saw them, in a loud, estranged voice. In time, when the wretched filth began to make its way into gas stations and the lot, he nearly screamed at them - "What are you doing to your sacred marriages made in heaven? Have you lowered your marriages to the filth, the grease and plastic of the filling stations? You are becoming like the pigs, you evildoers." Earl Potter would have scared the Hell out of many a Catholic parish today. Yes, scared the Hell out of them and brought them back to purity. To this day, the tools of the birth control trade are not sold in, nor allowed in Schuster by a town ordinance. To Hell with the federal statutes.

Reverend Earl would not take to the secret societies either. When the Freemasons from Birmingham were recruiting and just beginning construction on a lodge in downtown Schuster, Reverend Earl drove them out with an ax. He demolished a thirty-foot long two by six wall with that ax. The foreigners (Birmingham Masons) went home. The local Masons repented and recanted Masonry. They published the actual demonic Masonic oaths that they had taken, and were now recanting in the newspaper for all to see what a Mason was. When the men tried to argue that they might be killed by the Lodge, Rev. Earl told them that he might kill them himself if they didn't publish the recantations. Of course Rev.

Earl had to drive them down to the Schuster News for the occasion... There is no Lodge or affiliate there to this day. No black masses, no occult. The Lodge in Birmingham decided to leave Earl alone. They could have killed him or driven him out. They figured the man was demented and was no threat. They left him alone. Alas, Rev. Earl Potter was no friend of Papistry either. His heart was, however, a heart of gold. He was quite capable of looking beyond Rome, and into an individual's soul, and in there, finding God. Rev. Potter died in 1985 at the age of 84. He was the mentor of John Wesley. In one sense, they were opposites. Rev. Earl was fire and brimstone, and John Wesley was as meek as a lamb. Yet, everyone in Schuster old enough to have known the Rev. Potter could not look at John Wesley, nor hear him speak, without hearing and seeing Rev. Potter. Rev. Potter preached for 59 years. He preached until his dying day. He preached in all the Churches in Schuster, including the Methodist Church. He preached in Churches for hundreds of miles around - in Alabama, Georgia, and Tennessee. His flock, especially the pastors of Schuster had the foresight to tape him on cassette, and in his later years to even videotape him in his sermons. Sometimes when the pastors of Schuster thought that they were about to lose the war with their congregation against artificial birth control, Freemasonry, or pornography, they would simply put on a cassette or video of Rev. Earl, and have a seat for the next hour. "What are you doing to your sacred marriages made in heaven? Have you lowered your marriage to the filth, the grease and plastic of the filling stations? You are becoming like pigs you evildoers! Repent and therefore ye shall be saved!"

In order to know John Wesley it was imperative to have had some knowledge of Rev. Earl Potter. On this earth they were inseparable. John Wesley stepped out of a mold formed by the Rev. Earl Potter. God added additional improvements to boot - with John's education, humility, and meekness. John Wesley was a scholar. John Wesley was not a coward, not to imply that Rev. Earl was, of course. So, when the Church elders asked John Wesley to preach on John 6:48-70 at their city wide tent revival on Saturday night, June 27th, 1998, he told them he would be happy to, not actually remembering what the readings were about at that moment. When he asked why – why they were asking him to preach on those particular passages one of the elders told him "I don't believe I'd ever heard a proper preaching on the matter". John was happy to preach on whatever the elders would have him cover – it's all the Word of God.

"Sure, no problem" said John, wondering what in the world was in John 6:48-70. He didn't have a clue, and that just wasn't like John.

The revival was a tremendous success. All of the town's ministers had participated. John was to do the closing preaching, and have a follow-up question and answer period. That was the usual format for Schuster's tent revivals. The beautiful event would end with prayers, live Gospel music, more food, discussions, and prayers again.

As usual, a few hundred people in attendance were in tears when John Wesley had finished his sermon. John was not a fire and brimstone Baptist preacher, as mentioned. John's soft voice and holy presence was enough. John spoke and the people listened. It was if Christ Himself was giving the lesson, no gimmicks attached. When he was done, he asked if anyone had any questions. Larry Romero, a senior in John Wesley's high school, and about the biggest rascal the town of Schuster had to boast of, quickly looked around to see if anyone else had a hand up. Not seeing anyone else in a hurry to ask a question, he himself asked a question that he had never before thought of in his life. He wasn't even sure why he asked it. He felt like he was even pushed out of his chair by some unseen hand. He felt like a prisoner at gunpoint, until he said the words. "Why'd the disciples leave?" Then he sat down relieved and unfettered, smiling, and giggling at his friends around him as doing so.

Rev. Wesley knew that not everyone had heard Larry, so he repeated the question. "Larry Romero asked the question, 'Why did the disciples leave Jesus?'" John simply responded by saying "At this juncture in Christ's speech, some of the disciples simply thought that Jesus was speaking of cannibalism, and they just couldn't take hearing it. However, Jesus had just finished his discourse speaking of things of the spirit, not flesh, as we have from John 6:64." John thought he was done with the question. But God was not done with John. "Other questions?" said Rev. Wesley.

The same unseen perpetrators that had brought Larry Romero to his feet and opened his mouth and inspired thought and words were at it again. Larry was giving his best pimpled smile and giggle to Susan Duckworth two seats away from him, his partially opened mouth going a mile a minute chewing his gum. Up he went. His mouth moved again. They were back, these good guys, though unseen. "Did Jesus call them back?" said Larry, knowing that this is indeed what he was thinking, but wondering why he was thinking such things. Larry was there for the food and girls.

"No, umm, lets see, no, Jesus did not call them back," said John. The audience knew that something was wrong. That was the first "umm" that they had ever heard John say. John's first audible "umm" was triggered by the class clown. Everyone became silent, excluding a few babies recovering from crying spells. All ears were pealed. Rev. Wesley tried to run. "One last question before we eat?"

No, not my pimple faced class idiot. Oh, I don't mean that God. But why him? What now?, thought John.

Up again had gone Larry, starting to enjoy the attention, and beginning to realize that something profound was happening. He still managed to keep his jovial attitude as he winked at Susan as he was standing up. "Would you have called them back?"

"Well, I am certainly not Jesus Christ, and I would certainly not second guess Jesus, so I must say that I would not have called them back" said John.

Larry was starting to sit down now when his mind was prodded again. Indeed he pondered the particular thought, but still he was wondering why his mouth was so quick to action. He was beginning to get suspicious. He failed to smile or giggle this time. "Did they come back?" said Larry, unrelenting in his barrage of perplexing questions.

"Ummm, that we don't know, but, oh, John 6:67, 'and they walked no more with him'. Apparently many of his disciples left him for good." Two ummms. No one wanted to have the evening end. Even the babies had stopped crying by the grace of God. The Gospel singers put down their instruments, walked away from the piano, and sat down with the audience.

Larry's mouth moved again. He was refusing to yield the floor. He was not even sitting down now between questions. Several more questions came. The scholar was tripping. More questions. "What happens when *you don't make a commitment to Jesus* and choose instead to walk away from Him and you don't go back to Him?" shot Larry.

"The true lasting consequence would be Hell," said Rev. Wesley.

The barrage continued. For some unexplained reason, Larry was undergoing a conversion experience. He was now thinking and even praying in his heart even without the same intensity of heavenly inspirations from the holy angels and saints. He wanted answers. "Would you have let me walk away Reverend John? You know me personally. I am not the best student. I've had to stay after for help often. I'm amazed I'm probably going to be graduating on time. What if I didn't understand you? Would you have let me walk to Hell as you yourself had said would be the consequence?" said Larry.

A baby cried but everyone else got quieter.

"No, I would not have let you walk to Hell Larry" said John, now for the first time in the known history of Schuster, assuming a defeatist attitude and tone. But it was a happy defeat. John too felt the presence of God. Out of the mouths of babes. Unless you become like this little child... John knew the exact question that Larry was about to ask him. Susan Duckworth's mouth was open. Her father didn't want her to have anything to do with Larry, and called him a ne'er-do-well. She was resting her head with her hand on her jaw and her elbow on her knee, bent over looking around Robert Smith. She always thought Larry was a jerk. Now she could marry him she thought. Ahh, to be a teenager.

The barrage went forth. "Then if God is Love, why would Love let them walk to Hell, knowing their *misconception*?" said John.

The wording of Larry's question was exactly as John had "heard" it in his mind, just a split second before Larry had said it! Rev. Wesley stared out over the audience. A gentle wind was blowing in off the southernmost hills of the Appalachians, carrying with it the angels and saints of heaven. Not even Padre Pio could have seen a demon here, with his gift of spiritual vision. The prayers of the faithful had chased them all away. Gone. Banished for a moment. The family that prays together stays together. The town that prays together stays together. This town had set up demon net stronger than those used to catch U-boats many years ago. Light, and Light only had penetrated the net.

"Thank you for that culminating question Larry. I think all of the adults here now know the answer to that question. A light has shone in the darkness. The people who were in darkness have seen a great light." John was reaching for words to conclude his sermon. He realized it was God's sermon, so he just said a quick prayer like Jimmy Stewart at the bar - at Martini's, in "It's a Wonderful Life", and spoke. "The answer to that question is that the disciples were not misconceived. Jesus had said specifically in John 6:48-59, referencing either His Flesh or His Blood eleven or twelve times implicitly and explicitly 'For my flesh is meat indeed: and my blood is drink indeed. He that eateth my flesh, and drinketh my blood, abideth in me, and I in him.'" John paused for almost a whole minute. He was in tears.

Workers manning hot dogs, sauerkraut, buns and butter came from all over the grounds. Everyone was paying close attention to this man whom they all felt by now was a prophet. John was praying as he stared out over the crowd. He felt God rushing into his heart as never before. Some altar call he thought. That's it. It was an altar call. John was being called to the altar, to eat the Flesh, and drink the Blood of Our Lord and Savior Jesus Christ. That was the True Purpose of the altar, to bring the Body and Blood of Christ to everyone in the whole world. John spoke more words that he was compelled to speak. His heart was given the words through an inner locution. "I think that if we look at this under the right light, the only Light, God's Light, and we're really honest with ourselves, I think that we'll find that when Jesus said, once again, 'For my flesh is meat indeed: and my blood is drink indeed. He that eateth my flesh, and drinketh my blood, abideth in me, and I in him', I think that we'll find that what He really meant, what He really literally meant was 'For my flesh is meat indeed: and my blood is drink indeed. He that eateth my flesh, and drinketh my blood, abideth in me, and I in him.' Jesus Christ said what he meant." John paused again. The word "Catholic" was going off in the heads of 500 adults in the audience like a light flickering without pause in an arcade.

After this last pause, John began his final discourse as Reverend John Wesley. John had a mysterious infusion of light and knowledge into his soul. "There is only one Church that I know of that offers the Body and Blood of Christ. All of my life I have been an enemy of this Church, not their people whom I love, but their Church. This night I have come to find that the Body of Christ is not just His people, but is also His visible Church - including altars, buildings, bread and wine. The ministers of His Church call down His Precious Body, and His Precious Blood, and what was once bread and wine becomes this Body and Blood, though in appearance nothing has changed. His ministers are called priests. He lost many of His disciples because they did not want to stay with Him because they thought He was referencing something that was hard for them to stomach. He was. Peter, upon whom Christ built His Church, did not even have a good answer. 'Lord, to whom should we go'. As for myself, I know where I must go my friends. I fear that this is the last time I will be speaking to you as your pastor. I must defect to Rome. No, I must go home to Rome. I invite you all to come with me, to put a smile on sweet Jesus' face, to make up for those who walked away. I am going to become a Catholic.

The last crying baby stopped crying. John's family ran up to him at the podium and hugged him as he backed away from the microphone. John walked away with tears streaming down his face like a waterfall, his family too was crying. As the huddled mass walked away from the tent and towards their residence, John took one last look back at pimple faced Larry. Larry looked up at him at that moment, with tears in his eyes too. Their eyes made a contact that will last forever. Larry now knew what he had to do. He put his face back down in his hands, and his elbows on his knees and cried. Susan was crying. Hundreds of others were crying. The prayer had stopped though, and the black demons rushed back into Schuster in a furry, too late to repair the major damage that they had inflicted upon them. They did what they could, however, and the voices of a few angry Baptists and Methodists were heard, laity and pastors alike. It was John's victory, however. The crowd was with him for now.

Meanwhile, in Bar Harbor, Maine, the fog was setting in. A foghorn was sounding. In Schuster, Alabama, the fog was still there, but thanks be to God the fog that had settled over John 6:48-70 was beginning to break up. At least the people now had the benefit of having heard the foghorn.

In the Schuster residence, John and Paulette were seated at their kitchen table, and the children were gathered around them. "My God what have I done Paulette?" said John.

Paulette's world, in matters of God, religion, family, finance, and status had just fallen apart. She was near irrational now. She spoke the only words she could. "I don't know honey but we can try and figure it out tomorrow in the van. I taped your whole sermon...Do you think we can we go away. I feel like I need to go to Canada or Mexico. What I mean is - I just want to get away dear – it's not that I'm embarrassed. I just want to get out of here. Can we move our plans to go camping up a week", she said in machine gun like fire. She was stressed out but loving at the same time. "And instead of the Gulf, could we go someplace else a little, I don't know...? Can you take me to Maine tomorrow? Maine would be far enough for now," said Paulette.

"Maine?" said John.

"Thank you honey. Go pack up your bags kids. Take enough clothes and stuff for three weeks. Your father is taking us to Maine tomorrow. The kids were ecstatic when they heard they were going to Maine. "Mommy, can you get me a pet lobster?"

Paulette walked away from her husband, sat down in a chair in the corner of the kitchen, put her head against the wall, and began to cry. It was more than a normal cry. It was a wailing of sorts, with long gasps for air between wails. She knew of no divorce lawyers, but she was going through the "L" section of the yellow pages in her mind.

But she would have liked to have seen Maine... Let the lawyers wait. Maine. Ah, Maine. I don't know anybody in Maine. Paulette cried herself to sleep, as did the older children and the former preacher too.

****

Earlier in the Bohatch family journey, when they were about 20 minutes north of Pittsburgh on I-79, everyone but Paul was either asleep or feigning sleep. Paul turned on the radio and pressed the select button a few times. It was a replay of a Franciscan University produced show in which Father Bartolomeo Gucci had given a talk on the "The End of An Era" - not the end of the world, "The End of An Era". Father was using as his primary source material the Book "Mary and The Clergy", in which Father Stephen Nairobi had recorded messages that he had received through "inner locutions" from the Blessed Virgin Mary, since 1975. In the particular passage that Father Stephen was covering, Our Lady was warning Christ's priesthood and the laity about the infiltration of Freemasonry, and also the lesser antichrists into the heart of the Catholic Church. She spoke of the proximity of the coming of the mark of the beast, and the constancy that would be needed by the faithful in times of persecution. "We are entering the times when all who follow the idol will receive its mark on their forehead and on their hand... The faithful will need constancy to resist the mark of the beast... Those who adore the beast and its statue and will receive its mark will meet with the wrath of God... For this reason I am calling all of my children to live close to my Immaculate Heart in union with my Son Jesus to pass safely through the rapidly approaching storm, the approaching battle and the fall of Babylon... I invite all of my children to look to me this day, the day that the Church celebrates the Assumption of my glorified body into Heaven... in order to thus be true witnesses of constancy for the Church and for all of mankind...

Paul had actually come in on the end of Father Stephen's discourse. Father was indicating to the audience how we should put Our Lady's words in practice. "Our Lady is asking for our hearts. She needs nothing more than our prayers and sacrifices, our good confessions, our participation in the Holy Sacrifice of the Mass, our Rosaries - she needs nothing more than these to give to Her Son, Jesus Christ, as a spiritual bouquet through which the Father, Son, and Holy Spirit will bring about the conversion of the world, the era of peace spoken of by Our Lady at Fatima so long ago ... She does not want us to hold a conference. She does not want us to run out and write a book..."

"Oh God, two strikes against me... a conference and a book", thought Paul. Aside from the conference that he had just thrown together, there was also a book in his closet. Paul's uncle had asked him to write a biography of sorts - a pamphlet or small book about him (the Uncle Mack) and his wife, Paul's Aunt Jane. They had been brought back into the Church after a 30-year absence through a long series of God incidences and outright miracles from 1994-1996. Paul was halfway done with the booklet. *What am I doing? I hope this isn't the conference from Hell...*, thought Paul as made a right hand turn onto Route 80 just North of Slippery Rock Pennsylvania. Bar Harbor was now 610 interstate miles away. The first annual Acadia Medjugorje Conference, or "whatever I called it conference" was going to start in about 48 hours. He couldn't even remember the title he had given it. Paul wondered how the weather was in Nova Scotia this time of year. Then he thought about the merits of a much warmer New Jersey in July. *A family could swim in the Atlantic on the Jersey coast this time of year. Now Maine, on the other hand...* No, he would go to his sentencing in Maine. *I didn't even bring a microphone, thought Paul. That's OK, I don't have any speakers anyhow.* If Paul did not know it was a mortal sin, he might have been tempted to curl up and die. *Why was he such an idiot? Look out Bar Harbor, there's an idiot on* *the loose, he thought. Do they still hang idiots?...*He clenched his Rosary and began another decade.

Paul's daydreaming had slowed him down some. His speed had dropped from 66 to about 59 mph for just a few minutes. Paul hated when that happened. The last time he drove across Pennsylvania three months ago to visit his folks with his family he accidentally drove for four hours with the cruise control set at just under 55 mph. Things like that bugged him. He figured he lost three quarters of an hour on that trip. *Hey, I'm losing time he thought.* Two thousand feet ahead of him a gas tanker truck tried to avoid two large deer that jumped out in front of him. The truck jackknifed and rolled squarely down the middle of the highway taking up more than the two lanes, spilling its contents as it rolled and erupting into a ball of flame that reached higher to heaven than the tower of Babel. In one of those rare instances that defy the laws of statistics, Joe Manneson was lucky that he did not have his seat belt on. He was thrown from the cab 120 feet just before the explosion. All of his rolling was done just of the edge of the pavement in tall grass that should have been cut by the highway department weeks ago. Joe Manneson would live. Paul lent assistance, including calling in the accident.

Paul did not see an incident ten miles back on I-80, but he saw the aftermath of that also. Well, he saw the brick in the road. It wasn't moving at the time. He had to swerve around it. About 15 seconds before he saw it, the brick was falling at a rate of 32 feet per second squared. It had fallen off a construction truck traveling overhead on an overpass across I-80, smack into the middle of the right lane of I-80 East, just seconds before Paul started with his nonsensical, useless daydreaming, leading to a decrease in speed. For the rest of the trip to Maine, the Bohatch family left a swath of accidents and incidents everywhere they went; though they were oblivious to them all. Now Satan was not a happy camper. *Why can't he get what he wants just once in a while? Why do the good guys always win? He was furious, as time would tell...*

****

Sally and Henry Wijnen from Dubuque, Iowa were leaving Saint Francis Hospital at nine in the morning on Tuesday, June 30th, 1998. Sally was only 41 years old, but her heart was failing. She was being discharged from the hospital following her second mild heart attack. They met their six children in the hospital lobby, and were now on their way to their station wagon.

Though the configuration of the seating in their station wagon allowed for eight seat belts, they were breaking the law. Eight-year-old Amy was the prime offender, sitting in the front seat, safely buckled in next to her mother and father. She was under age for the front seat, in violation of a new Federal and International Law effective in the developed nations of the west. Strange, nobody winked when the law was proposed by the National Transportation Safety Board in 1997. Few noticed when Congress passed the bill and the new law took effect. Three out of four Catholic Home School families where the parents were over the age of 35 could no longer transport themselves and their children legally. Christians in general who fled from the disease of prophylactics now found themselves breaking the law daily. What family of six or seven or more individuals could now get around legally to go anywhere, to do anything together?

Some 'silly' Christians might speak of the laws as having been written against them, and against their civil rights - to bring them in line, and decrease their family size. Surely, however, it must be that these international power brokers who have been behind these laws had our best interests in mind, right? After all, they don't want our 7th or 8th child to die, do they? *Gosh. These monied people can be so good to us sometimes, can't they? They've got our best interests in mind, don't they? Some might wonder about their inconsistency in regards to wanting to kill our unborn babies. There's a can of worms though. We mustn't be too scrupulous now. We don't want to see Big Brother over our shoulders at every turn. We mustn't think that they just want to control our lives, to have us fall in line into the New World Order. We're supposed to be intelligent people...*

The Wijnens were being watched by a Dubuque policeman in a brand new squad car parked near the main entrance of the hospital. He radioed someone. A minute later he was pulling the Wijnens over. This was their third seat belt violation this year. They would be fined seventy-five dollars this day. The fourth violation required a mandatory jail sentence.

"Were any of you forced into this car?" said the patrolman to the children.

Amy cried. Sally Wijnen's heart raced back into an irregular beat. Just the day before her heart had been electronically stabilized. The pressure continued to get to her...

Ticket in hand, Henry Wijnen prepared to drive away. "Thank you officer", he said. He was sincerely offering up his pain, anger, and wallet to God for the conversion of the policeman. He looked and sounded unperturbed, but inside he felt great pain. He felt like he and his family had been violated - raped, in a sense.

"Watch your lip there Mr. Wijnen, this town has had about enough of you and the Mrs.", he said. He did not believe that anyone could really be thankful, at least outwardly cheerful when receiving a ticket. He took Henry's "thank you" as an insult, and walked away.

Sally Wijnen grasped her chest with her hands as Henry was pulling out.

"Do you need to go back to the hospital honey?" said Henry.

"No, please, just take me home."

Nine years before, you could not have found a healthier 32-year-old mother in the world. Nine years of fighting Outcome Based Education/Values Clarification had nearly killed her. More than that, her doctor suspected poisoning in 1996. She was hospitalized due to a suspicious inorganic poison that was subsequently found in her body, immediately after a social event that her non-profit group had sponsored in Dubuque to bring about public awareness of the social, academic, political, and demonic dangers of Outcome Based Education. Dinner had been catered. Sally's health had been failing for eight years. After the poisoning her heart was severely damaged.

Across the nation, Sally was known as the "Fighting Mom" of *Truth in Education*. She had taken on the Iowa Department of Education, the National Education Association, Department of Labor, and various local, county, state, and federal offices that had anything to do with the education of children. She had won several court battles. In one instance, a federal court had ruled that the Iowa School Board had to cease using Outcome Based testing materials. The school board changed the test provider, and the name of the series of tests, and completely neglected the courts ruling. Full steam ahead for those in power. They were still on schedule.

The harassments had come at all hours of the evening. The threats of bodily harm, too. The pressure had nearly broken the marriage of the Wijnens. Yet, gold is tried as if by fire, and the Wijnens were the strongest family in the country. Saints of the Lord.

A few years into the battle the Wijnens had pulled their children out of public school and had begun homeschooling. Sally was a trooper, and continued to fight for the rest of the nation's children, even after hers were back safe in their mother's arms. Safe for the time being at any rate. This nation has pending bills that would consider homeschooling a form of child abuse. Tighter and tighter controls are being put on homeschool families too - in areas of teacher accreditation, and the testing of the children. Even there, Satan is trying to sink his claws by crushing the ability of a family to teach their children in the ways of God, in the privacy of their own home. *To Hell with Satan and those who would deprive a child of his or her home-based education. We will teach our children at home until they come to haul us away. It will be over our dead bodies that we bow to Satan and his filthy United States and One World Governments...*

You could not find six more intelligent, well behaved, and well groomed, happier children in the country, or the world. A microcosm of Heaven, this Wijnens family. Sally Wijnen had one goal in mind for her family, to make them, each and every one, saints before the Lord. Saints for Jesus and Mary. The Wijnens were Catholic.

Sally always wanted to develop, or work in a Catholic apostolate. She never really wanted to take on the secular world and those who are the little people, the worker bees who are going about their tasks of trying to mold the new generation for the coming New World Order. Often, she felt her life had been wasted - but this near despair lasted only briefly. Prayer and priestly spiritual direction brought her right from such thoughts. Her physical wounds were not superficial however. They were reminders, scars of the battle. She continued to wish, however, that they had been for some nobler purpose, more directly related to the cause of God in the world. Yet, she had done her job exactly as God had asked her to do, the little way, as proposed by Saint Therese of Lisieux. Sally had no idea that over 1700 children had been brought into the safety of homeschooling directly through her efforts. The little way that had nearly killed her at the young age of 41 had been so beneficial to thousands of others unbeknownst to Sally.

In the most recent years, Sally had been battling Outcome Based/Values Clarification at the state and federal levels. She was unstoppable. She was the first to expose the link of this pagan method of teaching to the Department of Labor, and over them, the Big Corporations, and the Boards who control them. She even tackled those who pulled the strings of the 'Boards' - the untouchables. Masonry - Freemasonry and its many tentacles was not inactive in this battle against our children and families, and the battle for the control of the world. *This battle starts with the control of the minds of your children.*

Sally was the first also to expose the links of Outcome Based Education to perversions of all sorts, from militant homosexuality to the propagation of promiscuity and murder. Yes, murder, rape, and crime of all sorts were propelled forward by the federal government. *No values, no morals.* Sure - state values to be sure, the debauchery of the state served as the example. The Feds told the states what they must do to get their money. The states told the local school boards what they must do to get their money - *always saying they could implement their mandated plans however the saw fit.* Strange, however, *the education plans in Dubuque, Iowa look the same as those in Milford, Connecticut, and Topeka, Kansas.*

Outcome Based Education/Values Clarification is from Hell. If the nation had chosen to use the values of Jesus Christ we would have the opposite scenario. The values would be truth. Truth based in God, and

His ways. Today, we have the modern day Pontius Pilates, wretched puppets sitting on state and local school boards asking, when the subject is so often brought up, **"What is Truth?"**. *The truth of the State is the Big Lie, from the Father of all lies. Who are you going to believe? So often in the last few years have seemingly honest parents/concerned citizens tearfully run for election on state and local school boards only to turn traitor upon election. A turncoat at every corner. Absolute power corrupts absolutely.*

As Sally began to nationally expose more and more about the computerized portfolio tracking of individual students, about the disciplining of those bright students who continued to ask *"But what of the Truth? What of Virtue?"* and the hidden machinations really behind Outcome Based Education, the pressures, threats, and stress peaked, once again, until she was hospitalized on June 27th, 1998, for a several day stay.

Henry and Sally had been praying on the subject for several years now, and Sally was now going to step down from the helm of the fight against the pagan educators in government, national and now international in recent years. They knew that the world was about to change soon, that great things were afoot. They knew that the world had entered the end times - no, not the end of the world, but the end times, as Our Lady has so often spoken of to Father Nairobi and so many other mystics of our days. Even at this hour, Allied Van Lines was at the Wijnen home beginning to load the family belongings onto the truck. Sally and Henry and children were leaving the local, state, and federal battle for the souls of the children facing the pagan elite in the hands of capable Christians. They had been too long on the front lines, and the battle had cost them dearly. They were moving to a place where it seemed many Catholics and other Christians were gathering to face these end times in proximity to other die-hard Christian homeschoolers - Steubenville, Ohio, and the surrounding area.

Henry Wijnen had been faithfully attending the Men's Conferences at Franciscan University since 1989. Over the years he had become a good friend of another conference attendee he had met - Paul Bohatch, who had moved to Steubenville in recent years. Paul and Barbara Bohatch were letting the Wijnens move into a small, run-down house they owned on seven acres, in nearby Bloomingdale, Ohio, rent-free for as long as they needed it. Paul felt bad about making the offer, because the house was somewhat of a wreck. The Wijnens jumped at the opportunity, since their economic situation was somewhat in arrears due to court battles and the related costs of challenging the pagans. In September, Paul and Barbara were going to build a new small home on this property and begin preparations for facing harder times. Many in their area, and the whole country were expecting severe changes in the economy, the political winds, and the religious toleration arenas in the coming months and next few years, in the wake of expected environmental catastrophes (earthquakes, floods, hurricanes, droughts, etc).   Many were seeking to at least be somewhat self-sufficient, perhaps in the raising of chickens for eggs or meat, or goats for milk.   Many an educated man with clean fingernails in the area was learning the art of gardening.

The Wijnens family would be taking their Medjugorje Center with them to Bloomingdale.   For seven years they had provided the Dubuque area with volumes of tapes, books, Rosaries, scapulars, and pamphlets.   Many had come to know Jesus and Mary through their few hours a week of evangelizing for the Faith.   The Bohatch family was looking forward to working with the Wijnens in this endeavor.   Even in the Bohatch neck of the woods, there was a great need for the spreading of Our Lady's current messages to the world.   So much pride had kept so many away. **Our Lady did not die at Fatima. She is alive and doing well!**

The Allied Van Lines truck rolled out of town, on its way to Bloomingdale, Ohio. The Wijnens followed within the hour. They would see to the unloading of their belongings into the home in Bloomingdale, and then depart forthwith to rendezvous with the Bohatch family for a two-week camping vacation in Maine. A wealthy, older gentleman who had been one of the first recipients of the free Medjugorje tapes from the Wijnens Medjugorje Center, and who had subsequently become a good friend of the family, had insisted that Henry take Sally and the kids on vacation somewhere. He "forced" a thousand dollars upon them for the trip. He had seen Sally in battle, a Joan of Arc fighting for Jesus. He had come to see them off. "Henry, you make sure Sally gets plenty of rest in Maine, or I'll hear about it..."

****

After Rick Tremont's meeting of the Pierponts, he quickly put on a sweatshirt to cover up his "Eat More Whales" banner. He thought it best to go clothes shopping incognito! He walked down Jordan Street, two shops past Rosalie's, and entered One World Clothing. A young man about 29 years old approached him. "Hey man, what can I help you with?" he said.

"Yeah. Do you have any 'Save The Whale' or 'Save The Seal' shirts?" said Rick.

"Hey, another earth brother! Sure, we've got 50% hemp blend shirts - but don't smoke 'em dude - the cotton blend will kill you!"

Rick figured that since both he and the salesman had a few external characteristics in common - long hair, a little grubby looking, a little earthy, that the fellow had taken him for his "earth brother".

"Here's our dress shirts and our T-shirts. There's a dressing room over there if you need it man. I'm Eric, Eric Frick, what your name?"

"Rick" said the young man from Ohio.

"You're an artist, aren't you" said Eric Frick.

"Engineer" said Rick.

"Heavy!" said Eric.

Rick picked out a couple of tourist shirts and walked up to the register. A young lady was waiting for him at the register.

"Just these please" said Rick.

Eric walked up to the counter. "Hey Lys", he said to the young lady, "This is Rick the engineer. I can't believe he's not an artist. Look at this dude. We were just talking a minute ago". Rick, this is my fiancee and chief cook, bottle washer and owner of One World Clothing, Dr. Alyssa Palmer.

They exchanged educated pleasant greetings. "And your title Alyssa, you're a doctor in what field?" said Rick.

"Environmental Sciences" said Alyssa. Alyssa sensed something special in this young man that she couldn't put her finger on. She wasn't sure if it was a pleasant or annoying attraction. She felt she would see him again, and didn't want to delay knowing something about him, so she stalled as she was giving Rick his change.

"What type of engineer, Rick?" she said.

"I'm a chemical engineer - Ohio State" said Rick as he was about to walk out the door

"Really, I'm a Purdue grad. Goodbye Big Ten", she said flirtingly. "I hope to see you around".

Eric the live-in fiancé was no longer happy to have met Rick the engineer.

****

By 1 PM Rick had made his way down the street to Acadia Park Cyclery. He picked out a low-end combination mountain bike/touring bike, 15 speeds, used but in excellent shape, and paid cash for it. Though he'd been on the Island before, he asked about camping at the bike shop. The closest option for him was Bar Harbor Campground, a private campground 2 miles out of town, back east on Route 3. He had passed it on his way in. It wouldn't be roughing it, as he would prefer, but it would get him settled in a hurry so he could get back out on the bike and try to find out just why

God had brought him here. Yes, he thought, *God had introduced me to Therese, and it seems that we are destined to become friends, maybe more, but I have the feeling there is more to it than that. If God brought me here, then there is a spiritual dimension to this picture also. He'll show me in His time.*

Rick had actually had his mind set on backcountry camping in Acadia, but he had come to find out at the bike shop that Acadia didn't allow back country camping. Regardless, all he needed for now was a spot anywhere nearby to set up his two-man tent and throw his belongings into. As he made his way back down Route 3, he did his best to do so on his bike, trying to hold both of his bags over back with his right hand, holding onto the bike with his left. He had to get off the bike on the larger hills, legging it awkwardly with his possessions and the bike.

When he arrived at Bar Harbor Campground, he placed his bike and bags down on the ground on the side of the log cabin that serves as an office and went in. "Hi, I'd like to tent camp for one night, I'm on a bike" said Rick.

"Just go ahead in and pick out any empty site, and then come back and register. Make sure it's empty," said Brian at the counter.

Rick meandered into the campground. It was beautiful, looking like a familiar picture post card of the large eastern state! It was Maine in a nutshell - balsams, rock maples, hemlocks and spruce trees, with tremendous views of the mountains and the astonishingly beautiful Frenchman's Bay. Blueberries were everywhere, though it was somewhat early in the season. The air had never seemed cleaner to Rick. The aromas of the blueberries and balsam firs reminded Rick of being in a craft shop in anywhere USA, amid the decorative pillows filled with balsam needles and the potpourris of a myriad of spices and plants giving off their respective odors. This was the real McCoy however, July on the coast of Maine, away from the hustle and bustle of the rest of the world.

As Rick was heading about 15 miles an hour down a slightly inclined road into the heart of the campground, the bags on his back swung quickly to the left as he hit a speed bump, wheeling his whole body around with them. He came down to the asphalt with a crash. His left knee was torn up and his left pants leg was all bloody. Welcome to Maine he thought. He wished that he had not come for an instant, as he was limping around, and only half groping for his bags, because he was really quite incapable of pressing on for the next few minutes. He sat down in the middle of the road. A large Winnebago drove slowly around him. The occupants waved as they went by. What was he doing here? Just out of jail. He was 29 years old and feeling every bit of 40 at this particular moment. No job, no future. Nobody will hire him now, an ex-con. All that he wanted to do at this moment was crawl into the Maine woods and build a small cabin overlooking the ocean, in the middle of a thick stand of balsams. He felt like a bum. What had he done with his life? All of the friends of his youth were married by now, some of them two or three times by this time! If he didn't marry soon, he'd probably never have children! What right does a 29 year old jobless, unshaven, unkempt man have to be camping in a park on an island off the coast of Maine? He should be in an office or a factory or chemical plant somewhere adding to the gross national product.

Such thoughts crashed through Rick's mind as he recovered through the physical crash, and began to put himself back up on the bike again. A comforting thought came into his mind. I've been with Jesus and Mary for the last four years, in jail with them. They were happy I was with them. Rick began a Rosary to help remove his near despair. Just what he needed, a string of loose beads hanging from his left hand on the bike, passing through his fingers. He could hardly hang on as it was. Our Lady landed his ship safely, however, on the shores of site K-2, a trailer site that he knew he would be paying extra for because of the electric and water hook-up. He would splurge. He would treat himself to the best campground site at Bar Harbor Campground with an impeccable view of Frenchman's Bay. Actually, it was the second best view. He passed a furtive jealous eye across to the site labeled K-1, occupied by a Wilderness RV, positioned a little higher, with less obstructions blocking the view of the historic bay. *K-2 will have to do!*

After setting up camp, Rick finished the Rosary, but was still not terribly far from the brink of despair. He felt like a nobody. He was upset that for four years he had missed the great outdoors, which had been one of his few passions. To have been locked away from the ocean for four years was cruel and unusual punishment. He tried to think of what the sacrifice had been for - for those who would never see the light of day, let alone the ocean. For those who would be torn apart in the womb, with the pieces put back together when the job was done to be sure the baby was completely removed. *Babies.* They weren't his babies. Why did he care? Rick's knee was killing him. It was probably in need of a stitch or two, but Rick put his hope in a clean T-shirt wrapped tightly around it. He thought of the pain of the babies. The abortionists always said the babies didn't feel being ripped apart. *Yeah, sure!* Rick thought, as he tended to his still bleeding knee. *No pain. No soul. Tissue. The babies received a certificate allowing them to have pain starting on their birthday. The doctor* spanks them, they cry with pain, and then they get their *certificate. At that point you can't kill them, at least in the United States, at least for now...*

Rick was sitting on his rolled out sleeping bag in the tent, with the flaps open, and the front screen doors serving as the window to Frenchman's Bay. Something had changed the moment he had met the asphalt back on the road a half an hour before. He now had an attitude. Anything and everything went through his mind. Beautiful Therese. He wished they were already married. *Maybe marriage would help his poor miserable state. Wait. He had not been this miserable for five years. What's going on. Maybe he was just a fish out of water. Maybe it was the materialism rushing back in after a four-year absence. He was finding himself wanting one of everything.* He wished that he was married to Therese. He thought it would be nice to own this campground, and run it with her. He thought he'd like a boat - maybe a seaplane - they keep them on Long Pond right here in the Park. After all, he was a private pilot, but not current. He thought of other business potentials in Bar Harbor. He was jealous of the Rockefellers, Fords, and the other wealthy families that had summer cottages (mansions) and estates on the island. He thought it would be nice to own a stable on the island. He thought it would be great to own a small yacht club on the island, bordering the park. He wondered if they ever came on the market. Then again, maybe he would be better off with an estate outside of Baxter State Park, a huge wilderness area in northern Maine that he was beginning to get to know well not so many years ago. He was calculating how much money he would need to build a place and get a small business up and running - maybe that campground, or dock, or stable, or whatever. Anything but the chemical plant. He never wanted to go there again. Dupont treated him and all their engineers with the greatest respect. They were paid well, too. Oh God, but he just couldn't go back there again. He needed to be in the woods, or near the ocean, or just outside anywhere. He couldn't go back to the sights and smells of a chemical plant - endless buildings, pipes, smokestacks, danger zones. God, not that! Maybe I could live on a yacht. Did he become a rescuer just to get out of the chemical plant? Was he just a quitter? Not everyone involved in the rescue movement was a canonized saint yet. Many of them had a handful of their own problems. Some had had many abortions, many were divorced, many were broke, a few were homeless even prior to the rescuing exploits. One or two that he had met did not even believe in the one true God, and many had just been raked over the coals so many times that they were fried. Yet, is this not what we call humanity? Is this not the beginnings of the stuff that makes saints? Most of the rescuers that Rick had known had actually been very saintly. The kind of people you would trust your life with. The kind of people you would trust your kids with. Some of these people were praying 5 hours a day even when they weren't in jail, and maybe 12 hours a day when they were in jail. Most of these people would have stormed the gates of Auschwitz to be with Saint Maximilian Kolbe in his death cell. Where did Rick fit into this? Was he indeed the token chemical engineer, now rescuer who just didn't want to work anymore?

Thank God a horn beeped outside the tent. The friends of darkness were not happy. Satan's cohorts had put the squeeze on Rick in a painful, tired moment, and caught him off guard. They were about to reintroduce to him in his mind all of the pleasures that the world has to offer. They were off to a good start. The campground workers had interfered however. Rick poked his head out the tent door. He looked up at a beat up brown pickup truck with Bar Harbor Campground painted on the driver door. A brown haired man called over to him. "Have yah checked in yet?"

"No, I was about to head up to the office," said Rick.

"Just wanted to let yah know. We're filling up fast. Somebody's having a religious conference in Acadia, and people are coming in from all over, and the Park Service doesn't know anything about it. They're not real excited about it. The Park Superintendent stopped by earlier, but we didn't have anyone here yet by the name he gave us. Oh, and somebody wanted K-2. I thought that's where I saw yah walk your bike into before, so I thought I'd check it out. I'll tell them you're at K-2, but do get up there when you're settled," said the man.

"Sure thing" said Rick.

"Hey, you know you're gonna be paying more for this trailer lot, don't you?" said the fellow in the pick-up.

"No problem, I'm a millionaire from Wall Street" said Rick.

"What's your name, by the way?" Rick asked him.

"Hank", he said.

"I'm Rick, Rick Tremont. Nice to meet you." Rick said goodbye as he was getting out of the tent, as Hank was driving off.

Rick checked for his wallet, hobbled over to his new bike, and aimed it for the front gate. The honking of the horn was a grace from heaven, brought from the angels. Now Rick was thinking of all of the graces that God had brought to him and many others through his four years of rescuing. *God has been so good to me he thought as he peddled along.* He thought of everything his heroes like Saint Louis Marie de Montfort, Saint John Vianney, Saints Francis and Anthony, The Little Flower, Saint Catherine of Sienna, Saint Kateri Tekawitha, and Saint Maximilian Kolbe and Padre Pio had gone through. They suffered tremendously. Yet their suffering brought about untold graces and conversions. He thought that his four sacrificed years of his life must have been a picnic compared to the lives of most of the saints. *Where was my head at a few minutes ago? I know what I did with those four years. I gave them to God. If nothing more, I gave them to God. That's enough, period. Look what he gave me in return. My brother Luke, arch enemy of the Catholic Faith since he fell away from his Catholic Faith at Notre Dame University of all places. The first time I was arrested he came to yell at me in jail. He told me I was going to kill the family. He said I put I knife into the heart of the family that would never be taken out. He didn't say it. He screamed it in front of a fair portion of the population of Pittsburgh, at least a good number of the uniformed men of Pittsburgh - policemen and inmates included. One year later, where was it?..., Miami, Florida, we were cell mates! Praise the Lord. Now he's in the seminary. He'll be a priest in two years, a deacon next year! Jail has been so good for the Tremonts. God I miss it already!*

****

"Hi" said Rick to an older couple emerging from a tent. He was surprised they weren't in a fancy trailer like most of the older campers he had seen so far today.

"Beautiful day" said the wife.

"Gorgeous" said Rick. Rick was going slowly on this slightly inclined portion of the main road in the campground. The couple was still close enough for the husband to get in a word or two.

"You're here for the conference too, aren't you", he said.

"You mean this mysterious Medjugorje gathering?" said Rick. "I can't believe you said that. I've only had about four discussions longer than thirty seconds since I've been here, and you're the second person to say that to me. You guessed correctly, but I didn't even know about the conference till this morning, well after I arrived in Bar Harbor. How did you know?" said Rick.

"I saw your scapular" said the man.

"Wait a minute, my scapular doesn't exactly have a neon sign on it saying I'm here for Medjugorje?" said Rick.

"To tell you the truth, I really felt prompted to ask you as we were coming from the tent. Its almost like I was going to say that even if there was nobody there. Strange. I think we should have a beer sometime and try to figure that one out. Of course we know its just one of those signal graces God seems to be handing out by the bushel full these days - take the reason we're here for example...Wait; let us introduce ourselves first. I'm Wayne Sherman, and this is my wife Betsy. We're from Dallas, Texas," said Wayne.

"I'm Rick Tremont, hailing from Ohio," said the engineer.

Wayne continued with his story, while Rick relaxed himself on his bike. "Have a seat at the picnic table Rick," said Wayne.

Betsy asked Rick if he wanted a coke.

"Sure" said Rick, "thanks".

"Here we are down in Texas yesterday afternoon at this very hour, about 2 PM, and my wife gets this call from a lady friend she's been in Medjugorje with, Marge Scott. Now Marge tells her to get her tail up to Boston tonight because there's going to be a major Medjugorje Conference this week in Bar Harbor, rather in Acadia National Park near Bar Harbor. They ran an ad in the Boston Globe. I've got a copy of it here," said Wayne, handing Rick a copy of the same ad he had seen in the Bar Harbor Times. "Now Marge faxes this thing to us and says 'you got to get up here, I just have a feeling about this. I think you're supposed to be here', she says."

"Even at the moment Marge said this, I think we were both leaning towards coming up here, amazingly. It was like Marge didn't even have to convince us," said Betsy. "Wayne has a brother Frank who lives in Connecticut, and we were going to be visiting him and his family hopefully this summer anyhow, and I wanted to get to see Marge and meet her family too. But something stuck out at what Marge had said. So even though I was rapidly deciding that I wanted to come up here, I had to ask a question first. I had the fax in hand - Marge got the fax through on our second line, and I'm thinking Marge just said this was going to be a major conference. You see I've been to Acadia, twice in my life, and the last time was just three years ago. You can't have a major conference at Sand Beach, or Cadillac Mountain, or even Jordan Pond. There aren't any facilities to speak of. O.K., so I'm thinking it's a tent conference. Tents, that's it. But to have any size conference at Sand Beach, you'd have to use every square inch on that small beach. It's usually packed in July. There are tremendous parking problems. No Way. What is this I'm thinking - but at this point I already knew I was going to be there. As far as Cadillac Mountain is concerned, I think any tent you put up on top of that hill is going to be in the Atlantic in fifteen minutes. You can't set up a big tent on Cadillac. The only place you could have a large gathering at Jordan Pond is at the tea green, the dining area outside of the restaurant on the lakeside. I told Marge all this. I asked her why she thought it was going to be a major conference. She told me she didn't say major. She told me that she couldn't reach the organizer on the cellular phone number that was given. She didn't however tell me that Bar Harbor Campground knew nothing about it. She had called the campground and they told her she knew more about the conference than they did. *If she had told me* that the campground knew nothing about it, we probably wouldn't have come. Anyhow, we felt like we were supposed to come. We were lucky to get a flight out last night on US Air. All of the hotels that we called were supposedly booked for tonight," said Betsy.

"Yeah" said Wayne. "So here we are heading up to Boston last night, with no hotel rooms to look forward to near Bar Harbor. Marge and her husband picked us up at the airport, and we stayed at their house in Boston last night. They've got a great family. Three of their kids are still at home. Angels, you should see them - oh, you will! So we called the hotels again this morning before we left. No room. Everybody's out of rooms. Marge said to us 'Why don't you use our tent and camp in the park'. Now I think tents are OK for boy scouts and hippies, but I hate tents. I really hate tents. But here we are driving along this morning and Betsy says to me 'Why don't we buy a tent. There's a Wal-Mart over there. If we don't get a tent, we may not be able to stay anywhere near the conference.' I joked with her - 'what conference?' - this Mr. Paul Bohatch is nowhere to be found. I told her he must be an idiot. Either that or this whole thing is a very bad and costly joke. I think Our Lady brought us here though. I think its going to happen. This guy may still prove to be a jerk though, we'll see," said Wayne.

Betsy poked him in the ribs. "So I said 'Please Wayne, lets go get a tent and two pillows and two sleeping bags. They won't cost much. We can camp right in the park. We'll be right where all the action is. What if one or two of the visionaries are camping out in the park during the conference? They'll be up talking to the pilgrims all night without us! Our Lady appears to these young folks! We'll have to excuse ourselves from the invisible Virgin Mary and these visionaries that people fly 7,000 miles to see in a former Soviet Block country, and you want to drive off to Portland to get a hotel'. Needless to say, Wayne pulled into Wal-Mart."

We spent $600 on camping equipment. I did tell you how I felt about tents, didn't I?" said Wayne.

"Anyhow" said Betsy, "we finally got here five hours later and discovered that the park campgrounds are full. So much for camping out with Our Lady and the visionaries. This was best place we could find close to the park. But no kidding, this is a great place. I just wish I were in one of those Winnebagos! In all honesty, I'm ready for the trailer life... Well, anyhow we walked into the registration office and asked them which site Paul Bohatch was at. The fellow looked through a card file and said there was no one there by that name. I asked him if anyone was here from the Medjugorje Conference yet, and he said 'what'. Then he said 'Oh, that Mary thing. As far as I know, there isn't going to be a conference. That's what the park ranger said. I think it was actually the park superintendent that spoke to my boss - Craig. Not a happy fellow - that superintendent.' So here we are" said Betsy, "Now you know the rest of the story", trying to make her voice sound like what's his name...

"Rick, we've known you for ten minutes, but we haven't let you get a word in edgewise. Must be all the coffee I had on the road. Where are you from, and what brought you here in the first place?" said Wayne. "You mentioned that you didn't originally come for the conference", he said.

"Well there I was, laying in jail a week ago..." said Rick as he was interrupted by Wayne.

"Oh God, don't tell me you were arrested for false advertising - bilking the public for phantom Medjugorje Conferences - was it you?" laughed Wayne.

"No, not me, I've got witnesses. A bunch of other jailbirds" said Rick. "Anyhow, there I was laying in jail in the top bunk of my cell..." before Wayne interrupted him again.

Wayne laughed so hard he had Coke coming out his nose. "I thought you were kidding! What in the world were you in jail for? You don't seem like the jail house type!" he chuckled. Wayne instantly felt a little self-conscious. Betsy poked him in the rib again kidding with him, but really trying to get him to shut up so Rick could tell him their story."

Just then the brown truck beeped again. "Hey Rick, d'yah register yet? Somebody wanted your site at the office.... Hey, is the Pope coming or something? There's a lot of talk going on. The boss wants to send somebody a bill for all the incoming calls. I think he's going to bill the fellow that just pulled in with his family. They're here for the conference too. It seems like the show is going to go on. The guy in question is one Mr. Paul Bohatch; none other than the Mr. Paul Bohatch of Medjugorje fame that everyone has been looking for. I now have in my possession a newspaper called Weedle Columns, courtesy of Mr. Paul Bohatch himself. Now I know what everyone is talking about. You may see me there. The office told me that you had asked about the conference too, so I just thought I'd let you know. By the way, This Mr. Bohatch settled for another site. He just beat out a Winnebago for it. Last trailer site in the camp. He's gonna be at K-3. He's your new neighbor. Look for a white van and pop-up camper. Oh, if you're a praying man you'd better get to work on it. It seems this guy didn't tell his wife about the conference. She's ready to kill him. My wife would have killed me already. She about did when I brought my last boat home. But things worked out..., see yah. Hey, that's them coming down the road. Bye".

****

Paul had made a lot of mistakes in his life. He had done a lot of things that a lot of wives would have left their husbands for, and many have. Without considering many forms of these, Paul's offenses, one might just consider the financial ones. They were always in debt, and Paul was the one who controlled the money. It was his fault. Often the big ticket items involved something of a hazy noble cause, perhaps something with a religious flair, like a few expensive trips to a small town in Bosnia-Herzegovina, the purchasing of hundreds, well, thousands of books, booklets, Rosaries, and the whole works for free distribution. OK so far. Sometimes however, unilateral, purely secular, usually recreationally flavored decisions were made without the other party's knowing - decisions about buying used boats, land on the lake, a hang-glider, and so forth. Not that often, but it happened. So, when this little thing about the Medjugorje "Conference" came to light, there was what you might call a difference of opinions that one might say openly surfaced right there in the log cabin-of-an-office. Some would call it an argument. One might use a stronger word. Before they left the office, the owner reminded them that quiet hours were between 10PM and 7AM, and that they were strictly enforced. Mr. Busch, the owner, seeing the current predicament of the couple, and the concerned children awaiting them in the van, did not want to add to their burden and discuss the Park Superintendents feelings with them at this time. "Have a great night", he said, as he handed Paul a bunch of messages from a notepad when Barbara wasn't looking.

"If that's what Medjugorje's about then I'm not going to this stupid conference", Mr. Busch said out loud to himself after Paul and Barbara had pulled away, shaking his hand up in the air at someone or something unseen. "You're not going to see me there God! I'm no Catholic", he said again. "OK.., I'll go God. But just for Mom. She wanted to go to Medjugorje before she died. I'll go for her", he said. He started to cry. His mother had just died two years ago. They were coming off a bad season at the time of her illness. The family couldn't afford to send his mother to Medjugorje. His Presbyterian Mother had died praying a Rosary, asking Mary to come and take her home to Jesus...

****

As the white Ford Van and Jayco pop-up trailer approached, Rick's heart was pounding. Something was afoot. He felt like he was on a pilgrimage to Medjugorje itself, or Fatima, or Betania, or to any major Marian Shrine the world over. Something special was definitely going on here. Wayne and Betsy felt it too - and they had not even heard Rick's side of the story. They had more than a feeling that he was a special man, a man of God.

Now, here was this young man trying to peer into, with all his heart, with all his might right into the Ford van that was about to pass them by. Rick stood up. He dashed over to the edge of the Sherman's campsite, forgetting the pain in his knee. He did the inevitable. He flagged the Bohatch family with his hand. It was Barbara who had to put down her window to see what he wanted. When he saw Barbara's face, he realized he had made a big mistake. "Would you be the Bohatch family?" he said with an inappropriate smile on his face (he was trying to adjust his facial contortions to fit the situation, but he just gave up and smiled). The Bohatch family had been through another war. Their faces were angry, sad, and tear filled at the same time. The whole pack of them. Two wars in two days. Not a good record. Not very healthy. Something had to give.

"Yes, I'm Paul Bohatch, and this is my wife Barbara, and our children", Paul said leaning over towards Barbara to get a better look at Rick, and then looking towards the children. "Can I help you", he said.

Rick realized at this moment, perhaps through the inspiration of his guardian angel that the Bohatchs' needed a word or two to snap them out of despair and lift them up as never before. "I'm Rick Tremont from Ohio. I'm out here mainly for the conference at this point. I don't know how to say this but I think what you're doing is great. I've already met a handful of people that are going to be going and God is doing something very special with this gathering. I think this is going to be the greatest thing that ever happened to Maine since lobster. I just wanted to say thanks. See you there. Oh, Wayne and Betsy Sherman flew up from Texas last night after they heard about the conference from a friend in Boston" said Rick turning to look at and nod to the Shermans who had walked over to the car.

The Shermans said hello. Barbara was looking someplace far away. She was thinking of the baby in her womb that Paul was as of yet unaware of. She wanted to be alone on a deserted isle at the present moment. The Shermans and Rick felt very awkward.

"Oh God, you're not going to believe this but this thing may not be more than a Rosary rally. I don't know how to explain this but the only thing I've done for this gathering is to send three faxes and make three phone calls. I faxed the ads to the Ellsworth American, the Boston Glob, and the Bar Harbor Times. Then I called them to give them my American Express card number. I didn't tell my wife about it and she just found out. That's why we look a little disposed right now.

"Daddy, can we go fishing now?..."

Paul continued. "To tell you the truth, I don't know where my head was at. I was up till 5 in the morning praying the Rosary, and reading True Devotion To Mary for the 100th time. I got a supposed fax from

Medjugorje relayed to me after I woke up from just a few hours sleep - just dreaming about Medjugorje, I'm not even sure if I got to sleep, well then, anyhow, I just felt like I was supposed to do it. Please pray for us. Things are rough right now. We'd better go set up camp so the kids can get out and stretch. Nice meeting you". Everybody said goodbye. Barbara nodded a half smile to the fellow campers. Rick's words were comforting. She was happy to have met him and the Shermans. She felt that God was at work....

"Hey, umm, there's several of us that have been praying for all of you since this morning" said Paul, before the van had moved a foot. And as far as the conference... I think God is putting it together. Something is happening up here. I think Mary knows we're here. I think Jesus & Mary know that you just pulled into Bar Harbor Campground. I think they're up to something. Hey, God bless you," said Rick as Paul and Barbara nodded again and the van started to move. "Let us know if you need anything, or need any help with the conference - I've been to Medjugorje...", Rick said a little louder as the van was pulling away.

"Man, I gotta go register," said Rick. "Somebody may pay for my spot and I'll be evicted" said Rick to Wayne and Betsy, laughing as he did so. He started to jump on his bike.

"Your story!" said Wayne.

"I'll be right back," said Rick. "You'd better put the coffee on! Make mine a double", he said.

****

A little earlier on Thursday, a Militiaman from Montana arrived via Boston and Bar Harbor Airport on a small twin prop plane. His name was John Trudeau. The man behind him on the plane, following him unbeknownst to John, was an ATF agent. The folks who invited John to Bar Harbor, the Militia of Acadia, had experienced enough of the New World Order already. They were preparing to do direct battle with the United Nations that had taken over one of the islands of Acadia National Park, to use it as a so-called "environmental headquarters". The militia knew the truth of the matter. The militia was actually going to go in and take back this heavily fortified high tech operations center for the New World Order. They brought in John to give them the spark that they needed to kick UN butt. Harold Lipinski made the arrangements for John's visit. Harold had just picked up John from his hotel on Friday, July 3rd, 1998. They were going to have breakfast and talk strategy for their evening meeting. They never made it to the restaurant. Harold "made the mistake" of taking John to Jordan Pond to see what all the hub-hub was about. Apparently, large numbers of pilgrims were coming out of nowhere to attend a religious conference in Acadia National Park. John and Harold never left Jordan Pond that day. Something happened to John as he stepped out of the Jeep about a mile from the Pond. It was bumper to bumper traffic. John fell down as if he was dead. Harold thought he was dead. The people passing by in cars and offering to lend assistance thought he was dead. When John came to, he mentioned something about a Warning... This did not fit in with the scenario the ATF agent had expected. *What in Hell was going on here?*, he thought as he watched as John was attended to by several people.

John T. Trudeau was now destined to be a speaker at the 1998 Acadia Medjugorje Conference. His theology had changed somewhat that morning. He was no longer a Revisionist Christian Patriot. As he lay on the road leading to Jordan Pond, while many were thinking he was dead, **John got religion**.

****

Who were these people arriving at the United Nations in the most expensive limousines to ever drive the streets of New York? Who were these people that had just flown in from all around the world on their private, governmental, and military jets? Most of these same individuals had met frequently, at secret meetings the world over, from Rome to Honolulu, Paris to Miami, and Mexico City to Melbourne. By and large, most of these few dozen world travelers were not Presidents, Ambassadors, or even Secretaries of States. They all had one thing in common. Old money. Mostly old European money. They carried about the wealth of ages past that had so often influenced history, including the initiation of two world wars so far. There were a few newcomers to wealth that had forced their way into the world scene and would not be deprived a stake in the global political agenda. They claimed it. Their "new" money had come from computers and commerce, slave labor, and energy. They were accepted as long as they bowed to the same worldview as those with the "old money". There was an even greater consolidation of power and wealth above them all, the bearers of this "old and new money", but that is neither here, nor there, for the time being.

So, they arrived. They trickled in starting on Monday, June 29th, 1998. The press knew. The press was not allowed to cover the situation. The press bowed to Mammon.

There was even a big honcho from the EWTG World Headquarters, now located on Burnt Porcupine Island, formerly an island managed by the

United States Department of The Interior (Park Service), formerly belonging to the people of the formerly sovereign United States of America. *George Washington, if you're up there send help...*

There was an agenda for this emergency meeting. The United States of America was the last major player in the world to have its people broken from its freedom and molded into the One World mindset. Plainly put, the people of the United States were not falling into line quick enough. George Bush had taken the country far into the One World Universe. Bill Clinton had taken us amazing far along the same path to perdition. Yet, the country had a long way to go. This top secret meeting was to plan emergency moves in order to bring about the rapid transition of the United States from a sovereign democracy to a land of world citizens controlled by the very ones meeting in New York.

There was good cause for this emergency meeting. Satan has ears too. He knew that certain things were about to befall the world, and in particular, the United States of America. If the world did not listen to the Mother of Jesus, at least Satan knew she spoke the truth. Our Lady had mobilized a vast number of people in recent days - mobilized them into prayer and fasting offered up to Her Son, Jesus Christ. Satan was not blind to it. Word went out to the forces of darkness, those in the netherworld, and those walking for yet a little while longer on earth. Thus the New York meeting.

Those who had come for the meeting were briefed that the United States was soon to be placed in a position of weakness from nature. Yes, somehow they knew.

High on the agenda were the following items:

• The elimination of the majority of private American vehicles (a nation dependent upon mass transportation is dependent on the government)

• Higher Energy Prices (The average unleaded gas price was already at $2.25, primarily due to a new international tax imposed through the UN on the United States). This is related to the above item, and would also have the effect of keeping the public at the right degree of "agitation" due to insufficient income (individual and industry) to maintain heating and cooling levels in homes and businesses at comfortable temperatures.

• The removal of all registered guns from the Americans

• The elimination of the financial and material presence of Catholicism in the United States. This meant more lawsuits against the Church in regards to pedophiles and other areas. The goal was to bring about 24 more lawsuits in the country in the next few months that would break the back of the Roman Catholic Church in the United States, forcing it to surrender all material possessions (land, buildings, seminaries, churches, bank accounts, etc.). If necessary, lawsuits would be fabricated by the government and its cohorts. Money and witnesses would be provided if necessary. Unfortunately, the Judas' in the Church were doing enough damage to eliminate the need to require the government to do much fabricating of their own against the Church.

• The elimination of small arms producers (those supplying arms for sportsmen including high powered bows and cross bows)

• Tougher laws against religion in general, primarily Catholicism.

• The elimination of all building and development within vast distances of "National Parks" and forests to "preserve the global biosphere". This would prevent religious groups and others from seeking refuge and a means of carrying on their Christian apostolates somewhat distant geographically from government intervention.

• The registering of all Active Catholics

• Direct government action to enable the "ordination" of women "priests" within six months. This action would be covert, yet massive. The Catholic Liturgy would be neutered also in this program.

• A tougher permitting system for all religious gatherings.

• The Unveiling of the New World Religion.

• The elimination of the means of survival for those who would seek to avoid the New World Order through subsidence farming and hunting, and would attempt to avoid governmental agencies in general. The insurance industry was pressing for deer herd decreases nationwide, and was pushing for contraceptive salt licks to be placed by the millions across all known deer lands, public and private. The meat of such deer feeding at the contraceptive salt licks would be rendered inedible due to high estrogen levels. Two birds with one stone. Less accidents from deer, and the elimination of subsidence hunting by individuals. Subsidence farming elimination would be tougher to bring about, but a committee would be set up to bring about such a plan of action. Initial possibilities were stiff seed tariffs, "quarantining of vast amounts of "contaminated seeds" in the hands of the seed companies - if necessary, the government would provide the contamination, and a permitting system regarding seeds, fertilizer, weed killers, etc.

• The elimination of all businesses that provide goods and materials for food storage for the homeowner, including do-it yourself steamers, mason jars, and metal storage cans and containers.

• The elimination of all residential wood and coal stove manufacturers. Those who would seek to avoid the coming changes would probably be seeking energy independence. This cannot be.

- Inspection and certification of every wood stove in the United States of America under the guise of particulate emissions control. Stiff sentences for those caught burning wood and coal in unregistered stoves. The burning of wood or coal in fireplaces would simply be illegal, without a stove insert (registered and inspected). Inspectors will also have a free reign in firearms inspection/removal, and will assume other duties as the need for keeping the populace under control heats up.

New York, New York. I want to be a part of it. New York, New York...

****

"I'd like to pay for tonight at K-2 please," said Rick to a middle-aged lady now running the front desk. Rick looked around the office. This was the Maine he had known, yes, indeed. Tourist Maine. There were brochures of every description, offering a smorgasbord of recreational and sightseeing opportunities for everything from whale watching to glider plane flights, and horseback riding to small brewery tours. Most of these opportunities would cost the average adult twenty to seventy bucks. Seventy bucks times two million is a lot of bucks. The park was now averaging about two million visitors per year. If you weren't an independently wealthy landowner from stateside, and you lived on the island, your income probably depended on these 2 million visitors.

"You're the fellow on the bike, aren't you" said the lady reaching for a blank customer form.

·"Yes" said Rick.

"Did you know you're at a trailer site that costs six dollars more than a bike tent site?" she said

"Yeah, that's fine said Rick. I love the view of the Bay", he said.

"Sorry about the weather", she told him as he was filling out the paperwork.

Now, it was about 81 degrees, partly sunny, with a gentle breeze blowing in off of Frenchman's Bay. Rick was wondering what she was talking about. "What do you mean?" he said.

"Oh, you're the only one who hasn't heard the forecast. We've got four days, maybe a week of rain coming", she said. "We're coming off one of our hottest, driest summers, and now we're going to be in for a deluge. The weather has gone nuts. I think the tabloids are right. Well, the thunderstorms that are coming tonight are courtesy of the Midwest. They think that hurricane Michael might be pushing moisture up to our neck of the woods after it beats its way up the coast in the next few days. They say this one's in a hurry!" she said.

"Is it a big one?" said Rick

"Yeah, they're calling it the 500 year storm. Florida is in a panic. They're evacuating a big part of the coastline," said the attendant.

"I'm Rick Tremont by the way."

"I'm Brenda Lafayette, native Acadian, native Catholic. My relatives didn't go to Louisiana with the rest of the Catholics. Somehow the English missed a few of us. I see your scapular - that's why I thought I'd mention this to you. Did you come for this Medjugorje gathering?" she said.

"Nice to meet you Brenda. In a way, I guess you could say that's why I'm here. Will you be going?" Rick said.

"Whenever I can said Brenda. I'll be working part of the time. You know there's a handful of people in the area that have been to Medjugorje. A few of the rich and famous have been there too. I'm sure the ad in the Bar Harbor times and the Ellsworth American was a pleasant shock for some of them. Not everyone, however, likes Our Lady Down East. The liberals, if you can call them Christians own the turf. God is kept in the closet as something you can bring out and pet once in a while, like a whale or seal or something. Babies are out up here too."

"Brenda, do you think there will be many people that come out to the park for Our Lady for the next few days", Rick said.

"I know about 20 people that have rearranged their whole weekend to be there every minute. This is the oddest blessing the area has had since the Jesuits came. Basically, the people from two prayer groups that I know of will be here. Pray for my daughters and their husbands. I hope they come. The world about killed them and their families, but Jesus & Mary have resurrected them. They could all use a shot in the arm though. I have three daughters. My husband went down in bad weather dragging for shellfish in 1992. They only found a few items from his boat."

"Sorry to hear that Brenda. I'll keep you all in my prayers said Rick, handing her the campground form and the cash."

"Thanks" said Brenda. "God bless you."

"No Problem. God bless you," said Rick heading for the door.

****

Steve Lebroq was a good man and who loved his job dearly. Steve had one of the most coveted jobs in the United States. He was the Park Superintendent for Acadia National Park. Surprisingly, Steve's job was more sought after by career federal workers than the superintendent's job at Yellowstone. Strange though, Steve himself would have taken Yellowstone if the situation had presented itself in 1994 when he took over the reign's at Acadia. Now however, the devil in the White House in

Washington couldn't get him out with an executive order if he wanted to. Steve had become a part of Acadia, and Acadia was a part of Steve. His family felt the same way. They lived in the Superintendent's residence right inside the Park. His wife and children thought they were in heaven. Bikes, horses, fishing, the ocean, boats – you name it, they had it, and they loved it. Emily, Steve's wife, would have found it hard to ever adjust to a life anywhere else. She rubbed elbows with some of the most interesting people in the world, and the social life was without end. Steve Jr., and William (Bill), their children, aged 12 and 10 respectively, were the happiest kids you could find anywhere, on the surface, at least. Steve had been one of those wonder boys in the government world that went far in a hurry. He was one of the youngest Park Superintendents in the country. A lot of questions were raised when he was chosen for Acadia. The questions went unanswered. Being a yes man has its benefits.

The Lebroqs were a typical American family. They were dead for the most part. That is, their souls were dead or dying. Is not mortal sin death of the soul? Is it not better to cut off our hand or pluck out our eyes than to die to God? The Lebroqs were mortally wounded and in need of confession. Confession did not seem to be too soon in coming, however. Steve was raised a Catholic. His father was in the Knights of Columbus. Steve hated the knights of Columbus. His father was often there when Steve was growing up. Sure, the knights spread the Catholic Faith, they defended the Faith, and they assisted the poor and provided insurance for Catholics. On the down side, they also had a bar. It was the bar that Steve really hated. His father was an alcoholic, a low down drunk as a buzzard alcoholic, who seemed to get along fine at the factory, but was a holy terror at home. Steve stopped going to church at age 12. His father died at age 59, and Steve remembered both feelings of relief and sorrow. Steve's mother took the brunt of the pain the father inflicted on the family with his addiction, but through prayer, she came out the better for it. The four children received deep emotional scars that even now, had not yet healed. They had all left the Catholic faith. Steve and his sister Marsha tried not to ever think about God. Alice and Frank, the remaining siblings, thought about God on Sundays.

Unbeknownst to Steve, his father was also a Mason, and had died many years before his reported death. Steve's father was buried on December 27, 1992, his body having expired on Christmas day. His father's soul had died on January 4, 1962, the day he became a Freemason. His father's soul was resurrected on the same day of his body's expiration – on December 25, 1992, through the sacrament of Reconciliation (Confession). That always bugged Steve, seeing the priest around on Christmas at his father's deathbed. Where had the priests been in the last few decades when his family needed help? More than that, why would this devil of his father get a shot at heaven now, after the hidden life he had lead?

One of the gifts of God to mankind is that we bounce back. We can bounce back from death in the family, the loss of a job, a cold, a serious illness – even cancer, cancer of the body, and cancer of the soul. Steve had the latter, and was about to recover even though he didn't want too. His mother's prayers for him and all of her children were going to be answered soon. She had been to daily Mass since the age of twenty, rarely missing a day. Since the day of her marriage, her main prayer was that God would make her family a family of saints. In many ways hers was the worst, most dysfunctional family on the block. More than the drink, it was the cancer of Freemasonry that had torn through her family like a demon possessed, with ax in hand, and able to cross from the netherworld to our world. The demons of darkness had all but destroyed their family. Yet death, where is your sting? Where is your sting now?

For a little while yet, darkness still had hold of Steve. Some demons can only be cast out by much prayer and fasting. The good news is that the process had begun. There were many people now praying for the impending situation that was about to occur in the park. Steve was at the top of this whole park pyramid. He and the devils around him were being bombarded with the Son's rays – and the prayers of the faithful and their petitions to Jesus through Mary.

Steve was enjoying his morning donut and coffee with his feet up on the table reading the latest in government news. He put down that paper and picked up the Bar Harbor times. The headlines looked the same. There were tourists on the front page, a story of the plight of the lobster fishermen, and some national news related to the Park System of the United States which was now, at least on paper under the jurisdiction of the United Nations, thanks to the treason of Bill Clinton, enemy of the Republic. Bill had been giving away our country for years, but it was not until 1997 that things began to move rapidly. This day's news in that regard considered personnel changes that the UN was making in *our Sovereign Parks!* Steve's job was secure from current changes, so he just glanced over that article. He flipped the page, and there it was. Page three. Right before his eyes. **"The First Annual Acadia Medjugorje Conference, Acadia National Park, July 3,4, and 5th, 1998."**

Not here, sorry! The Jesuits hit the road a long time ago and Steve wasn't going to let them back in his park. His thoughts didn't make sense, but his mind had just jumped to the early Catholic history of the area. The Catholics got their butts kicked out of Acadia by the English. That's why we have Cajuns in Louisiana. *What the hell are these people doing?*

They're not bringing their God baggage into my park. Conference? I'm the boss. Nobody called me about a conference. The Park Service is not going to be happy. My job is in jeopardy. They've told us unequivocally that God is out. I'm all for it.

"Helen?" Steve called to his secretary. "Have you heard anything about this so called religious conference?" he said.

"I saw that this morning. I was going to ask you about it. How are they going to do that without buildings? Do you think it's a joke? Can they do that legally in the park?" she said.

"I'm going to call this guy on his cellular phone and tell him to stay home this weekend" said Steve, red faced, feeling like someone had just stolen an apple from his prized tree.

He went into his office and dialed. No answer except for the recorded message *"We're sorry, the Cellular West customer that you are trying to reach is not available. Please try again later"*. Paul Bohatch did not want to spend the extra three dollars per month on the messaging service, so Steve was unable to leave his message.

"I'm going over to Bar Harbor Campground to talk to them about this so called conference that is definitely not going to happen!" said Steve. He left in a huff.

At the campground, they were just as surprised as Steve was about the conference. Steve was even angry with Mr. Busch, the owner. He lost his temper with him. "Tell that son of a... that we'll have him arrested if he sets foot in the park. And I'll appreciate it if you guys cease cooperating with this idiot" said Steve. He pushed the door open wide, as he left hurriedly. The door was pulled back to a slam by the spring. Mr. Busch checked the customer cards again. No Paul Bohatch. *Bohatch? What kind of a name is that?*

Steve bugged several more people with such questions and rudeness before he gave up looking for clues in this case and went back to the office. There was a fax awaiting him when he got back:

Environmental Worldwide Task Group

United Nations

UN Building

New York, NY

Superintendent Steve Lebroq

July 2, 1998

Acadia National Park

Bar Harbor, Maine

Dear Mr. Lebroq:

Our office has been informed of a supposed religious gathering to be held July 3,4, and 5th at Acadia National Park.

This gathering is against International Law. See that it is not held. Such gatherings will not be tolerated in Acadia National Park, or in any other lands controlled by the United Nations.

Under no circumstances will this gathering be allowed, now or in the future. Your position in the park, and the future of your career depends upon this.

Boutros H. Sage

President

EWTG

In the future, such directives would be coming from the new headquarters on Burnt Porcupine Island. At this time however, the new headquarters was not yet fully operational.

****

Luke and Alice Miller had rarely been out of Michigan prior to the trip that they were now undertaking. Luke was 27 years old, and Alice was 26. They had been high school sweethearts and married when he was 19. When others were concerned with football and college, Luke was concerned with motorcycles and cars. Since her freshman year in high school, Alice was usually concerned about what Luke was concerned about. They had not lived the most chaste high school life together, and from that came Shawna, their first born. Shawna brought about the marriage of Luke and Alice. Luke and Alice had two more children after this, Robert, and Jenny. They lived in Rawlins, a suburb of Dearborn, in a trailer on Alice's mother's property, 10 acres on the edge of town.

Upon marriage, Luke secured a job as a pump jockey at an Exxon station in Rawlins in 1990. For a while, they thought the world was theirs, in their young love, and used trailer – their very own home, their very own bedroom. For a while, five dollars an hour did pay the bills. They could even get out once in a while on a date with Alice's mother doing the baby-sitting. Then came Robert and Jenny, and more bills. In this period of transition, Luke did manage to move up to the position of a full time mechanic at six fifty per hour, where his wage still stands. Luke was a boon for business. The customers loved him for his skill and courtesy. On a car, he had the hands of a surgeon, and in his speech the courtesy of a diplomat, but he was neither, and their pantry, their trailer, their one car - a well-traveled 1986 Ford Escort, and their clothing spoke of this. Strange that it does not seem to be hard to be a pauper these days. Even a working man can do it.

Luke and Alice had never really found God. Well, they never went looking for Him either. God was for the wealthy they thought, those who didn't have to work on Sunday. Luke made time and a half on Sundays, and was usually at the Exxon Station on these days of obligation for one-fifth of the rest of mankind. One might have guessed that the Millers were Christians, however. In many ways their life spoke of it. Alice had been baptized, to a degree, but baptism not being scored the same as horseshoes, her Baptism was lacking the grace of the Father, Son, and Holy Spirit, and held no ground in heaven. Her mother's church at the time did not recognize the Trinity. Luke had never received the waters of baptism.

Luke had an older brother Ron, who used to drive for Roadway Express. Back in 1989, Ron's cab decided it was time for a new valve job when Ron was on the road in a place called Ellsworth, Maine. Roadway Express had to send in another tractor-trailer to pick up Ron's load. Ron had 20 hours to kill. When he heard the striped bass were running up the Penobscot at the gas station where he was making his phone calls, he walked across the street to a K-Mart and bought a salt water fishing rig. If he hadn't caught that 37 inch bass on his 7th cast into the Penobscot, he probably wouldn't have quit his job and stayed behind in Ellsworth. Things being as they were however, Ron became an Ellsworth resident, and was making a fair living with a very small seafood restaurant that he had started. By 1995 the business had grown into a restaurant/gift shop. He married his cashier Emily in 1991. Emily first had him promise he would be baptized before their wedding. He joined her church, the Ellsworth Open Bible Chapel. There were only 33 in the congregation, 34 now with Ron. Ron and Emily had two children by 1998, and were reading the Bible together almost every day with their children.

Luke was very thankful for his children, but he knew that they could not afford any more. He talked it over with Alice, and they decided to check into a sterilization program that the state of Michigan offered. Washington State had pioneered a similar program, and now almost every state was following in rapid succession. The program offered free sterilization for those who met certain educational, financial, and moral requirements. Hitler would have been proud of the program. Basically, Michigan and the rest of the country were now prepared to sterilize those who weren't going to amount to much. True, many middle class and wealthy, intelligent individuals choose to make the same decision. Some of the most well known, intelligent people in the United States had opted for such surgery. Such as these, however, were not the target of this program, however. Michigan was after the imbeciles. Why should they have progeny? Better to end their line deemed those in control.

Luke was scheduled to be under the knife on July 3rd, 1998. By the grace of God, he made the "mistake" of telling Ron what he was about to do one day. Now Ron's church was all for any and every form of birth control, even if it smelled like abortion, but didn't go by the name of abortion. Of course they did hold that abortion was a great sin "usually". There were two children in Ron and Emily's church under the age of seven. They were the beautiful children of Ron and Emily. Ron had often wondered "where had all the children gone?" He and Emily had fought on occasion because Ron wanted to find a church with lots of children, so their children would have playmates on Sundays and Wednesdays. Emily was a diehard for the Open Bible Chapel, and would never consider leaving. Ron's concerns over the lack of children in his church, and elsewhere for that matter, introduced him to the works of the deceased *(by the grace of God)* Margaret Sanger, pioneering enemy of babies, blacks, Catholics, and humanity in general, who had given birth to Planned Parenthood. ***Now Ron knew where all the babies had gone***.

Luke called Ron about a month after Ron's enlightenment on the subject of babies, or rather the lack of babies. Luke had never spoken with anyone but Alice before on the subject of the bedroom or what it entails. He had a great amount of modesty, a preconception of sorts of the way that Christians are supposed to handle that which is uniquely proper to the sacrament of marriage. He felt prodded by an unseen force. After the usual "what's up", "how is everything", Luke dropped the bombshell. Ron read Luke the riot act, and then he read him the *unabridged* Margaret Sanger. He quoted her works. Alice heard it all on another phone. Luke and Alice were ashamed. Ron felt so strong about it that he wanted Luke and Alice and the kids to come out and visit. He said he'd send them $500 in traveling money if they would come out and visit at the end of July or the first week of August. Ron told Luke that he thought they should sit down together and talk about Jesus Christ. They could camp, fish, drink beer, whatever, but Ron told Luke he needed to get his butt out of Michigan. The next day Ron Fed-Ex'd a $500 check to Luke & Alice. Having never seen that much money in one fell swoop before, and wanting to see his brother, Luke called and told Ron he'd see him around July 1st.

****

The sign read "Carey Ohio", next exit. The secondary signs showed food, gas, lodging, and religion would be found at the next exit. Religion? Well, there was something about a shrine. At first Luke thought it was the Masons.

Luke never could hold his coffee, but he sure could put it down. It was two in the morning, and all that coffee had to be relieved. "Alice" said Luke, "did I pass the rest area? The sign said two miles. I gotta hit the bathroom or we're gonna have to call out the National Guard. This is serious." Alice was half-asleep. At first she didn't answer. Luke realized he could not put much value in the answer of his sleepy wife. "What, oh, no. I don't know", she said, though rather convincingly. Luke did not want to take a chance. "I'm gonna get off here, we're in Carey, Ohio, wherever the Hell that is. There's supposed to be gas here." Luke exited and turned left at the stop sign. *There's that sign for the shrine,* he thought. He still couldn't read the whole sign as it flashed by.

"Damn, the Speedway gas station is closed", he said. "What, a McDonalds out in the middle of the cornfields. What's the world coming to", he said to himself. The McDonalds was closed of course at this late hour. "I'm gonna go look into town. Then I'm probably gonna fertilize some corn out there."

As is often the case in flat farm country, the lightning from storms 50 or 75 miles away was lighting up the sky in an assortment of compass directions. Because of the distance, however, not a sound could be heard. The sky was black and partly cloudy, and broken fog was here and there. As Luke approached the town, which was about a mile from the highway, he took his first left. He thought it was useless. As he felt an even more urgent call to do what only he himself could do, he gasped out an "oh God, help me", inaudible to his wife. Whether it was Saint Jimmy Stewart, or Clarence himself, it worked. Right in front of him was the biggest church in town. There were more lights on in this church than one might expect for the early morning hours. This church did not seem to be dead. Indeed, the church was not dead; God himself, Jesus Christ in the Blessed Sacrament was waiting for him. Luke turned left, and left again into a visitors parking lot. He ran out of the car after saying he'd be right back to his wife. She'd thought he'd gone to get religion at this hour. He thought he'd gone to find a toilet. He got both. He ran up the steps on the left side of the church, pulled on the handle of the first door he saw and it opened. First miracle! He ran up another set of steps inside the church and bingo! He couldn't read the sign in the somewhat darkened church, but he just knew it had to be. *Yes! Yes! Yes! A toilet!*

Luke wanted to leave in a hurry. He was afraid that someone might see his car and call the police, or maybe they saw him go into the church. He actually felt a fear that had never come over him before. It was the devil. The devil never really had a need to scare the Hell out of him before, because Satan was already in control, in an exterior way, so to speak, because Luke had not opted for the Lord. As Luke was leaving the bathroom, his body shuddered with fear. His short hair actually stood on end more than before. He kept looking behind him. Waves, physical waves of fear shot through his body. He instantly had goosebumps, and his hair stood on end like a porcupine. This was not normal. *Hey, if this was a Catholic Church as he guessed, he'd seen his last. Let me out of here was all he could think of as he ran back down the steps.* "**Stop**", an unknown voice called. As he was about to explode out of the church, beginning to push the door open, he felt the fear inside him immediately intensify, and peak. Then, it was as if the fear turned into an explosion, and then suddenly dissipated as quickly as it had set over him. He then was no longer afraid. "**Stop**", he heard again. He let the door go back in its place. With apprehension he walked back up the steps. He passed the bathroom, walked across the huge foyer, and then started to walk down the middle isle of the church. *What, who, had called him back?,* he thought. He knew it was a friend of God. It was a woman's voice. But the woman was not nearby and calling in the usual audible voice that one might hear when called by another. The voice was in his head. As he walked down the aisle he immediately saw the flickering of hundreds of candles lit by pilgrims from all over the country earlier in the day. He was indeed at the Shrine. The Shrine of Our Lady of Consolation in Carey, Ohio

There was a mysterious stillness in the church. It was quieter than quiet. Candlelight gave some illumination to the darkened church. Luke felt his goosebumps coming back. The flickering candles played games with Luke - putting darting dark figures in places were there were none. Now they were here. Now they were gone. At the same time, it was as if he was alone in the world. He had long forgotten about his wife and children out in the car, and his purpose for being here. It seemed as if he was walking up to a great curtain, looking for the voice of the Great Oz, but this was not Oz, this was a Catholic Church, and he knew that God was here. That was beyond a doubt. He suspected the presence of God was in a gold colored metal box he saw in the center tabernacle behind the main altar in the church. He could see the flickering singular light that he thought stood for something powerful, but he did not understand more than that. It was just enough to know that God was mysteriously here somehow. He looked up at the ceilings. Surely those must be the apostles up there, dancing above his head in the flickering light. Those are not the idols that I have heard of. Those are Christ's beloved apostles! He approached the end of the aisle, the front of the church, and knelt before the tabernacle, perhaps at his guardian angel's inspiration. He looked to his right and back – it looked like a doll dressed up as the baby Jesus. It was The Infant of Prague. It was indeed a statue of the baby Jesus, the miraculous Infant of

Prague! As he turned to his left and walked back toward the front of the church he knelt before an altar to the right of the main altar, above which was a statue of Mary, holding the baby Jesus. *How beautiful*, he thought. He did not know that this was the beautiful statue of Our Lady of Consolation brought over from Bohemia in 1875. So many miracles have been attributed it – to Jesus through Mary. To Luke it was simply a beautiful statue, but somehow he felt its importance. "Did you call me?" he said, half-believing she did. He walked to the left of the church and saw another altar.

Beneath the altar was the most beautiful statue of Jesus Christ in the tomb. Unseen to Luke, underneath the neck of Jesus Christ, away from the opening, was a piece of paper, a check deposit slip, with a petition scribbled on it. *Dear Jesus & Mary, please bless my sister who has cancer. She is dying. And please let Alice and Luke Miller know of your love. Please bring them into the One, Holy, Catholic and Apostolic Faith. I love you Jesus. I love you Mary. Charlene Clark.* Charlene and Timmy Clark were neighbors of Alice and Luke. They had been to the shrine before.

Suddenly there was the most frightful crash that Luke had ever heard. For no reason, no reason visibly seen, the silence in this church, this huge basilica was shattered. A glass enclosure covering one of the larger candles on the right of the church near Our Lady's statue crashed to the ground, sounding like an explosion from Hell in the midst of this huge, just moments ago silent basilica. Luke's fear at the door a few minutes ago came back with a vengeance, a hundred fold. His somewhat short hair was now standing straight out from his head. His body gave new meaning the word goosebumps. He turned around instantly with the noise. At first he saw nothing. Then he saw the ugliest 8-foot creature of a man with fiery green glowing eyes that ever walked the streets of Hell. The demon or head honcho himself disappeared as fast as he came, but Luke did not need a formal invitation to leave. He ran up the left side isle of the church as fast as he could go, yelling out "Jesus, Jesus, Jesus, Mary!" Then he looked up, as he was about to exit the church into the foyer. "God", he yelled. No, it wasn't God. It wasn't Satan. It was Alice.

"What are you doing Luke?" do you want these people to call the police on you. You probably woke up the neighborhood." Luke was still shaking as he was standing next to his wife in the back of the church. He had to remind himself that his wife had not just seen the same horror show that he had.

"Alice. Alice. Oh God, I'm glad you came in. The kids..." said Luke.

"I locked the door, they're all sleeping safe and sound. I need to use the restroom too. Where is it? What in the world are you doing in here anyway?" she said as she walked to the restroom, having spotted the door behind her.

Alice walked out of the restroom and saw Luke in the middle of the foyer, reading a pamphlet. "Come on Luke. We got to get going. I think we still have an hour and a half to my brother's house", she said. They were going to visit her brother in Columbus before continuing on to Maine. "Let's get out of here," said Alice, "this place is spooky", she said. Alice peeked into the church again, looking up the middle isle. For some reason she started to walk up it. She walked up to the front of the isle. She noticed red glass all over the floor where she was standing. She turned around and looked at Luke who was following her very sheepishly. "Look at this glass", she said.

"Tell me about it" said Luke.

"What" said Alice.

Luke was now next to Alice. "Alice, do you believe in God?"

"What", she said.

"Do you believe in God?" said Luke again.

"I guess he's out there somewhere. Do you?" said Alice.

"I think he's in here. I think God is up there. It's so mysterious. Look up there" he said pointing to the tabernacle and its light. "Do you believe in the devil?" he said. As he spoke the words a chill came over him this time, and his goosebumps hit record heights again, as he relived what had happened minutes before.

"Maybe I believe God, but I think the devil is just that Catholic stuff....", she said.

"I just saw him" said Luke.

"God?", she said.

"The Devil", he said.

"Luke, don't scare me like this. Don't ever do that. Let's get out of here," said Alice.

"Wait, you see that glass. He did it. The devil did it. I saw him there - about 8 feet tall with fiery green eyes and all. I hope to never see him again. I didn't think I was afraid of much. This ain't kid stuff. It was worse than the movies, believe me", he said. "Can we sit down a minute?"

He told her the whole story, including the voice at the door as he was first about to leave. "Do you think it was some kind of Catholic devil or something – something these people bring around or honor because of their superstitions?" said Luke.

"I don't know, why would you think that?" said Alice.

"I don't think that," said Luke. I don't think that ugly guy wanted me here. I think he wanted me to run. I think the people honor God here. I think Satan was trying to scare me out of here.

Alice did not want to believe Luke, though Luke had never lied to her since they were married as far as she knew. She did not want to believe in devils. God, O.K., He was pleasant. But Luke could keep this stuff that exorcism movies are made of. She felt it however. Deep down she knew he was not lying or even mistaken. She felt as scared as he did now. "Well, if there is a God, and there is a Devil, what in the world is going on? What would it mean?"

"Why didn't God appear to you instead. That might have made it simpler. Jesus could have just come and said 'Clean up your act or something'. You had to get the Devil. You're scaring the heck out of me", she said.

"I picked up these pamphlets in the back of the church. This one's about the church history. This is what these people call the Saint Michael Prayer. He was in the Bible I think. "Would you say this prayer with me", he said. "I think that's what we need to do. It says Saint Michael is powerful against evil. That guy was one bad dude I saw, and I'm still shaking" said Luke.

"Will you stop scaring the living daylights out of me? You pray? God, you must have seen that ugly thing. I never saw you pray" said Alice. "Give me the card", she said.

"Saint Michael the Archangel, defend us in the day of battle, be our protection against the wickedness and snares of the devil, and do thou oh prince of the Heavenly Host, by the power of God, cast into Hell Satan and all of the evil spirits who prowl throughout the world seeking the ruin of souls, Amen" they said together.

"Can we keep saying the prayers for a little while honey? " said Luke.

"Oh God" she said, half-scared, half-angry. "What about the kids?", she said.

"The kids will be fine, just a few minutes", he said.

"Saint Michael the Archangel, defend us in the day of battle, be our protection against the wickedness and snares of the Devil..."

Twenty minutes later they stopped. They had now prayed together for about 25 minutes all told. They had never prayed together before. Alice and Luke were no longer the same people that had walked into the church not long ago. They were a praying family now. They were no longer pagans. There's a Hell of a difference between the two.

"We'd better go get the kids honey. God, what if they woke up. They'd be scared. Let's go," said Alice.

As they were about to walk out the door of the church, Luke said, "Wait, what's down there?" He started to walk downstairs. "Honey, the kids", she said. She followed him downstairs. "Oh, so this is where they hide most of the statues," said Alice.

"Honey, I don't think they're hiding them. I think we found the only unlocked doors in Carey, Ohio tonight. Maybe the only unlocked doors in Ohio. They want people to come to their church, anytime. They want us to come down here too. Look, people come here from all over," said Luke.

Luke and Alice were standing in front of several cases of crutches, prosthetics, eyeglasses, cigarette packs, needles, and the most somber looking medical devices that man has known in the last 100 years. Somber because of the pain and sufferings that the bearers must have borne. They had all been left here by people who had been cured. Some of them had been medically verified, just like at Lourdes, France, Fatima, Portugal, and Medjugorje, Bosnia. There were pictures of loved ones, with notes on them from people who were asking Our Lady to intercede with Jesus for them. One could not read the letters on writing paper, on cardboard, on pictures, on bottles, on cards, etc., without having tears in the eyes.

So, for a few minutes more they forgot about the children, and walked in the darkened church basement amidst the flickering lights. They passed the life-size and lifelike statues of the saints, works of art, and the already mentioned cases holding the testimonies in ink and other forms of the pilgrims who had passed by. They came to the statue of Saint Francis. It was marked so, that's how they knew who it was. A few candles were burning around him. The saint look so peaceful, so humble, so Christ like, they knew there was nothing harmful here in this statue. There was nothing here related to the thing that Luke had seen upstairs a little while ago. Then another statue – Saint Anthony of Padua. Surely Luke and Alice could only see the testimony of goodness and joy in the statue's face here, too. He was holding the Christ Child. Another statue of Our Lady. Did she resemble anything like what he had just seen upstairs? No! No! No! The statue looked like every mother, like everyone should look like. All one could think of was Love! Praise to the artist thought Luke! Praise to her Maker, he thought! He was trying to remember and say the Saint Michael prayer as he and Alice walked around the mysterious, dimly lit downstairs of the Basilica church. Alice was trying to do the same.

If there was something frightening here in this darkness - if there was something ugly here, amidst the lifelike statues, the holy pictures with lights dancing in front of them, and the occasional heart stopping sounds of a long length of wood or metal expanding with a great sound amidst the silence – then it was the realization of the battle that is. Jesus is here. Mary is here. The saints are here. But the battle is also here. The wicked combatants are also here. The battle is for eternal life or eternal death. So, yes, Satan is also here. Jesus, however, Lord of all, has told us to choose him – to choose life. Satan has no power over us unless we willingly choose to give it to him.

A heating duct overhead suddenly expanded and caused a loud noise shattering the silence. Alice jumped and hugged Luke in fear. Where in the world were they now she thought. A little while ago they were on a highway going 65 miles an hour southeast across Ohio, heading for Columbus. What happened? Where were they? Where were they really?

They came back to the glass cases. Luke read with a whisper. *'From P.J. Columbus, Lima, Ohio. In thanksgiving for being cured at Carey, Ohio, of blindness, February 22nd, 1916, after having been blind for two years, and of paralysis June 12, 1917, with which I was afflicted for seven months. I was taken in a basket to the shrine where it is today. I walked home and to this day I can see perfectly and am enjoying full health. Thanks to almighty God and the Virgin Mary. Sincerely, P.J. Columbus, February 22, 1919.'* He read another. *'To sell business and get my family back together. Hear my prayer Lord. J.K.'* The latter was written on the back of an A.I. Root candle label!

Alice, taking Luke's cue, whispered a few of the notes. *'Mary, I give you this bracelet. Help me not to cry too much. I'm 4 years old. Belinda Zefin'.* And another: *'Lord, Thank you for sparing my baby from having any more seizures. Gloria'*

"Look at this," said Alice. "Did you see the picture of the poor baby there hooked up to the medical instruments? They requested God to heal him on that one, that picture. Look, way over here, it's the same boy 10 months later. Hector Mikelo Ramirez. He looks like he's ready for soccer. It says *'Hector Mikelo Ramirez, 10 Mo. old, Thank you God, Hector Mikelo is doing well! Thank you Lord!'* "They came back to say thanks" said Alice, "wow, that's powerful".

"Here's another: *'Please Dear Blessed Mother, heal Danny's right eye. Please keep him & all our families in your loving care.'*

"Oh God, look at this" said Luke. *'Michael Thomas Serra, 3 years old, Leukemia, Please pray for me.'* – "The note is on a pair of baby socks. Man...."

"Look," said Alice: *'Dominic, Cindie, Don Saxer. Thank you O Blessed Mother, for this little miracle (there's a picture of the parents and the baby) you helped us to deliver on January 7, 1997. After 3 horrible miscarriages we became pregnant through His divine help and came to you last summer (1996) and sought your Most Holy Help in carrying this child to full term. Not only did we have a healthy 10-lb. boy, he is the calmest & most content & happy baby we've ever seen. He is here because of you, Mary! We love you very much!!!'* "They've even got his ultrasound here!" said Alice. "Oh God, the kids... Let's get out of here..."

Luke and Alice ran back out of the basement to the stairway they came down. They dashed up the stairs and out the door. "Oh my God, Alice said. They're crying. The kids didn't know where we were," said Alice. They got to the car, unlocked it, and went into the kids and closed the doors.

"Mommy. Mommy! Mommy! Mommy! Screamed Shawna, the oldest daughter, age 7. Robert age 5, and Jenny age 2 were also screaming, but decreasing in magnitude now that mom and dad had finally arrived. They had been screaming for over a half an hour. They had never experienced fear like this. Shawna told them that a giant beast like a man with green fire in his eyes was throwing balls of fire at them...."

After calming the children down, and giving them something to drink, they carried the children, pillows, and blankets back into the church and down into the basement, where a hundred church pews were welcoming them to get some well-deserved rest. Robert and Jenny were asleep before they hit the pews. Shawna fell asleep quite content as Dad was laying her down on a blanket and a pillow. Alice and Luke hugged each other, standing next to the sleeping children who were laid out in the front pew on the right, in front of the statue of Saint Francis of Assisi. They both felt like they had been waiting all of their life to get to this very church – as if the doors had been open for decades, just waiting for them to walk in. They had found God tonight, and they knew they were surrounded by his friends - not the plaster, plastic, and oil paint, but the saints that the materials represented. They felt safer now than they'd ever felt before. They felt like they were at home. *How sterile, cold, and lonely must be the Heaven in the minds of those who think the saints are dead, or perhaps just no longer the friends and benefactors of those of us here below,* thought Shawna. They were crying tears of sorrow and tears of joy. The tears of sorrow were for lost time. The tears of joy were in thanksgiving for the present and the future.

Over the years that the huge Basilica had been in existence, many a pilgrim had ventured to spend an evening in the church above, or in the basement below, in this beautiful, heavenly haven, known by thousands upon thousands in the eastern United States as the "unlocked" Basilica. The Basilica doors had never been locked, outside of the testing of the locks upon installation. So many souls had been saved through the intercession of Our Lady of Consolation. So many times, Our Lady had dispatched her friends, the angels and saints to bring forth a wayfarer from the highways and byways nearby, to bring them to this Basilica. Here Her Son waited for them in the Blessed Sacrament, in that golden box that Luke was yet to learn the secret of. They had come, these pilgrims, sometimes at midnight, or two or four in the morning - they had been hailed down, sometimes quite mysteriously as allowed by God, and brought, sometimes unawares to this place by the soldiers of heaven. They were brought in the wee hours, from the worst tempests and storms that raged in Northwestern Ohio, or in the hearts, minds, and souls of the wayfarers and pilgrims. They were hog tied and carried by the angels, and brought to this sanctuary, as they aimed their vehicle for this "shrine" that they had just heard about for the first time through the signs along the way. They came and they were consoled. They came and they were healed. They went away ready for the Heaven of heavens, with or without their crutches, sometimes healed in body, always blessed within.

Having arrived at the hour that they did, in the midst of late hours, all of the traces of the attacks that modernism had laid at the walls of this Jericho in reverse remained hidden from them, by the grace of God and Our Lady. After all, the attack was broad based, from Miami to Seattle, and points between, and around the globe. They would meet none of the scoffers, not one feminist, not one doubter of Our Lady of Consolation, Fatima, or Medjugorje. They would see no myriad of altar girls hovering around the altar this day, where once only young men - boys, maturing in age, stature, spirit and wisdom were found, often receiving the very foundation for their eventual ordination to the priesthood. Ah, but what would become of those who replaced the boys? Many a one, with the backing of their parents, would like them to climb the ecclesiastical ranks, and some few were being encouraged to do so in this "Land Of The Free", this "democracy", at least formerly, of ours. It was the will of the people after all! So what if Karol Wojtyla and company had said 'nay' infallibly, regarding the sought after breach in the ecclesiastical ladder. Indeed, some Bishops were already grooming their seminaries to welcome mixed gender! *In with the new, out with the old...*

A few hours later, the Millers took part in their first Catholic Mass. They were surprised that the Scriptures were read several times during the service. They didn't think that was so. Afterward they spoke to Brother Joel and Father Richard together, and told them everything that had happened just hours ago. They were invited to the rectory for breakfast and further talk. Father Richard and Brother Joel had seen and heard of such stories before. Brother Joel, a better storyteller than Father Richard, told the Miller family countless stories of the miraculous and mysterious connected with the Shrine. Father Richard answered the many questions that Luke and Alice had about the Catholic Faith. The Miller's were blessed to have such fine tour guides and spiritual directors in Father Richard and Brother Joel. Sister Mary Immaculata assisted Brother Joel in giving the Miller's a historic, detailed tour of the Basilica after breakfast.

Later on that day, the Miller's took their story to Alice's brother's house. Alice's brother said he was going to take the family to the shrine the next day. Her brother's family had never been inside a church together. God's graces were following the Miller's wherever they went, leaving miracles and conversions at every turn.

Soon Brother Ron in Ellsworth would find that Luke and Alice got religion along the trail, though not the kind the he and Emily had hoped to introduce them to. Luke, Alice, Shawna, and Robert had the Rosary memorized before they got to Ellsworth two days later, having picked up Rosary pamphlets and a dozen free plastic Rosaries in the church. Jenny would learn the Rosary in a year or two.

****

Steve Lebroq calmed down by the end of the day. He was sorry for the way he had acted. He knew that he had still not gotten over his father's alcoholism and its effect on his family. His anger was not at a religious conference, a Catholic gathering. He followed the books this day, however, and got a memo out to every available Park Service Ranger on the island that they were to report to him personally in the morning. He didn't tell them what it was about. They already knew. They just didn't know how Steve was going to deal with the situation. Steve wanted everyone there, from the naturalists and janitors, to the secretaries and lifeguards. There was work to be done, and Steve might need an army to do the job. Little did he know that he might just get an army. From the way this conference had started off, though, the unknown conference from nowhere, he rather doubted that there would be more than a few dozen what he thought would be properly called 'religious groupies'. Steve never called the cellular phone of Paul Bohatch again. He never called Bar Harbor Campground again. He really thought this supposed event would just blow over. *It was obvious to him that Paul Bohatch had very poor organizing skills!*

Well, *something was about to blow over*, at least over a portion of our country. Tropical Storm Michael was now a hurricane, fast heading for the shores of Florida. The storm was gyrating so much that the National Hurricane Center in Miami couldn't pick a landfall. They were guessing a wide mark, somewhere between Miami and Melbourne. One thing for sure, nobody in Florida would have to water his or her gardens this week. Michael was pushing wind speeds of 250 miles per hour, and had been gaining speed every hour for the last 8 hours. The hurricane was packing record amounts of moisture and that meant record amounts of rain for a lot of places in the next few days. The East Coast of Florida, from Homestead to Titusville was being evacuated for 10 miles inland. The conditions were so right for this hurricane to continue to gain strength until landfall, that the computer models were saying it was a 500-year storm. If this storm was to prove itself to be just such a storm, it would make its way into the history books, albeit possibly wet history books as being the largest hurricane ever known to hit the Americas. Florida was in a panic. Landfall was guestimated to be at 3PM, Eastern Standard Time, somewhere in the wide swath of shoreline being outlined by the National Hurricane Center on the screen that was now being viewed by millions of North Americans from the comfort of their own homes.

Steve was watching the 10 PM news with his wife on Thursday night, July 2, and taking in everything about the hurricane. He found it fascinating. He was glad he was not the park superintendent at the Everglades right now. The weather he loved though, any kind of it. That's what made Acadia so special. You never knew what the Atlantic was going to serve up. When he was off duty, he and Emily, and the kids would ride their bikes to Thunder Hole in all kinds of weather, barring snow and ice, and sit for hours and watch the surf, and listen to the roar of the Atlantic.

The television station was wrapping up the hurricane news and forecast for the time being, and Paul was about to flip over to the weather station to follow it more closely. They came right out with another story however, that caught an equal share of Steve's attention. A small to moderate earthquake had struck Virginia, Maryland, Delaware, and the Washington DC area sometime around 7 PM EST. There was little damage outside of fine china, but the scientists and the seismologists were scratching their head over this one. They were not ready for this. Channel 7 gave the quake news little time consideration. Outside of the scientists being a little perplexed, it had hardly made the news, despite the fact that tremors were felt as far north as Cape Cod, and as far south as Charleston, South Carolina. One gentleman, an apparent millionaire, judging from his Cape Cod mansion that was shown on the station, was running his home VCR recorder at the time of the earthquake, focusing on a martini on a glass table on a cement slab porch. All of a sudden the martini looked like Frenchman's Bay with waves going back and forth across the top of the wide mouthed glass, for just a few seconds. There was no wind; it was an enclosed porch. The fellow called his wife in while he was still filming the martini, and she's heard telling him that there's been a quake in DC. He questioned her on the tape "DC? Look at the martini!" She thought she heard something in the kitchen in retrospect, at that moment, but wasn't sure. The station had about 4 such interviews with people who said they felt the quake or lost some china off a high shelf.

But enough about earthquakes. It was off to a national commercial for AT&T Wireless. The AT&T boycotts from the Christian groups, due to AT&T's support for militant homosexuality and anti-family programs had borne little fruit. *AT&T was bursting with new business...*

So, aside from the hurricane news, Steve and Emily had experienced about 55 seconds of earthquake footage and comment, and then it was off to Martha's Vineyard with President Bill Clinton and family, enjoying a three-week vacation at an estate owned by Ted Glitzen the movie star. They showed Bill walking around in his shorts with the First Lady on the estate grounds. Bill was also wearing that tremendously sickening "I'm so impure and disgusting but you love me and I can do anything I want including killing babies because you voted for me and we control the media snicker of a look" on his face. Some people call it a smile. Others see right through the black eyes of this voracious shark and call an antichrist an antichrist without mincing words. Bill's current burden is not his sick sexual appetites or his selling out of America to the militant homosexuals and foreign governments. Bill's problem is that he does not repent. Who of us are better than Saint Mary Magdalene before we begin to tell God we are sorry and ask Him to change our ways? Bill continues to grovel in his slime, peering out from it once in a while to mock both man and God. One day Bill Clinton may be a great saint. We must pray for that day, but prepare also for the worst – through prayer!

Emily was heading off to bed, but Steve couldn't get enough of the hurricane news. He somehow wanted to feel its energy; to be a part of it, to take in all of the expert's advise that he could and digest it himself. He said goodnight to Emily, told her he was going to stay up and watch the hurricane news on the weather channel, and went to find his Atlantic Coast maps. The children had already gone to bed without their prayers at 9:30. They always went to bed without their prayers, and it was beginning to show. They had no prayers, nor did their father or mother. All things in God's time, however.

Steve went to the refrigerator and grabbed a Moose Butt Beer. Moose Butt was one of those local beers that tasted a little worse than a Michelob or Miller, but cost 3 times as much. Bill knew the owner, so he didn't mind giving him the business. There was something about it too, maybe it was the fact that it was made right here on the wild Atlantic or maybe there was something mystical about it. It was beyond Steve, but he bought his share of Moose Butt. Steve was well aware of the effect that alcoholism had on his family, so he didn't really drink that often, and he didn't really drink that much. Two beers was usually the max for this cheap date, and on the rarest occasions, three. Moose Butt was a bottled beer, no one could imagine drinking Moose Butt Beer from a can. It would be un-Acadian. Steve popped the lid off the Moose Butt and turned to the weather station. *Five hundred-year storm*, he thought. *What do you do with a five hundred-year storm? What conference? There was a hurricane to follow! Now, if he could only get one of those reporters hanging on to a pier support for dear life that you sometimes see during the coverage of the hurricanes. That would be exciting...*

****

El Nino must have had the week off. Dust was everywhere. The old Ford Station Wagon was leaving a huge tunnel of a cloud behind it as it rattled down the driveway of the farm of Isaac and Eliza Yoder, near Kidron, Ohio. Ralph slammed on the brakes as he came to the farmhouse. Amish children went into hiding, fearing the worst of this Englishman in a hurry. Even the chickens headed for cover. The man was barely out of his car and he began yelling something that was totally foreign and abstract to Isaac and Eliza Yoder, who had just come to the front door of their house. The date was July 2, 1998. He screamed it out "Isaac, pack your bags we're going to the coast of Maine. Get along now. God sent me. You're supposed to go with me. Your whole family...

Following proper Amish protocol, Isaac had tried to refrain from most things "English". Yet, he would have to admit it before God, he had some science fiction reading under his belt. Isaac now felt that he was in one of the middle chapters of Ray Bradbury's "The Martian Chronicles". This couldn't be happening.

"Isaac, who is this man?" said Eliza.

"I have no idea Eliza".

Ralph made it to the porch at the instant that Isaac had just denied knowledge of the man with the '79 Ford. Then it hit him. "Ralph. Ralph Piccarreta. Oh my God. It's really you. Honey, this is Ralph Piccarreta. He's the man behind our praying the Rosary. He's the man that God sent to me a year ago."

"Please come in," said Eliza. "I have been wanting to meet you."

"There's no time, there's no time" said the strange man from Wheeling in a loud voice. "We need to get to Maine. We need to go now. We need to get to Maine..."

No, thought Isaac. He was mistaken. The mad man in front of him reminded him of George Bailey's uncle in "It's A Wonderful Life", after he had lost the bank deposit. It wasn't the Martian Chronicles after all... Isaac had seen the movie at a Mennonite's home many years prior.

"Maine?" said Isaac in a calm voice.

"Maine" said Ralph. There's going to be a Medjugorje Conference. I think Our Lady wants you to be there.

"We can't possibly go. The community. The... The..."

"Look, didn't you say something about needing a new draft horse harness when we met last year" said Ralph.

"No" said Isaac.

"You must have" said Ralph, waving a copy of the Bar Harbor Times classified section in front of him. "Belgium Draft Horse Harness, custom made for team of three. Many extras. Call 282-3322 (Bar Harbor)"

"I work with Morgans," said Isaac. "Belgiums weigh 2000 pounds". My Morgans are half that. It won't fit."

"I know a good tailor," said Ralph.

"I'll go pack now Isaac," said Eliza. She called the children in and told them to pack enough clothes for two weeks.

"Hank will want to go Ralph. He's my Baptist neighbor. Our families have been praying the Rosary together for six months. I'll run over to his house. Forget that, there he is, with his family" said Isaac, pointing to a Ford Van pulling up in front of the house.

Hank and his family were all packed and on their way to Glacier National Park for a three-week camping trip to Montana. They were pulling a trailer behind them. They were coming to say goodbye to the Yoders. Isaac explained what had just taken place. Hank Harper's family had all emerged from the van and stepped outside onto the dirt driveway, each bearing a Rosary in their hand.

"Honey, how do you feel about Maine?" said Hank to his wife.

"I've always wanted to see Maine," said Marsha Harper. "Let's go to Maine, Honey", she said.

In fifteen minutes the Yoder family had packed and was about to embark with Ralph Piccarreta for the coast of Maine and Acadia National Park. Hank Harper had made a call with his cellular phone and made arrangements with a Mennonite family to take care of the Yoder farm for the next two weeks. They had done so before. Ralph and Isaac were the last two to get into the car. As they were opening their doors and motioning to get in, Isaac took a good look at the old Ford. "Ralph, do you think she'll make it to Maine?"

"Guaranteed, Isaac. When Our Lady wants you somewhere she gets you there. I might not get you home though," he said looking at Isaac with a straight face that broke into a smile!

Isaac thought of his poor milking cows that are so fond of being milked twice a day...

The old wagon headed back down the driveway followed by a van pulling a late model Airstream Trailer.

Another adventure in Amish land had begun. The Yoder children felt like they were already in Heaven. MAINE! Lobsters, Whales, Dolphins, Bears. MAINE!

****

At Bar Harbor Campground a little earlier in the day, the pop up trailer was made ready for camping. The van was unpacked. The lines for water & electric connected. Paul Bohatch threw the last of the firewood from the back of the van towards the grill provided by the campground. He had hardly said anything during the unpacking and setup. Some of the youngsters were picking blueberries. Everyone was blissfully happy to be back in a blueberry patch overlooking the Atlantic Ocean. Paul however was in never never land.

Things were looking up around dinnertime. The Bohatch family was all settled in and enjoying a cookout of hot-dogs and hamburgers. Rick Tremont was entertaining Wayne and Betsy Sherman about 15 feet away at the next campsite. Though the Bohatch family was shuffling around with preparing and eating their dinner around the picnic table, the new friends were exchanging words across the campsites.

The Bohatchs' had spent much of the afternoon at two very special places on the island – Sand Beach and Cadillac Mountain. They would see them again in the next few days too! At Sand Beach the older children jumped in the 56-degree water. It wouldn't be proper to say swam, though they made several attempts at it. Most people run out of the water at Sand Beach after just a half a minute or so of wading up to their ankles. They run out screaming. As Mary and Bernadette slept, Paul and Barbara rested and talked on a sheet spread out on the white sand, half watching their wading children. Though they were only at Sand Beach for a few hours, it was the rest of a lifetime for Barbara, and a great blessing that the two younger girls had decided it was naptime. Such simple things in life like a napping baby can only be truly appreciated by a mother. Barbara and Paul spoke about the conference. Having had a chance to rest, she was now actually looking forward to a little gathering, but had just wished that Paul had decided to do it for one day, instead of three. Paul and Barbara were glad that they had met Rick, and Wayne and Betsy Sherman. Paul had been talking with Barbara about the faxes that he received concerning Medjugorje before they left on their trip. He knew that if he had been on the receiving end of these faxes, then tens of thousands of others had received the same faxes also. They wondered what it all meant. "I wonder if Rick, or Wayne and his wife know about the faxes honey," said Paul to Barbara.

While trying to find the latest weather forecast on the radio, in the van between Sand Beach and Cadillac Mountain, Paul and his family heard more than they bargained for about the weather. The earthquake tremors had not yet hit the East Coast, but they learned of the hurricane for the first time. "Man, and they're expecting it to hit Florida tomorrow at three in the afternoon. Can you believe it, three o'clock, when we'll be at Jordan Pond, for the first day of the First Annual Acadia Medjugorje Conference", half smiling at Barbara knowing that the gathering might well have been better called the first annual Bohatch, Tremont, and Sherman Rosary Picnic. What do you think honey, is this possibly tied into the first fax. You know it all seems like so much science fiction. I mean, why would anybody believe in Medjugorje. Yet, look at Fatima, the sun comes down crashing to the earth just about. Seventy Thousand people witness the event. Yet, if you weren't there, it's like something out of C.S. Lewis. Who would believe?" said Paul.

"A five hundred year storm. What do they mean exactly by the worst storm in 500 years Paul" said Barbara.

"Its just statistics, that's all. The existing data gives you what the worst storm in 5, 10, 20, or 100 years is. Extrapolation is used to give the numbers you're looking for whether it's the storm of the century or the storm of the millennium" said Paul.

"They said they're evacuating everybody within a ten mile radius of the shore, from Homestead to what was it, Titusville. Titusville is way up the coast I think. They did call it a voluntary evacuation at this time, but you know what, I think they're just trying to space out traffic flow right now. If it was a mandatory evacuation, there's no way they could evacuate that much of the Florida coast in less than a day. Yeah, less than a day, because it's going to be Hell down there this time tomorrow. Where are those people going to go?" said Barbara.

"They must be heading for western Florida, Georgia, and the Carolinas. Of course, who'd want to go far from their home at a time like this, but I don't think they'll have enough hotel rooms and emergency centers in central and western Florida. Some of those people are going to have to go out of state", Paul replied.

"I wonder how they feel in Charleston, South Carolina right now, where my sister is. Why don't we call Lynn on the cellular phone? Do the rates go down at a certain time?" said Barbara.

"They go down after 7PM" said Paul. "Call her now if you want", he said.

"I'll call her later after we eat. Besides, she's probably at the beach with the kids, getting in a last swim before the weather hits" said Barbara.

"Honey. You know even as we're talking about all of this, I mean, even though I believe in all this – the warning, the chastisements, and everything, it still seems nuts, far out, whatever. I mean if they polled a million people and asked who believes in the times that we're in as told to us by say Our Lady at Akita, or Medjugorje, or Our Lady's words to Father Nairobi, and only one person put their hand up it would be me. Yet, it is kind of like watching a movie. Where does reality end or begin?" said Paul.

"You think too much. All I know is that one rather large hurricane is heading for our coast. I feel a need to call everyone we know near the shore in several states and talk to them. Even the ones that don't care for Our Lady or even for God. How many people is that? Who do we know near the shore?" said Barbara?

"Counting New York, New Jersey, and Connecticut – and Massachusetts?" said Paul.

"No, not yet, maybe just those up to Delaware. The storm can do a lot in the next few days. It may even go back to sea. We don't need to give all of our northern friends a crash course on Marian Apparitions in one easy phone call. We'll wait a day or two and see what's up. I wonder if you can get calls into the East Coast of Florida right now. I bet its tough. Let's see, as far as our coastal friends – Jane & Phil in Daytona, Rob & Sue in Charleston, Benny in Delaware, Aunt Jean in – what's her town in North Carolina? I think I'll call Franny too. She's an hour from the Georgia coast, but I feel like I should call her" said Barbara.

"Donny is on the coast, and Hank, Red, and Bart," said Paul.

"I don't think Bart believes that tomorrow is coming, let alone in God. He should live in Missouri," said Barbara.

"Good old Bart. Did I ever tell you about the time he put Budweiser in the coke machine at the gas station that he worked at next to school? I'll never forget it – he put it in the diet iced tea column, figuring nobody would want any. For the next few days diet iced tea was very popular amongst the students. He lost his job but made a lot of friends" said Paul.

"Honey, I'm sorry I can be so, you know. You know," said Paul.

"Get it out honey. Confession is good for the conscience," said Barbara.

"It's just that sometimes I'm less than perfect, that's all I'm trying to say," said Paul with a big smile.

"Turn right!", shouted Barbara. "You're gonna miss Cadillac Mountain!" Paul screeched to a halt, checked the mirrors and backed up a few feet. He aimed the car for the summit of Cadillac Mountain. The sky was mostly sunny, and there was hardly any wind. Who could imagine that storms were raging, one off the coast of Florida, and one right there on Mount Desert Isle.

****

In Florida, late afternoon on Thursday, July 2, 1998, there was no plywood left in the building supply stores from Key Largo to Titusville. Fifty miles up the coast in the Daytona Beach area there were a few warped boards left, here and there, in the lumberyards. Ninety miles up the coast from Daytona Beach in Jacksonville, lumber supply managers were wondering if they had enough plywood in stock. They did not.

Some years ago Pope John Paul II was addressing a German audience. The reporters were firing questions at him left and right. Inevitably he was asked about the third secret of Fatima. Did the third secret of Fatima mention great chastisements, including floods? Was Florida mentioned? The Pope indicated that what was of primary importance was the souls of the people, not whether or not millions of people would perish from one moment to the next. In essence that is the heart of the Christian message. The boarded up homes and buildings may help minimize the damages from hurricanes, but they can not aid the souls of the people. We can't protect our souls with plywood from 84 lumber, Lowe's or the Home Depot. Prayer is our answer. Our Lady has told us from many points around the world not to wait for the chastisements, not to wait for the warning, not to wait, to turn back to God today. The most frightening thing about a great chastisement from God is not the death of the body, but the potential instant death of the soul. One of the prayers of the Church is a request that the Lord protect us from sudden death. A sudden death to those in a state of mortal sin – eternal death, so to speak. A sudden death to those in a state of grace is eternal life, life forever with Jesus Christ. In Medjugorje, Our Lady spends so little time warning us about what's to come in the form of chastisements. Her messages are simply of hope. Her monthly message for the world is typically several sentences asking us to convert our hearts by prayer, fasting, penance, forgiveness, daily Mass, and confession. She has told us that peace would come if the western world would go to monthly confession. Think about that! Who goes to confession? Catholics! Did she say that if all of the Protestants, Jews, Muslims, and pagans would go to confession there would be peace in the world? No! Great if they would and could, but in a world that is one-fifth Catholic, Our Lady tells us that if the Catholics go to confession once a month the world will be converted. After all, what is peace if not conversion of the heart? It is true that indeed Our Lady's messages from other sources, such as Akita, LaSalette, and even Fatima – all approved apparitions and messages are sometimes hard to bear. The severities of chastisements yet pending have been spoken of in great detail – fire falling from heaven, nations being annihilated, many pastors and Bishops leading the faithful astray - *but Our Lady never once proposed plywood as the remedy - only prayer.* Our Lady had told us that prayer can even change the course of natural disasters. Yet who has the faith to believe this today?

So, on this day, hundreds of thousands of coastal Florida homeowners purchased the last boards of available plywood, and in haste went home to secure them as best they could to their homes and buildings. Too many cursed the weather, God, and man in their haste and unrepentance as they went about the arduous task of securing as best they could their material possessions, leaving behind in the dust, soon to be mud, their spiritual possessions, their souls. A small minority prayed their hearts out, with every swing of the hammer, with every nail driven, with every suitcase loaded into the car or truck, with every tear falling from their eyes. They prayed to Jesus. They prayed to Mary His mother. They prayed and they left their homes, their livelihoods, and their material and spiritual well beings in the hands of God. Even as far south as Homestead, Florida, I-95 was beginning to see a lot of traffic. One young couple and their two pre-school children, who had secured their home, and had already pushed north 10 miles on I-95, turned around and went home when they realized that they had left behind the crucifix, holy water, and Rosaries on the home-made altar in their living room. They would return to get them, despite the fact that they knew how much more difficult their way would be when they would once again resume their northward trek, facing even greater traffic and delays as a consequence. They talked about it and decided that more time together in the car in this crisis would simply be more time to pray for the souls of all the people in Florida as they headed northwest to Tampa where they would stay with relatives. The Virgin Mary's heart leapt for joy, in seeing the faith of this one family. Jesus, her Son, was so pleased to see His Mother's heart lifted up so. He would do anything for His mother. Would the world have perished he would have spared this family that without ceasing called upon Him and His mother. *What is man that Thou art mindful of him, O Lord?* What is a hurricane if God is with man?

****

In the middle of nowhere in northern Minnesota, at a rustic, but ever popular retreat house, two Sisters of Saint Joseph The Laborer, if you could call them that (sisters, nuns), and 24 elderly retreatants began their New Age rituals searching for inner conscienceness. They were calling on various spirits, none of the recognizable to the average Protestant, Catholic, or Pope. They were offering up their prayers as they called them for the poor souls in Florida, about to face a major hurricane.

In the octagonal meeting building, as well as in every extant cabin, there was no trace of Jesus Christ, Mary, the saints, or anything holy. God was not to be found here indeed. For this was a place of devils, of the ugliest demons. These were the demons of the worst sort, for they caused their human counterparts to call themselves Catholic. Many looked at these nuns and the typical retreatants who attended retreats at this center and thought if that is what Catholicism is all about, then they would have nothing to do with that New Age, demonic idolatry. If they had only remembered that Jesus Christ had his Judas too. The descendants of Judas are numerous. Where else would they wish to leave their mark but in the historic Catholic Church? The characteristic that made Judas a traitor was his proximity to Jesus Christ, temporal and spiritual. Pope John Paul II, the Vicar of Christ on earth, has many such descendants of Judas - both in Rome dressed as cardinals and bishops, and throughout the world. They're found in the ranks of the laity, priesthood, brotherhood, and sadly too, in the ranks of some nuns too - a typical cross section of mankind.

While many Protestants and Catholics were scandalized by these nuns and their devil worship (for that is what it is really), and many fell away because of their scandal - many joined their ranks because of the temporary joy of their worldliness. There were also many that prayed against them and the demons that they walked hand in hand with. Many were made stronger because of the weakness of these nuns, as they prayed and prayed for the conversion of the two sisters and their clientele, their very wealthy clientele.

As the gong sounded, and the incense went up in smoke, and the sisters lead in the sinister chanting, a neighbor down the road, Angela Jacobs still could not get through to her Bishop. It was her fourth try this Thursday. The Bishop did not return her calls in regards to the sisters of Saint Joseph. A widow, all alone now, she spent her time in prayer. She prayed the Rosary constantly. She prayed for the conversion of the nuns - her neighbors. She wanted to move; she wanted to be on the other side of the world from these demons. She felt alone in her battle. No one knew the battle she was in, the spiritual warfare she faced. It was a living hell. Angela bore it with that blessed spirit and smile on her face and in her heart that could only be seen in one other place on earth in our times – on the face of Mother Teresa of Calcutta. She had in fact long wished she could join the Sisters of Charity, but it was only a wish of her heart, for she was aging, and would soon be in need of the type of services that only the Sisters of Charity could render. Her bones pained her, and her motion was slowed. Yet, she took care of the goats and chickens that fed her, and managed her affairs better than most. More than that, she had great help from the hosts of heaven, the angels and the saints. Sometimes it was mysterious, supernatural help that even crossed the mystical lines to assist her materially. Yet, she was not a mystic. Old Angela only suspected Divine Intervention on many an occasion, and was never a witness to the outward assistance that she received. You wouldn't have known it however, the way she talked to the angels and saints. She often thought to herself that it was a one way conversation. It wasn't however, and these angels and saints would keep her going if they had to keep her physically propped upped, fed, and washed and cared for themselves. She was winning the battle for souls next-door, and many of the elderly and other clientele who had been with the nuns were returning to their true Catholic faith. This woman Angela was a great light of hope for Minnesota, unsuspected as she was.

Angela usually retired about 10PM, but at the close of this day she surrendered much needed sleep for the souls in Florida, and would not be in bed till well after 2 AM. She was calling down upon the mercy of God for all of the souls in Florida. She forgot to pray for their homes, their bank accounts, and their material well being. "Dear God, take my life this night in exchange for the salvation of the poor souls in Florida in danger of eternal death on this day. I give you my fasting, my prayers, my all. Save them O Lord; take me this night if it is your will. Bring all those in need to true repentance through the intercession of Your most Holy Mother Mary..."

****

At the National Hurricane Center in Miami, officials were dumbfounded with the radar, satellite, and visual reports (from center aircraft) that they were receiving. This was not a hurricane; this was a chastisement waiting to happen. Non-essential personnel were excused to go home and make preparations of their own at 4 PM, Thursday, July 2, 1998. Off the air, the scientists were definitely referring to this one as the "wrath of God sitting off the coast of Florida". No, it wasn't sitting. That was part of the problem. This hurricane, now packing winds up to 250 miles per hour was racing toward the coast of Florida. The scientists involved, and the emergency personnel that they were working with knew that the evacuation of the necessary areas would never be done in time given the present conditions and forward speed of the hurricane. All they could do was calm the people and get as many out as possible. The problem was this hurricane was not cooperating with the scientists. At noon on Thursday it was heading straight for Miami. At 3PM it was heading for Titusville. At 4PM it was headed for Cape Canaveral. The largest hurricane on record was now the most unpredictable hurricane on record. It was early too, for the hurricane season had not yet arrived. *Tell that to Michael....*

****

Father Albert Green was greatly relieved to be off on a break he had been looking forward to for five years. This diocesan priest was on the first leg of a trip that would take him from Overlook Bluffs, Oklahoma, to Bar Harbor, Maine. He was on a well-deserved leave of absence that some of his upset parishioners were calling an all expenses paid vacation to Maine. He was going to serve as a temporary summer assistant to the greatly understaffed Catholic Churches of Mount Desert Island, Maine, and surrounding areas. During the summers, when this part of coastal Maine swelled with tourists, 35% of them Catholics, the few priests in the area were simply not enough. The local Bishop was forever seeking assistance from points afar. Yes, Father Green would have some time to relax, but he would have his hands full just the same, saying Mass, hearing confessions, and lending pastoral assistance to the area all around Acadia National Park, the summer playground of New England.

It was Thursday night about 7PM when his plane began its final approach to Logan International Airport. Within two hours he would be on a small turboprop plane heading for Bar Harbor Airport. About an hour from now, a gentleman in a business suit, a father of six, Louis Longmire, Esquire, who was living in adultery, and looking forward to a rendezvous in Bar Harbor Maine, would be making his first confession in 15 years, right there in the airport, to Father Green.

Though Louis lived and worked in Boston, and his estranged family was in the Boston Suburbs, as well as his mistress, Louis did not originate this trip in Boston. In the last 48 hours he had been jockeying between business meetings and airports that took him from Seattle, to Memphis, to Dallas, and Charleston, South Carolina. In Seattle, by 'chance' meeting, Louis had dinner with a former co-worker, another lawyer, whose faith in God was so strong that this lawyer, Ramon Nogales, had to keep his fire in check, less he burn others with the heat. Ramon was the greatest lay evangelist that Washington State ever saw. Given another ten years, everybody in Washington State would have been Catholic. Ramon was a wealthy man, making a very healthy salary, with his own law firm. Yes, Ramon was a wealthy man. Note the word 'was'. Ramon and his wife Mary, and 5 children, lived in a moderate home in the Seattle Suburbs, and had no known enemies excepting Satan and his cohorts. They gave, and they gave, and they gave till it hurt. They gave their time, their money, and their possessions to anyone who asked. The Jews were asked by God, as well as all Christians are asked by God to give 10% of their income to God, to the Church, to Christian charity. Ramon and Mary gave everything they had back to God. Ramon was the wealthiest man in Seattle to receive 3 default notices on his mortgage in the first half of 1998. His mortgage was only $667.50 per month. There were times however, when others needed that money more than Ramon and Mary. A homeschooling family, Ramon and Mary were the teachers of their children. They used Holy Rosary Home Schooling for their curriculum, though several good curriculums were available. God came first in everything, including the children's education. Their worst fear that was something would happen to them and that their children would be forced to attend public school again, or even a modernist Catholic school, where the darkness of sex education, values clarification, sinister catechisms, and warped anti-Catholic twisted history were the norms. These fears were only fleeting however, and their only real, lasting fear, was the fear of God, the beginning of *all* Wisdom. That fear, ever present with the Nogales family, was lost in the sea of joy in living a holy Christian life in the Body of Christ. This was the Ramon Nogales that Louis Longmire had the "accidental grace" of meeting on Tuesday, June 30, 1998. As all things work for the glory of God, however, this meeting was no accident. More than that, it was a precipitated by a phone call to Ramon and Mary from Louis' estranged wife. Ramon knew where Louis would be on this day. He knew his flight schedule. He tried to act surprised to see Louis when the "chance" meeting happened.

"Ramon, how the Hell you doing? What the heck are you doing out here? Shouldn't Seattle's most famous criminal lawyer be in court?" said Louis.

Ramon knew where the battle was. He knew how to attack. A frontal approach would fail in a hurry. Over dinner, Ramon talked about "guy things" with Louis. He tried to avoid family talk as much as he could. Louis had not come out and mentioned his adulterous situation, and was avoiding mentioning his family, who Ramon knew. Ramon played the same game, and they enjoyed great conversation in other areas. They covered football, basketball, fishing in Minnesota and Washington State, and business. God was not mentioned although that was all that Ramon was thinking about. At one point, Ramon knew that he had to mention their respective families, so he wouldn't let on to the game. If he had avoided the subject completely, the gig would have been up – Louis was a crackerjack lawyer and he would have guessed that Ramon had inside information on his marriage. That might have brought any hope for a happy spiritual ending of their meeting to a rapid failed close. "So how's Nancy and the kids…" dropped Ramon.

"Just great. The kids are growing like weeds. Unfortunately everybody's playing soccer and my kids look like they're giraffes on ice when I try to shoot hoops with them. It's embarrassing. This soccer is spreading like a disease. I'm afraid it may be affecting the pool of available basketball players in the near future..." joked Louis. "How's everybody at home Ramon?" said Louis.

"Just great. The kids are so happy to be near the water now. They live for fishing" said Ramon stretching the truth a little bit. Mary says to say hello..." said Ramon. *Oh God, what am I saying,* thought Ramon. "That is she wanted me to say hello from her the next time we talked. I forgot to tell you when we spoke last month... Is your new firm treating you well?" he said.

"It should be, I'm the boss!" said Louis. "We're handling almost exclusively accidents and injuries right now. We have to turn great cases away by the wheelbarrow-full because we're so busy" said Louis. "I'm a millionaire several times over. I could retire at the young age of 43 right now but the money is falling off the tree right in to my lap and I hate to turn it away", joked Louis. "You should see my house on Cape Cod, God you'd love it. I'm heading up to Bar Harbor in a couple of days for some R&R," Louis let slip out, though he was sorry he did. He didn't want to bring about any awkward questions from Ramon. Ramon was ahead of the game however, and knew what kind of questions to field. Ramon mentioned Cadillac Mountain, Frenchman's Bay, and how he loved it up there at Acadia.

"Speaking of Acadia, there's gonna be a....", *Ramon accidentally blurted out.* A friend of his from Colebrook, New Hampshire called earlier in the day to ask him if he knew any of the speakers who would be talking at the Acadia Medjugorje Conference. The conference was news to him, and that was strange because he was generally kept aware of such events across the US and Canada because of his involvement with the Seattle Marian Center. Ramon had almost lost the battle again by mentioning the conference. When Satan has someone in the grip of mortal sin, the walls of darkness sometimes have to be taken down block by block before the individual is washed clean through the Sacrament of Confession. Ramon was glad he was not in court, he might have lost his case already. Ramon continued, "there's gonna be a chance, uh, uh, that I, that I could get up to fish with you for a day at Bar Harbor. I've got to get to Portland on business sometime this month, and it might work out..." Ramon hardly knew what he was saying, he was getting flustered, but at some point in the next half a year, he would be looking at a trip to Portland on business. Satan's cohorts were inspiring Ramon to stutter, fall, trap himself, and let on what he knows. Ramon felt sick. He wanted to leave. Perhaps it was the stench of sin. He found himself not liking his friend. He wished he had not left his office to go to the airport. He almost told Louis that he thought it was disgusting what he did to Nancy and the kids... Yet, these were the inspired thoughts of the demons, and did not belong to Ramon.

Louis now had two options, as he saw it. He could tell Ramon to come up and join him at some point, and still manage to spend time with his girlfriend, when Ramon wasn't around, or he could just tell Ramon that they probably couldn't meet at Bar Harbor, for some as of yet, un-thought of excuse. "Great man, try to get up there. I'm looking at buying a house on the island. Maybe you could check one or two out with me," said Louis. In a split second, he had decided that his friendship was more important than lying right now. He really liked, maybe loved Ramon, and he liked being around him. Sherry would understand if he had to leave her for a little while. "Here, I'll give you my cellular phone number. Call me" said Louis passing Ramon his card. "I gotta run Ramon, they've just called my flight. Hey, what are you doing here anyway?", he said.

"Oh, I'm meeting someone... Have a great trip. I'll try to see you in Bar Harbor. You're gonna be there when?" said Ramon.

"Very late Thursday night. Maybe 11PM or so by the time I'm settled. See ya. Great seeing you" he said as he headed over to the flight gate.

Ramon realized he had just lost the battle. He wanted to say a thousand things. He wanted to entrap Louis as only he the crack lawyer could do. He failed. He couldn't get God into the conversation even through the back door. He was praying a Hail Mary after he had just said goodbye to Louis. He was about 50 feet from Louis and he felt inspired to call out. "Louis, hold on, hold it", he yelled.

Louis walked out of line and back over to Ramon. "Yeah buddy, what's up," said Louis happy to have a chance to give his friend another goodbye.

"I wonder if you can do me a tremendous favor? I could sure use your help," said Ramon.

"Sure, anything Ramon! Name it," said Louis.

Louis' heart exploded with joy. God was holding out on him to make victory seem that much sweeter. The battle was already over and all Louis had to do was think of what to say now. He really didn't know what to say. For four or five seconds he said nothing. *Great, now the cat had his tongue. Well,* he thought, *I will open my mouth and the Mother of God will put words in it for me.* "Come over here a minute, will you?" Ramon was looking in the direction of a large bench.

A jet was preparing for take-off. It was rather hard to hear for a moment. It came to him. The Mother of God explained to him how the victory would be won, not in words, not in a locution, but just in a sense of peace, and knowing, with ideas now filtering into his head from somewhere above. Ramon put his briefcase on the red vinyl covered bench next to the window. He started to open it. Louis looked back at the last of the boarding passengers on his flight. He was somewhat anxious now. Ramon saw him looking. Ramon swiftly moved into the heart of the battle and trusted in God.

"Louis, I'm a huge supporter of this non-profit group that I think is doing a heck of a good job to help a lot of people out. I'm not going to even mention how much Mary and I have been sending them." Since this was the finale of the words between friends, a final climax, Ramon now knew by inspiration, that Louis would not be offended by a last minute mention of God. He went for it. "Well, in the last few years, let's just say I've been a major supporter of a group called The Mary Foundation, out of Ohio. They've got a few great books they distribute, and some of the most heart wrenching, earth shaking cassette tapes you've ever heard. It's pretty much Catholic stuff, but a large number of the people that they're getting the stuff out to are Protestants or people of no faith. I've got one of their books here, "Pierced By A Sword", by a fellow called Bud MacFarly Jr. Sometimes I wonder if I'm doing the right thing helping them. You know, you get into something for some reason or another, and you wonder what's up and what's down. There's a lot of crazy stuff being published and circulated out there today, and it makes you wonder" said Ramon.

Ramon was trying to build up the interest of Louis without really saying much of anything, particularly about God or the Church. That would come soon, but not today. He just knew it now. But he also knew he had one minute or less to make his case. "I was wondering if you could read this book for me? *No, could you study this book for me?* Everything that the Mary Foundation is doing is related in some way to the type of material in this book. I need help. If you would take a look at this for me, it would help me tremendously. If you see anything, anything at all wrong with what this guy is writing, you could let me know, and I will stop supporting them 'yesterday'. I was thinking since you're going to be on the plane a lot in the next few days... I know its asking a lot", said Ramon. It was exactly three o'clock. Ramon called upon the Divine Mercy of God. He called upon the assistance of Blessed Faustina Kawalska. Ramon knew it was all over at that point. God won...

****

Back in Salem, Massachusetts, Nancy Longmire was on her knees in front a crucifix at Saint Mary's church at three o'clock on Tuesday, June 30, 1998. They were praying the Chaplet of Divine Mercy for the conversion of her runaway husband, her self-seeking husband who had left her for another younger, prettier, sexier woman. They were praying hard with conviction. Almost with anger on Nancy's part, but with knowledge that something holy was afoot, Nancy yelled at the younger children who were not cooperating. "Do you want your father to come back? Stop fooling around, all of you. Pray hard. Jesus said that his Father would not deny anyone their request at this holy hour, the hour Jesus died. And this is the prayer He gave to Sister Faustina. Pray. Do you want your father back?..." She was yelling at them as reverently and quietly as her nerves would allow her to. It was an inspired yell. She now had their full attention as they continued their chaplet in front of the Blessed Sacrament.

****

Louis was repulsed at Ramon's request. *What the Hell did he care about the Virgin Mary?* Then, for some unknown reason he started to think about his toe-headed two-year-old back home, and his heart softened. He pictured him in a church on his knees praying.... Louis was not really mad at Ramon. Ramon did not know where he was at in life right now. He couldn't possibly know. Besides, Ramon had known Louis for many years, and even back in time when Louis took his Catholic Faith half seriously. And that was where their friendship had left off years ago, at least geographically. "No problem buddy. I said anything and I meant it. I'll have this puppy read, no – studied and graded before Bar Harbor. I'll give you a call. Gotta run, last call..." said Louis. He hugged Ramon and dashed off to his awaiting jet. They yelled goodbye to each other. Grace won. The battle was over here. God 1, Satan 0. God always won. There was just some mopping up to be done here and there, nothing major outside of Confession. Ramon would have died a happy man if he had been called home at that moment. He stayed praying a Rosary until Louis' jet was in the air and out of sight. God he loved airports...

"Thank you Jesus and Mary" said Ramon as he about skipped out of the airport back to his car, continuing the Five Sorrowful Mysteries of the Rosary...

****

As Father Albert Green was making his way over from terminal he had arrived at from Oklahoma, to the terminal he would depart from on a direct flight to Bar Harbor, Maine, the enemies of truth were not letting up on their sinuous inspirations that they were throwing at him. *God, what am I doing here? Priests shouldn't be taking leaves of absence from God. I don't remember Saint Francis of Assisi going to the beach for a half of* summer. What right do I have to go to the coast of Maine? Maybe I'm not worthy to be a priest. Maybe I shouldn't be. I've always doubted my vocation. Well, I'll have the time to consider what to do while I'm in Maine. My family never appreciated me being a priest either.... Half of them didn't keep their faith. Maybe I'm just like the half that didn't keep their faith. I could have been living in a place like Bar Harbor all of these years. And women, if I'm supposed to be a priest, why do I spend so much time thinking of beautiful women? Father Green saw an elderly lady walk out of her way to say hello as he was making his way along.

"Hello father, God bless you! Thank you for being a priest. Could I have your blessing father?" she said.

Father gave her his priestly blessing in Latin. She thanked him and he continued on. *I guess God 'heard' me thinking. Sorry God, but you know, I'm no visionary, its just me, Father Albert Green. I can't fast like the saints, I can't pray like them, I can't stay up all night adoring you like many of them did, and I don't seem to like pain any more than the rest of mankind. I think I eat too much, I feel just as much a part of the world as the next guy perhaps. I don't feel anything special about being a priest. I feel like John Q. Smith in the clothing of a priest. Could you do me a favor and give me an immediate stamp of approval. I feel like I need you to tell me tonight that you're the one that called me to be a priest. Hey, I do appreciate the elderly Lady coming up to me, thanks.* Father was falling into a depressed state, even as he was thinking these thoughts.

He arrived at his terminal exhausted and ready for bed, yet he had hours to go yet in his evening before he could catch some shut-eye. He would try to sleep anyhow. Then it happened. It could have been his guardian angel letting him know the impending situation. He looked up and he saw the businessman sitting down bent over, trying to hide the tears rolling off his face. He had one hand to his head, his hand partially on his chin, his thumb picking his teeth. He knew that this man would be over bothering him to go to confession within five minutes. Next time he would have to travel incognito he thought. *I just want to go away and hide.* The man with the tears had not looked up yet. A book, *Pierced By A Sword*, was sitting on his lap. Father could not completely read the title, but he knew the cover, the book had swept through his parish, and already caused him extended stays in the confessional. He would have to read that book someday. The crying man looked a wreck. He looked as though he had never cried a tear in his life, this big fellow, who did not have the soft look about him. *Virgin tears*, father thought. Father knew it was sin. He knew what type of sin too. Father also knew that this particular sin was being washed away from the man with every tear. He gave the man 30 seconds to approach him for confession, even though he had not yet looked up enough to see Father. Within 15 seconds, the man looked up, saw Father, looked around for a moment, dried his eyes, and walked over to the priest. *Wait, God, thought Father Albert. This could be it, the confirmation I was looking for. But I want it to be big. I want to know it's from You. Would you let Francis of Assisi be part of this confession? Everyone else asks for roses from Saint Therese of Lisieux as a confirmation. She must be terribly busy. But surely Francis of Assisi must be available! He can't possibly be as busy as Saint Therese! Please bring Francis into this Sacrament of Confession in a way that only you could!*

"Hi Father", the man said. "Would you be able to hear my confession?" said Louis Longmire.

"Certainly" said Father, "Where would you like to go?"

"Right here is fine Father," said Louis. The gate waiting area was packed with people. Father Albert realized that this man must have a heavy burden to have the courage to go to confession in this crowd. Father took out his stole and put it on, and they started the confession. Louis first started by telling Father Green how he had left his wife and children 7 months ago for a beautiful young lady that was in love with his money. She seemed to have a type of love for Louis too, but Louis knew now that it was an affair stamped with the approval of Hell. Louis told him everything, about his addictions and lusts, and growing passion for money and material objects too. Father Green seemed to know Louis well in just a few short minutes. After confessing the most serious of his sins, Louis told him about meeting his wife, having his first child, second, third, fourth, fifth, mentioning them all by name and their ages, not yet mentioning the sixth child. He spoke of the chance meeting with Ramon Nogales. He told him almost every detail of his discussions with Ramon. He said he now knew that Ramon had set him up. Louis laughed, he cried. Knowing that Ramon set him up made him happy in a certain way. He told Father he now believed that he, Louis, was the 'only one that Ramon was waiting to meet at the airport.' "Now I see the hand of God all over this Father. God used Ramon to bring me to you. I thank God and I thank Ramon, and I thank you" said Louis. "Now, if I can only get my wife and children back. And Sherry, what am I going to do about Sherry. O God, I want to run away and die... I can't face any of them..."

"Louis. Look. Your being here is from God. When I first came here a short while ago I knew that you were going to come to confession. God told me. I gave you 30 seconds from the moment you saw me. You were here in half that time. Your coming to confession to me is also a confirmation for me. I have been doubting certain things about my own life, and believe it or not, I just asked a little while ago for something like this. Now, if you had mentioned the name Francis of Assisi, I'd have been so happy I could have died, because as I was sitting there moments ago looking at you…" said Father before he was cut off.

"Father, my two year old…, the one I told you that I saw in my head praying in the church. His name is Francis and he was conceived in Assisi, we believe. I took the family to Italy three years ago. I had the nerve to name our boy Francis after the saint, and then I was cheating on my wife soon after. O God, Father, I could just die… I hate what I have done… How can I ever forgive myself, let alone ask my wife to forgive me? I haven't seen any of them or called them for three months. I couldn't talk to the kids. What would they say, 'Daddy, how's your girlfriend. Why'd you leave us Daddy?' Oh, God…"

Everyone in the gate area heard the last minute of Louis' confession as he belted it out in big sobs. He didn't care about being embarrassed at this point. He had already embarrassed his family and God. He was supposed to have been a Catholic…

Of the forty-nine people in the gate area, most of whom were waiting on the next flight to Bar Harbor, twenty-one of them were Catholic, and had some understanding of what Louis was going through in the Sacrament Of Confession. Three of those Catholics were praying for Louis and his family even as he spoke now to Father. Two of them were praying the Rosary. One was saying the Saint Michael prayer to fend off the devils so Louis could have a holy confession and a life changing sacramental experience. Two of the Protestants were praying for Louis also, not quite understanding the full impact of "Forgive men's sins and they are forgiven, hold them bound and they are held bound", but realizing just the same that something profound was happening. They were beseeching Jesus to help the poor sinner.

One of these Protestants had often been taught by various preachers that the Confession of the Catholics was a blasphemous twisting of scriptures, yet, he saw great merit in what Louis was going through. This young man thought that he would never have the nerve to confess some of his sins to a minister, to a priest, whatever, as Louis was doing. He had sins that he hoped no one would ever know of, especially his family. In one or two gatherings in the last few years where the members of his church were openly confessing their sins amidst the preacher's volumous preaching and coercion, and loud 'Amens' and 'Hallelujahs' from both the pulpit and the congregation, he had blurted out his bigger sins in a fashion that would not have been decipherable by the person in the seat closest to him. He thereafter tried to wash his hands of these sins, but they kept recurring, and the guilt never left him. He wondered if there was any unseen strength afforded one to carry on in purity and holiness after 'going to confession' to a priest as this man was doing.

Father tried to now reassure Louis. He spoke very quietly so no one could hear except Louis. Louis was on his knees. People were being considerate and trying not to look. "Louis, you are exactly where God wants you right now. For your own benefit, you have become broken, a formless puddle of water, a pile of used bricks sinking in the mud. That's good. None of this 'I'm O.K., you're O.K.' garbage. None of this we don't want to hurt your self-esteem New Age garbage. You've lived a questionable life in the last few years. You've hurt your wife and children. You had to be stripped of all of your pride – that's why you're on your knees right now in the middle of all these people. You had to die to yourself, just as Christ died on the cross. You had to suffer through all of this. Christ spent a lot of time talking about foundations for someone who was not in the construction business. You needed a new foundation. What if you found someone to tell you 'its O.K., you're a good person, you're doing the right thing'. Or, just as dangerous, what if someone had told you to just trim back on your sinning somewhat and everything will be O.K. You'd be building on sand. What if you went back to your wife and children resolved to continue in adultery. If you continued unrepentant and died this way, you'd go to Hell forever. Your children would see your example, and perhaps follow you in your sins. You would be living a lie. Your life would be miserable even though your passions fulfilled. You had to be made nothing. Now, believe me, God is going to build a new foundation for you, because you have turned in your old one. You're going to have pain, great pain again, especially when you contact and meet with your wife and children the first few times. Your next few weeks are going to be a 'living Hell', but you would be best to think of it as Purgatory, a purging of your soul. It beats Hell, and it's how saints are tried. Most of all you must have faith in God. You must believe that as impossible as your family situation is right now, God can move the mountains that need to be moved. Incessantly call on the aid of Saint Mary Magdalene. Also, Jesus told Sister Faustina that 'the bigger the sinner, the greater their right to His Mercy. Think about that. In a certain sense – the bigger the sinner – the better. No one, not even the worst sinner in the world should ever despair. And think about this Louis, if you fall a million times into the same addictive sin – the greater your right to His Mercy! All you have to do is try," said Father.

"Father, what if I had gone so far as divorcing and remarrying once or twice. How could God have mended that? I won't have to burn those bridges thank God, but so many of my friends... How can God fix that? What is done is done."

"You don't have that problem, and you shouldn't be thinking about it. You have enough burdens. But for your friends in such a scenario, there can only be one Christian marriage, not two, not three. Only one is valid, even if it is not lived out or abandoned. One cannot be married again in the eyes of God if one is already married. Divorce is not recognized by God or the Church, except in those cases that Christ Himself and the Gospels addressed, and the Church recognizes this. As for yourself, you need to immediately break relations with your friend, and then contact your wife, and begin to pray again. Pray the Rosary if you have the time. I recommend daily Mass if you can make it. I will keep you in my prayers. Now make a good act of contrition and I will give you absolution in the name of the Father, the Son, and the Holy Spirit..."

****

In a few minutes Louis was on his feet drying his eyes the best he could. Father hugged Louis as only a brother could, a brother in Christ, and a spiritual father in Christ as well - 'I am your Father in Christ' - the words of Saint Paul came to Father's mind, but he left them unspoken.

A tall gentleman was standing nearby waiting for the same flight. He was a Protestant minister, the pastor of Holden Bible Church; the man was traveling to meet the rest of his family already vacationing on Mount Desert Island. This Rev. Paul Braun was a fire and brimstone minister with walls of steel built around his very anti-Catholic beliefs. Until this evening, he knew, in his own mind, that Roman Catholicism was the Whore of Babylon. Many a Catholic apologetic that had run into him walked away realizing that they had run into a rock wall, strong as Gibraltar, yet grounded in error. Not even Karl Keating could have gotten a word in edgewise with Rev. Braun. Nor had Rev. Braun ever consented to study any of the true Catholic apologetic tracts that had been given to him over the years. "I won't read the Devil's lies..." had always been his groundless defense. The Scriptures in his mind's eye kept jumping out in front of him, as he watched Louis Longmire receiving absolution in the name of the Father, Son, and Holy Spirit. Rev. Braun kept pondering the scriptures in his mind - "Forgive men's sins and they are forgiven. Hold them bound and they are held bound..." A crack had just appeared in the foundation of Rev. Braun's anti-Catholicism. He looked at the face of Louis Longmire as Louis was leaving Father. It was a look of hope, of joy, of relief, albeit wounded from the sins of man. Rev. Braun knew that something profound had just happened to Louis. *What did Christ mean?* pondered Rev. Braun, as he continued to stare at the departing Louis Longmire. *Forgive men's sins and they are forgiven. Hold them bound and...*

Louis made his way through the crowded airport to the nearest public phone. He had two phone calls to make... In his newfound joy he had almost lost his sense of the here and now, of time and place. He had forgotten that he had his cellular phone in his pants pocket. He fumbled through his pockets for change for the phone call. He pulled out several items from his pockets so he could better get at his change. After gathering his needed coins, he put the miscellaneous items back into his pocket, including his cellular phone. *Please deposit one dollar and ten cents..."Hello, Honey?..."*

****

At Bar Harbor Campground, the Bohatch Family, Rick Tremont, and Wayne and Betsy Sherman started a Rosary together, around a campfire at 8PM. Evening comes early in Maine, and tonight was no exception. Despite the problems of the last few days, the Bohatch family had bounced back as if they already had one foot in heaven. The kids were exuberant. They felt like they were on a wilderness adventure on par with Swiss Family Robinson. The sky was filled with an uncountable number of diamonds glistening in the sky, as they had never seen them before. The clouds from the southwest had not yet begun to roll in as they would later on in the evening. The wind was coming in at just the right speed off of Frenchman's Bay – just enough to put the temperature exactly where it should be after a hot July day.

Two of the younger Bohatch children had already fallen asleep. One more would be out like a light before the Rosary was finished. They didn't rush through the Rosary; they tried to think of every word as they prayed, since Wayne had just spoken of this before they started. He had reminded this rag-tag group of pilgrims that Our Lady spent several weeks teaching the visionaries of Medjugorje how to pray from the heart, beginning with the Our Father and Hail Mary. The Bohatch family would too often find themselves coasting through the Rosary at a good clip. It was good to have another non-family member remind them to take their time with the Rosary, and really concentrate on the meaning of the words and the mysteries.

When they finished the Rosary, Paul asked Rick if he would tell them some personal stories from Medjugorje – since he was the only one who had been there of those gathered around the fire. Though both Paul and Barbara, and Wayne and Betsy spread the messages of Our Lady, from Medjugorje, none of them had been there, but had come to believe in their validity some years before.

The friends all gathered in more closely around the campfire, as the sparks jumped ten or fifteen feet into the air every time a piece of wood cracked with exploding gases in the fire.

Rick thought for a minute, and then began. Four of the Bohatch children had already been tucked in bed, asleep with smiles and adventure written all over their faces. The remaining audience was all ears. Rick was a born storyteller, and may have missed his mark with chemical engineering. "Well, I'd like to back up a little, and bring you back to the events that happened just before my first trip to Medjugorje, and then I'll briskly bring you to Bosnia-Herzegovina for the grand finale of this first trip. I've pretty much been a tightwad all of my life. My mother used to ask me what I was going to be when I grow up if I never learned to share. Right out of college I was making big bucks as a chemical engineer with Union Carbide – my first employer. I was told that I was the highest paid new recruit that they hired in the United States upon my graduation in 1991. For four years I squirreled away every penny. I might look like a pauper, but the money I saved as an engineer for four years continued make as salary for me in the stock market and other investments while I was rescuing. In some ways I had to dissociate myself from this money because of my rescuing activities. My parents have helped me on that. Well anyway, there I was, Mr. Sunday Catholic putting five bucks on a good day in the collection basket at church. Sometimes I put in two bucks. Remember, I told you I was not a big spender said Rick laughing. My Catholic Faith was typical of most Catholics today. I was on a road to Hell. I was a pick and choose Catholic. I won't go into the fields of picking and choosing that I differed with the Pope on – they were the biggies that the press is always covering. One night I get a call from a Jewish friend of mine in Charleston, West Virginia, Adam Rubiowitz. Adam and I both graduated from Ohio State in chemical engineering, in the same class. Well, this dude is now Catholic he tells me, and he's laying all this Catholic stuff on me over the phone like he's an ambassador for the Pope or something. He's starting to make me sick, right. O.K., we had never mentioned God once while we were at school. And now he's a Holy Roller working for Jesus & Mary. All right. He asks me if I want to go on a rescue. I told him Gilligan already got off the island, didn't you hear? He tells me he's talking about a rescue at an abortion clinic in Charleston. I said, "Hey Adam, they arrest people for that and then write bad things about you in the paper." He tells me he's serious. I asked him when he was doing it, and he told me tomorrow. I was four hours away from him in Chillicothe, Ohio. I told him I was driving down 'tonight" to have him reconsider his strange decision over a beer. I get to his house about nine that night, and there's all these freaky people sitting around praying a Rosary. Then I was introduced and came to find out they seem to be typical Americans – a lawyer, a plumber, a grandmother, a nurse, a housewife, a policeman, and you name it - typical Americans with typical jobs."

...The policeman blew my mind away. He told me that up until about eight hours ago he was an atheist. Eight hours prior he was sent to arrest Adam who was in the garbage bin at one of Charleston's two baby-killing centers. He went through the pre-packaged arrest verbiage speaking to Adam who didn't even bother to stop and look at him. Adam was looking for something. Adam pulls up a plastic bag as this policeman is about to pull him out by the neck, and as Adam is being pulled out by two officers, a baby falls out of the bag. A dead baby, with no arms and one leg. It was a baby girl. The arms and legs were in the garbage bag. Everybody in the clinic was outside watching just about, including the workers. The manager, Lanny Hyath was burning red with rage and hate. She started screaming at Rick to leave her Dumpster alone. The officers had to control her. The very dead baby was still warm. A girl, a victim of abortion. It was perfectly legal. Girls and ladies who were waiting to kill their babies were running out to their cars with boyfriends crying and screaming. Some of them had just killed their babies. They were screaming the loudest. Miss Hyath goes in and turns the shingle saying "Sorry We're Closed", and calls her lawyer. The policeman in question starts crying as if he was at his best friend's funeral. He comes to believe in God at this moment. In his rage, he walks in and arrests Lanny, the clinic operator, for first-degree murder, knowing she has done nothing illegal. His buddy is trying to calm him down and just get him back to the squad car, but it's no go. He arrests her in front of the crowd that was left, with his deputy just wiping his hands of the whole thing, and they go off to the police station. Adam takes the baby, and gives her a proper funeral with the aid of a priest friend and others. The policeman finds himself in hot water, and every politician in the country wants him strung up..."

I rescued with them the next day. Basically, we just went in peacefully, sat down and prayed a Rosary. We were arrested. Well, the night before, Adam was telling me all about his conversion because of Medjugorje. He chewed my head off till four in the morning."

As we're being dragged out of the abortion clinic by the police, I yelled to Lanny Hyath that if she wanted to go to Medjugorje for free to visit me in jail, and I'd make arrangements. She called me a..., ah, well, we'll skip that part. That first night in jail we all offered up our fasting and prayers for the conversion of Lanny Hyath and all of the workers. Lanny Hyath saw something very ugly beside her bed that night, and given the mixed audience, and approaching bedtime for our younger campers here, I'll spare the details. Lanny was at the jail at 7AM the day after our arrest, begging to see me. I couldn't believe it. For 12 hours I didn't think of money once. Very untypical of me. When I saw Lanny coming down the hall escorted by a police officer, dollar signs began to roll in front of my eyes. I momentarily forgot about God and babies."

"Did you mean what you said about Medjugorje?" she started off.

"I'm still thinking money and I got mad for a second. I'm thinking, oh great, she's had this great conversion experience like Adam, and now this very, very, wealthy young lady wants me to buy her pilgrimage ticket. I don't know why, but I almost called her a devil and told her to take a hike. At the same time I'm thinking maybe this is a test, for her, for me, whatever. I'm good at tests, and I wanted to pass this one. "God, Yes!" I said, "If I can go with you..."

We went with Medjugorje Travel Center out of Buffalo – about four weeks later. Lanny is now a Sister of Charity, somewhere. At her and the order's request, she's trying to live a quiet life as she works hard to assist Jesus in the poorest of the poor with the other Sisters of the order. Lanny's clinic, by the way, was closed for two days. Two precious days."

I know I skipped the wonderful things that happened on this first trip to Medjugorje, particularly to Lanny, but you know, God wants tuna that tastes good, not tuna with good taste. He wants our hearts. He doesn't want everyone chasing after bells and whistles wherever Mary is appearing. Our Lady converted Lanny before she left for Medjugorje. She believed the whole package instantly. However, it wasn't until she was physically in Medjugorje for several days that she knew Our Lady was calling her to be a nun for Jesus."

As for me on that trip, well, everything pointed to dollar signs, the readings were about tithing, sharing, whatever. It was the first time that I learned that Christians should be tithing ten percent of their gross income. I couldn't believe it. I thought that stuff was for the ancient wealthy Jews. But God showed me what He'll do for us when we give our tithing back to him. It's actually His. In a sense, if we don't give Him that ten percent, we're stealing from Him. So I shoot for at least ten percent today, all because of Medjugorje. However, finding the right Catholic Bishops, priests, and groups to give this money to is a little tough these days. So many Bishops, priests, nuns, and Catholic lay people are leading the faithful straight to Hell with their New Age or feminist theologies and Liturgies. I don't go to Mass where there's altar girls. The vast majority of priests have historically come up through the ranks as altar boys. In some churches today you can't find an altar boy, just the girls. Are the boys dead? Satan has taken their jobs and given them to the girls. The Bishops are cutting off the flow of priests themselves. God continues to call His priests, however. Then we have the diocesan newspapers and national so-called Catholic Magazines that run the same crap about "this group meeting to discuss women priests", "this group calls for pope to step down because of senility", "Most Catholics Prefer Artificial Birth Control", whatever. They run these news service articles or their own stuff, tear down the Church in a questioning sort of way, without presenting the true church teaching next to the dissident articles, without a cautionary statement warning us of the diabolical content of the article in question. The diocesan paper here in Maine is still carrying McBrien's garbage. Oh, I just meant to say that sometimes it's not easy to distribute your ten percent! Even in some great churches, look at the filth they're carrying in their bulletins. It makes you want to vomit. Almost all of the stock Catholic bulletins are this way. Check out the authors of the cutesy articles. You'll find them in the who's who section of the anti-Pope, feminist, witchcraft, and gay pride section of your local library. Thank God we still have a handful of orthodox priests, nuns, and Bishops. I give my money to them."

By this time, all of the Bohatch children were asleep. None of the adults were ready for bed. The evening was young, and there was great expectation in the air over the coming events of tomorrow and the next few days.

"O.K. Rick said Barbara. That's one story. Give us another story about Medjugorje. Barbara was really enjoying the evening now, as was all of the company. It was a combination of the night air, the smell of the ocean, the balsams, the blueberries surrounding them, and the mystery of the coming together of all of these Christians at this special time.

"Another story, all right... Ummm... All right. A television reporter. Don Blum is his name. Don Blum is from Nashville, Tennessee. Now, as you know, television - that is secular television is not exactly a full cookie jar of die-hard Christians. Well, somehow this fellow Don Blum, a very devout Baptist fellow was working for WADC in Nashville. Don is one of those guys that think the Virgin Mary of the Catholics is some kind of Draconian nightmarish demon. In Don's own words, he did not have a lot of good to say about Our Lady before his conversion. Don, and a lot of Christians like him, knew that Jesus had a mother named Mary. That's where they draw the line. She gets mentioned sometimes at Christmas. End of story. Beyond that and you're in "pagan Catholic country".

I was with Don by the grace of God on my second trip to Medjugorje in 1993. Now, we've heard stories like this before, and some of them have made the news and made it into books and magazines, but I don't think Don's has. He's a quiet guy. The station decided to send Don to Medjugorje to do a story. Don balks, but then says he'll go, but he has to take his minister. They liked that idea, so they let the minister go too, all expenses paid. Well this minister is no friend of Mary, but the guy loved to travel. Traveling was his passion. So the minister jumped on board. There were 114 pilgrims on this pilgrimage. About 112 of us were praying the Rosary for about 24 hours once we gathered at JFK Airport for the flight over. Don and his minister were really upset, but they didn't say anything. They just read their Bibles. The Rosary made them very tense. They prayed against demons all the while. They thought now that they were traveling with Satan and his cohorts. Don told me subsequently that his minister - Fred Pauley went and called his wife and told him to have the congregation pray hard for him and Don, because they were amidst the wolves, traveling right in the thick of this group practicing Satanism, repeating their repetitious prayers to some god. Don and Fred were surrounded by all of us at the airport. There was no getting around it; there was a lot of paperwork and tagging and so forth to be done. Meanwhile its "Hail Mary, full of Grace..."'

We got on this 747 and most of the people on board are going to this little town in Bosnia-Herzegovina called – guess what? - Medjugorje. So, now there's a few hundred of us praying the Rosary, even as some slept in turn, during the day, and into the evening. Then, as we're touching down in Dubrovnik, it's still "Hail Mary, Full of grace..." The priest I was with had been to Medjugorje 14 times, and had never heard of this before. I mean, we had a continuous Rosary. The pilot could hardly get our attention to tell us the details of the flight, like when to fasten our belts, or what mountain range we were flying over. An hour later, we're getting on the buses and its "Hail Mary, full of Grace..." One of the buses broke down an hour into the trip. The other buses waited on it to keep our group together. Hours later we're on our way and its "Hail Mary, full of Grace..." Don and Pastor Pauley were so sick of being with us that they were trying to evangelize us out of our faith as we rode along. When we arrived in Medjugorje, everyone on all of the buses exploded into a loud chorus of cheering and excitement. Many of the people had been waiting years and years for that moment, to come to Our Lady's land. All of the buses turned up Sivric Street, and parked in series. We all got off the buses and were gathered together in the street. We were told that Father, oh, what's his name; the skinny balding Franciscan would be giving us a talk in about 30 minutes. It was then about 6:40 PM, and the visionaries that were in town were having their vision with Our Lady upon our arrival. I think Our Lady knew that Don and Fred were on the bus. From what I gather, Our Lady mentioned a certain situation to one of the visionaries, and the visionary told Father what's his name. Fred and Don were not going to go to the church. They had agreed that they would meet out in front of the house they were staying at shortly, after they had found their room. They would go somewhere and pray, and maybe get a soft drink. Now, even though they still thought they were among heathens, they had a great excitement themselves, being in a foreign country, a former Soviet Bloc nation, with a chance to evangelize to thousands. Fred was fully intending to stand on the street corners and preach the Hell out of these Catholics, Protestants, and even Muslim pilgrims. At the last moment, as they were walking away from Saint James, Don told me that he said to Fred that he felt a call to go into the church. Fred took it as if it was a call from God to call these Catholics back to Jesus in their own church. He was ready to be bold."

They walked in the church, and the visionary and Father 'what's his name' were about 10 feet from the door. Fred and Don saw them, and knew immediately who they were. The visionary whispered something to Father, if I may drop the 'what's his name', and Father looked at him with his dark eyes that seem to pierce one's soul and looked right at Fred as the visionary spoke. The visionary was nodding his head looking at Father. When Kurt, the organizer, thought that everyone had arrived, Father went to the podium. In his very good, but strongly Slavic accented English, Father spoke. "Dear pilgrims, I know you have come a long way and are tired. Yet, you have gathered here, even over sleep or food, you have gathered here in this church, to honor Jesus Christ and his Mother Mary." The pilgrims were on the edge of their seats while they were listening to this world famous priest who has often been compared to Francis of Assisi, and himself a living mystic. "Before I speak further...", he said. Rev. Pauley was just about to stand up and give these people a "what for", straight from the Bible. Yet, Rev. Pauley made no motion as of yet. No one knew what he was about to do. Almost. "Before I speak further, there is someone in your group who would like to speak to you. Though he is not of our faith, he has something that he would like to tell you about Our Lady that we can all benefit from" said Father. Fred was wondering whom this confused non-Catholic friend of Mary was. "Reverend Pauley, would you please speak to the pilgrims for a few minutes. Fred's heart about stopped. He told me later that his heart actually did jump momentarily to an irregular beat, and it caused a momentary shortness of breath in this healthy young minister. Father waved him up with his hand and he approached the podium, bringing his Bible. Fred was touched by a sudden feeling of deference."

"But what do you want me to say Father", Oh God, he used that word, *Father*, he thought.

"Whatever is on your heart", Father said. Everyone in the church was hearing their discourse.

"But *Father*, what topic?" said Fred. Oh God, he did it again.

Father walked back to him a few steps and leaned over and said to him a little softer. "Let God talk. Open the Bible blindly, and put your finger on it, and then read what God gives you. Do that twice. Use your Bible. Use your Protestant Bible....", Father said."

Fred was cowering. Suddenly he did not think that Father represented the enemy. He seemed like a saint. Yet, Fred would try to correct these Catholics and other pilgrims of their errors just the same. He placed his Bible on the podium, faced the people said a quick verbal prayer "Jesus, give me your words so that the blind shall see", closed his eyes, opened his bible, and put his finger on Luke 1:28, opened his eyes and read: *Hail, full of grace, the Lord is with thee, Blessed art thou among women...* read Fred. He was in shock from the events of the last five minutes. He couldn't believe what he had just read. He felt like he was misleading the people. Then he caught himself – *he was only reading the Bible.* He thought of the last 24 hours, the airports, the jet, and the buses. That's all he heard, "Hail Mary, full of Grace...." **Then he remembered, thank God,** he thought, *the problem was that these Catholics use this prayer in vain repetition. That was the heart of the problem.* The problem is that they continually repeat that stuff like a broken record, in this vain repetition, as do the hypocrites in the Bible. All these things flashed through his mind in just a half a minute or so after reading the verse to the pilgrims. He closed the Bible, **"Father, that they may see"**, he said loudly, with his eyes closed, and then opening the Bible he put his finger on Revelations 4:8, "And the four living creatures had each of them six wings; and round about and within they are full of eyes. And they rested not day and night, saying, 'Holy, holy, holy, Lord God almighty who was, and who is, and who is to come', he said. Fred's heart was beating fast. My God thought Fred - *Rested not day and night saying, Holy, holy, holy, Lord God... These angels were forever repeating. Forever repeating. Forever repeating. How many times? Rested not day and night, saying.... How many times did the angels say this in repetitive prayer? Certainly not as many times as the Catholics repeat the Hail Marys and the Lord's Prayer thought Fred. Forever Repeating. Forever Repeating. Forever repeating, thought Fred.* His heart continued to race. *Oh my God thought Fred. Oh God, that's it. It must be O.K. to repeat your prayers continuously, as long as you mean it! As long as you are PRAYING FROM THE HEART!"*

Fred addressed the people now giving them a different message than he thought he would ever do. He summed up his reasons for coming, and his thoughts of the last 24 hours. Another man was in tears, this Reverend Fred Pauley. To Jesus through Mary. That's the road Fred took. "Fred is now a Catholic. He is studying to be a deacon for the Nashville diocese. He is one fired-up gentleman. You know, when things like this have happened before, the first question that comes to the mind of other Catholics is "Did anyone else follow him into the Catholic Church? Usually the answer is no, or well, just his wife, but generally most of the friends of such people think the convert is crazy, that he lost it..."

In Fred's case, 72 other people swiftly followed him into the Catholic Church, not including his family" said Rick. "Now, I know this story was supposed to be about Don, and indeed it is. Don did not go home to the United States. Don lives in Medjugorje, where he has worked with an American named Tim and an Irish nurse named Kay in setting up a make-shift pharmacy to get vital medicines all over the war torn area of Bosnia-Hercegovina. Now that Tim and Kay are married and living in the United States, Don has inherited the "pharmacy". Fred and Don still see each other when Fred leads pilgrimages to Medjugorje every few months. Father, 'what's his name' said that Don and Fred have the two most unique, interesting conversion stories that he has ever heard of."

The fire was roaring, and crackling with a sound that was music to campers' ears. The smoke was delicious. Why is it that the smoke from a campfire can be the most inviting, pleasant aroma, that even an avid non-smoker loves to be around? Especially in the north woods (or coast) of Maine, provided some of the logs are Balsam Fir.

"Beautiful stories" said Betsy Sherman, "I wish I had been there on those trips". Everyone agreed with her.

"Hey, it's almost ten. Let's see if we can get the weather," said Paul, reaching for a small portable radio on the picnic table. Wayne got to it first and handed it to him. They were all jolted back, away from Saint James Church and Medjugorje, as they all heard about the weather. Yes, the forecast said they were locked in for 5 days of rain. More than that, a tremendous hurricane was racing for the coast of Florida. They were all silent, as they knew what they needed to pray for with the rest of their prayers tonight – the people of Florida. And then, a bombshell. A small bombshell yes, because it seemed so insignificant. Yet, Rick and Paul, unbeknownst to the other were stirred to their souls. Paul knew why. Rick was not sure why, but was inspired with thoughts from his guardian angel.

"Did anybody hear of a recent fax from Medjugorje, maybe about something important happening there?" said Rick? "I mean in the last few days", he said.

Wayne and Betsy shook their heads and said no. Paul and Barbara just looked at each other for a second or two, and then Paul went to the van to fetch his series of three faxes, one of them being from Medjugorje, at least reportedly. "I have, he finally said, walking back to his friends with not one, but the three faxes in his hand. And so began another turn in the conversation...

****

The clouds were rolling in. The sky was now half covered with an approaching thunderstorm. Lightning was striking in many places in the distance. The thunder however, was barely heard at Bar Harbor Campground, or at points within the park just several hundred yards away, with the strikes being so far in the distance. The winds were beginning to pick up and tell a story. There was a great convergence approaching Bar Harbor and Mount Desert Isle. Many tourists, soon to be pilgrims by Divine Providence, were heading for the island from many places on the globe. The third most traveled National Park; Acadia was unrivaled in the percentage of international tourists. Our Lady was bringing together a motley bunch of sinners from around the world. None of them were saints, yet, and most of them were far from it. The angels and saints of heaven were preparing for a battle with the devils of Hell. A great battle for souls was about to take place. This battle was universal in nature, and surely was not centered in the little town of Bar Harbor, or even on this island. The battle was worldwide, and was the ongoing battle between the forces of Love, and the forces of Hate. The gathering at Acadia was merely a microcosm of what was taking place throughout the world at this time, and yet, there were certain things about to take place here that would effect the whole world indeed.

And so they were coming. The tent campers, those with trailers, the hotel and motel clientele, and even those unwary of pending world events, were approaching the island on yachts and cruise ships, and 747s from around the globe. Some small number - but a growing number, were approaching Acadia because of an ad that they or a friend in a prayer group or some other fraternity had told them about. In the United States, over a half a million people had now heard of a reported fax from a land far away. Confusion still reigned, however, as faxes begot faxes, rumors begot rumors, rebuttals begot rebuttals, jealousy begot jealousy, power and importance begot the same, and pride won a small battle.

If anyone was going to convey a message or series of messages from a Lovely Lady in a land far away, in a time of need, it would be those who had been working for Her the longest. It would be those who had suffered the most for Her and Her Son, those who had been in the trenches for years. It would be those who thought they owned the messages from Heaven. Surely, God would honor their fidelity, wouldn't He? Wouldn't he give them the seat of most importance? Surely, he would pass the ball to them, these important people with fax machines and newsletters who manned offices day in and day out, and traveled the world conveying the messages. It had to be. They had even met the visionaries, they'd brought hundreds and in some cases thousands of pilgrims to the village, spoken with them, they've stayed in their homes, and called them on the phone now and then. Surely, God has been privy to this. God would have to notify them among the first, right? Ahh, but these owners of fax machines are a jealous lot. Just like the world. It just might be that God might one day allow the messages of the 8th, 9th, and 10th secrets of Medjugorje to become divulged at the proper time, perhaps not necessarily through the Marian Centers, but in spite of them. And so it was. God knows they tried. It was a hard task to do however, given the sensitivity of the material. What if the Marian centers with the original faxes were wrong? Despite their faults, like the rest of us, the organizers and members of such centers tried their best to walk through the quagmire or information. Was it from Heaven? Was what from heaven? The best original fax was quite incomplete. Nobody was getting through to Bosnia. Things were tough all over. But then, we can see the hand of the devils in this, this confusion, this jealousy, and yes even the ongoing mechanical failures of phones, faxes, and machines.

Look out Acadia, here come 25,000 happy campers!

****

It rained as hard as it ever did that night along the East Coast, from Cape May, New Jersey, to Pemaquid Point, Maine. The lightning storms were ferocious, and in several instances the strikes were the direct cause of death. The flash flooding was more sudden and widespread than the name implies, complete with millions of dollars in damage, and loss of life. The rain came with a vengeance, and for much of the coast, was promising to be around for several more days. Delaware was now in a state of emergency, as the storms pushed into the area, close on the heels of the rain that fell on New England and surrounding states and Canadian Provinces. The governor of Delaware was dragged out of bed by his associates at 4 AM to declare the situation an emergency. Half of Delaware was without power. The governor himself was walking around with the aid of flashlights. The power plants of New England, having been struggling in the last several years to keep up with power requirements considering its diminished nuclear energy sources, were now having *no problems* keeping up with the electrical demands. The demands, that is, of those still connected to the grid with live wires. Twenty percent of the area was now without power. There would be more states of emergency declared the next day, in parts of other states. Miraculously, the loss of life had been minimal in the United States before sunrise, on this Friday, July 3rd, 1998. These storms, seemingly present everywhere, had the ferocity a grizzly bear whose cubs had just been threatened. It was a wonder the loss of life was so minimal. On the coast, from Maine to Maryland, there were some evacuations, unrelated to the monster pending off the coast of Florida.

Pennsylvania had its worst flooding on record Thursday evening and into Friday morning. The governor of Pennsylvania was a Catholic Judas. He was a baby killer – a pro-death supporter. He went through the outward motions of being a Catholic as he did his part to tear down Christ's Church. He faithfully attended Sunday Mass with his family. Thousands of babies were killed through abortion directly because of this governor. He was no different than thousands of other Catholic and other Christian governors, senators, and congressmen. If they were to get ahead in politics, power, and wealth, they had to buy into the secret societies, the clubs, and the New World Order. That night Governor Kennedy was awakened at 2 AM by a loud thunder burst. The governor's mansion was without power for the next 33 hours. Governor Kennedy left his bed with a flashlight in hand and made his way to the kitchen to make a cup of coffee. *Wait a minute, no power, he thought.* As he was walking back to the bedroom, he stared out into his magnificent back yard gardens, trying to get a glimpse of the yard despite the raging torrents from Heaven. There was a huge lightning strike 50 feet from the mansion at that moment, with a corresponding deafening clap. In a flash, the Governor thought he saw thousands of dead, decapitated babies strewn about the back yard, many without limbs. In the next moment he clearly saw a vision of the saintly pro-life rescuer Joan Langley in front of him, amidst these unborn, just outside the doors of the mansion. He had refused to release his fellow Catholic sister in Christ from jail just months before. God had to release her Himself. Governor Kennedy then fell dead from a heart attack, onto the cold, hard marble floor. His flashlight bounced across the floor. Blood from his mouth dripped out onto his Playboy Magazine that opened up to the centerfold as he fell. His "Catholic" wife and 1.7 children came running out of their bedrooms when they heard his dying scream. He had not been to confession in 17 years... Satan had snagged another Irishman running after a pot-o-gold.

****

By 7 AM, Friday, July 3rd, 1998, there were confirmed reports of 213 Tornadoes having wreaked their havoc from Texas to Arkansas, to Ohio and back to Colorado. Now, by this hour, hundreds had actually died from direct injuries from the tornadoes. Major structures were damaged and destroyed. In Arkansas, a major chicken processing facility owned by a friend of President Bill Clinton, with dubious ties to drugs and racketeering was no longer on the face of the earth. Grass and forest fires that had sprung up overnight in California, Washington and Oregon were spreading quickly with furious dry winds coming in off the coast, in part spurred on by El Nino.

A small earthquake, 5.9 on the Richter scale occurred at 5AM, in the area centered around Hollywood California. A few Los Angeles buildings had minor damage, but worst hit were indeed the Hollywood Hills. Once again, in just a few years, the pornography industry centered in Hollywood was devastated. Several studios were damaged severely. An abortion clinic in Hollywood was destroyed by fire, apparently due to a related gas leak from the earthquake. The owner of the building, a Catholic who rented out the facility was away in Maine, on holiday.

Crime was down dramatically, indeed it was almost non-existent in much of the country from Thursday evening to Friday morning and beyond. It would be this way for a time, as men laid down all weapons of harm, and put aside all ideas of stealing and hurting others in order to lend a hand to those in need. There were plenty in need all over the country, and into Canada and Mexico, where strange weather was surging like never before. Half of the abortions that were scheduled for the United States on this Friday would be canceled before 3 PM. After 3 PM, there was nary a clinic to be found with doors open. The country was reeling and would do so even more on this day. The churches were flooded, with people, not with water, away from the low-lying areas of the East Coast. More Catholics were in Catholic Churches by 9 AM this day than had been in a Catholic Church on any given day since 1958. For some, the reborn faith would hold. For others, the Church was only a temporary security blanket that they would no longer need once their lights were back on and their refrigerator was again operating.

So, with the news relating of tremors, floods, hurricanes, death, tornadoes, and the like, it was to the great surprise of many on Mount Desert Isle to awaken to not only such reports from the media, but to also awaken to the most beautiful kind of day imaginable. It was one filled with sunshine, clean misty air, and a coastline full of large waves breaking against the rocks and forming a temporary explosion of millions of diamonds glistening with the sun, then crashing their way back to the rocks and sand, and water. Such a day it was that could invigorate the dying, and restore life to the lame. It was the kind of day we all have known at least several times in our life, when we felt as if we were walking in God's paradise, free from all stain of sin. Indeed, if there was an earthly representation of a foretaste of heaven almost completely lacking in crime of all sorts – abortion, murder of other sorts, divorce, theft, impurity, slander, and what have you; it would have been Mount Desert Isle. This miracle was not just in the great outdoors; it was in the hearts of all whom were present on the isle.   The island was temporarily transported to sobriety, which is near holiness, not far from Paradise.

The whole world was awakening to the happenings in North America in the last day or so, and the north coast of Maine, and Mount Desert Isle was no exception. The talk everywhere was on the disasters. It was not a morbid talk however; it was concerned talk, one full of compassion, and even holy action. The churches had flung open their doors by sun-up, their pastors awaiting the throngs of people as if their angels alerted them. By 8 AM, many churches were full. The Catholic Churches could not hold the many thousands of Catholic tourists from the world over. Indeed, it was strange to see. One might have been in Saint Peter's Catholic Church in Bar Harbor, or Saint Ignatious' Church in Northeast Harbor, but you might have had the impression that you were in Rome due to the international flavor of the pilgrims.   There were Chinese, Russians, Brazilians, our brothers the Canadians of course, Germans, Irish, English, South Africans and Kenyans, to name a few of the countries represented. Truly, this word "catholic", which means simply "universal" was true to form today. The Church was indeed universal, on Mount Desert Island, on this frightening but blessed day in history. In the Catholic Churches, the priests were having Masses continually for the people - aided by the many visiting priests, and for all the victims of the Natural Disasters. For those who could not hear any part of the Masses outside, the Rosary was prayed in continuum. When one Mass was finished, those who were inside had the foresight to leave orderly, and make room for those standing outside. And when the shuffling was completed, the Mass would begin again. And the Rosary went on.

In the Protestant Churches, and in those congregations with a similar protest, but preferring to drop this word 'protest' from their denomination, the prayers, the services continued in like manner. In the hearts of most people on the island, the lines of denomination, sometimes used as lines of demarcation in war, came tumbling down. Yes, the Catholics were celebrating Mass, where Christ becomes what was once bread and wine, upon the Priest's words of consecration. They had their Mary. The Protestants, the Bible believers read their Bibles and had their prayers and services for those now distressed in this country too. Ahh, if only all of the

"Bible Only" believers could see the Blessed Masses going on around them on this island today. Readings from the same psalms, from Gospels, from the letters of Scripture, and the Old Testament too. The erasing of some of the denominational lines was evident as those of little faith or no faith began to make their appearances, to bring their newfound prayers to God in the first church they could find. The rush to prayer, whether in the home, or in a church or temple, was evident not only in this secluded part of Maine, but throughout the nation.

There were very few on the island on this Friday, July 3rd, 1998, whose thoughts did not go out to loved ones and friends or acquaintances in far away places; these places where nature, or God's wrath, had surfaced – California, Colorado, Arkansas, Illinois, Delaware, New Jersey, and in many other states and two other countries. Mexico and Canada had seen and continued to see their share of fires and storms. Perhaps less than one percent of the people on the island now were from these affected areas of North America. Of these, fewer than 25% of them started their long trek home. Some simply put their homes and possessions in the hands of God, prayed for the victims, and tried to carry on with their planned course of rest and relaxation, adventure and trekking. Other vacationers forgot to pray, either for themselves, their neighbors, their states, or their country. Most of them had enough insurance to get them through anything, and they were going to have a good time at Acadia if it killed them. A large number of vacationers could not get in touch with relatives or friends back home. Travelers were being urged to stay away from the hardest hit areas, and there was little that residents in many of these locations would have been able to do on this day if they returned home. In many locations, even residents were being turned away by police and rescue forces, due to bridge and road problems. This was particularly true along the East Coast, from Maryland to New Jersey.

Strange, or blessed, however one looks at it - but when the earthquakes, monsoons, floods, and volcanoes strike countries other than the United States, such as China, India, Japan, Bangladesh, or the countries in Africa, wherever, we often hear of massive destruction and loss of life. Sometimes the casualties are in the tens of thousands, and sometimes that by a factor of ten. Yet, when God allows nature to wreak its havoc on the United States, in one sense we seem to get off with a light slap on the wrist, even in the most devastating natural disasters, yes, even in the five and ten billion dollar hurricanes, earthquakes or floods. Often, the United States walks away from such events with the loss of life that can be counted on one hand, usually on no more than ten hands. Incredible. True, the loss of one unprepared soul, a soul in a state of mortal sin at an untimely death, a loss of one soul to the fires of Hell is a tremendous expense, an infinite expense known only to God Himself. In the United States, we mourn for a few days for the victims of the Hugos, the earthquakes, floods, and whatever, we collect our insurance settlements, rebuild, and then we return to the status quo. Normal, that is, being our mortal sin. Normal being our Disney movies that defame the Catholic Church and all of Christianity. Normal being our orgy minded presidents, our One-World Politicians, our anti-God clinics, our anti-children developments and societies. And if we hear of the progeny of Bonzo dying, there is a feeling of a great loss in our country. In this case, the schools will comfort us with their be kind to the environment movements (initiated by the One World Propagandists and their environmental societies), and perhaps a collection will be taken up for monkey habitat protection in Africa sponsored by a United Nations affiliate. And on that day, tens of thousands, perhaps hundreds of thousands of babies will be murdered through abortion and abortifacients – our birth controls that kick the fertilized eggs, the conceived babies, out into the wilderness of death. Business as usual.

On this day, however, this Friday, the United States would see less than half of its murders by abortion and death by abortifacients. A cleansing had begun to take place. "Perhaps" God, however, would like to see all murders cease. *Perhaps he is not looking at percentages. Perhaps he is looking at the child in "your particular womb".*

The news reports were devastating. The largest fires on record were now sweeping California. Homes, houses, grasslands, and redwoods - California was ablaze. Washington, Oregon, and now Idaho, Wyoming, and Montana were now sharing in the forest and grass fires. As if to add insult to injury, Yellowstone was burning again. With recent scars not yet healed, Yellowstone was once again engulfed in smoke. Grizzly bears, wolves, elk, and moose were all to be seen in the streets of West Yellowstone, Idaho. Both Boy Scouts and Winnebagos were sent packing. There was not a campsite or cabin at Yellowstone that was not in danger of fire or smoke. Old Faithful would be putting on its show every sixty-three minutes for diminishing and non-existent crowds for the time being. Ahh, but that was just the West and the blazes. The real damage was on the East Coast. An East Coast that had not yet even seen Hurricane Michael, though the surf was indeed up, and rising fast. The news reports almost jumped from the West Coast and Yellowstone, nearly bypassing the tornado and flooding activity in the plains and Midwestern states, and jumped to the predicament of the East Coast. Almost every coastal county from Maryland to North Jersey was a declared disaster area. Power was still out in vast areas. Though breaks in storms appeared, other storms were on their heels on the mid-U.S. Coast. Rescue, electric, and phone crews could hardly begin to make a dent in the cleanup when the storms had not yet abated by Friday morning. At least now there was daylight. Precious daylight to aid the workers and volunteers. *Some of them were wearing strange uniforms.*

Many airports in the east were closed from damage and debris. A few small airports and one international airport out west were closed. The available airports were jammed full of waiting jets and passengers.

The reports on loss of life were conflicting. At 9AM, such reports from around the nation were placing the death toll at anywhere from 190 to 750 people from the disasters of the last dozen hours. Several thousand people were missing or unaccounted for in various states. The monetary loss was being pegged at between 12 and 30 billion dollars all told. The reporters and interviewees were rightfully praising the heroic and unrelenting aid of tens of thousands of volunteer firefighters, medics, first aid workers, boat owners; and those other volunteers that were offering their brawn and brains to remove dangerous tree limbs and rescue stranded persons amidst the wreckage that was plentiful in many areas.

News reports indicated that these disasters would not in any way affect the insurance industry on the whole, though some smaller individual corporations would have a tough go at it. They assured homeowners and businesses and other interested parties that though the loss of life was indeed a tremendous loss that cannot be made up for, the insurance end of things would easily cover the material loss from fires, floods, and even earthquakes. All of the analysts agreed on this. It would take an event or series of events ten times this severe to begin to have a negative effect on the industry, as one insurance industry analyst had indicated. The media had not yet the time to begin to forecast the effect on the economy as reflected on the prices at the grocery store, clothing store, and the building supply center. Who could yet forecast such things, as the flux of environmental disasters had not yet abated? And there's that Hurricane yet to deal with...

A special day was arising on the largest island on either of our coasts, Mount Desert Island.

It would be a gross tragedy to say the spirit on the island was one of devastation. No, the spirit on the island was one of hope and of cheer. Not a morbid cheer for evil. No, this was a cheer that despite the great affront of nature, the United States had been spared. We were still a United States - at least for the time being. Many felt that God had spoken to us, had warned us, and there was indeed an exuberance in the air that so many people had turned back to God, at least for an hour, perhaps a morning or a day, perhaps for their lifetime. Over one third of everyone on the island, visitors and residents included, on this special Friday had been to church as least for a short visit, to bring their petitions to God. But what of the two thirds, on the island, and elsewhere? Was God not speaking to everyone? Did He not leave His calling card for us all? Certainly, not everyone could go, because of jobs, health, or lack of transportation. God saw some of them praying from wherever the day found them. Yet, so many forgot to turn back to God. They would have another chance however, as God had not finished His call.

Things were rather exciting for the campers on the island on Thursday night and early Friday morning, before sunrise. The storms were tremendous. Lightning had even caused two fires in the park. They were quickly extinguished by the torrential rains accompanying the storms. Several trailers had been overturned at various campgrounds, with only a few dents and bruises to show for it. May God bless the tent campers! Many of the poor tent campers vowed that they had camped their last night out in the great outdoors. A handful of their tents had become pools of water and mangled aluminum and steel tubes, and broken fiberglass stretch poles. Every tent camper was excited to see the beautiful sunrise. A handful of the rookie tent campers indeed packed their belongings and headed off the island at first light. Most however, stayed behind to continue with their very eventful vacation.

Praise God, there were many pilgrims among those who stayed on. A fair percentage of tent and trailer campers that had been coming onto the island in the last day or two were there for a solemn purpose. They had come to honor the Blessed Virgin Mary. They had heard of a Medjugorje Conference to be held of all places in Acadia National Park. Yes, the greatest numbers of pilgrims had come from New England, New York, and New Jersey, but every state was represented, and over 37 countries as well. In the case of those from foreign countries, Canada excluded, and those from distant states, most of those who would come to Our Lady's gathering would be accidentals, like puffins blown onto the shores of Connecticut by some great storm. They, for the most part would become hardened pilgrims, with firm holy resolve, however, in the next few days. The Canadians were in full force.

****

There is a certain hierarchy of sorts in the world of camping. The first to wake are the tent campers, followed by those in pop-up campers, and then those in the full-fledged travel trailers. This rule is unbendable as the norm, but exceptions will happen. One of the last to bed, and the first to rise at Bar Harbor Campground this Friday, July 3rd, 1997, was none other than Rick Tremont. Rick did not arise in a condition that would have won any beauty contests. At 5:30 AM Rick possessed the type of bags under his eyes that one would think might be proper only on a happy camper well passed the age of 60, suffering from an assortment of illnesses including high blood pressure. Yet, in spirit, Rick felt like a million bucks. Rick stepped out of his tent, and took a right past tents and trailers, and traveled about 300 feet to the rest room. Upon his return, he promptly took to the task of rebuilding the blaze from the night before back to its previous temperament. He took out one of the few utensils that he had with him, a 7 inch coffee pot, or tea pot, if you will, filled it with water, and placed it on the grate over the now sizzling campfire. Courteous to the campers around him, he tried to be as quiet as a mouse. He went back into the tent and brought out a tiny short wave radio. Rick rarely left home without that short wave, always hoping to catch whatever programs he could on Mother Regina's station. This morning, however, Rick was desperately trying to catch some news and weather. He, like the rest of America, was anxious for the news on the storms and fires and so forth, and was hoping against all odds for a break in the weather by 3 PM. That fateful 3PM, on this First Friday of the month of July. Once again those strange thoughts, those questions that come along in life were racing through his head. *Why am I here? What am I going to do in life? Am I going to have children? What am I doing on this island? It's freezing and its July? What is it like here in January? Where is my bed? Is it in Ohio, or heaven? Have I wasted my life away? Where is that beautiful girl I met? Oh God, what is her name – oh, Therese. Therese Pierpont. What if she doesn't come back? God, she's gorgeous. Why isn't she married? What's wrong with her? Am I dreaming?*

…sshhhh..ckkshss…b

z… the radio crackled. Rick was holding the radio close to his ear so as not to have the noise disturb anyone. As he pressed the button on the digital tuner, the unused frequencies flied by. Suddenly Rick passed two channels coming in very loudly. He hoped he didn't wake anyone up, especially the Bohatch family that was sleeping about twenty feet from where he was. God knows they needed their sleep. Something stirred in the Bohatch pop-up. A being emerged, with characteristics much like Rick, baggy eyes with a general lack of luster and life in the face. Paul nodded to Rick without saying anything as he made his way over to the fire.

"Pinch me Rick. What does this all mean? What am I doing here? Somehow I know this was meant to be, and you're a part of it. We were meant to meet you. It's almost like I've read the book, if you know what I mean. But I feel really strange", whispered Paul.

"Well good morning to you buddy!" said Rick in a louder whisper, smiling back at Paul feeling the same sentiments.

"Oh yeah, good morning", excuse me said Paul. "Do you have any coffee by any chance, to go with that steaming water. I know it's Friday, but to tell you the truth, if I don't have some coffee in my fast today I may not make it to my conference. I'm not a very good example for fasting as Our Lady requests, bread and water, if one can. Several times I've done it, but usually I have my crutches – bread, plain biscuits, and tea or coffee to boot on demand. I'll probably have coffee dangled in front of my mouth in purgatory, and fresh McDonalds biscuits," said Paul.

"Me too on those accounts" said Rick. "It's like if everything is going perfect for me on that Wednesday or Friday, I can do it on bread and water, if not, I use a crutch or two or three like you said" said Rick.

"What are you hearing on the radio?" said Paul.

"Look at that!" said Rick pointing to a shooting star, heading northward on a track over the Atlantic that to the eye could only end at the North Pole. "Man, that was the brightest shooting star I ever saw. It lit up the sky like noon", he said.

"Wow" said Paul. "A few minutes later and we wouldn't have seen that, with the approach of daylight", he said.

"The radio. I haven't heard anything since I crawled out of bed. But all night long everyone was talking about what's going on in nature right now. They're saying 200 to 700 dead across the country overnight from one of about every kind of natural disaster known to man. There's the forest fires all over the place, including Yellowstone again, tornadoes for the heart of the nation, floods too, and floods and storms with near hurricane force winds for the mid-coast – all without the aid of a hurricane. Hurricane Michael is just now beginning to be felt in Florida, with winds coming in at up to 60 miles per hour right now. They're expecting the brunt of it at about 3PM - what a coincidence. And then there are the tremors in California and the DC area. Quite a 24 hour period!" said Rick. Believe it or not, but one secular station mentioned the fax from Medjugorje. They believed in it", he said.

****

All day long, the storms ran northeast, and northwest, avoiding the whole area for many miles around Mount Desert Island. It was as if some object in a giant wind tunnel was deflecting the winds aloft, coming up off of New Hampshire and Massachusetts below, and forcing them to miss the island by strange happenstance. And the people came. People were coming by the thousands. They were not coming for the lobster and surf.

They were not coming to catch the trophy stripers, or to go for a pleasant horse carriage ride on the Rockefeller's roads. No, they were coming to pray. To pray and to honor Jesus' Mother. If the rest of the world would turn their eyes from her, they would not. If the circumstances surrounding a questionable fax from Medjugorje were not enough, it was rumored that one of the Medjugorje visionaries, Boris Baric, who was now living in Portland with his American wife, would be speaking at the conference. How this rumor started was beyond knowledge. Perhaps his proximity to the park, less than four hours driving time, which was known by tens of thousands of people in New England alone, was simply enough to drive the winds of rumor. Since Father Zdenko Pavlic, the "Saint Francis" of Medjugorje was in the United States at the time, trying to raise money for the churches and orphans of Bosnia-Herzegovina and Croatia, it was also rumored that he would be accompanying Boris. By ten AM, the Bohatch family, Rick Tremont, the Shermans, the Pierponts, and countless others on the island, enroute to the island, or even in homes, cars, and businesses far away were learning of these rumors. This combined with the current environmental events sent a logjam of cars on all roads leading to Acadia National Park. As soon as Paul learned of this, he felt sick. *What sin was this that he was guilty of? If he had only used the word picnic, or gathering, instead of Conference, he felt he could look God in the eye if such a thing could be done.* Yes, all along, he was thinking that there would perhaps be a handful of people that would come and meet, and that they would make a fine blessed time of their fellowshipping and praying over the course of the three days. He had even guessed that there would be at least a couple among the pilgrims who had been to Medjugorje, that would not mind talking for several hours, all combined. That, plus the possibility of a Mass on one or two days, combined with the Rosary and Chaplet of Divine Mercy, and some readings from Our Lady's messages at Medjugorje would do the trick – would fill in the slots, the hours which Paul had written of in his advertisements. Now, Paul was beginning to feel as if he was a condemned man. He was close to despair. The environment, the natural disasters and their timing had made this whole thing exponentially more than he had planned. *What if this was from Satan? Thousands were on their way.*

"Paul and Barbara, Wayne and Betsy Sherman, and Rick Tremont were sitting around the campfire talking just after ten AM. The Bohatch children except for the baby were out picking blueberries and riding bikes. They were talking. Paul was not saying much, but again, he was thinking too hard. They had just started to gather in the children to say a morning Rosary, and pray for the day's events. Paul was planning on driving into town after the Rosary, getting the family something to eat in Bar Harbor, and then taking everyone over to Saint Peter's to spend an hour or two there storming heaven. Rick and the Shermans were going to do the same, but then head up early to Jordan Pond to spread a blanket of prayer up there where they would soon be meeting with perhaps thousands of pilgrims.

When they finished the Rosary, a most surprising event took place. Walking on the small road in front of Rick's campsite was the Pierpont family, at least three of them. "Therese!" yelled Rick.

Therese turned around in sudden surprise. "Rick, wow, how'd you pick out this campground. We're at K-15", she said.

"Logistics said Rick. It was the closest to Ron's Shop and Carry", he said with a smile. "Let me introduce you to this "major conference" organizer, Paul Bohatch and his family, and the Shermans" said Rick. Rick made the introductions. "Is this your father?" said Rick.

"Yes, this is my father, Francis Pierpont, he came over on the Bluenose Ferry early this morning. It may be the last run for the Bluenose for a day or two; the water is kicking up out there with these storms. We're thankful he made it". We came early to try to find sites for my mother's sister and brother, and their families. Everyone's here now, they're down by us", she said. "It was good we came in at sunrise, because I think all of the sites are taken right now. I don't think Bar Harbor has ever seen the likes of a day like this", she said.

After the introductions were over, the families and friends began to fill each other in on the weather reports, disaster reports, and "Conference" news.

"Mr. Bohatch" said Therese....

"Call me Paul," said Paul.

"Paul, I don't know how to tell you this, but from the very little that I heard at 2AM this morning from a friend in Boston, you're in hot water with the Marian Centers", Therese said. "They're all saying that you lied about the speakers and they say there's one very unhappy Croatian visionary in Portland, and his priest friend as well", she said.

"I knew I should have called this a Rosary rally. My life would have been much simpler, and my prospects for jail considerably less", Paul half-joked. "Well, since there is probably going to be thousands of pilgrims at Jordan Pond this afternoon, looking for a famous visionary, how do you think they are going to react. You don't think it will get out of hand, do you?", he said.

Wayne Sherman jumped into the conversation. "I think these people are coming to honor Our Lady and pray for our struggling country. They're driving through horrendous storms to get here. They don't even know that it's like paradise out here with our strange weather. For all they know, they're driving into more storms for what they can only figure is an outdoor event. We'll be O.K. I think a lot of these folks are already on God's side," said Wayne.

"Honey, if they lock you up, ask them for a room with a view and a telephone", laughed Barbara. Paul was greatly relieved that Barbara was beginning to make light of these serious matters. He knew at that moment that everything was going to be all right. Barbara was a barometer for him at stressful times like this. The barometric readings were almost always better than Paul had bargained for.

"You know they know about this in Nova Scotia, Paul" said Francis Pierpont. "They still hang fly-by-night conference sponsors there, but they'd have to extradite you, and that could take time", laughed Mr. Pierpont.

"Thanks Mr. Pierpont" said Paul beginning to feel better with the current of reverse psychology taking place under his nose.

"Rick, how's jail food?" said Paul.

"Didn't you hear the man" said Rick, "We're talking hanging. Hung men don't eat," said Rick nonchalantly.

"Paul" said Barbara, Lets get this scary task underway. Lets get some food in town, visit Jesus in the tabernacle, and head out for tea time at Jordan Pond."

"Get it done Johnny Reb," said Rick to Paul.

"O.K. my John Wayne fan, very funny. We'll see you there, if not at church," said Paul.

"Therese, do you have enough room for a tired bicyclist in your car?" said Rick.

"Dad, is that O.K.?" said Therese to her Dad.

"Sure honey", he said.

The Bohatch family rounded up their youngsters, and quickly left in the van. The Shermans were going to follow the Pierponts and their relatives into town to have lunch together, and then they would follow each other on a great adventure to Jordan Pond. What a day was awaiting all parties, on the island, and in the United States! A day to not be forgotten.

****

Steve Lebroq had a dream early Friday morning that shook him more than any tremor could. He thought of it as a dream, but it seemed more real to him than day to day life. Around three in the morning, he was sleeping sound in bed, and he had a vision in this dream that he was standing next to his father, who had an angelic look about him, a heavenly look, not a look that one might have from down under. Next to his father was a lovely Lady dressed in blue. Steve did not want to venture at her identity, but his early years as a practicing Catholic gave him the general idea. The man, his father in the dream said, "I love you. I'm sorry. I love you". And the woman just smiled a heavenly smile as if she had nothing else to do. Rick seemed to have been shown a small portion of his father's life, from youth to his last days on earth. He was shown his trials, tribulations, his weaknesses, and his tremendous sufferings. Even the liquor seemed a suffering. A demon of drunkenness had his grips deep into his father's skull most of his life. Though not possessed, his father's very thoughts and actions were nearly always shaded by this ghoul. His own fault, his own sins, had invited the demon to him. Steve was shown how his father prayed a thousand times for his healing, but he was never healed. God allowed Steve to see how his father suffered in causing suffering for his own family. An addict. An addict by choice. He tried to leave the alcohol, which was simply beer. He never did. Yet Steve's father prayed, and several others spent many years praying for him. Steve was shown the Knights of Columbus praying for him often, when he was not around, even trying to refuse him even a single beer, at the conclusion of business meetings, when his father was among them. Yet, are prayers lost in God? No. Prayers won the day. Steve now knew, even in this sleep, through this vision, that his father was in heaven. *But what about the family God? Father tore us apart? What of the prayers for our family?* Yet even these questions in his mind were answered by a renewed confidence on Steve's part that all things work for the glory of God. Steve's family was about to undergo a radical conversion.

In a sense, Steve was happy to be a part of this dream; these things were good and profitable to know. Then, Steve was taken through the dark tunnel that was his life. He had his warning, as some number have already had throughout the world. God would not have him wait for this general warning of mankind, that many prophets had spoken of that was said to be imminent. Steve had his day in court. Not judgment day. Just an arraignment day in court. *He lost, but he won. He was shown all of his sins since he reached the age of reason, and the effect that they had on everyone. He was shown his actual sins, and his sins of negligence and omission.* It has been proposed by many that Hell is the cutting oneself off from God. A physical place yes, but a place where souls have parted from God. Sin parts us from God. Steve had seen Hell, at least from a distance, and he had even seen the place reserved for him by God if he continued on in his current ways, his lukewarmness to Jesus Christ. At 4 AM, he woke up screaming in a tremendous drenching sweat. His wife thought he was one possessed. In actuality, it was the birth pangs of Steve Lebroq, being born again. Yes, confession would follow to bring to a climax what had begun. No one in the Lebroq household could go back to sleep, after learning what had just happened to Dad. The kids were just informed that they were going to go to a religious conference tomorrow and that they were going to love it. Emily told him she was now looking forward to going with excitement. Her soul had been longing for God and things heavenly. She had seen bits and pieces of news on the events in Medjugorje. Funny, she believed every word of it, but had not acted upon her knowledge.

Steve put on enough bacon and eggs to feed an army. As the family was enjoying an early breakfast, the phone rang at 6 AM. A ranger, working under Steve, was calling him to advise him to expect huge crowds and big problems today. Pilgrims were flocking in by the thousands... Steve sat down to work out a game plan. By 7 AM, all he had written down were plans for parking and traffic control, portable rest room facilities, and a speaker system for this conference. I bet this guy didn't even bring a microphone with him... *We've got a lot of work to do...*

At 1 PM all of the normal Jordan Pond parking sites, including the overflow parking further north on the one-way Park Loop Road were filled. Cars were now beginning to park along the side of the road, on both the left and the right. Steven Lebroq had pulled every available Park Service worker from their normal jobs to work at Jordan Pond on traffic control, porta-john placement, and other work in regards to last minute facility upgrades. There was not yet a soul around who had any first hand information on this Conference. Yet, in faith, he went forward, spending Uncle Sam's money on a worthy cause, a public cause. *Damn the torpedoes. Damn his job if he was to lose it.* All for Jesus & Mary, that Lovely Lady dressed in blue. Steve remembered a poem he had learned about Mary as a young child, of that same title – Lovely Lady Dressed in blue. With all his heart, Steve had this undying urge to leave right now, and catch the first flight into war torn Bosnia, and visit Our Lady and tell her how sorry he was for denying her Son. He was crying the whole time he was working. Crying, laughing, but always smiling as the tears came down. *God, what if there aren't any organizers or speakers. Oh God, then I become the scapegoat, the idiot. Good! I deserve it. I want to be an idiot for God. I hope nobody shows up. I want to offer my embarrassment up to Jesus through Mary. I hope this thing fails! What am I saying? Come Jesus, Come. Come into my life. Bring Mary, your Mother. Come here, too, to this island of vacationers and thrill-seekers. Turn us all into pilgrims on our way to you!*

By 1:30 PM, no one had yet arrived who knew anything about the planning of this gathering. Steve had taken the liberty to have a thirty by twenty-foot stage erected right at the foot of Jordan Pond. It had been used before for various park gatherings, and had seen its better days. As things were now, he could do little about the protection from the rain that was falling on most of the mainland. God would have to provide on that account. A brand new Fender Public Address System, including six microphones, four 150-Watt Speakers, and an eight-channel equalizer had been set up, complete with chairs and microphone stands. Steve was trying to figure out how he could keep himself from getting fired for the next few days. After all, the Park Service would be tearing down and setting up this stage and accompanying facilities two more times this weekend, using park services materials, labor, and property. As everyone knows, Uncle Sam no longer holds with the motto "In God We Trust", and as of late relations between God and the Uncle had become estranged. More than that, since Uncle Clinton, the traitor, had turned over our national parks to Aunt UN in 1997, Steve would have to answer to even higher authorities. One ranger had already approached him about separation of church and state, and Park Service regulations.

"Excuse me", a young lady with a French accent asked Steve Lebroq who was directing traffic near the entrance of Jordan Pond, "who arranged for all of this?", she said. The young lady and her companions had just come from the edge of the pond.

"*Are you with God or against him*?" said Steve with a smile.

"With Him", she said.

"Then God did. God did. And She did", Steve said, pointing to the sky, mispronouncing the name of a small town in Bosnia "Our Lady of Mejugoorski, she did it", he said.

"Excuse me, is this where the conference is?", an elderly Lady with four equally aged lady passengers asked Steve Lebroq who was standing in the road ushering traffic along to the roadside parking available further on.

"Yes, sorry though, you'll have to park about 500 feet down the road, the lots are jam packed", Steve replied.

"Thanks", she said, as she headed down the road.

"But are those Park Service facilities?", inquired the young lady again? She was referring to the stage and rest room facilities, and even several large tables set up here and there on the huge lawn that stretches out and away from Jordan Pond House to the pond itself.

"Park Service" said Steve, waving on traffic with his hands at the same time.

"Who did it?" said Wayne Sherman. "Who arranged for it. Mr. Bohatch said no one knew about this", he said.

"Ahh, are you with this conference, or this Mr. Bohatch?" said Steve.

"No, well…, yes, I guess, but we probably haven't known about it any longer than you. In fact, Mr. Bohatch who ran the ad probably hasn't known about it much longer than you. He just ran the ad hoping to get a few people together to pray the Rosary and talk about Mary's messages" said Mr. Sherman.

"Well, he's got himself a conference on his hands. Is he here yet? I want to kill him!" said Steve with a smile suggesting his jesting. *"That is, I wanted to kill him, figuratively, until 4 this morning!* Something happened to me this morning. I was shown things in my life..." said Steve trailing off.

"The Warning" said Rick.

"Warning?" said Steve.

"The Warning that is coming for all of the world at a given time in the near future, that has been prophesied by many saints and holy people, and seers in the last few hundred years" said the tired and formerly quiet Mrs. Anna Pierpont. "Our Lady spoke of it at Garabandal, Spain, in the 1960s to four visionaries also. In essence, Our Lady also spoke of the warning to Father Nairobi - the spiritual leader of the Marian Movement of Clergy. Right now Garabandal is being dragged through the mud, sadly by many Marian leaders, even though it hasn't been condemned - nearly, but not so. Anyhow, there are some people who have had a foretaste of what is to come for the rest of us – through this general warning for all mankind. A prime example of another person that I know of that has experienced the warning is Father Steven Schreir. I'm glad you survived. I hope I do", she said lightly.

The group introduced themselves formally to Steve Lebroq.

"Hey, I guess you're one of our speakers today," said Rick Tremont to Steve.

"Oh God, I don't want to relive that, not yet at least. It almost killed me. I'm still sweating...." said Steve.

Rick looked off in the distance, down the road. "Paul, you're not gonna believe this...", yelled Rick, to Paul who was approaching the main entrance to Jordan Pond on foot with his family.

And so the stage was set, literally...

****

Just before three o'clock, two priests were found in the crowd who would open the conference, and lead the faithful in the Chaplet of Divine Mercy. The priests asked the heavenly assistance of Sister Faustina, now Blessed Faustina, to whom Jesus gave the Chaplet several decades ago in Poland. There were over 5,000 people jammed into the Jordan Pond area, many into the woods, and many along the shoreline further up along the pond behind the stage. There were dozens of canoes and kayaks full of happy pilgrims, floating right behind the stage. They had some of the best seats! What a day! If it was not for the PA system, and the stage, fewer than 100 people would probably have been able to hear the speakers and the prayers and talks to come. As it was now, all of the people for thousands of feet around were able to hear the speakers clearly.

When the Chaplet was done, and the two priests had made a few remarks on Medjugorje, a brief summary of Our Lady's visits there, a waitress from the Jordan Pond House Restaurant came running up to the stage. She was shouting at the top of her lungs, "Father, tell the people to pray hard. Washington DC has just been hit with a major earthquake. Congress is being called in and sent to back up underground Congressional facilities at the Greenbrier Resort, near White Sulpher Springs, West Virginia. God, and that hurricane....". The waitress was trying to regain her breath. "Michael is ripping Florida apart right now. Its bigger than they thought, they couldn't get the coast evacuated...", she stammered loudly.

One of the priests, Father Albert Green, had an instant of disbelief when West Virginia was mentioned. *What in the world would Congress be going to a resort in West Virginia for? This is a hoax.* He instantly leaned over to the other priest, Father Daniel Spaulding. "Father, what is she talking about - West Virginia. Is this a joke?", he whispered quietly.

"For many years the Greenbrier has been an emergency alternate for Congress. It's always been there waiting. They've got underground facilities awaiting them," said Father Spaulding. "It's one of the most famous East Coast resorts too. Golfers go there from all around the world too. I've been there. The facilities were designed for a day such as this..."

The crowd was silent. The waitress was only four feet from the microphone, looking up to Father Green up on the stage. He had turned the microphone toward her as she started to speak. The pilgrims now knew what they were doing on a pristine island off the coast of Maine, on a beautiful day when storms were raging all around them. They were battling the gates of Hell. They were called together to pray. There were three other priests in the crowd. People started approaching the priests asking to go to confession. Confession lines instantly started to form. The people, this microcosm of America, at least those of goodwill, had started to turn back to God. Perhaps they remembered Niniveh, that great city which God spared. The city of gentiles nevertheless!

The priests on the stage were reassuring the people that the best thing they could do now was to pray for the victims of the disasters, and to pray for the conversion of their nation. A small percentage of the crowd dashed off to pay phones or cell phones to call loved ones or friends in the effected areas. Paul Bohatch now knew the reason he had been prompted to put this gathering together - which now, indeed, was a conference! Yes, he had a Medjugorje Conference on his hands. Aside from all of his prayer, Paul had really only taken two steps to put the conference together. He had placed the ads in the paper. Secondly, just a few minutes before, he had asked the two priests now on the stage, for their assistance. He was now about to make his third and final move as the general director of this what was now a large conference. "Rick" said Paul, as they were standing in the crowded front of the stage. "Rick", he said again. "You're in charge. This is now your conference. Ever since we met last night, I knew that's the way it was supposed to be", he said.

"Woe buddy, hold on there bubbalooie. What do you mean?" said Rick.

"Just what I said. Look, at least be the emcee, and help me call the shots. I think we have to give this gathering a shot in the arm of organization" said Paul. "I may be changing diapers or taking the kids to the porta-potties at any given moment. I think God wants you up there on that stage, that's all. I'll do all the running around I can do. I bet we have a hundred potential speakers amongst these lay people, priests, and the six nuns I've seen so far. I'll start putting a schedule together. I've got a portable computer and printer with me. I think we're in business, but I need your help. Can you guys help too?" said Rick, looking at Therese, her Mom and Dad, the Shermans, and also glimpsing up at the priests. Everyone agreed whole-heartedly. It was an organization thrown together by Heaven, as only God could do. "Rick, get up there and announce that we're going to start the Rosary in 5 minutes. Then see if you can commandeer the attention and a portion of the time of these priests for the next few days. Fill them in on what has happened to this impromptu Rosary rally. Tell them we could sure use their help. I'm going to see if I can get the other three priests up there with you in the next minute so you can give them the play-by-play too. Therese, could you go invite all those nuns to listen to Rick for a minute too? Maybe one of them, or all of them would like to participate", he said.

"O.K. buddy, sounds like a winner" said Rick jumping up onto the stage.

"Sure" said Therese, starting off after the nuns.

"Rick, wait a minute. After you talk to the priests, fill in the crowd on what this conference is about and how it came to be. You don't have to mention my name, but just indicate that we need their prayers and support, and that it looks like it was meant to be, whatever. Oh, see if you can beat down some of those rumors we've heard about the conference too. Oh..., one last thing. Try to indicate to them that we're looking for speakers with great stories, whether they're priests or lay persons, nuns, whatever. You're going to have to couch that somehow, however, otherwise we'll have 2000 would be speakers. Tell them they can talk to me down at the end of the stage over there" said Rick pointing to the east side of the stage.

It worked. Within two minutes there were five priests and six nuns on the stage, talking with Rick Tremont. Rick filled them in on everything. After all, he knew just about as much as Paul knew about this conference, which was just about nothing. Paul had also dashed off after Steve Lebroq whom his friends had introduced him to earlier. Superintendent Steve walked up onto the stage also at Paul's request. Steve was a key part of this conference, and Paul saw the hand of God in his role for sure.

In the meantime, the two youngest Bohatch children were screaming and carrying on. Barbara was having a tough time managing the children. She was quite happy that her husband swallowed some pride and turned over the keys of the conference to Rick, at least in part. He still however was quite busy for the moment. She offered up her sufferings, the sufferings of a busy, typical mother to God for those who were suffering in the United States right now, and for those whose souls were in danger of Hell. She gathered the children together and walked over in the direction of her husband, east of the stage, and brought them upon the pond bank, had everyone sit down, and started a Rosary in advance of the rest of the pilgrims.

If one was honest, it would have to be admitted that a few thousand of the more than 5000 pilgrims had only just become pilgrims. A larger number of these converted vacationers were only incidentally in the area, and had become a part of the crowd of pilgrims, some of them quite by accident. Amongst them were Jews, Muslims, Hindus, Catholics, Protestants, and even atheists. Amongst the avid atheists was the owner of "One World Clothing", and her live-in fiancee. Few of the 'incidentals' withdrew from the area upon learning their predicament. Indeed, if the Church did not use certain discretion in catechesis, half of them would have become Catholic 15 minutes into the conference, with a nominal push – perhaps an invitation.

It is true that Our Lady at Medjugorje has never asked a single person to become a Catholic. She just tells them to turn back to her Son, Jesus Christ. Many do become Catholic for their own reasons. There was indeed here in this place, there must have been, at least, a sudden infusion of the Holy Spirit, strong enough to shatter the prejudices and bigotries of generations upon generations. Certainly, the turmoil in parts of our country, perhaps especially in the nation's capitol, and the subsequent need for an infusion of prayer lead to this fervor. But God was at the center of all that was spoken of from that stage. It was God that these people were turning to. These vacationers, these pilgrims were far from falling bricks, floodwaters, and hurricanes. No, it was not a fear of chastisements, not an unwarranted fear of visionaries' reports, true or false, of such chastisements that caused the people to pray. Charity and love of one's neighbor had won the day.

In the interim after Rick had announced an impending Rosary, and prior to the Rosary, the crowd was, as might be expected, talking amongst themselves in reserved tones, while many were already kneeling down, standing, or sitting in prayer. Now there were people from all over, from near and far, individuals and families. There were the chaste and unchaste, sinners and bigger sinners, - those in a state of Grace, and those not in a state of Grace – those in mortal sin. The latter were in larger numbers. The people however, had received an influx of virtue, and as the priests came back off the stage, mortal sins, though unseen, were to be found fleeing from the island in droves, as the masses went to sacramental confession.

Prior to this, on-stage, Holy Fate had won a victory. All five of the priests would be able to assist in Masses, Confession, and as speakers if needed, for at least part of each day of the conference. Only two of the priests had come believing in Medjugorje. Two others said they had scorned Medjugorje up until an hour ago, but now believed. The fifth priest indicated he had not the time to think about Medjugorje prior to today, but that he now had the beginnings of belief. One of the nuns had been to Medjugorje, and said she had some very moving stories to tell if they were in need of speakers. They had come from Boston to specifically attend the conference. And then came Steve Lebroq. "I think God wants me to talk", he said. He told Rick and the others gathered around what had happened to him the night before.

"Steve, God wants you to tell your story. I think you're right. There's a whole bunch of Steve Lebroqs out there who need to hear you" said Father Green.

"Steve, this is just day one", cut in Rick. "I think we're going to see at least two or three times as many people tomorrow and Sunday. We're going to need more of everything – speakers - porta-johns, you name it. Because of the special circumstances of today, most of these people are going to leave here tonight and call their friends and loved ones and tell them to get their butts up here. We need to be ready," said Rick. "Oh yeah, and Paul's idea about changing the location of the conference each day – he's nuts. *I'll tell him. We're staying right here.* We'll have to put up signs at the other locations. Can you do all this, he said.

"I guess. If President Clinton doesn't fire me directly the uncivil libertarians will catch up to me as things are right now. As I was thinking before, if I can only delay getting fired for a couple more days, maybe I can be of assistance. I'll get to work on it. God, I'm going to miss this job. I'm glad to be on God's payroll now though!" said Steve.

"Steve, if Our Lady wants you to keep this job, you'll be here till they bury you on Cadillac Mountain at a very old age" said Rick.

"They'll be nobody here tomorrow if we get the weather they say is coming at us," said one of the priests with an Irish accent.

"Ahh, Father, had you not heard the weather for today? Severe storms all day long, but I've never seen a finer day. Yet, if you were on Cadillac Mountain right now you would see the thunderstorms battling Nova Scotia to the east, and the mainland to the west of Ellsworth. It's truly a miracle," said the most petite of the six Sisters of Charity. "All we need to do is come, and God will do the rest. Thank God ahead of time as the saintly American Franciscan Father Solanus Casey used to say", she said.

Five minutes had gone on to ten minutes, and the Rosary had not yet begun. It was now 25 minutes after 3 PM, and the gathering was nearly a half-hour old. The people continued to talk and pray. The Jordan Pond House Restaurant had never seen such a day. To say they were understaffed was to put it lightly. Long known as a depot for tea and lunch for the rich and famous in the past 100 years, their tea supply was running desperately low. Many would have to make do with coffee...

The priests, nuns, and Steve Lebroq gathered in chairs at one end of the stage, and talked quietly amongst themselves while Rick went to the center microphone. "Ladies and gentlemen, could I please have your attention for a few minutes, well, for perhaps ten minutes before we begin the Rosary. I'd like to first introduce myself, my name is Rick Tremont, and I'm going to be your emcee for the conference. You might find it hard to believe, but let me go way, way, back in time to some of the events that took place in the early planning stages for this conference, say about 24 hours ago...". Rick went on to introduce the conception of this conference, the Bohatch family, the Pierponts, the Shermans, Steve Lebroq and his family, the priests and nuns on the stage, and others that he had met in the "planning stages" in the last hour. He dispelled with the rumors that were circulating among Marian groups and lay persons about this conference. And then a very wonderful thing happened. Rick was about to set a spark to the bed of a very, very dry forest floor. He was about to start a fire that could not be put out except by God Himself. Oh, but even the spark originated with God. There would be no need for extinguishing the fire. Rick was about to say some words that would bring together people of such diversity, people with such profound stories of conversion and hope that nary an eye at Jordan Pond would not be losing many a tear in the next few days. These tears would be followed by the conversion of the heart of many a pilgrim...

"Lastly, though God has already brought a number of speakers forth, if there are perhaps three or four of you in the audience who feel called to speak regarding Medjugorje or Our Lady in general, would you please see the gentleman to the right of the stage. That fellow with his right hand in the air. Paul, your right hand please" said Rick. Paul put his hand in the air.

A hundred people wanted to dash up to Paul from throughout the audience. They were people who had experienced miraculous cures in Medjugorje, or had their marriages healed, or were brought back to God by Our Lady, and in one case, a former Mason wanted to come forth and give his painful life's story until his conversion in that little hamlet in Bosnia-Herzegovina. They all prayed for discernment. Then some of them started their long walk to the left of the stage to meet the man who placed the ads. There was a man from New York State who had often wanted his neighbor to drop dead concerning a property and right-of-way/gate dispute. At times he and the neighbor had actually been at arms. *With his wife's approval, he made his move and headed for Paul Bohatch.*

Another potential speaker was a young Purdue graduate, who was a Methodist turned pantheist New Age environmentalist, doctor of science, and United Nations consultant in sustainable environment and population affairs. In the last half-hour, it seems, she was undergoing a rapid conversion to Jesus Christ, and as Rick was speaking she was just finishing reading a flyer on Medjugorje by Wayne Weedle. She would be going home to her bed alone this evening. She had this sudden urge to tell these people that she had considerable inside information on the coming extreme measures of forced population control and extreme environmentalism that would be coming to the western world shortly, on the heals of such episodes of natural disasters as they were now seeing. She had great insight into the diabolical spirit that was behind this planned historical movement, and she wanted to expose it so as to allow the people to pray against such coming events. She began to walk to the stage after excusing herself from her boyfriend and her family that was visiting with her. She remembered her 'chance' meeting with Rick. *I believe in God...* she thought as she headed for the stage.

Mohammed and Gloria Jackson looked at each other and walked toward the front of the crowd. The newlyweds had just recently arrived from the nation's capitol. They were tense over the fate of their relatives back in the DC area, but knowing that their families were in the suburbs gave them some comfort. God had brought them here for a purpose. They had a story to tell that would touch the lives of thousands... "Mr. Bohatch..."

Another prospective speaker was just starting to step forward - a man from Alabama with a very, very Protestant name. A young pimple-faced wise guy back in Alabama had shaken this Bible Scholar's comfortable Bible-only beliefs. This Baptist minister now had a desire for the Eucharist. He wondered how long he would have to wait. Would the priests have a special dispensation for him? He didn't want to wait. He would protest! No, he couldn't! That wasn't Catholic. What about the dispensation? He was ready. He didn't know the whole Catholic Catechism, but he now knew more than most Catholics. At a rest stop in Tennessee, some crazy uppity young Catholic housewife had placed two cassette tapes on his windshield. They were killer tapes of the worst sort – the conversion story of Tom Rutbensky, and the conversion story of Scott Zahn. Real killers. The kind of tapes you don't walk away from. You just keep playing them over and over again until you're Catholic. The housewife saw the "Clergy" bumper sticker on the man's front bumper. Perfect target she thought. The man saw her as he was going back to his car with his family. He yelled, but she and her husband and young family made a clean getaway down the interstate. He would never know who she was, in this world. Those tapes were killers. Then there was the tape that the man's wife had made at a revival a few days ago. That one was haunting. She read the referenced Bible passages to him over and over on their way from Alabama to Maine, between the Tom Rutbensky and Scott Zahn tapes. *They can't make me wait till Easter, can they, before allowing me to become Catholic? He reached the stage and put out his hand to Paul's hand.*

Another young lady was elbowing her husband to prompt him to go up to Mr. Bohatch and volunteer for a talk. She finally dragged him up. The children followed in the rear. This Michigan family had just spent a very interesting night in a Basilica in Ohio two days ago. They had done some priority reorganization on the way to Maine.

There was a lawyer from the Boston suburbs who started to make his way up to see Paul. This was hard for him, for he had a difficult story to tell, and the priest he had just divulged this nightmare to the night before was right up there on stage. He was a resolute man, however, now adding virtue to temper his resoluteness. Unknown to him, a lawyer friend of his from Washington State was also in the crowd with his family. They had flown in to do what they could to help their friends get back on their feet. They had not yet seen each other.

Way in the back, far from the stage and close to the Jordan Pond House, a middle aged man and his wife and family and his brother and sister-in-law and their children were on their knees praying a Rosary for the disaster victims. They were in the middle of the Rosary when the speaker was inviting other potential speakers to come forth. This fellow who had just flown out from California with his family was still recovering from a Medjugorje Conference gone awry, at least in part, several days ago. He was the conference organizer. God, could he tell stories about Medjugorje! He brought his younger brother back into the faith with his storytelling.

All of the stories were true. The younger brother nodded to the older. The older brother just continued to pray. "Get up there," said the younger brother. The older brother headed for one Mr. Paul Bohatch, down by Jordan Pond.

Rick saw all of the people converging on Paul. *God, he thought, what have I done? I bet we've got some real winners there.* Well, we can always shorten the conference he thought. After all, he was in charge now! Rick snapped back to the current moment. *The Rosary he thought. What should I say? We've been going a half an hour and some of these people have just arrived. I don't want to lose anybody either. I'll recap, add a few lines and get to the Rosary.* Rick summed up once again what the conference was about, what had taken place in our country about 3 o'clock in regards to the disasters, and let the people know that they were about to go to the Five Joyful Mysteries of the Rosary. He pointed out a table with about 2,500 cheap plastic, but free and guaranteed effective Rosaries on it (Paul's supplies), and Rosary Pamphlets to boot. He asked Father DiNardo to lead the group in the Rosary, which he happily consented to, and joined Rick at the microphone. Rick mentioned that immediately following the Rosary Father DiNardo, whom Rick had now known for about 30 minutes, would give a 10-minute discussion on the origins and Biblical nature of the Rosary. Father looked at him with a surprised smile.

"We pray now for the victims of the natural disasters, for the Pope's intentions, and for Our Lady's intentions" said Father. "In the Name of the Father, the Son, and the Holy Spirit... I believe in God, the Father Almighty, Creator of Heaven and Earth, and in Jesus Christ, His only Son..." And so the conference was well under way. Never before had so many Rosaries, so many prayers and petitions been carried to the throne of Heaven - having Mount Desert Isle as their origin....

...The Rosary was finished with the Hail Holy Queen: "Hail Holy Queen, Mother of Mercy, Our Life, Our Sweetness, and our Hope. To thee do we cry, poor banished children of Eve. To the do we send up our sighs, morning and weeping in this vale of tears. Turn then most gracious advocate, thine eyes of mercy toward us, and after this, our exile, show unto us the Blessed Fruit of thy womb, Jesus. O clement, o loving, O sweet Virgin Mary, pray for us, O holy Mother of God, that we may be made worthy of the promises of Christ..."

Father DiNardo then went into his "ten" minute talk on the history and scriptural nature of the Rosary. A half an hour later he was done. Saint Louis Marie de Montfort could not have given a better discussion, a better history of the Rosary. Indeed, it was as if Father had de Montfort's writings, his "Secret of The Rosary", and "True Devotion To Mary" memorized in his heart. The parables and stories he told were from these writings, as retold by this master storyteller. "And now ladies and gentleman, as we move on, let us please stay in constant prayer and understanding of the suffering that many in our nation are experiencing at this time. Let us remember the unborn too, the world over, as we pray for those who are suffering" said Father DiNardo. "Everyday in our country, thousands of babies are killed through abortion and "birth control". And please, if any of you are thinking that I am speaking just to certain ones in this prayerful group today, you are mistaken. For who amongst us can 'cast the first stone'. We are all sinners. Perhaps it will be uplifting for some of you, who have not yet started your walk back to God to know this - Most of the very, very saintly people that I have known for many years were once deeply entrenched in sin! Deeply! Thank you for your attention", he said. "I bless you in the name of the Father, Son, and Holy Spirit". Father handed the microphone back to Rick, nodding a thank you to him as he did.

Rick thanked Father on behalf of the crowd, and walked over and whispered something to Paul Bohatch. In a minute, Rick was standing up addressing the crowd. "Excuse me, could I please have your attention. At this time we would like to have a ten-minute break so that you can say hello to the people that you find yourselves next to. Also, please use the restrooms, or get something to eat or drink as needed. I do have two very important messages to cover however. The first item is that the whole conference will take place right here at Jordan Pond. So please, let your friends and relatives know that we will be at Jordan Pond the whole three days, and not at Cadillac Mountain or Sand Beach for the remaining two days. Secondly, as those of you who were here earlier are now aware, this was a rather impromptu Medjugorje gathering that Mr. Paul Bohatch, a layman from Steubenville, Ohio, put together starting just a few days ago. Paul made zero arrangements for this conference that he thought might amount to no more than a small Rosary Rally. He placed ads in three papers. Many of you saw the ads. He did that and he prayed. The facilities, right down to the last microphone, porta-john, and extension cord were provided for us here, unbeknownst to us, hours before the Bohatch family arrived. The few of us that have been helping Paul for a day or so now have only just today met the man who put all of the facilities together for the conference! This man is Mr. Steve Lebroq. Please pray very hard for Mr. Steve Lebroq, the Park Superintendent, and all of the Park Service employees who worked very hard to set this all up. As you know, our country is becoming less and less friendly to Christians as we head toward the end of this era, as Our Lady calls it. There may be repercussions for Mr. Lebroq, so please pray hard for him and his family, and again, all of the workers that you see around you.

We will be hearing from Mr. Lebroq, who had been away from Jesus Christ for a few dozen years until about 4 AM this morning. You won't want to miss his talk. Oh, and one other item. As I've already informed you of Mr. Bohatchs' non-intensive planning for this gathering, we seem to find ourselves short on musicians and proper hymns and Christian music that befits such a conference. If any of you are musicians for the Lord, and would like to assist us, please feel free to come forward to the stage at this time. It would be great if we could have some music during this brief break. As soon as Rick had said this, Allison Welday, a Christian musician, guitar player, and Franciscan University graduate started to walk up the stairs to the stage with her guitar in hand. "Praise the Lord, we have music" said Rick as she came up. "Oooh my God, and I think I know who our musician is. Are you, oh, I've heard you at Franciscan University and elsewhere" said Rick. "Welday, Amy Welday, right?"

"Close" said the young musician. "I'm Allison Welday, and yes, perhaps you've heard me at Franciscan University", she said.

"Ladies and gentlemen, Allison Welday will sing for God and us at this time" said Rick. "If I recall correctly, Allison has been singing at half of the Marian Conferences in our country in the last decade or so. Perhaps after some music, she can tell us the details of how God brought her here this weekend," said Rick. "Oh, we will have Mass each day of the conference, and rough schedules for you tomorrow. Tonight's Mass will be at 6:30 PM, so we'll be running somewhat later than was originally published in the ad" said Rick. God bless you... Allison..." said Rick

Allison Welday, with a generous selection of microphones, chairs, stands, and other musical/sound peripherals to choose from, had already set herself up to play by the time Paul had finished speaking. She started with a soft instrumental that increased in volume from a whisper up a crescendo trail to a still hushed sound and everyone longing for the words to follow. Many knew what words would indeed follow.

"Oh my God", thought Rick, as he finished moving other microphones and a chair or two around as Allison was starting. "Not that one. Oh God, get me off this stage. I gotta get out of here. Rick had tears streaming down his face as he headed for the rear stage exit, anxious to go hide himself somewhere amidst the balsam fir trees only hundreds of feet away. There was no rear stage exit proper, however, and Rick had to jump off the stage onto a narrow strip of land separating Jordan Pond from the stage. His long black hair hid his river of tears. Each time he had been to Medjugorje, he had dashed back into Saint James Church for a quick goodbye to Jesus & Mary. Each time a group of pilgrims was singing that same song. Allison was singing it now. It was about to crush Rick with both joy and sorrow. It reminded him of his pick-and-choose Catholic past life, and life yet to come, Heavenly life with Jesus & Mary, that does in fact, begin today. Rick could not explain his tears to anyone. How can any young man, with an earthly mother already his own, explain a powerful, undying, pure, chaste, and blazing love for the Mother of God? The song was too much for him. Paul called to him as he ran to the balsams, half-tiptoeing along the pond edge, dodging pilgrims and water alike. He heard Paul's call but ran away despite it. He just needed a few minutes. Allison sang the powerful song written by Maria Parkinson: 'As... I kneel... before you..., As... I bow... my head in prayer... Ave... Maria, ... gratia plena... Ev'ry thought, ev'ry word... is lost in your embrace...' Rick disappeared into the balsams. A young lady from Nova Scotia, and hundreds of others watched his exit from the stage and his disappearance into the woods.

Yes, Therese Pierpont had in fact been studying Rick since he first jumped onto the stage to initiate the conference. She was hoping that God was not calling him to the priesthood. At the same time she was telling God that it was O.K. if he was calling him to the priesthood. She wanted to spend the rest of her life with that tall, handsome, gentle young man that looked more like an Indian brave in "I Will Fight No More Forever", than a former Union Carbide engineer. She knew that his demeanor, from the few times she had been with him now had all the indications of one potentially called to the priesthood. His evident meekness and his years of bravery on the front lines of the fight for life, combined with his still unmarried state spoke of a possible life-long dedication to God in the celibate life. Therese had been in love with two people in life. The first had become a priest. And now Rick. *Would she lose Rick? That is, would God gain Rick?* she thought. When Therese and her first love had parted, he went to the seminary, and she went to convent in Texas. She was the perfect novice. She was ready for a 100 years of hard work and service and prayer for her Lord, Jesus Christ. Then, her superiors, with all their concerns for social justice, left Jesus & Mary in the name of such social justice, putting the cart before the horse, and the convent floundered, and was disbanded by the Bishop. Therese found herself back in Nova Scotia with her family, helping in the family business. Suitors abounded, but none of them, she felt, were from God. So for years she had prayed, and worked.

Therese continued to stare at the balsam forest far to the left of the stage. She was replaying her life in her mind. She was happy, because life in a state of grace, free from mortal sin, is akin to heavenly things, amidst the crosses that one bears in day to day life. Yet, she found herself now longing for the warmth and companionship of a husband, and children, as never before. What was the meaning of this weekend? Had the chastisements spoken of at Akita, at LaSalette, and at Fatima finally come to the west? Not just the west, but to North America? Had the Canadian Dream, so proximate to the often-mentioned American Dream finally been burst? Was this the beginning of the demise of baseball, hot-dogs, and apple pie? What future could Therese have with Rick? What was the future of the United States economy, and the economy of their northern neighbor? The United States Congress can longer call Washington DC home. What does this mean? Will the rest of the world behave while the United States is staggering? Will any superpowers move against the United States now? Will the United States lose its sovereignty by default, or by inviting in the world powers to assist, never to leave? Will this usher in the New World Order brought to us in care of monied families of the world, their clubs and organizations, and their masons - the disposable worker bees?

"Therese. Therese?" said Anna Pierpont. Your father and I are going to see if we can get a cup of coffee at the Jordan Pond Restaurant. Would you like anything?" she said.

"No thanks mom. I'm O.K.," said Therese. She was thankful that her mother had snapped her out of thoughts of near despair. "I'll wait here Mom", she said. Therese realized that she had given in to evil thoughts in the last few minutes, instead of remembering that in the end, God wins! True, these things might soon come to pass, but she momentarily let her soul be dragged down with these ideas. She now remembered some light hearted thoughts from a priest, Father Daniel Anje, at a Notre Dame Medjugorje Conference several years before. The priest was reminding everyone that the message from Medjugorje was pure hope, not despair. In fact, Mary hardly ever mentioned "tough times" from Medjugorje. Her message was pray, hope, fast, penance, peace. Be ever joyful. Mary is with us. One could count the messages concerning tough times, or chastisements on one hand, amidst the thousands of messages of hope, and a call to return to her Son, Jesus Christ, and His Mercy. The priest told the audience that at one point Mary told the visionaries that she wanted them, the villagers, to have the happiest Christmas ever, she wanted them to be more joyful now than they had ever been. Wasn't that something said the priest, as if "She didn't know that there was a war going on all around them in Bosnia". Yes, there was war, but Mary was bringing the Scriptural message that if God is for us, who can be against us. Peace! Mir! Therese smiled inwardly and outwardly. She began to walk to the balsam forest to the left of the stage. She had seen Rick crying. She knew why he was crying. It was a killer song. What friend of Our Lady could stand this song, without buckling under the pressure to cry? One might cry because Our Lady's messages have gone largely unheeded. One might cry out for not having done more for Jesus and Mary, at whatever stage one's life is at. One might cry because of all the infighting that has taken place among Marian groups, visionaries, so-called visionaries, priests, religious, and lay persons, regarding Our Lady's supposed messages from heaven. Jealousy ruled the day. My visionaries. My messages. My church. My Pope, not your Pope. Fatima not Medjugorje. My apostolate. My money. My conference. We must have a merciful God, thought Therese as she approached the woods. He has put up with us for so long. Therese entered the sparse forest, filled 50 feet deep with pilgrims standing, sitting, and leaning on trees, listening to Allison Welday fill the valley with praises in song to God. She finally spotted Rick, and headed off in his direction. She was going to find out, in not so many words, what this young man was doing the rest of his life. After all, she thought, we have a Pope of Hope! God will need followers - mothers and fathers and children when he makes all things new again!

The phones at the Jordan Pond Restaurant were in constant use. Vacationers, now pilgrims were calling all over the island, all over New England, and all over North America. The cellular phones were in use too, hundreds of them. Calls were being made to loved ones and friends who might have been in danger from the recent calls of nature. The hurricane continued to pound the Florida Coast, half onshore, half offshore, and heading northward, leaving debris, death, and poverty in its wake. The earthquake victims on the East Coast were numerous. Washington, DC was no longer an operating city. Suburbs survived with bridge, road, and foundation damage everywhere, but many cities near the center of the quake were facing the same crisis as the nation's capitol. Fires and floods raged elsewhere in the country. So the pilgrims called distant places, and most received assurances that all was O.K. Some could not get through on their calls. Some callers received news that was hard to bear. Amidst the calls to check on loved ones and friends were the calls to urge loved ones and friends to hurry to the island! To pray! To come as quickly as they could to Bar Harbor. Many of these latter calls did not fall on deaf ears. They came from Ellsworth a half an hour away. They were coming from Portland, Bangor, Boston, Montpelier, and Nashua, hours away. And many others too, at more distant locations, were beginning their two and three-day journeys to come and honor Our Lady on God's island. The island towns were fast becoming ghost towns, as all roads now lead to the quaint Jordan Pond.

Several rangers came jogging, as fast as they could, with a long haired, partially balding gentleman, across the green in front of the stage, carrying with them thirty thousand dollars in state-of-the-art recording equipment. Starting in about 5 minutes from now, every word of the conference would be recorded, thanks to a phone call made by Alyssa Palmer, to her friend Joshua Pauley. Joshua was a middle aged man from Southeast Harbor who did most of the recording on the island for the New Age 'save the world and whales and stuff like that' soloist musicians and singing groups, whose albums went worldwide in large numbers. John was twice divorced, and had moved to the island in the late 1980s seeking freedom, his inner self, and a self-sustainable food supply independent of world economies and artificial fertilizers. John was free, except for alimony, child support, and taxes. His garden had grown over with weeds. He was watching a rerun of McHale's Navy when Alyssa had called him on her cellular phone. He took it as a sign from God. There had to be more to life than McHale's Navy while our country was on a fast track to Hell running from Mother Nature – no, running from God. Something had snapped in the inner recesses of Joshua's soul as soon as Alyssa had asked for his help on the phone. Joshua now believed in God, again. It was as if scales had fallen from the eyes of his soul. He packed his van as fast as he could, with enough tapes for a week of recording. As he ran out the door with the last microphone in his hand, his summer neighbors could hear him screaming, "Yes! Yes! Yes! I'm coming God! I'm back. I'm back. I'm coming! I'm coming Mary! Hold on! I'm sorry! I'm sorry! God, I'm sorry! The middle aged hippie jumped into his van, started the engine, and skidded around his circular driveway. Looking both ways, he darted out into the road a little too quickly. He came to a screeching halt. His hand painted sign, which served as the arm holding up his mailbox, was stuck in his mind, making him sick. He had babies on his mind. Two dead babies that he had helped bring to conception on this very island that never made it home, at least to life on earth. He backed into his driveway, and then some more. He stared at the sign: 'PRO-CHOICE PAULEY'. There were whales and sailboats on the sign too. "Damn the whales" he said. "Save the babies. Oh God, I'm sorry my children", he screamed as he ran over his mailbox and sign and continued on in a hurry for a date with God at Jordan Pond. The demons were screaming too, though they had not yet had their exorcise, they knew that they would soon be forced to flee from this aging hippie. Yes, this hippie who by the power of the Holy Spirit, through the intercession of the Virgin Mary, through the prayers of his first wife, and his mother had just come home to rest in Him. Besides, Our Lady needed a "sound man". Joshua was available. Joshua's tapes would soon be traveling the world to help a multitude of others.

****

In the vast crowd on the lawn of Jordan Pond was an Amish family with their Baptist friends. They had come all the way from the Ohio Heartland to be here, where they knew God wanted them to be. They pondered the events of recent days in their hearts. What did it all mean? Oh, they were thrilled that God had brought them there. They felt like they never wanted to go home. They had come to more fully understand Jesus Christ and the Church he founded so long ago. They had come to understand the role of His Mother in calling back all of mankind back to Jesus Christ, while there was yet time!

Isaac never would see that Belgium Horse harness. The Harpers never would see Glacier National Park. Who in the world though, would wish to be anywhere else, but at Acadia National Park, Jordan Pond, where God was working his prodigies, and one more time calling out to his people before the Advent of His Justice! Isaac Yoder passed another bead through his fingers...

The man from Wheeling with the '79 Ford Station Wagon was away from his friends at the moment. He had just driven 600 miles to come to this conference, and now he was up walking on the mountains surrounding Jordan Pond praying his Rosary! He was crying as he was walking along, nudging pine cones off the trail with his shoes, pulling pine needles off the branches of the stunted trees he was passing along the way. He felt all alone in the world. He missed his deceased wife. He missed his children who didn't want to be around him and his Catholicity. The kids had scorned him as he invited them all to come with him to Acadia to the conference. One of his daughters, Megan, her husband Don and their children had changed their minds and had just crossed the bridge to Mount Desert Isle. Ralph Piccarreta had no idea he was about to see his daughter in the middle of an island off the coast of Maine. Of all of his children, he thought that she would be the least inclined to ever pray again. Soon Megan and her family would be praying a Rosary.

****

Paul Bohatch was trying to turn most everything he could about the conference over to Rick Tremont. He didn't feel like he deserved to be a part of it anymore. He felt quite inadequate in doing what delegating he had been doing in these first few hours of the conference. Rick Tremont and two priests had to about drag him back onto the stage. They were telling him that he needed to give a short talk on the circumstances that had brought about his initiating this conference. It was those circumstances exactly that he wished to avoid. Rick and the priests prevailed. Paul was about to address the audience that had now grown to about 6500 people since three o'clock. Several hundred of those people did not yet know what was taking place at Jordan Pond. "Dear Friends, could we please say together a prayer to the Holy Spirit. 'Come Holy Spirit, come by the means of the powerful intercession of the Blessed Virgin Mary, Your well Beloved Spouse. Jesus, Mary, and Joseph, I love you, save souls. Save priests souls. And we ask you Lord to come to the aid of those in our country now suffering from natural disasters" said Paul. "Several days ago I was at home like many of you looking forward to a trip to Acadia National Park with my family. We've tried to come camping here when we could afford to in the last eight years. We've probably been here six times now – from Ohio, Steubenville. The last several times we were here, I wanted to go down to the Bar Harbor Times and run an ad something like this: 'Rosary will be prayed at Bar Harbor Campground, 8 PM, site XYZ, July 1-10th'. I never did and it bugged me. That's all I was going to do several days ago - finally place that ad. I probably would have if I had a campsite number, but they don't take reservations at Bar Harbor Campground! So, I thought, hey, we could meet with people in the park! I can place an ad for that now. As I would guess a fair number of you have, I have given out a good number of books, cassettes, videotapes, and so forth on Medjugorje. I support a handful of the Marian Centers in the country, like many of you. Just before leaving, I received three faxes concerning a reported fax from Medjugorje dated June 30, 1998. I will come back to that in a moment. In light of the faxes I thought, well, we'll call it a Medjugorje Conference. I bet we can get a few dozen people. After all, they'll be several thousand vacationers there each day, and a fair percentage of them will have heard of or already believe in Medjugorje. Some of those people are bound to have a story to tell, I thought. Well, here we are. Now, in light of the faxes I received, the purpose, at least in light of current events, is defunct, in a way. However, as I'm sure many of you have heard something of such faxes by now, I will cover the subject in case it has created confusion for anyone. It was reported in one fax circulating among Marian groups and the laity that the 8th secret given to the visionaries in Medjugorje was imminent. Furthermore, the spiritual director of Marie (one of the six visionaries) - Father Andrieu had been told by Marie that in ten days the event concerned in this 8th secret was to come to pass. Marie, as requested by Our Lady years before, had pre-selected Father Andrieu to be the one to pray and fast for seven days after she had divulged the secret to him at Our Lady's instructions. On June 30th, a few days ago, it may have been that Father Andrieu passed on the information concerning the 8th secret to the world after his seven days of fasting and prayer. I say may have been, because the original reported fax was incomplete and by and large illegible. The word America did appear in the original supposed fax from Medjugorje. I received two follow-up faxes that were passed on to me, tenth hand, mind you, that the fax from Medjugorje was, in effect, a fraud. Now you know more than I do on that subject. Perhaps more light will be shed on that during the conference. It does appear that the validity of the 8th secret is a moot point, as our country has now already passed a point of no return in regards to many areas, in light of the catastrophes upon us. In particular, CBCN news has just broken a story from leading insurance analysts that the backbone of the insurance industry in the United States is broken. This news comes to us when Hurricane Michael is just now beginning to push northward with its destruction. We are being told also by CBCN news that the hurricane is a 500-year storm. The National Hurricane Center in Florida is not sure if there has ever been one like it. They're calling it the Hurricane from Hell. Our job is to pray, hope, and don't worry, as Padre Pio has told us, and Our Lady too, in effect. Since CBCN news is here already, and I see others that look like they are reporters arriving and setting up cameras and so forth, I would like to put it on the record that the message from Medjugorje is a happy one filled with hope. If there are any doomsayer groupies in the audience, I am afraid that you have come to the wrong conference. If there are some sticky situations for the world to be tested with, perhaps now, perhaps in the near future, and if Our Lady has on rare occasions mentioned them, it is not to cast us in to fear and doubt, but to walk us safely through the quagmire that we have created from our own sins. She wouldn't be appearing the world over if there was no hope. She is the Queen of Peace, looking after us like her little children. I have one last item to mention. One of our priest friends here would like to storm heaven with prayers from Cadillac Mountain this evening, after our gathering here. If any of you would like to join him, he is going to be staying up there all night. I know the signs say closed at midnight, but we have it from a good source that the park rangers will be home in bed this evening, getting ready for tomorrow. We will be here for two more days, starting tomorrow at 9 AM. We'll have schedules for everyone tomorrow too. Thank you for coming, and God bless you!" said Paul. "Oh, one other thing, if you will. Please keep my family in your prayers. We've just been through a war, in part because of what I wanted to do in regards to this gathering, and in part because of my temper. God has brought us out of the depths in the last day or so, but we need your prayers. Thanks, God bless you," said Paul.

Father Green, Paul Bohatch, and Rick Tremont had a hard time convincing Louis Longmire to get up on the stage so quickly after he had come forth to offer his services as a speaker. Yes, it was his idea to go up to the stage, and speak with the people in charge, after Rick Tremont had invited the audience to do so. Yet, Louis was still quite frightened at the prospect of turning state's evidence, as this sharp lawyer framed the thought in his mind. Was he really ready? His wife and children were in the crowd. He had come to the gathering with them, by accident, he thought. Now he knew without a doubt that Our Lady of Medjugorje, this Virgin Mary, Mother of God, had invited him. He talked with Father Green, yes, this Father Green from the airport, about his situation. Father Green told him that this day and yesterday had the hand of God all over it and that Louis was a part of this story also. Father told him that he was confident that his story would be a great balm for many broken hearts and families, and would perhaps lead hundreds or thousands of others away from the same circumstances that Louis had found himself in until yesterday. He walked to the front of the stage with Rick Tremont, and Rick introduced him.

"Good evening. As Rick Tremont has told you, my name is Louis Longmire. I'm married with six children, and my wife and children are among you now. This is the first time in many months that our family has been together. I have been living the life of a pagan playboy in this time, though I was raised a Catholic. I was heading here initially to meet my live-in girlfriend and to buy as large a piece of real estate as I could find on this island in the next few days. I am a multi-millionaire, and in retrospect, as I have learned in the last few days, the only problem that I don't have is a financial problem. I am in need of God's mercy and forgiveness more than all of you, I am sure, because I had taken my most precious gift, my family, and scattered those that I love to the wind. I have cried very few times in my life, but I, I think that has changed. I seem to, I..., seem to be having a hard time talking to you now, amidst my tears, and the great tightness in my throat, that feels like it is strangling me." Louis was speaking in broken phrases, as he fought back the emotions overwhelming him at this crucial point in his life. "As hard as this is for me now, to speak to you, please pray for my family, because their burden must be even greater, as I seem to have become an expert at inflicting pain. I took a circuitous route in coming here, having been away on business and pleasure in several cities in the last few days. Most memorable now is my stop in Seattle, where God sent a great criminal lawyer, Ramon Nogales, an old friend of mine, to "accidentally" meet up with me at the airport..." Louis was now crying audibly, with long sobs between phrases, and sometimes between individual words. "God, in his mercy, sent this angel to me... He sent Ramon to me to pull me from the vomit of my sins..." Louis paused again in sobs. "Ramon was at the airport to meet me. I did not know this initially, and he never told me. Circumstances told me, well after our meeting. I could have decked him if I had known why he was there. But then, you see, God knew this, so he sent a crafty lawyer. A crafty lawyer as cunning as a serpent, and wise as a fox. I only wish that at this moment Ramon and his family were here. You see, this saint of God still thinks that I am on the road to Hell"...sobs... I haven't called him yet.... I... Oh God here he is, and his family" said Louis. Louis was looking down in front of the stage, where Ramon and his family had just now made their way up to. Louis went to his knees in tears. His wife and older children were in tears farther off in the crowd. Ramon had seen Louis' family. He whispered to his wife their whereabouts and a few other words. She and the children walked off to find them, to comfort them, and Ramon stepped up onto the stage to be with Louis. He lifted Louis back to his feet, from his kneeling position. Louis cried into the microphone, though not intentionally for three minutes. Ramon just stood there holding him, with a Rosary in his hand, praying silently. "This is my dear friend Ramon Nogales", whimpered Louis Longmire into the microphone finally.

"Good evening" said Ramon.

"Here I am balling in front of you, and I haven't even let you in on the story yet", snuffled Louis, with a crying laugh. "A few days ago," sniff, "a few days ago, I ran into Ramon" said Louis. "Oh God, he seemed so surprised to see me," said Louis, nearly laughing. "We talked for hours. Small talk mostly. I should have known something was up. It wasn't until long in the discussion that he asked me about my family, whom he knows quite well, as we once worked together. Years ago our families spent a lot of time together. He knew it might ruin his chance to convert me by bringing it up right away, so he put aside such talk for the most part. God, we had a boring conversation", Louis sniffled. "I'm saying goodbye to Louis, happy as a liar could be, and I'm dashing off to get in line to board my jet, and uh, sniff, Ramon must have been praying real hard, because he shouts out 'Louis, hold on, Come 'ere for a minute', or something like that. I jumped out of line and dashed over to him. I said 'Yeah, what's up buddy'. Now Ramon still didn't have his act together, I think he was waiting for Moses to speak or something, because he didn't know what to say to me for a few seconds. Sniff. He stalls and drags me over to a bench, and puts his briefcase down, and God or maybe Mary of Medjugorje must have jumped in at this point, because Ramon was now on fire with his smooth talking courtroom craftiness that no other human being possesses. As he's fiddling with his briefcase, he said to me 'Louis, I wonder if you can do me a big favor'. I told him 'Anything buddy, just name it', as I'm looking over my shoulder to my gate and jet ready to take off. I almost told him to call me and ran off to my jet at that point. Ramon gave me this big sob story about how he was helping out this Catholic group called the Mary Foundation, and how he wanted my advice - no, he needed my advice. I told him 'Sure, I said anything Ramon', and I meant it. He pulls out this book, this one here," said Louis, his sniffing dissipating. It's called 'Pierced by A Sword'. If you've got any relatives who have walked away from God or the Faith, I highly recommended it.

Well, anyhow, I felt like telling Ramon, who I now considered an ex-friend at this point, to take a hike. I didn't need any of that God stuff. But, at this stage in my life I had become a good liar, and we once were the best of friends, and I did tell him 'anything', so I said 'sure, I'll read it, no problem'. Oh, I forgot. Sniff. - He didn't just ask me to read it. *He asked me to study it.* **Oh, God, I studied it**. A few days and several more airports later I found God again. I met a priest in Boston, where I was waiting for a flight to meet this lady whom I said was not my wife. The priest was Father Albert Green. *That's him over there.* I went to confession for the first time in many years. Now I'm a broken man, sniff, but I think that's where God wanted me. With the grace of God, my wife, children, and I are now going to piece our family back together. I can't say much more, because, sniff, I, I can hardly stand up right now. I want to tell you though, that perhaps my biggest detraction from going to confession and starting the hike back to God and my family was guilt. I mean, I didn't know how my wife and children could ever forgive me, let alone God. I had tremendous false joy in my sin, but all along I knew I had chosen, well, Hell, I guess."

A man in mortal sin cannot be happy. It is impossible. I felt like I was damned forever, even though I was living and acting as a happy-go-lucky lawyer and playboy. I was in despair, driven by my passions and desires for material things. I felt like I could never go home - to my family or God. I felt, I don't know - I felt like I was possessed and it was impossible for me to, like I said, go home.... I felt dirty. I, I was dirty... Sniff. That book though.... Sniff. This one....", he said holding 'Pierced By A Sword' up in his right hand. "Without Ramon, this book, and Father Green, I... Sniff. Sniff. Look, if any of you out there feel that you cannot go home to God or family... don't buy that lie. Father Green helped me in such a way that he cannot imagine in the Sacrament of Confession. My sins are forgiven... Christ told the apostles "Forgive men's sins and they are forgiven..." Who can do that today? Our priests, and our priests only. Jesus Christ has said this. Why don't we believe?... Sniff. I was helped most by Father when he told me that, in a way, Christ has a special love for me, that in human terms, is a great love, a love - again in human terms, that is greater for me, than for many others. Sniff. You see, I once was lost, but.... Sniff. But, now, but now..., am found. To Jesus through Mary... She's just our Mom, that's all. She brought me home to Jesus

Christ. Who can speak against that?" Louis burst out into a fit of tears and bent over again - this man that 'doesn't cry'.

A half a minute later, when he regained control of himself, he spoke again. "If you don't mind, sniff, I'm going to end here, because I can hardly stand up for the crying and wrenching in my whole body. If I was a praying man, which I now hope to become, I would say that it was the disease of sin being wrenched from my soul. I thank you for listening to me, sniff, and I hope that my story might help some of you. Men, if any of you have done what I have done, please, sniff, please go home to your families. Please pray for me and my family, and my friend Ramon and his family. We will pray for you. Thank you" said Louis, and then left the stage with Ramon.

After Louis' brief talk, there was dead silence for a few moments. Then, a solitary person in the vast crowd began to applaud. Do not the angels rejoice for the conversion of one sinner? Then the conversion of this sinner, an individual but representative cross section in a way of the western world deserved great rejoicing. A few others joined in. A few seconds more and over six thousand people were clapping, themselves rejoicing with the angels of heaven. The applause lasted for six minutes. Louis had left out so many wonderful God incidences and adjoining miracles from the last few days, but they would be brought to light once again - on Sunday, when the crowd, many thousands of them who had not yet heard his story would hear it for the first time. Those who had heard him this evening would demand to hear from him again, as if Louis was a mirror in which they saw themselves for the first time, and were reflected back to God as quickly as one can say the word remorse. Not everyone in attendance was a virgin or chaste husband, wife, or obedient child. There were sinners in the crowd, sinners who were beginning to now wish to walk on the straight and narrow road to God. God "demanded" it, as a freewill offering from everyone. The country and its disasters and now suffering people demanded it. And Louis demanded it, in his broken appeal to the hearts, minds, and bodies of everyone present. He had exposed the little man behind the curtain in the Land of Oz. That particular carpetbagger of Oz, however, had the best of intentions, and in the end gave all that he could to aid his friends. The carpetbagger that Louis had actually exposed however, was none other than the devil and his deceitful, lying, passionate ways. So many that day were on the yellow brick road to the precipice, running with Louis in the lead, formerly. It was time for everyone to click their heels and go home - not to leave Mount Desert Island this day – but to go home, to turn back to God. **Our souls are restless until they rest in Thee (God)**, as the good doctor said.

The conference was beginning to take on form. More than half of the employees of Jordan Pond Restaurant and gift shop had become active participants in the conference, though not abandoning their posts for the most part. Truth be known, the numbers were higher. Half of these employees had already undergone a tremendous conversion, and were now praying people, no longer New Agers, fallen away Christians, or people of little or no faith. Half of these employees were now ready to take up their cross and follow Him to the end. As for the other half, they were well on their way to the Wellspring of all Hope. Furthermore, these summer residents of this beautiful island were somewhat closer to the weather reports, news reports, and now wholesome gossip than were most of the pilgrims and former vacationers. They were not unaware of the current state of their country. They were not unaware of the miraculous weather that they were experiencing either. They were looking out from their buildings of employment, toward the stage that was only hours old, and miraculous in itself. They were aware that great thunderstorms were raging to their north, south, east, and west - in Canada and in the land of the formerly free and formerly brave. The many park rangers and other Park Service personnel were also touched by the events of day one of this miraculous gathering.

After Louis' talk, Rick Tremont again took to the microphone and let the crowd know that they were going to pray the Five Sorrowful Mysteries of the Rosary at this point, followed by music from Allison Welday, and then the Holy Sacrifice of the Mass. That would conclude the evening, with the conference taking up where it left off, tomorrow, Saturday, at 9 AM. He reminded them that Father Albert Green would be spending the evening up on Cadillac Mountain for an evening of prayer for the conversion of our nation and world, and for those suffering in the current chastisements.

****

It was almost midnight now, and thousands were gathered with Father Green on Cadillac Mountain, praying the Rosary, having small informal talks amongst each other, as well as raising joyful songs unto the Lord. Many had brought their musical instruments with them, mostly guitars, violins, harmonicas, and a few other instruments. Many groups, large and small, were heading off to nearby knolls and peaks to bed down for the evening, or to have some quiet time to themselves. Many hundreds remained right in the immediate area of Cadillac Mountain. All told, there were over a thousand souls staying on the peaks of Cadillac that evening. Many had gone back to their campsites and hotels earlier in the evening to gather supplies or check on their camp. Paul and Barbara Bohatch and their family had gone back to Bar Harbor Campground, as well as the Pierponts, Rick Tremont, the Shermans, and others, and had returned with sleeping gear to Cadillac. Mrs. Sherman, however, wanted to stay behind at the campground, and suggested to Paul & Barbara that she would be happy to stay and watch over their sleeping children if they both wanted to go up to the mountain. They jumped at the idea, as it had actually been years since they had a date! Many of those who had already spoken or were yet to speak at the conference also headed up to Cadillac sometime after the conference had ended. Hundreds of pilgrims and vacationers - now converted pilgrims who were late arriving on the island today who had not attended the conference had also gone to the summit of Cadillac, as the word of the conference had spread like wildfire to all parts of the island, mainland, and points afar.

There were many campfires going across the mountaintops, a first for Acadia in this formerly off-limits to camping area. There was a myriad of stars in the sky, and yet the fireworks display - the thunderstorms pounding the East Coast in the last day had not begun to dissipate at points distant. Nova Scotia and most of New England were still experiencing the deluge. Mount Desert Island had some fair winds blowing through from time to time, but the miracle continued - storms all around, visible lightning strikes could now be seen to the North, South, East, and West. However, it was clear skies for miles around the island. It was even a great night for shooting stars. Everyone on Cadillac knew that they were witnessing the power of God. Everyone on Cadillac knew that Jesus and Mary were smiling down upon them as they continued their Rosaries, songs, and other prayers and talk of and with God.

From a distance, earlier in the day, Paul Bohatch thought he saw a Franciscan brother, or priest, west of the stage along the banks of Jordan Pond. There was another somewhat shorter man with him. They were in Paul's sight for a few seconds, and were gone, lost in the crowd, balsams, poplars, and spruce. When he saw them, his heart leapt furiously for just a moment, but he forced the physical and mental aspects of his thought far from him. It was vain of him to even think of it. After all, prudence would preclude visionaries, be they lay persons or priests from attending this irresponsibly unplanned event that was at least in part, a thorn in the side of many Marian groups at this time. Anything could go wrong at this event. There were no controls, speakers had not been properly screened and questioned as to their orthodoxy or beliefs, and accommodations were an afterthought. It had taken many groups years of praying and fasting to finally have the grace of having one or more of the Medjugorje visionaries or priests to speak at or attend a Marian Conference in the United States.

Paul was thinking of such things, sitting around a campfire with 500 other Christians who had just finished the Rosary.

Rick Tremont and Therese Pierpont were hiking the hills and valleys close by, hand in hand. They had just finished the Five Glorious Mysteries of the Rosary together. Rick was telling Therese how much the tops of the hills around Cadillac reminded him of being on Podbro, or Krizevac (Cross Mountain) in Medjugorje. Podbro was the hill where Our Lady first appeared to the visionaries on June 24th, 1981. "Yeah, these rocky footpaths and boulders scattered everywhere are just like the ones on Podbro and Krizevac. "Oh, God" said Rick, stubbing his toe on one of the very rocks he was looking down at.

"You O.K. Rick?" said Therese.

"It's nothing. I've got another foot", he said smiling in the moonlight. Moonlight. "The East Coast is awash in thunderstorms and flooding and we've got moonlight. I feel like heaven has lowered a ladder to this place. Look - another shooting star" said Rick.

"When we get back to the summit, let's try to find out what's happening in North America with the disasters. That was a radio I saw you with before, wasn't it?" said Therese.

"Yes" said Rick," short wave, AM, and FM", he said. "You know the media is only feeding us a portion of the truth, as we were speaking about before - along with all of the propaganda. I don't think we'll even be able to trust the media to divulge to us the major events that will be taking place in the world in the next few days, weeks, months, and years", he said. "I think that we're at a turning point now, a turning point that the One World and New Age crowd have been waiting for. Christians have been waiting for this era too, this era preceding the reign of the Immaculate Heart of Mary that she spoke about at Fatima. Unfortunately, we've got a few battles ahead of us, but its always been the same for us Christians since day one", he said.

"You know," said Therese, "I wonder what kind of government you're going to have in the next few days. I'm assuming your President and Vice President are alive, and your senators and congressman, whom I am sure, are flocking to West Virginia at this time according to the news. I think things are over, as the Americans have known them. I can only imagine that your president is now going to be bringing in more and more of the world's military forces, the United Nations perhaps, to subdue your people. God knows what he is doing though; we can count on that. And we have Saint Antony of the Desert to remind us that 'When the enjoyments of the body are weak, then is the power of the soul strong'. America will start to grow in holiness, perhaps starting this day, as things seem to get worse economically, materially, and politically" said Therese, finding a large round boulder to climb up on. "Let's sit down up here for a while Rick, and look at the stars and the ocean."

Cadillac Mountain does not have a rival hill anywhere on the eastern coast of the United States. Tucked away in the heart of Acadia National Park, yet, only a few thousand feet from the Atlantic Ocean, it offers vistas of Northern Spruce and hardwood forests, the Atlantic Ocean and enchanted historical bays and coves. In view also are mountain ranges in central and northern Maine, a dark evening sky with a myriad of stars on cloudless evenings, and a stark beauty that is powerful enough to spark life and hope back into a tired soul. Wildlife abounds. It's the tallest mountain on the East Coast of the Americas, north of Rio de Janeiro, Brazil. The mountain and its vistas are most impressive at dusk and dawn, yet evening is a special time up there too. Never before had there been an evening like this on Cadillac Mountain. Storms still raged here and there, but none posed an immediate threat to Acadia.

"I have the same feeling that I've had when I've been on Mounts Podbro and Krizevac," said Rick, as they sat down on the boulder together. Two figures sat by a fire burning about 100 feet away, they were talking in subdued voices, sometimes happy, sometimes solemn, but their words were not recognizable. "One feels a great sense of Peace in Medjugorje. It's like having one foot in heaven and one on earth. That's the way I've often described Medjugorje. You know I didn't want to leave each time I went to Medjugorje. Few people do. You feel the battle between Heaven and Hell there too. Our Lady has said to one of the visionaries there that wherever she goes, Satan follows. You see evidence of this too. "The bad guy knows where Medjugorje is too", he said.

"I know, I've read where Satan appeared to Emiliana there. Our Lady came shortly thereafter and explained that She wanted Emiliana to know how real Satan was, how real the battle was. She was scared out of her wits when he appeared to her," said Therese.

Rick asked Therese if he could put his arm around her. She nodded with a smile. She followed in suit.

On my second trip to Medjugorje, in June of 1993, we pulled into Medjugorje on bus after midnight. We had been passing in and around the war zones for hours. We saw the wake of destruction in Croatia and Bosnia. The buses came to a halt, their air brakes expired with a loud noise, and then the air was filled with machine gun fire all around us. I was thinking, great, we've made it this far to be mowed down right here in Medjugorje. The first pilgrims to go. My guess is that some of the pilgrims had need of a laundry service upon hearing the machine gun fire. It was pitch black, because of the potential for night air attacks, and everyone knew the Serbs and Muslims weren't using rock salt as ammunition. Real bullets. Our tour leader, who bravely got off the bus to investigate, came back on and told us "nothing to worry about, they're celebrating our arrival". I could have done without the 21-gun salute. Anyhow, as we're getting off the bus, I spoke up some and mentioned that if anyone would like to go up Mount Krizevac in a little while that I was going to head up. A fellow Don something or other from Upper Sandusky, Ohio said he'd go up with me. I must have missed Don, but I wound up going up with a young American high school senior living in Germany with his family - his dad was in the military. We went up barefoot. It was no problem for me, my feet are tough from playing soccer barefoot, but he about killed himself. His feet were all bloody. He told me in a subsequent letter that he had broken a toe. To bring this wagon train back to full circle, I'll get back to Don now - and the fact that you really do feel the battle between good and evil there. Oh, by the way, I had never been more scared in my life, going up Krizevac there, even though I had this huge linebacker high school senior to protect me from the enemy, be they corporal or spiritual. It was the spiritual ones that I most feared. The path up Krizevac is long and hard, even in the daytime. At night it takes an eternity to get to the top. When you get to that cross though, you feel like you're knocking on the door to heaven. It's great. I could live up there in a tent for the rest of my life," said Rick.

"Do you know what a tangent is Rick?" said Therese with a smile and a laugh.

Rick had a tendency to go off on these geometrical figures. "Oh yeah, you're forgetting I'm an engineer. I specialize in tangents. Back to Don though. Don missed me somehow that night, and not finding me, went back to his room and went to sleep. When I saw him the next day, he told me about not finding me. Then he told me why he was not about to go up by himself. Don was also on his second trip to Medjugorje. On his last trip he climbed up Krizevac on a pitch-black night late in the evening. There was no one around. He wove himself by shear luck through the streets of Medjugorje, past rock homes, gravel roads and drives, potholes, barking dogs, and unpeopled alleys. He finally found the main path up Krizevac. He had just started his ascent, when he began to hear a howling, like a wolf, but a more sinister howling. His hair stood on end he said. He, like me, had never been more scared in his life. The howling got closer and closer. He knew that what was howling was not of this world, and he did not want to meet it. Not that he necessarily thought he could beat such a thing in a foot race mind you, but his instinct was to run as he was blurting out the Saint Michael prayer at the same time. He fell a dozen times before he even made it to the first Station of the Cross going up the mountain. He was bleeding from several cuts now. He was a grown educated man with a large family back in the corn fields of western Ohio, and he felt like his heart was going to burst and he would never see his family again. He staggered on. He ran on. The howling was so loud now that he almost felt like it was on top of him. He fell down again and looked up, and there's this beast staring him right in the eye. Taller than a man, looking half human and half straight from Hell, Don swears that the presence oozed hate and slime and fear. The thing was on fire, and flames were leaping behind it and all around it. Its ears looked like Spock's, and its eyes were fiery green. The hands were claws, and the feet too. Then the howl came again, and Don fell down in fear, praying harder now to Jesus and Mary and Saint Michael. He anticipated that the thing would step on his neck and crush him as he had gone down onto the ground. He felt a burning breathing on his neck. He remembered that Jesus said that the only one we had to fear was the One who has the power over men's souls, God Himself. He stood up and looked the thing in the eyes and said 'Get behind me Satan. You're a jerk'. That didn't work.

Therese, who had wanted to change the subject for the last few minutes now, let out a frightened laugh. "You're a jerk?" she said.

"Yeah, that's what he told me," said Rick. He said he was having a hard time thinking of what to say to this dude's face. Then he screamed out "In the name of Jesus Christ I command you to be gone you idiot!" said Rick.

"No, he didn't" said Therese. "Not you idiot".

"You idiot" said Rick. He said it was a combination of his being at a loss for words, scared to Hell, and angry at this ghoulish thing. He said he really did want to let this devil know he was an idiot" said Rick. "The thing disappeared. Don was at the cross ten minutes later, praying at two in the morning with a dozen pilgrims from Ireland who were pouring out their hearts to Jesus & Mary, crying for their country and families. He said it was the greatest night in his life, but he wouldn't do it again alone without an armed guard, preferably a priest with a bottle of holy water of recent vintage" said Rick. "Anyhow, several things having a similar flair like this happened to me over there, but I guess I'd best defer such talk, you being 'womanfolk' and all, and the hour being late!" he said.

"Yeah, Rick, lets talk about the weather" said Therese. "Listen", she said. "What are those guys praying?"

"Zdravo Marijo, milosti puna, Gospodin s tombom...

"It's the Hail Mary. I think they're praying the Rosary in Croatian. I can't believe it," said Rick.

....blagoslovljena ti medju zenama I blagoslovljen plod utrobe tvoje, Isus. Sveta Marijo, Majko Bozja, moli za nas gresnike sada I na cas smrti nase. Amen", went the prayers of the two men by the fire nearby. Others were walking in the area from time to time. A couple speaking French walked by on the path next to Rick and Therese. They said hello to each other.

"They're just finishing up the Rosary," said Rick. I don't think they say the Hail Holy Queen at the end like we do in North America. Let's go say hello. I've got a strange feeling about this," said Rick.

Rick and Therese made their way over the campfire. They weren't the same willows of Podbro, but the vegetation consisting of short scrub pines, blueberry bushes, spruce, and briars reminded one of similarly fashioned growth on the hills around Medjugorje. The men were now laughing in low voices. The two by the fire glanced up the hill at the same time and saw Rick and Therese making their way down to them. It was now obvious that the taller of the two men was a Franciscan. "Gospodin s vama! (The Lord be with you!)" said the Franciscan in the brown habit.

"I s duhom tvojim (and also with you)" said Rick in his best Croatian. Therese felt like she was in a movie. She was awestruck that Rick understood the words.

"You know Croatian?", she whispered.

"I had a Croatian/English prayer book in jail for four years. I know a lot of Croatian prayers and common words and phrases. If they ask us to dinner though we could be in trouble. I might end up ordering sneakers or something," said Rick.

"Welcome" said the Franciscan.

"Welcome" said the other man.

Rick and Therese exchanged polite greetings, and then introduced themselves.

"Ah, Rick, I was going to, what you say, have a word with you. Good to meet you. I am Father Zdenko. This young man I believe you know, Boris Baric, a friend of Our Lady, from Medjugorje. He now lives in Portland, Maine, with his young family. They all shook hands.

"Well, what brings you to Acadia National Park", quipped Rick with a broad smile.

"Blueberries. They are in season," said the priest. "We wanted to see if they were as good as ours back home! "Now we find we are at a Medjugorje Conference!", joked Father.

"Please, pull up a Rock" said Boris, in better English than Father Zdenko. "Please have a seat".

Rick and Therese found places to sit around the fire. Father and Boris sat back down too.

"Boris, as we understand, your visions with Our Lady continue daily at 6:40 PM Croatian time, 12:40 PM Eastern Standard Time. Can I ask you a silly question in this regards?" said Therese.

Boris nodded. "Sure".

"Does Our Lady know we are here? I'm saying that figuratively, because I know she does. And I know God knows that we are here. I'm not sure what I am trying to say...," said Therese.

The two Croats spoke together for several seconds. Father Zdenko then said "Do you mean does Our Lady, ah, let see, ... recognize this conference, is she happy with it?" said Father.

"Exactly" said Therese.

"I asked her that question today before the conference began. You see, we were so close to this place, but we did not know it was going to be, um, to be held here on this island. We heard about if from friends last night. Father was visiting with us and with your people here in this country to raise funds for the Church in Croatia and Bosnia, and for the orphans. We are what you would say, that is, we just happened to be near – in Portland. We did not plan to ... attend. We did not know. Oh, you did not know either! Well, because of this, I did ask Our Lady what this was...about. I asked her this today. She smiled. She no..., um, no answer came. She smiled. She does that sometimes...," said Boris. "So, I don't know your answer".

"Father, do you know if the world has supposedly been warned of the 8th secret. Is that what we are seeing happening in our country now?" said Rick.

"I am the wrong priest to answer that, I am no..., not Father Andrieu. We cannot call Medjugorje at this time. Something is happening that we..., we do not know exactly", he said.

"Boris. Do you know?" said Rick.

"I asked Our Lady this too. Guess what. She smiled. She told me I asked too many questions when I should be, ...that is, I need to pray more, and um, talk less. Yes. She told me to pray for the victims of the disasters and for the conversion of the United States. She did say that. And all of the west. She said she holds all the victims close to Her, but she needs our prayers. Pray always she said. Just like Jesus said. Pray always" said Boris.

"Father, would you and Boris like to speak to the pilgrims tomorrow?" said Rick.

Boris spoke first. "I, I ask Virgin Mary, before I speak, wherever, if she wants me to do this, wherever. Before any conference or other place. I don't think she knows where Acadia National Park is," said Boris laughing. The others joined in. "No, seriously, I don't have an answer from her. At this time, now, I have to say no thank you. Please also, don't tell anyone we are here, or the crowds, will..., they will not leave us. We will be there though. Maybe Our Lady will let us know - that is to speak. For now, we have come as pilgrims like you. This is all very strange to

Father and I. I think Our Lady is very happy though. I think she brought everyone here. The devil is so..., uh, cunning - tricky, though, and we have to be sure. What if this is not from God? There are many people here...," said Boris.

Rick felt uneasy. *What if he had become part of Satan's plan? What if this was Satan's Conference?*

"Mir Gospodnji bio vazda s vama" (The peace of the Lord be with you always) said Father Zdenko, who had just read Rick's heart and soul. "You are working for God Rick, put those, put such other thoughts far from you. What do you see, above, that is, above this island?" he said.

"Stars" said Rick.

"What do you see everywhere else?" said Father.

"Storms" said Rick.

"Our Lady told Boris that the two of us would not need a tent for this trip. She said, "The weather is, ah, how you say, the weather is ideal, no rain" said Father. "Later, when Boris told me, I asked him three times about this. I asked him if she'd seen the radar slides, um, pictures. The rain is hard everywhere but here", he said. "Our Lady knows the pilgrims have come. *This is her conference.* She is protecting this place."

The four pilgrims spoke for a half an hour longer, after which Father heard the confessions of Rick and Therese. As Rick and Therese were heading back to Cadillac's summit, where her relatives and others were still praying, talking, and singing, Father called out to the two of them. "Rick, Therese, Gospa (Our Lady) said that she blesses you and your future children."

Marriage is your, uh, your vocation Rick, not the priesthood.

"Thank you father, they both said simultaneously. Good night Father. Goodnight Boris."

"You told him you had thoughts of marrying me?" said Therese in wonderment.

"Not me. I told him we just met!" said Rick. "Did you talk about marriage?"

"Not me" said Therese.

"I didn't even mention the seminary or priesthood," said Rick. "They say he is another Saint Francis, and another Padre Pio combined. I think I believe the rumors now. That's the third time he has prayed over me in the last five years now. Something profound has happened each time. About this marriage thing..."

"Rather rude of him, don't you think?" said Therese beaming with joy.

"Well, Therese. To tell you the truth, I don't want you to be an old maid," said Rick. "Oh, God, Therese, will you marry me?" he said, turning several shades of red in the moonlight.

"Yes, Rick. I think our marriage has been arranged by Heaven. I'm not going to argue with Heaven", she said.

"The Church will have us wait at least a half a year to prepare for marriage" said Rick. "But your parents, how are we going to tell them. They'll think we're loonies", he said.

"No, not quite. My parents know the holiness and sanctity of Father Zdenko. If they can have a word with him they'll understand" said Therese.

"But we've been asked to be silent on their visit here" said Rick.

"For now" said Therese. "How long do you think this Franciscan can hide himself in his habit with thousands of pilgrims all about for the next few days. Besides, I have a feeling that we will have two more speakers at this conference before we are through on Sunday!" she said.

As Therese and Rick came back to "camp", the fires were beginning to diminish. Only a few were going strong now, here and there. The rest had been reduced to coals. A few of those who would be speaking in the next few days were still up speaking with one priest and Paul Bohatch. Barbara Bohatch was settled down in a small tent that they had set up near the campfire. Mr. and Mrs. Pierpont were among those still awake and talking.

"We were about to send the hounds out for you" said Mr. Pierpont.

"Such a night Dad. We've been all over the summit, and wound up spending some time talking with a couple of pilgrims who had been to Medjugorje a few times like Rick. They had some great stories," said Therese. Mr. and Mrs. Pierpont noticed that Rick and Therese were holding hands. They realized what they were doing in front of her parents and both began to turn a little red. Here they were, thirty-something, behaving as high school sweethearts. Chaste high school sweethearts.

The thunderous waves pounded the exposed eastern shores of Mount Desert Island in the early hours of Saturday, July 4th, 1998. Storms raged all around, from the Florida Keys to Eastern Canada, yet, not here, in this newfound land of Our Lady. Mir was the word. Not mum. Mir. Peace.

****

There would be no Fourth of July parade in Washington DC this year. There would be search parties, excavation crews, and soldiers and machines of every description combing the ruins of our nation's capitol. The seven abortion clinics within biking distance of 1600 Pennsylvania Avenue would all be closed today, tomorrow, and until Jesus returns, whenever that Day of the Lord comes. They were no more. Their signs dangled freely from cable or bolts across bent and twisted metal and piles of rubble. One of these buildings, a smaller wood framed and sided structure received very little damage however. A rescue was in operation at 3 PM, when the earthquake hit. The twelve rescuers had chained themselves into the building at 2:55 PM, and the Chaplet of Divine Mercy, followed by the Rosary, asking Our Lord to spare the lives of the children still alive in the building at the time. They prayed too for the conversion of our nation and the end of abortion. All of the children that were still alive and doing well at 2:55 PM were indeed saved. They would later be born into God's creation, and raised as saints to walk in the ways of the Lord. "Vengeance is mine saith the Lord".

In a strange twist of events the rescuers were still in chains inside of the building at 2 AM on Saturday, July 4th, 1998. Everyone - doctors, nurses, would-be patients, and those who had already sacrificed their unborn had fled during the earthquake. Unlike Lot's wife, they didn't look back. The police were called to the scene by the manager of the clinic, Laura Petit, at 2:56 PM, just as the rescuers had stepped in the door. However, before the police had a chance to arrive, they found themselves with a host of more serious matters at 3 PM. Bridges out, buildings destroyed, and life extinguished all around them. There were more important things to do than to arrest 12 people for praying the Rosary at 3418 Staunton Avenue, Washington, DC. After all, they were praying for the protection of life. As the quake hit, the officers in the three responding squad cars had the immediate awareness that it was because of abortion that God had sent this chastisement. All six officers had been on many pro-life arrests before.

So there they were, these twelve rescuers, all chained up and nowhere to go. They prayed, and then they prayed some more...

****

The formerly responding police officers experienced sudden remorse, for having willingly chosen the side of death at past arrests. One of their members, two years prior, assisting at a pro-life arrest in Washington, had in turn chained himself to the rescuers. He in turn was arrested and jailed. He was jailed for just over two years prior to his release on July 1st, 1998. He was the secret hero of half of the DC police force. These timid, but better than lukewarm faithful visited their hero from time to time in a penitentiary in Virginia. The other half of the DC police force looked upon Mohammed Jackson, this pro-life former police officer turned rescuer as a turncoat enemy of all that America stood for. Such varied opinions. On July 1st, 1998, at 7 PM, Cardinal Rickey baptized Mohammed Jackson in the Basilica of the Immaculate Conception in Washington, DC. On July 2nd, 1998, Mohammed Jackson married Gloria Steinlen, a fellow pro-life rescuer.   Cardinal Rickey also presided at the wedding.   Both were impoverished through their pro-life activities.   The wedding, reception, and honeymoon were paid for by and at the insistence of Thomas Dominici, the founder and president of Dominici's Pizza, the national chain.   In financial terms, Thomas Dominici is the greatest promoter of bringing babies into the world alive, that ever walked the face of the earth. Almost a year prior, the world had lost the single greatest spokeswoman for babies and life, on par with Pope John Paul II, the beatified by the faithful Mother Teresa of Calcutta.   She was Heaven's gain, however, and the faithful, the remnant, knew that as Saint Therese the Little Flower had written, she would do even more good now from Heaven.   The unborn still had Pope John Paul II here on earth, and this Thomas Dominici, and the millions of pro-life families and individuals throughout the world.   And now God was intervening directly Himself, through nature, to call us to be people of life, to choose Life, to choose His Son, Jesus Christ.

At 5 PM, July 2nd, 1998, Washington DC was sending forth a native son and a native daughter on their way to their honeymoon in Acadia National Park, Maine.   After a two-week honeymoon of camping in the park, Mohammed was to assume the position as Youth Director for the growing Saint Paul's Parish of Ellsworth, Maine.   He had followed a course of study in Catholicism and religious education through the diocese of Washington, DC, and had received an associate degree in prison specializing in religious education.   In Ellsworth, the strong hand of Thomas Dominici would again soon be exercised, in the form of a check for $100,000, made payable to Shore Realty.   Aside from the wedding, Thomas Dominici had only met Mohammed and Gloria one time in 1997, when he visited Mohammed in jail with a priest and a friend of the priest, Gloria Steinlen. By the end of June 1998, Thomas was thinking that such faith ought to be rewarded.   Oh, he knew that God would reward him greatly.   Thomas just wanted to speed things up.   Before they had left on their honeymoon, Thomas had mentioned to the young couple something about wanting to see if he could help them with a down payment on a house.   He told them to keep in touch.   Shore realty would be calling the Jacksons in two weeks, to take the newlyweds out looking for the mini farm of their dreams, to the great and happy surprise of Mohammed and Gloria Jackson.   For now though, the Jacksons were rushing north on I-95, wishing to put great distance between them and the rains and winds preceding that great storm Michael, rushing northward on a path of destruction.   Rain they would have though, and torrents they would see, until shortly before their arrival to Mount Desert Isle, two thirds of the way up the rocky coast of Maine. Our Lady had been expecting them.   They would have sunshine for much of the balance of their honeymoon.   Such faith ought to be rewarded.

A busy day in the nation's capital. Is it a punishment when a Father strongly corrects the dangerous behavior of a child playing on the edge of a precipice, or is it Mercy?

At 2:15 AM, a distraught DC policeman, in a battered, torn, bloody uniform entered the clinic. This fallen away Catholic, divorced man had come back to his Catholic Faith at 3:01 PM on Friday, just as his squad car skidded to a halt on a DC side-street as he was headed with his partner to an aborturarium, a house of murder. The street they were on became impassable from debris and stalled cars and trucks. He and his partner split up as they went about assisting the injured here and there. This officer in question, Frank Thompson, wound up jogging his way 8 miles to his former home, helping the distressed and injured along the way. When he arrived at his former Hillcrest Heights home, he was thankful that he and his former wife had not purchased a brick home years ago. Many of the brick structures in the neighborhood had severe structural damage.

There were bands of people roaming about, that Frank had passed along his jogging route. For the time they were friendly if not saintly, helpful bands of young men, older men, and a few women going about the task of rescuing a city in distress. There was no crime taking place in Washington DC at this time. Frank dashed up the driveway, passed bicycles, a watering hose, and downed gutters and waterspouts, and ran into the house. "Mary? Mary?" he screamed. A ragged looking woman with three young children gathered around her came out of the kitchen. They all had the look of fear in their eyes. They had seen death today. They felt the earth move today. Such a day had never been seen on the likes of the reruns of 'Mayberry RFD', which was blasting on the television in the living room. The program was being sent in via cable from Raleigh, North Carolina. Eighty-five percent of the area within 20 miles of Washington was without power. When the power came back on, Mary had turned on the TV as if to restore some normalcy to a shattered day and life for her and the children, and the United States. Mary and the children had managed to get back to the house from their errands downtown earlier. They had to walk the last three miles home after losing the car forever in an accident at 3 PM. The first thing Mary did when they returned home was to attempt to turn on that TV, the god in their life, the former god in Frank's life. They gathered in the kitchen around the smaller set they huddled around at dinnertime. It did not respond. Neither did the lights.

Just after what would have been dinnertime for them, the electricity again flowed into their home, and "Gilligan's Island" came on. They stared at their God, and Gilligan, and then Andy and Aunt Bea until Frank burst in the door. When he found his family, he walked over and turned off the blasting television. "Mary, I'm sorry. Please don't marry John. I want to come back home, that is, I want to be your husband again." He was hugging her and the children. They had been divorced for three years, and Mary was going to tie another knot next month to another former Catholic, John Williams.

The relief that Mary felt in seeing her husband, her real husband, alive and well, was incredible. She snapped back to reality. "John stopped by a little while ago. He had a Rosary in his hand. I didn't think he believed in God anymore. We both mutually called off the wedding. He was going home to his former wife. I told him that I could not marry him anyhow, that I was going to beg you to come home" said Mary. The two older children were as happy as they could be at the present moment, under the given circumstances. The youngest, the three-year-old was complaining that the television was off. She wanted it on, young Mary did. She would not get her way.

"Rosary" said Frank. Do you have any Rosaries? We need to pray right now. And then I need to go help some people. People are dying, injured, and trapped all over. I've got to get to the abortion clinic on Staunton Avenue. I was on call going to arrest them - that is a dozen rescuers. Then the quake. We were told that Mike Schmitt was in the group. If I know Mike like I think I do, he had all of the rescuers in chains and locks within 45 seconds of entering the building. It probably would have taken two hours for us and the Fire Department to unchain them. They chain themselves to buy an extra hour for the babies. It usually works. He's even been using special alloy steel lately. I used to think he was public enemy number one. I got to get back there with tools. Even if somebody comes off the street to help them, they're not going to get them out of there with household tools and cutters. I've got to get some tools from the station for this job. "Oh God, lets pray. You don't know what its like out there" said Frank.

"I do Frank, and the kids too", she said. "We were leaving the Shop-Rite downtown when it hit. I totaled the car. We had to walk three miles. We could have only gone another mile with the car anyway because of the bridges", she said.

"Oh God, honey, I'm sorry. Look, from now on we believe in God, right, and always will until our dying days, right. It's gotta be this way if we're going to make it in what's to come" said Frank.

"Yes Frank, yes. I know this is from God. He's trying to speak to our country, to our family," said Mary.

"Daddy, turn on Gilligan's Island" said the youngest. Frank walked over to the television in the kitchen, grabbed it and the one in the living room, and walked outside with the televisions and threw them into the street where they landed with resounding crashes. He walked back in smiling. He hadn't lost it. He just knew what had to be done. Mary had found some Rosaries. They fumbled through what they remembered of the Rosary together. Neither of the parents had prayed a Rosary since their childhood. They finished and Frank was out the door to help the rescuers and others along the way, after he saw that his family had something to eat and drink.

"I'll be back late tonight Mary, I'm going to try to help out till I drop, but then I'll be back", called Frank as he rode off on his old Schwinn 10 speed. He headed for the police station, 5 miles from his house, back towards the city. The station was abandoned; all living officers and personnel were on rescue missions of their own at 8 PM. He made his way to the supply room he was looking for. Most of the rescue equipment was already out being used. Frank spied one of the few tools left in the room, a large pair of state-of-the-art bolt cutters that had never been used. "Thank you Lord" said Frank, and he was out the door and back on his bike. He had the best of intentions to go directly to the rescuers. But every block offered its own share of the distressed, stranded, and trapped.

At 2:15 on Saturday morning, Officer Frank Thompson arrived at the Women's Health Center of DC. The Babies Death Center thought Frank. Bring money, we kill. "Hello", called Frank to the rescuers, waving his flashlight. "You all O.K.?" he said.

The rescuers were calmly praying a Rosary as Frank entered the building. The building looked like it was ready for another day of the killing fields, its wood structure having toughed out the quake. "We're fine" said Mike Schmitt, "but we were beginning to think that the old saying 'There's never a policeman around when you need one was true.' We were expecting you quite earlier in the day. We don't pack along our tools of escape, we leave that up to you guys!" said Mike.

"You don't know how bad things are out there, judging from appearances in here. This building is in good shape", he said. "It was a large quake, DC is largely gone as we knew it – the larger landmarks at least. I'm Frank Thompson, of the DC Police Force", he said.

"Everyone had been talking amongst themselves since Frank had come in, as well as thanking Frank. "You're not here to arrest us now, are you Frank?" said Anita Guernsey, one of the rescuers.

"God no. Anyone with a conscience knows that God allowed this quake for the sins of our country, and our individual sins. For the time being there is a great repentance, remorse, and feeling of charity in the air. There are thousands of people, volunteers helping with rescue efforts everywhere around here. You guys are the only sane people in town. I think everyone knows that now. At least everyone has to face that at this moment. I don't suppose God is done with us yet," said Frank, as he was halfway through freeing the twelve.

They were almost all freed now, as Frank had been quick with the bolt cutters. Frank freed the last person, a grandmother from Bethesda, June Linovic. "God bless you she said, for coming out here so late to help us!"

"I couldn't leave you here. I think my guardian angel must have been letting me know you were all still here. I couldn't stop thinking about you. We were rushing over to arrest you just before three o'clock and then boom" said Frank.

Everyone was standing up and stretching out. They had been in an awkward position for so long, that some of them might have needed medical treatment if their self-incarceration had gone on much longer.

"Frank, could I talk to you for a moment" said Mike. "Are you serious that you and the people you are coming across out there think that this is a chastisement from God for the sins of man?" said Mike.

"There's a few diehards out there that are cursing God, but yes, that is the general consensus, that God is punishing us for our sins, especially abortion. That word abortion has come up many times today, in different places that I've been helping out" said Frank, looking around at all of the rescuers, still stretching out.

Frank's flashlight was diminishing some, but Mike asked Frank and the others to take a walk around the building with him. Mike pointed out the various instruments of death, vacuum machines, and various plastic and metal devices that have one purpose. There was blood all over the floors of two of the rooms.

"There must be $100,000 worth of equipment in here that is used to destroy life. How can we make sure that this equipment is never used to kill babies again?" said Mike. "Frank, you know this is a wood building", he said.

"Here's another flashlight," said Frank. "Check every square inch of every room to make sure there's no one else in here. Let's split into two groups. The building is on a slab, with a one floor plan. We have ten rooms plus closets to check. Half of you go with Mike, and half of you come with me" said Frank.

Minutes later the twelve emerged from the building. A red glow was being emitted from inside the building, as seen through the windows. Inside, birth control pills and other life killing abortifacients in the form of plastic, creams, and fancy devices began to burn and melt away, returning back to Hell. Machines that might bring shivers to the spine of visitors to Auschwitz began to return to the elements and compounds from which they were originally formed. A cry was heard, above the rain, farther east on Staunton Avenue, perhaps from someone injured from falling debris or possibly even trapped by crumbled walls or ceilings. The thirteen now dashed off in the direction of the call to see if they could lend assistance. Frank Thompson and June Linovic scampered slowly behind the other rescuers. Frank was assisting the 65-year-old grandmother as best he could as they followed along. Such scenes would repeat themselves every several blocks or so until the group of tired Christians found themselves, miles and hours later, at the home of Frank and Mary Thompson. Mary and the children had waited up for Frank, in fear for his, and their lives. They were ecstatic to see Frank and his new found friends. They welcomed them all into their home for food and rest. New troubles or challenges lay ahead for all of them, for all humanity, but God wins in the long run, that's how The Book ends.

As the last of the campfires on Cadillac Mountain were sending their smoldering smoke heavenwards, and all pilgrims were now retired, the small crowd in the Thompson home at last fell off to sleep too, all hearts bent towards God as they closed the chapter on a long, long day. Sunrise was not far off.

****

Small jets and prop planes banked into the Greenbrier Valley Airport, in southeastern West Virginia all Friday night long, and into Saturday morning, carrying secretaries, Congressmen, Senators, a President of sordid sorts, politicians, an assortment of world leaders, and various military personnel. Vacations were all over for all of the guests at the Greenbrier Resort, one of the new homes of the United States Federal Government. Yes, the Shadow Government FEMA - the Federal Emergency Management Agency was really controlling the country, along with Freemasonry and George Bush, but there was important activity taking place at the Greenbrier too! Vacationers and some homeowners were sent packing for 25 miles around. West Virginia had also suddenly become one of the most militarily fortified states in the nation. Area private pilots were invited to keep their Cessnas and Cherokees on the ground, as the skies over the Greenbrier Valley and then some were now "no fly" zones, and very dangerous to say the least. A misguided young pilot, a dentist by trade, who was still so enamored with his brand new Cessna 152, like a child with a new ten speed at Christmas, ventured to attempt to fly over the Greenbrier Resort before sundown on Friday evening. He wanted a close-up view of history in the making. He wanted to experience the world coming to the Greenbrier Valley firsthand. An F-14 Tomcat blew him away. The pilot was a German whose squadron had just been called up by the UN from Holloman Air Force Base in New Mexico. The German pilot was just following orders.

****

It was now just past noon on Saturday, back at Acadia National Park. The sky was clear over the island, and the rains had ceased for hundreds of miles in all directions, though pockets of storms were still here and there. New storms were promising to arrive on the heels of, or in the wake of what would be left of 'Michael' in the next several days to come.

Since landfall on Friday, at 3 PM, Michael had been working its devastation northward at just over 20 miles per hour. Recorded winds reached over 200 miles per hour. Great damage was done even 20 miles inland as Michael hurried northward after hitting the coast at Miami. Fort Lauderdale, West Palm Beach, Vero Beach, Melbourne, and all coastal towns and resorts between were no longer viable entities. They would not see rebuilding in this era. The coast had been evacuated to a high degree, but the loss of life was still phenomenal. The material loss was uncountable. All along the coast up until Melbourne the storm was hugging the ocean to such a great degree to feed upon the warm moisture laden air hugging the shore, and thereby maintaining its ferocity and strength for the time being.

It was just after noon, Saturday, July 4th, 1998. The United States was not celebrating its birthday. All fireworks and parades had been canceled form coast to coast. The United States was in mourning, for the most part, or in anguish and pain, amazement, or sorrow. Much of the nation, and many Christian brothers and sisters in Canada and Mexico, and points distant were in deep prayer. As the United States goes, so goes the world, at least that is how the saying goes. A pity actually, for the United States has not always set the best of examples in ways of fidelity to God, in chastity and purity, and in money matters. In politics we have been utterly Masonic, and that should be enough said. But we had the world's attention now, and we, the great nation of exports, science, wheat, cars, tractors, computers and machinery were indeed the recipients of non-stop prayers from around the world. Not everyone approached the newfound situation in the United States with a noble heart. There were detractors in high places who were now poised for power, control, and action. Puppet strings were being set, checked, cross-checked, and checked again. A friend once asked Franklin Roosevelt about the power he yielded as President of the

United States. The president told him that if he really knew who had the power - who really controlled this country, it would scare him to death. Things had not changed much since then, politically.

Back at Acadia National Park, the pilgrims were spreading out with their picnic lunches on the front lawn of the Jordan Pond Restaurant that stretched down to Jordan Pond. They had just finished with the Mass. Over 4,000 had received Holy Communion on this day, at the Medjugorje Conference. This number did not include those of other faiths, and children who were not able to receive communion. All told, the attendance was swelling to well above 12,000 people. Whereas some cars were parked two miles or more from the conference area on Friday, there were now pilgrims parking their cars over four miles from the Jordan Pond main entrance. Shuttle busses were picking up passengers from all points. They had temporarily dispensed with their regular park tours, to assist with the flow of pilgrims. It was actually easy to get from Jordan Pond, to cars at distant points, thanks to the shuttle owners who had volunteered their services.

Prior to sunrise, Mount Desert Isle was covered in a think blanket of fog, leftover from the sinking of the PT 109. The pilgrims on Cadillac and elsewhere in the park were awaking to foghorns and the clanging bells of buoys, in Frenchman's Bay, and out on the ocean. Coffee supplies were quite low on the island, and it would take a lot of coffee on this morning to put life back into the veins of the happy campers, many of whom had stayed up well past their bed time. A few had stayed awake in prayer to welcome the morning fog and the dawn. On this morning, there had been a great migration from the summit of Cadillac Mountain, and from campgrounds, hotels, and motels for miles distant, to Jordan Pond. Jordan Pond had never seen such crowds or prayers. Nary a Rosary had been prayed there before. Now, the consecrated land could count her Rosaries in the tens of thousands, and rising, by the hour.

The conference had begun with the Five Joyful Mysteries of the Rosary. A priest, Father Marcel LeBeuf from Quebec, had then given another brief summary of the happenings at Medjugorje, Bosnia-Herzegovina since June 24, 1981, followed by a large sampling of readings from Our Lady of Medjugorje from the early days, on through the present. After his talk he answered over two dozen questions pertaining to the apparitions at Medjugorje.

Following Father LeBeuf's talk, the pilgrims had the pleasure of hearing the incredible story of Luke and Alice Miller. The audience heard the story of the evening spent in the Basilica of Our Lady of Consolation in Carey, Ohio. The story did not have the same dramatics that it would have had it been told late in the evening, but compelling it was. There were many in the audience, victims of the disease of birth control who were touched by this story more than all of the others. Few there were indeed, even amongst Our Lady's most ardent followers who had not been stained at some point or another, from these soils of darkness. Somewhere along the line in the last few days, Luke Miller had come across a revealing book on Margaret Sanger, the founder of Planned Parenthood, and spearhead against life. He read about ten minutes of passages from her writings, from this supposed saint of secularism and humanism. The pilgrims were appalled. She had no love or need for blacks, Catholics, Chinese, and those of various other religions and ethnic backgrounds. The passages that Luke read were not an environmentalist's plea for Mother Earth. They were simply demonically inspired words of hate. All this from a woman who had become a cornerstone of American civilization. No wonder God had begun to bring the United States down to its very foundations, with the onset of one disaster after another. Luke read statements from various sources prior to the early 1930s. Every Christian denomination was opposed to artificial birth control. He read several statements from Christian leaders, Protestant Bishops, ministers, and so forth, from this era, whose words have wrung prophetically true to our own day and age. They had warned that birth control would lead to increased rates of adultery, divorce, homosexuality, pornography, child molestation, and the list goes on.

 Luke was concluding his short talk and added further: "I know I've gotten off the trail of the main purpose of this conference, Mary's visions or apparitions in "Mejagooria", but I believe Mary brought us here for a purpose to speak to you. From having learned a little bit about her messages over there, it seems that she spends and awful lot of time speaking about purity and sins of the flesh. I don't think she's come just to talk, and talk, and talk. She wants action for Jesus. Being pure and putting aside birth control and other impurity is what she wants. That's action. Accepting God's greatest gifts to us, our children. That's action. That's following her messages. This book says that when the powers that be, these One World Order United Nations folks want to bring abortion into a country, even your Catholic countries, the first thing they do is blackmail them financially, threatening to cut off funds if they don't do this, and don't do that. This book says that Ireland is falling fast. And everybody, I mean everybody knows how Catholic Ireland was just a short time ago. So the countries accept the first round of money, and the first round of baby snuffing chemicals from America and Europe. Ten years later they're passing out condoms in your Catholic schools. That's how it works. That's what this Lady is coming to warn us about. She wants our purity and prayers. That's what my wife and I feel Mary brought us here for. Thank you all for listening." Luke and Alice thanked the people again.

Alice mentioned one more thing to the audience. "My husband and I have decided that we, with the children are all going to become Catholic. We wish that we could do so today, because we would like to join you at Communion. You see we now believe in the Body and Blood of Jesus Christ", she said. There was a great applause from a happy audience as they were walking off the stage with their children who were waiting for them in chairs to the left of the microphones.

The Holy Sacrifice of the Mass followed Luke and Alice Miller's talk. Father LeBeuf gave the homily on the theme "Conversion of the Heart". After Mass followed adoration, and over 12,000 people on the grass, in the woods, and on the hills around the area knelt in adoration. It was the largest crowd that had ever gathered in Maine to adore our Eucharistic Lord. To fulfill Our Lady's First Saturday requests, the Rosary was recited, and confessions were heard throughout the day. The crowd offered their prayers in reparation for sins against the Immaculate Heart of Mary.

As the crowd enjoyed their lunches, hundreds continued to go to confession, pray, and talk in large and small groups. A strong July sun beat down on the pilgrims, but shade was plentiful, and a strong but pleasant wind helped keep the weather conditions in line. Scattered storms to the north, south, east, and west continued, but Mount Desert Isle had the next best weather to Paradise. The waves continued to roll into the island from the ocean with great ferocity, but a ferocity that failed to pass beyond the boundary where water meets rock. Wasted energy apart from its sheer beauty and power!

At one-thirty Rick Tremont was again at the microphone. He summarized the purpose of the conference, how it came about, and gave a 30 second talk on the natural disasters that befell the country in the last day or so. He mentioned that the conference was being offered up for the sick and suffering from the disasters, and for the conversion of the nation and world. He then introduced two television personalities from WELL TV, Ellsworth Maine. The two, Henry Longchance, and Lonny McWitt, were a news anchorman and meteorologist, respectfully. Henry Longchance spent about 10 minutes summarizing the headline news for pilgrims. Perhaps an unusual move for a Marian conference, but the pilgrims were concerned for their loved ones, friends, and even neighbors back in the affected areas. On the whole, the insurance industry in the country was now belly up. Small insurance institutions and those not doing business in the affected areas would continue business as usual, for the time being. Fires out west were out of control. Several National Parks, forests, and suburbs were now embers still aglow. The manpower, planes, ground vehicles, and even dry fire-fighting chemicals had been exhausted or proven too little, too late. Large rivers and lakes were now the only sure fire-lines. Thousands of people were homeless and without jobs due to the floods in the Great Plains States, the Midwest, and the East Coast. Hundreds were dead and missing from tornadoes from Texas to the Dakotas. Hundreds of thousands of homes, apartments, and buildings on the coast of Florida were now reduced to concrete slabs, freshly awash in salt water. Most of the coastal residents of Florida affected by Hurricane Michael had time to "get out", as Henry had put it, but many did not. Millions could no longer go home in Florida. Bridges. Bridges took their beating. Those on islands, across causeways, or in any area heavily dependent upon bridges were in dire straits. If the hurricane was not strong enough to battle the bridge, the runaway barges, ships, boats and debris sent crashing into them took their toll on such structures. With a blast of his mighty nostrils God had returned parts of Florida to the alligators, crocodiles, and panthers, assuming of course, that some of Florida's 50 odd endangered panthers had weathered out the storm.

With regards to the Earthquake, centered around Washington, DC, Henry Longchance filled the people in the best he could. Congress was not likely to return to Washington, DC. The prognosis for DC was bleak. Hunger would be setting in soon for those who survived who remained on in the nation's capital. The outlying suburbs were operating O.K., with only moderate bridge and foundation damage to speak of, but surrounding major cities had also felt the brunt of the quake, and were limping quite badly. These cities included Philadelphia, Richmond, Virginia, Raleigh, North Carolina, Dover Delaware, and many cities within these bounds. Several major airports were closed due to damaged facilities and dangerously cracked tarmacs. The quake was even felt in the Greenbrier Valley area of West Virginia where Congress was now setting up office. Henry told the pilgrims that Congress was now in session and operating as best as could be expected from their new home at the Greenbrier Resort. There were new outbreaks of small wars the world over, due to the blinking of the United States, and there were more threats of war. Henry told of United Nations troops on U.S. soil. "Thank you for your attention. I want you to know that everyone at WELL in Ellsworth is praying for you now and our country. Several of us have returned to God in our hearts in the last day. If I can find a priest right now, I'm going to try to go to confession for the first time in 15 years. I'm glad you're all here. Thank you" said Henry, passing the microphone to Lonny McWitt, the meteorologist for WELL.

"Thank you said Lonny. I want you to know that God has not had a lot of friends in the media in modern times. I could elaborate on this, but I will just emphasize the positive. God has more friends in the media now than ever before... I have been asked up here to give you an update on Hurricane Michael. As you know, Michael found landfall at Miami yesterday, at about 3PM. Michael veered north-northwest up the coast of Florida, raking everything along the coast. It is safe to say that Florida is now the poorest state in the nation. The loss of life and material damage is vast. Winds have been clocked, onshore, at just over 200 miles per hour. The vast portion of the hurricane has remained off the coast, over the ocean, feeding Michael its destructive energy. Ten hours later Michael took a sudden left turn and went into Orlando. We have no meteorological explanations for this. Orlando has been hit hard, almost as hard as Miami. Orlando, as we knew it, no longer exists. The grounds at the former Walt Disney World Complex, yes, I said former, are being used as a tent camp for refugees. Michael's forward speed ceased in Orlando, but wind speeds continued at over 175 miles per hour. Michael began its retreat from Orlando at about 2AM this morning, and headed on a course for Saint Augustine, Florida. Three hours later Daytona Beach was part of American History. Palm Coast, Saint Augustine, and Jacksonville were to be next in Michael's wake. Now you are not going to hear this on the radio or television, or read about this in your newspapers or magazines. Over ten thousand people attended a Rosary Rally in Saint Augustine Friday evening, at 6PM, praying for protection for their families, their city, their state and nation. They prayed for an end of abortion and the conversion of the nation. They went home at 8 PM, after carrying a statue of Our Lady through the streets of Saint Augustine in Procession. They should have been hit with the hurricane. Michael went due east and now remains over the Atlantic, well off land, well north now of Saint Augustine. He's heading north at 25 miles per hour - well out at sea. The Carolinas are expected to be hit within the next eight hours. Why, might you ask, will you not be told about the Rosary Rally in Saint Augustine, and their apparent miracle? The media in our country is controlled by large corporations and the powers that be. Boards of directors control the large corporations. The elite among them share directorships among the largest and most powerful corporations in the world. On top of them you have the individuals and families that control the world, who are much more powerful than the pawns in Washington, DC, or formerly in Washington. At our station, WELL, we are already seeing the dragnet being pulled in during the last day or so. Something is afoot. The media is about to become your greatest enemy, so to speak. More and more you are going to be told half-truths, outright lies, and propaganda from the mainline media. I will give you one example and then I will step aside. Our station knows of the United Nations troops that are now in or on their way to our country. We know where they are and their numbers. We know of China's current naval activity off the U.S. coast. We know how decrepit is the state of the new Federal government and their operations center in West Virginia. Yet, we have been told that we can not pass on this information. Please pray for the news media. Many of us do not have the courage to stand up for God. Thank you". Lonny and Henry walked off the stage together.

Allison Welday began to play and sing Amazing Grace. Twelve thousand people joined in. The singing was heard 8 miles away at Bar Harbor, when the wind was right.

****

Next up on the stage to give a talk was a Freedom Fighter from Montana. John T. Trudeau had arrived on the island intending to speak at a "preparedness" gathering – a militia meeting. The meeting never took place. John got waylaid along the way. Here he was now, about to address several thousand pilgrims that he would have called "pagans" the day before. Life was starting to get interesting for John…

Rick introduced him. Many knew who John Trudeau was! John was already a hero to a handful of the pilgrims. There was a loud round of welcoming applause… "My Dear Friends: I am glad that I am meeting you today, and not an earlier day in this week, not an earlier day in the life of John T. Trudeau. My God, I have been labeled a "kook" by Rush Limbaugh, the MahaRushi himself, and thousands like me who believe that we are the most Blessed Nation that God has ever allowed to live on the face of the earth, *and* that a conspiracy is looming! My Dear God, wait till Rush hears the rest of the story… I came to this island to address the Acadia Militia. God however, had different plans for me. **I got addressed yesterday.** Yesterday I got religion. Oh, I had religion all right, but yesterday, God put the seven books back in my Bible that Martin Luther pulled out. God put the "Tradition" back into my Faith that Saint Paul told us to hold fast to. God put a Rosary in my hands from a lovely Lady dressed in Blue. I don't know how I'm going to explain this to my militia friends what these beads are all about. I'm new at this. I'm going to start with the Lord's Prayer however, one of the prayers in the Rosary. Then I'm going to flip the pages of my Bible and go the Gospel of Luke, Luke 1:28 and Luke 1:42 to show them where the "Hail Mary" prayer of the Rosary came from. Then, if they don't want to listen to what I'm saying, I'm going to tell them to take a hike. I sure as Hell don't want to be in a foxhole fighting the United Nations troops with folks who don't love the

Mother of Jesus Christ as the Bible tells us to do – to even go so far as to call her Blessed as Luke tells us. I wouldn't want to be in a foxhole with somebody who didn't like my earthly mother, let alone the Mother of Jesus Christ, my only Lord and Savior. Yesterday, for the first time, I realized that in my zeal to have Christ and Christ alone, I , I realized just how far I went, to, to push aside Mary. No, I did more than push aside Mary. I can't even tell you what I said of Jesus' Mother. I can't because of the children here." John had copious tears rolling off his face now. "Man" said John.

"Look, um, look," said John. "Um, look, I'm losing my voice." John was hardly audible. He put the microphone closer to his mouth. "I'm losing my voice. I can't... Look, I don't deserve to be a speaker here. I, I..." John stopped talking for close to a half a minute as he tried to dry his eyes. He had a flashback to his talk at Yale University in 1995. Things had changed for John. "Look, I'm with you. I hope the militias of America will still believe I am with them. I know we have some real battles ahead. We will see bullets. But I, I want you to know that this is now my most valuable weapon", he said, holding up his twenty cent corded Rosary that was given to him by a member of Our Lady's Rosary Makers, Auburn, Maine branch, on Friday. John stopped speaking again for another half a minute, continuing to hold up his Rosary. He started to walk away, but turned quickly back to the microphone. "I can't say any more now. And, and, I don't think God wants me to say anything more now. I just want you to know I'm with you, you Christians. I just want you to know that I now understand the battle we're in, a battle for souls. Please keep me in your prayers. Please keep the militias in you're prayers. As far as a military presence, they're about all we have right now to fight the physical battle here at home, to preserve our freedom, our United States Constitution. The traitors in Washington have sent our soldiers, your children abroad to fight in useless battles, to fight Satan's wars, exposing our soldiers to danger, and leaving our country wide open to a hostile takeover complete with concentration camps, martial law, and a very real Antichrist. Pray that all involved in the militias in North America will come to understand the true nature of the Beast. Pray that they too will soon get back the seven books of the Bible taken from them so long ago by proud and errant men. Pray that when these patriots, these proud, strong men and women are walking to Jesus Christ, that they won't be ashamed to have His Mother at their side." John left the stage in tears.

A thundering applause echoed across Jordan Pond, through the valleys all the way back to Bar Harbor. There were few in Bar Harbor to hear the echo though. Most were there on the scene at Jordan Pond

****

It was just past one in the afternoon on Saturday, July 4th, 1998. Rick Tremont had just brought up another speaker. "……Yet, I will have our next speaker introduce himself. He is a pilgrim, like yourselves, brought here by Our Lady to bring glory to Her Son, Jesus Christ. There is an old adage, and scripture to boot, that tells us that 'All things work towards the glory of God'. This gentleman here is living proof that this is so. And so, I give you the gentleman from New York" said Rick.

"Thank you, the tall man stated. I've never been much of a praying man, so I ask the Good Lord to guide my words at this time. May Mary, His Mother, and my former enemy, at least in my mind, help me to bring praise to Her Son. I believe that some of you, perhaps many of you will know who I am in just a moment or two. Yet, this will not be for any good I have done. Indeed, I have been the thorn in the side of a 21st Century Saint Paul whom many of you know. Perhaps he is who he is now, in part because he passed the test, albeit a treacherous one, that I helped put him through… A few generations ago, my ancestors were prosperous farmers in upstate New York, farming over 400 acres of fertile ground. Perhaps my ancestors were an oddity, because of our ancestral nationality. My great grandfather was killed, murdered, by someone who thought our kind ought not to live a life of prosperity, as our relatives did, a hardworking but prosperous life. The family lost most of the land. It was stolen after the murder. The murderer took the land, all legal-like. All of my life I have been wounded by this. It ate at me. It nearly killed me. I took this cross to school. I took this cross to work. I took this cross everywhere I went, and I never learned to forgive those who put the cross on our family's shoulders. I even took out my anger on innocent parties, such as those who became neighbors over the years, on what was really our land. I almost killed one of my neighbors with a gun. I daresay he almost killed me in his turn too. I however, was the aggressor. You see, he had bought the small farm adjacent us that was the site on which my great grandfather was killed. Their house was right where he died. I hated this fellow, and his wife, and their visitors too. I had a gate on the right of way to their house. I controlled it. I locked it often. It almost killed the fellow's elderly father when he came to visit his son, and couldn't get through the gate. The walking almost killed him. That's when this man, this fellow who now works for Jesus & Mary wanted to punch out my lights. I am sure that many of you know who he is by now – Tom Rutbensky of Medjugorje Missions. Yes, I am the one who made Tom's book so exciting. I was both the Hatfields and McCoys for the Rutbensky's. Everyday was an adventure living next to me, Victor Rushmiller. When Tom Rutbensky came to my house after his conversion experience to tell me that he was no longer going to argue with me and wanted to be my friend I could have decked him. I did not want to have cause to befriend this man I did not like, for no cause of his own. I would like to tell you that over the years we became the best of friends and learned to live and work together. However, this did not happen. A few days ago, as we were headed out the driveway beginning our trip on a vacation in Maine, as I suppose many of you were, I locked the gate across the right of way, that I had not locked in years. A few hours into the trip, something happened to me without anyone knowing it. God melted a few generations of built-up hatred in just a few moments. We stopped to eat, and I secretly wrote a letter of apology to Tom, for everything. I felt like a new man, though one wondering around aimlessly, though only in my mind, for I appeared as the same old husband, the same old father in the driver's seat of the family car, taking the family to Maine. Being with all of you here, meeting and talking, and praying with all of year here, has given my life purpose and meaning. Victor was crying. God emptied me out on the long ride here. He turned me into an empty vessel. Now, through the intercession of Mary, this Mary of Medjugorje who I have been fighting indirectly for many years, I have been made into a new creation...."

Victor spoke for a short while longer, broadening the story already told with details of his life, troubles, his neighbor Tom Rutbensky, and further bits and pieces on his conversion that took place in the last few days. All the while, he spoke with tears on his face, and sobs in his voice. They were happy tears, tears marking a new beginning of life with God – to Jesus through Mary. Hundreds in the crowd did know who he was, and were amazed at his story. Over 300 people in crowd had read "Apostles of These Times", Tom Rutbensky's book. They knew how hard it must have been for Victor to be up there speaking. Many were praying for him as he spoke.

There was a long applause after Victor finished speaking, as due any speaker who had just come home to God. Victor's coming home was a grand celebration in heaven and on earth. Many an unseen devil was sent packing from the vicinity of Victor Rushmiller and family during this gathering, especially when Victor and the family were prayed over by priests. Satan had tried to use Victor to bring an end, a permanent earthly end of an Apostle of the last time. Satan had failed, as usual.

****

The ugly one was not a happy camper. Perhaps he could at least bring about the demise of this gathering. One could only take so much from a Woman's heel. This however was The Woman who 'cometh forth as the morning rising, fair as the moon, bright as the sun, and terrible as an army set in battle array'. Try he would however. He would seek victories, small or large, wherever and whenever he could. A meeting was called. Nine choirs of angels responded. They were dark, ugly, ferocious, hateful, and blasphemous choirs of angels. These were not the friends of Thomas Aquinas who had defined their ranks for us. These were the other ones with a very bad attitude. They gathered in an old U.S. Coast Guard building on the island, in a quaint little town called Southwest Harbor, just miles away. It is strange to think that even angels need their real estate, so to speak. The Dumb Ox, the Angelic Doctor, this same Saint Thomas Aquinas the Dominican tells us that no two angels can occupy the same physical space. Imagine that. So, a meeting was held in an old empty building. Plans were made. Devilish plans.

****

Raphael Morales was the next speaker. He had been talking softly with Paul Bohatch, Rick Tremont, and Therese Pierpont during Victor's talk. They were planning strategy for the conference, and Raphael was going over what he should cover in his talk for the gathered pilgrims.

After the California Medjugorje conference last weekend, Raphael and his family had flown out to meet visit his sister Maria and her family in Augusta, Maine. They had arrived on Wednesday, and were all ready to start a joint family two-week trailer and tent camping tour of the Maine Coast. That was before Maria made the mistake, at least in her own estimation of pointing out the ad for the Medjugorje Conference in the Boston Globe. Now Raphael knew where they must start their shore vacation – Bar Harbor. Maria and her husband protested lightly. Raphael won. Two families headed off for Bar Harbor at noon on Thursday, July 2nd, 1998. The Morales family followed Maria's family's Winnebago non-stop to Bar Harbor. They were there in less than two hours. They pulled into the first trailer friendly campground they could find on the island – Mount Desert Narrows Campground, several miles from Bar Harbor, yet, still on Mount Desert Isle, and just a few miles from the park entrance. They were checked in by mid-Thursday afternoon, and went into town in Raphael's large rental van together, all fifteen of the clan. They had decided to live it up on the first day of their vacation together, they chose to dine at Captain Jim's Rusty Whale. Rusty Whale? Rusty Whale. The tourists flocked there like Mecca. Their lobster tasted like everyone else's on the island, but the tourists loved the Rusty Whale's décor, which was part whaleboat, part maritime museum, and part rusty old boat gear. For armchair hikers and vacationers, and 'Winnebagers', a dinner at the Rusty Whale was a highlight of the summer's vacation. Every child loved it. There were ship's boats to climb on, ship's wheels to turn, whales to ride on, and a little bit of science to learn for shipmates of all ages. Ship's bells, fog, and the ringing of danger buoys were all piped in. The Rusty Whale had a lighthouse you could climb up too.

Maria had left the Catholic Faith after high school. When she started her walk back to God years later, she became a Presbyterian. She was tired of hearing about priests who had molested children, nuns who wanted to be priests, priests who didn't have the time of day for her in times of crises, and tired of being told what to do by a celibate man from Vatican City. To Maria, the Church was half empty, not half full. She had forgotten that one-twelfth of the disciples of Jesus Christ betrayed Him. She had failed to notice how overworked and spread out the priests of God are today. For years, she fought her younger brother and his work with Medjugorje. As they had headed out of Mount Desert Narrows Campground, Raphael popped in his Scott Zahn conversion story cassette. Professor Zahn was a modern day Augustine, a former Presbyterian minister with an also former ax to grind against the Catholic Faith. This professor of theology studied and prayed his way right into the Catholic Faith, albeit against his utmost concerns for sanity. Yet, he had found his home in Rome, after a life of scriptural and historical study. His story had helped bring in hundreds of fellow Protestant ministers into the Catholic Church. Thousands of lay Protestants had come in through his efforts also. Tens of thousands of Catholics had come home to their faith, through, in a sense, the intercession of Scott Zahn. And now Maria, Raphael's sister, a very anti-Catholic scholarly medical doctor would be going to confession tomorrow for the first time in 22 years. The Scott Zahn tape was too much to take. Point by point Scott exposed the common fallacies, errors, and empty emotions often directed against the Catholic Faith. Point by point, through the Bible and historical facts, the scales fell away with every word spoken so eloquently by Professor Zahn. To think, he was once against the Faith. Perhaps God brought him over to ensure His victory. What a formidable opponent this man would have been.

So, at the last minute, Raphael, after talking it over with Paul Bohatch, Rick Tremont, and Therese Pierpont took his sister by the hand and brought her onto the stage with him. "God, but what am I going to say. What am I going to say? I'm not ready for this. You're crazy. Maria quieted down as they approached the microphone and she began to hear her own 'Protesting' voice reverberate throughout the valley. As Raphael began to speak and introduce himself and his sister, Maria was already deep in prayer. She knew that this had all been allowed by God. He had allowed her to run free from Him for years, all with a mind to this very day. Raphael let Maria speak first. She thought she would talk for perhaps four or five minutes. She spoke for a half an hour. Nearly everyone by the pond, in the forest, in the restaurant, and on the close by hills could relate to her story. She spoke so convincingly, so openly, with such force, that everyone knew she was speaking from her heart. She received a standing ovation for over a minute after she had left the microphone.

Raphael took to the microphone after his sister's talk. He had tears in his eyes. One more Latino had come home. That was his life's work, trying to stem the flood of the Latino's from the Church in North, Central, and South America. This was his whole life. He was constantly on the road throughout the Americas, bringing Our Lady to his brothers and sisters. She took it from there, and brought them home to Christ to complete their journey. Raphael received his call for his mission in Medjugorje. He was one of the first Americans to come to Our Lady's call from stateside. Raphael began to tell his story. He began with a prayer to Blessed Juan Diego, and then by telling the people to be of good cheer, for he felt that Our Lady was beginning to close the floodgates on the flow of faithful into the realm of perdition. "In spite of earthquakes, fires, floods, hurricanes, and politicians and their machines, we have good cause for joy. That joy is the peace of knowing, loving, and serving Jesus Christ, our Lord and Savior. At this time, on this day of turmoil for our nation, we can also look to Our Lady, who sees the master plan, who understands the crosses that we bear, who knows that Heaven remains unshaken despite our woes, despite hurricanes and earthquakes. She knows that all in Heaven await us with open arms. She is the same Lady who told Juan Diego 'Listen, my son, to what I tell you now: do not be troubled nor disturbed by anything: do not fear illness nor any other distressing occurrence, nor pain. Am I not your mother? Am I not life and health? Have I not placed you on my lap and made you my responsibility? Do you need anything else'…"

****

It was a disgruntled Acadia National Park Ranger who, through demonic inspiration, finally managed to get a fax through to the right people in their makeshift government offices in the Greenbrier Valley in West Virginia. The letter found its way into welcome hands.

Now this new government, now emerging from its cocoon, would in time, be usurping the rights of religion - that is true religion. The religion of the New Age, One World Order, this pantheistic chaotic environmental adoration would of course be upheld and protected, but Jesus and Mary would soon have to go. At least this would be the proposition from down under. A test case was now in order. The nation had enough things to ponder over and work through that such usurpation would go unnoticed in the beginning, present pilgrims excluded, of course. The Blue Hats were sent to Augusta Maine, by C-130s. Most states would see them soon regardless, as their deployment, in the name of National Security would be, in the near future, deemed necessary by those in charge. Augusta was to receive them in the long run anyhow, according to the blueprints. The time schedule was just perked up.

Several states were now under martial law and the President had ascended to his catbird seat. Yet his power, his throne was indeed just that, a bird's nest compared to that of those in control, call them the Illuminati if you will. Perhaps a 'big word' that might cause laughter amongst the scholars, but a word fit to describe how the wealthy elite might describe themselves. Yet there was darkness surrounding the name, and these elite also. The world knew these quiet people – that was true. The world did not know their power. The world would have shuddered had it known. Such types nodded ascent, and the open persecution of the Church in the United States began. The president signed the letter citing martial law. Yet Maine was not under martial law. Maine was doing just fine. Florida and the Carolinas were being racked, Washington DC ceased to be what it once was, but who would dare to write, or come bearing a letter citing martial law in Maine on July 4th, 1998?

A premature victory party was being held in Southwest Harbor, in the old Coast Guard Warehouse. The sinister laughter and blasphemies could not be heard by the uninitiated. It was rather cold in the warehouse. There was an actual physical drop in temperature that was noticed by a visiting Coast Guard officer who had to return prematurely from a local Medjugorje Conference to make his rounds. He saw his breath inside the building. He shuddered and rubbed his hands together as he was inspecting certain offices inside the warehouse. He wondered why it was so cold. Sometimes the fire of Hell exerts itself in a physical way that is as cold as ice, representing a lack of Love. The old Coast Guard building was in need of an exorcism. The propane heater would have been of no effect. The officer reached into his pocket and drew out a bottle of Holy Water – water blessed by a priest. He said the Saint Michael prayer and dispersed with a fair quantity of water in the suspect building. The temperature rose some. If he could hear the demons, he would have heard what sounded like the frightening sound of a disturbed group of bee boxes, an instant high pitched humming of thousands of frightened, angered bees. Yet bees

are a wonderful blessing. We were dealing with wasps here though.
Soiled mud wasps of the worse sort.

****

Rick Tremont had gone onstage to thank Raphael and his sister, and
their families. God, did he have news that was going to add to the fevered
pitch of the excitement and prayers of now more than 15,000 pilgrims.

Not even the shuttle buses could keep up with the influx of pilgrims now.
A handful of horse-drawn carriages were now being used to bring pilgrims
from their cars parked miles away. Big money had its hand here, too. A
blessed hand. In a strange twist of fate, the Rockefellers were the first ones
to put the horse carts in motion, by freeing up their stable and carriages
and personnel. J.D. was not at home. The Rockefeller estate bordered
closely to Jordan Pond. The vendor that ran the stables and carriage rides
for Acadia National Park followed in suit. The sound system, enhanced
overnight by the Park Service, was being pushed to the limits, yet was still
audible to the pilgrims who were the furthest from the speakers, barring
any loud background noises.

"Ladies and gentlemen, and children, could I please have your attention",
stated Rick Tremont. At this point were going to bring out Allison Welday
for 30 minutes of music and break, but several important developments
have lead to us changing the schedule. As I believe you now know, several
of our distressed states are operating under martial law. More than that, it
seems that our government has taken a broad step away from our U.S.
Constitution today, in its guarantee of religious freedom. We believe that
this is only the first step of what is to come in the very near future, as we
enter more deeply into those times spoken of by the Book of Revelations –
the Apocalypse, and Our Lady to Father Nairobi; and Her words to other
visionaries elsewhere in recent decades. With that in mind I have the sad
task to inform you that four Hundred Blue Hats, United Nations troops are
on their way to Acadia to squelch and disband our Conference. The
president of the United States has given them the power to do so in a letter
citing martial law. As far as I know, there are at least 6 local police
officers, and 3 state troopers that have joined, I will say, our ranks, and
have gone ahead to cut them off on the bridge to the island. Two Ellsworth
police tried to block Route 3 in Ellsworth and were fired at with a single
bullet, as a warning shot. Their patrol cars were pushed out of the way.
We have been told that our religious gathering is just a test case for what I
will call our new government, as they begin to exercise their ideologies.
That came to us from a government official in West Virginia who is on
God's side. Religious gatherings outside of Churches and cemeteries are

now forbidden in the United States." The crowd that had been gasping in low tones for the last minute instantly let out a fearfully loud gasp.

"The officers have asked us to pray for them. They are probably at the bridge now. They say they are David against Goliath. But David won, and they know that. If you don't mind, we will all say a Rosary now that the officers will be safe, and that these troops will depart, miraculously. I would like to have a priest and his young friend lead the Rosary for us at this time. Some of you may have heard of this Croatian Priest and his young friend from Medjugorje. The good priest has been called the Saint Francis of Medjugorje, though he would be upset at my saying so. He defended the children, the visionaries when the communists came for them. He was jailed for a year and a half defending them and Our Lady." Father Zdenko was blushing, tugging at Rick's clothing to have him dispense with the praise for this man of humility.

"This priest that many of you already know is Father Zdenko Pavlic. His young Croatian compatriot will need little introduction either, being one of the six chosen ones from Medjugorje - chosen by Our Lady to bear Her messages to the world" said Rick. "The young man is Boris Baric", he said, as he was passing Father his microphone, and walking a few feet to reach for another microphone for Boris.

"U ime Oca I Sina I Duha Svetoga. Amen" (In the name of the Father, and of the Son, and of the Holy Spirit. Amen.)" said Father Zdenko as Rick walked off the stage. Over 12,000 in the crowd made the Sign of the Cross. "Let us begin right away, without ado, as you say, further ado, on the Rosary. We pray that the soldiers go home, we pray for the good police, for the victims of the disasters in the United States and elsewhere. We pray to, for conversion, of this country, and Canada, Mexico, and all people of all of the Americas and world" said Father Zdenko. Father started the Rosary.

****

There were now seven police cars in the middle of the bridge on Route 3 leading to the island. The Blue Hats arrived. Officer Ron Feathers, a Maine State Trooper called out to their leader from the middle of the bridge, in front of the police cars. "This is the United States of America, a sovereign nation, under God. I command you by the authority invested in me by the State of Maine to leave here, and to leave Maine, and to return to your countries.

"In perfect English, a gentleman in a Blue Hat with a Continental French Accent called out. I am General Renney. I bear a letter from the President of the United States of America ordering our regiment to disband an illegal religious gathering in Acadia National Park. We are proceeding through in five minutes whether your cars are moved or not", he said.

"Then you have just declared war against the United States of America, and the state of Maine" said trooper Feathers.

"The letter is cosigned in ink by the governor of Maine" said General Renney.

"If this is so, *and I question the authenticity of such a letter*, then it would be that our President and Governor have also declared war against the United States and its Constitution. You cannot proceed, and I again order you to leave" said Ron Feathers.

"Five minutes. From your president. Five minutes" said officer Renney.

Cars, trucks, and Winnebagos were now piling up behind the police vehicles in a parking pattern that could only prove disastrous to the smooth flow of traffic at a McDonalds restaurant, or any bridge to any island. Armed millionaires and lobstermen together appeared on the bridge. The two-lane bridge stretched for over seven hundred feet between the mainland and the island, crossing a raised swampland at one point where shellfish made the best of it. At low tide, the water was indeed low, but impassable by any vehicle excluding those that might be amphibious. General Renney had only conventional troop carriers and jeeps. Their weapons were impressive for a small force, but any rifle could kill, including a deer gun.

"General Renney, you lose. Forget Bar Harbor Airport. Our forces have forbidden any military takeoffs or landings. You lose General. Why don't you just go back to France where you belong? It was you guys that sent us the Statue of Liberty, remember. You know about the Statue of Liberty General, don't you?" said Trooper Ron Feathers.

"One minute" said Officer Renney.

One minute elapsed. General Renney motioned with his hand to the driver of a Jeep. It was the best response that he could offer to Officer Ron Feathers and company. It had a machine gun mounted in the back. The machine gunner was placed high enough that he could shoot right over his driver's head with safety. It was an American Jeep with a UN logo on it. General Renney sent this, his most warlike equipment forward, with another motion of his hand. There was a driver, and an armed guard in the front seat, as well as the machine gunner. Several lobster fishermen moved forward in force. First they pulled down the machine gunner. "Wait, he said, in a strong Spanish Accent. I'm Catholic, look at my Rosary." He pulled out his Rosary as one large lobsterman with a red beard was single-handedly picking him up in the air and throwing him into the drink. He was yelling, almost politely though. He landed in two feet of raging current. He scrambled to his feet to hold onto part of the bridge above him. "I didn't want to do this. These crazy politicians. Help me. Help me. Pull me up", he said. He was joined by his fellow servicemen. One of them, an avid non-swimmer from Belgium had been thrown out somewhat further from the bridge in deeper water and was being swept out. A lobster boat came to his aid. The Spanish man continued to yell out. General Renney was not a happy General. He had sold God down the road a long time ago back in France. Ah, France, the first daughter of the Church. How far you had fallen with your self-illumination. General Renney, like most of France, was a baptized Catholic. That was then though, and this was now.

"Wait. Help", cried the very wet Spanish soldier. The third soldier, from Germany lost his hold on the bridge and was swept out toward a waiting lobster boat. The Spanish soldier continued his wailing. "I wish to defect. I claim asylum. Help me. I wish to defect". The same burly lobsterman with a long red beard reached down and pulled him up with the aid of a thirty-ish man from one of the island's monied families. The millionaire and the lobsterman talked to the Spanish soldier for five minutes, while General Renney stood smoking a cigarette.

The Spanish soldier was taking turns nodding at the handsome well dressed millionaire whose Mercedes was helping to block the bridge, and the lobsterman whose lobster traps were in need of their lobsterman, who was running late in his rounds. The Spanish soldier was apparently in agreement with whatever they had just asked of them. "Si. Si. Yes. Si."

The Spanish soldier walked halfway between General Renney and the lobsterman who had come out a ways with him. The lobsterman didn't need a weapon. You wouldn't want to get on this man's bad side. This gentle giant had lifted the Spanish soldier up over his head and stared in his eyes when they pulled him out of the water. He held him aloft for a minute or so asking him if he was serious about defecting. "General Renney. I now am, uh, am now defecting to the United States of America. I am defecting and putting myself in the hands of the highest-ranking officer on the side of justice, Officer Ron Feathers of the Maine State Police. I invite all of you, Catholics, other Christians, former Christians and those of other faiths or no faith, to defect also, and seek asylum on this island, which has been guaranteed. You have come here to end religious freedom, in the land of the free. You have come to fight God. You cannot fight God. I have been told that there is one on this island who has the power to sway armies, and you will again be safe should you defect. These people, these good Americans here do not wish to um, what you say surrender, to give up their Statue of Liberty, no their United States Constitution to a world government. They will fight to the death. I urge you to come with me, defect, and how you say, respect rights of a sovereign nation and its people", he said.

General Renney pulled a rifle out of a holder in his jeep. He aimed it at the Spanish soldier who stood perfectly still, showing the sincerity of his convictions. Another soldier stepped out of a troop truck and put a gun to General Renney's head. "General, before you go shooting anybody, I want you to consider this gun to your head. I'm a Catholic. I'm defecting and attending me a Medjugorje Conference" said the young Englishman. "You're coming with me, because I heard a rumor that there's a Croatian priest there who talks to God. I'm talking 'talks to God'. I'm going to introduce you to him, and then I'm gonna put my gun down. I won't need it after that. Now be a good bloke, and walk forward. You ever heard of Padre Pio General?"

Seventeen other soldiers followed General Renney and the English UN soldier. The remaining soldiers disembarked from their vehicles and watched the events from their side of the bridge. When General Renney and his escort, as well as the accompanying soldiers reached the lobsterman they all threw their guns into the water, all except for the Englishman with the gun to the head of General Renney. "We wish to defect they said in unison." Their English was as understandable to a Midwest farmer as the Down East accent of the Acadians. These men were part of an elite group that were to be the first of several waves of United Nation troops to conquer American soil in the name of 'lending assistance' to disaster victims, with the carte blanche of martial law in their back pockets. Several thousand of these troops, all thoroughly trained in the English language, and American customs were already stationed at several secret bases in the United States. Canada had its share of United Nations Troops also, as well as Mexico. Tens of thousands more UN troops were awaiting deployment to the United States. The troops were poised and waiting for such inevitable natural and economic disasters that had just struck the United States. Yes, the world leaders, the Gorbacevs and Prime ministers and presidents alike knew they were coming. God had sent his prophets. Satan had sent his apes, monkeys and decoys. He had used the information too. He had many scientists and environmentalists and false prophets on his side too. The enemy had prepared. The New World Order would come about soon, as soon as America would fall in line. The United States had to be broken first. There was too much freedom and free speech. That would come, with time, and with chastisements. The elite waited in comfort. The time came. The first wave of soldiers launched against Philadelphia Freedom had failed. Eighteen were now candidates for US citizenship, the Englishman included, and their former leader was held at gunpoint. Several hundred more were now watching the show from a distance. Word had just arrived that these United Nations troops would not likely receive other UN assistance in the next few days, if ever. The US military was still a possibility, but Trooper Ron Feathers took a gamble. There was now a hundred lobstermen, restaurant owners, and a few of these same resident and/or vacationing millionaires following directives from Trooper Feathers. They marched across the bridge, armed with their rifles. Several were on horseback. The United Nations troops did not arm themselves. Officer Feathers spoke: "Gentlemen, if you don't wish to defect, then you're under arrest by the authority invested in me by the state of Maine." He read them their rights. Many more of the soldiers wished to defect, but Trooper Feathers did not give them a chance to speak. Their defection would come later. Gentlemen, you can surrender your arms now, get in your vehicles and take them two miles back up the road whenst you came, to the Bar Harbor Airport, where they will be impounded and become the permanent property of the town of Bar Harbor. The other option is that we will forcibly take such things from you and deposit them in this here Atlantic Ocean on the double. Which will it be?" Nobody said anything at this point.

These foreign guys had seen enough American movies to feel like they were in a John Wayne western. They were actually enjoying themselves, you might say. Trooper Feathers nodded to the red bearded lobsterman, Mike Kopp. Mike threw a soldier out of the driver seat of the first jeep in line and told the others to get out, which they did. He drove it into the parking lot of the low budget outdoor lobster restaurant that hugged Route 3 and the bridge. He went over to talk to the owner, whom he knew, and came back to the jeep after addressing several patrons at the restaurant. He revved the engine, skidded forward and launched the jeep across a dock/lounge area, through a wooden railing and out into the swift, but thankfully shallow current racing through the narrows. Mike jumped from jeep just before impact. The jeep landed nose first, half covered with water, fell sideways, and there remained. Mike swam and walked to shore, to the cheering crowd of what was now thousands of people. The United Nations soldiers were leading the cheering. There was some freedom left in the press, and suddenly the whole country was told what was happening via satellite, television, radio, and computer, on an island off the coast of Maine. Millions had just seen lobsterman Mike Kopp in his first ever made for television jeep stunt. Suddenly the world's eyes were on Acadia National Park, and Bar Harbor. The UN soldiers were now about to follow Mike Kopp who had walked back to the UN troops and commandeered another jeep. "Follow me to the airport gentlemen", he yelled. A Ukrainian soldier had jumped into the front seat with Mike, and two Austrian soldiers joined them in the back seat. Mike pulled into the parking lot of the outdoor restaurant once more, which made his new found friends somewhat uneasy. They didn't have their bathing suits on...

"Hey, what are you doing?" said the Ukrainian who thought he was going to be driven to the airport. Mike walked over to the outdoor service window of the restaurant and asked his friend for four beers. He handed him a wet ten-dollar bill and walked back to the jeep, beers in hand.

"You guys ever had a Moose Butt?" said Mike, passing out the beers. He turned the jeep around, headed out of the parking lot onto Route 3 West. Fifty-five other UN vehicles turned around, each in their own turn, and followed the red bearded lobsterman down the road to Bar Harbor Airport. Bar Harbor Airport was not on the island, but was two miles west of the Atlantic on Route 3. The soldiers left a 7-foot pile of guns and weapons in a pile near the bridge.

On their return Mike Kopp lead the Catholic soldiers among them in the Rosary. They walked back towards the bridge that they had just left.

More than half of the European soldiers were baptized Catholics. Few of them knew their Faith. Fewer kept their Faith. Through the intercession of Mike Kopp, red necked, red bearded lobsterman from Somesville (a beautiful one-horse town on Mount Desert Isle), they now had their faith back. This old salt and now retired jeep driver had become their hero. Mike's faith grew abundantly that day too. Everybody's gotta serve someone, as the songwriter says. Mike hadn't been to Mass or confession for 10 years. He was a foul mouthed, beer drinking hell raiser until he met the United Nations soldiers who were about to tear asunder his US Constitution. He always carried his dear mother's Rosary in his pocket, however, by the grace of God. Now he was a 'born again' Catholic ready to die for his faith, for the faith of his fathers, for his belief in Jesus Christ as Lord and Savior, and Mother Mary, the simple Mother of Jesus. Yes, Mother Mary who would one day be proclaimed Coredemptrix, Mediatrix, and Advocate by dogmatic decree of Pope John Paul II.

Mike had initiated the Rosary with a Moose Butt in his left hand, and caught himself taking a swig after the Sign of the Cross. *Oh my* thought Mike, *I'm glad mom isn't here to see me*. He quickly tossed his bottle into a nearby garbage pail, and continued on.... Too late though, a cameraman had already immortalized Mike's opening prayers and swig of beer on film. *Don't try this at home kids...*

The Apostles Creed, an Our Father, and one Hail Mary having now been said, Mike launched into another Hail Mary as the cohort wove their way back to the great Atlantic, on foot. A German Protestant soldier in the group thought he remembered hearing some of the words of that prayer in the Bible. 'Yeah, the angel Michael, or was it Elizabeth', he thought. "Hail Mary, full of Grace, the Lord is with thee. Blessed art thou among women, and blessed is the Fruit of Thy Womb, Jesus...." *Maybe it was Michael and Elizabeth* thought the soldier. He found himself praying the Rosary before their march ended. Most of the soldiers began to join in on the Rosary. The world had never seen happier prisoners of war than it had on this day. Tears were coming down the eyes of many of the soldiers. It was the happiest day in the lives of nearly every one of these young men. They were so happy that God had won. And He never even fired a single shot – God, that is.

Oh God, thought Mike. *I'm gonna get these guys to walk all the way to Jordan Pond with me. They're gonna hear about Medjugorje. I'm gonna hear about Medjugorje. I bet I can get them to go if we can get a beer in them...* thought Mike in his best-intentioned old ways, with an evangelical twist. *We'll pray the Rosary the whole way...Wow*, thought Mike, glancing back at all the soldiers with a strange kind of look on his face. *These guys need some religion... Mary, please help me. Bring us all to Jesus..."*

****

One step forward, two steps backward. Communists preferred the reverse ratio. The world was now laughing at the New World Order, thanks to television, radio, and the Internet. Let them have their laugh thought the elite. Let them have their radio and television freedom a little longer. Let them print their evening news. Let them fly through cyberspace and the Internet laughing at the failed coup. They will be hungry soon, unemployed, and fighting amongst themselves. Then they will beg for us to come to their aid. We will come, noose in hand. Such were the thoughts of the presupposing high and mighty behind closed doors.

****

The English soldier, General Renney, and the seventeen former UN soldiers, and hundreds of others on the island side of the bridge had paused for a while to watch Mike Kopp and his one man show of his nautical knowledge as it relates to jeeps. The world cheered. Everyone on the bridge cheered. The English soldier put down his gun. General Renney had never been in a situation like this before. He realized that the One World Order was a lost cause should America prove to be a nation of Mike Kopps. Mike Kopp had captured nearly 400 troops single-handedly. Inside himself, General Renney was warming up to America. He had seen some John Wayne westerns too. Well, he owned them all. The Adventures of Mike Kopp beat them all. He was now planning his defection in his mind, though his countenance still displayed that stern, general-like look. All he wanted to do was get off his feet and have a beer with Mike Kopp. Suddenly the crowd on the island side of the bridge broke in two, and through their midst walked two Croatian men – a black haired, tall Franciscan Priest, and a shorter, younger man with a winning smile. The priest said a few words in Croatian, then began to speak French to the Frenchman, the general. "Can we speak on the island", he said to the general.   General Renney, the priest, the visionary, policemen, lobstermen, and a host of others made their way to the island to look for a comfortable place to sit and talk.

The town of Bar Harbor was preparing dinner for 1000 people. Lobster, fish, salad, bread, cheese, you name it. Volunteers were being mobilized. They had guests to feed. They would rise to the occasion.

****

After he had lead the pilgrims in the praying of the Rosary, Father Zdenko had the heavenly inspiration that he was needed at the bridge to the island. He was whisked off with Boris to the bridge by the Pierponts in their aged Chevy Blazer. They arrived just in time to see a jeep flying through the air into Mount Desert Narrows. Splash. What was that all about?

Several minutes later, Father Zdenko, Boris, the Pierponts, General Renney and the 18 UN troops, and several hundred others were walking back towards Thompson Island Information Center.   Thompson Information Center is on a little bit of an island that juts out to Mount Desert Narrows, where the bridge to the island crossed at its southernmost point. It was a small patch of land, a hundred acres at most, which was subject to flooding in severe tides. It was a mix of swamp grass, spruce, and balsams, with some hardwoods and brush thrown in for color. There was a parking area, and several large fields where hundreds could sit or stand.   The group headed for the largest field.   Father Zdenko had conferred with Trooper Feathers for a moment on the bridge, and Trooper Feathers initiated the removal of the friendly vehicles from the island side of the bridge. Their task was past. The first declared war against the United Nations was over. The UN had lost. Not a shot was fired, excluding the warning shot in Ellsworth. The sum of the casualties was one wet jeep that would be left in the water at Mount Desert Narrows, for posterity, and as a remembrance of the war.   Yes, the island, the newspapermen, the television and radio personalities were referring to the act of aggression as war. It was not a joke. They were saying that

President Clinton had declared war against the people of Mount Desert Isle, against the state of Maine.

The still free people were ready for two hangings that would not come – hangings of the President of the Republic, and the governor of the state, two turncoats who had shown their traitorous mettle. In this era, the press in North America was still clinging to a shadow of freedom, despite the fact that they were in on the take. Yes, the media, which was normally being used by the forces of darkness as a part of the plan, at least in the northern echelons of the media pyramid, would never again, in this era, be able to flex such unchecked, unedited, unrestrained reporting. Yet they would have the next few days at their disposal, to do and say what they may.

Perhaps God in His great mercy was allowing for one last roll call. He had sent his Mother, this EVER Virgin Mary, to LaSalette, Lourdes, Fatima, Akita, Betania, San Nicholas (Argentina), Kibeho (Rwanda), Seoul (South Korea), to Medjugorje and elsewhere. Some of the people heard Her call. Fewer listened to Her call. For some, Her messages fell upon rocky soil and died. For some, Her messages fell on fertile ground, sprouted, but were choked out by weeds. For a few million though, Her messages fell upon fertile soil, were nurtured and returned a hundred fold harvest. Yet, She came for everyone, not just millions. She spoke through Father Nairobi, yet most of Christ's priests pushed Her aside. The times she was preparing us for had arrived. True, they had arrived much sooner for Rwanda, and Bosnia, and the unborn of China and the west as well. But the times had come home to stateside now. Overnight, millions had joined the third world economy right here in the good old United States. And now, the press, our own devilish press was being allowed by God to spill the beans with headlines like: "New World Order Strikes Blow At Maine – UN Loses"; "President Sells Constitution Short – Land of The Former Free"; "A Nation Divided: 55% of Americans Say Impeach President"; "The Blue Hats: Who Invited Them?"; "Much Ado About Mary?"; "US Still A Sovereign Nation? – Guess Again"; "Big Money & The International Power Brokers – Who's Running The Country?"; "Christians Cry Foul: Say Apocalyptic Times Have Arrived"; "Pope Rebukes World Powers – Leave The Sovereign Nations Be"; "Bar Harbor: First of A Series of Coming UN Incursions?"; "Mike Kopp, Lobsterman: A Nation's Hero, A President's Downfall?"; "Mike Kopp: Put President Clinton In Chains"; "Mike Kopp: President Clinton Faces Arrest If Ever On Acadian Turf"; "The Neutering of a President: Its Time Has Come"; "Chastisements or Nature?"; "Bosnian Visionary Figures In Acadian Picture"; "The Saint Francis of Medjugorje?: Croatian Priest Brings Only Peace To Acadia"; "The New Age: An Old Devil In New Clothes?";

"Freemasonry Rallies Behind President: We Can't Go It Alone"; "One World Order On A Roll"; "Corking The Keg of World Power: Just Say No!"; "Old World Money: New World Order"; "Mike Kopp For President – Poll Shows Lobsterman Would Win 65% Of Vote"; "Lobsterman Leads Defeated United Nations Army In Rosary Rally – Captures 400 Troops, Then Converts Them", "Is The Virgin Mary Appearing At Acadia?: Reported Visionary Said To Be Having Daily Apparitions On Island"; "Words From Heaven Arriving At Acadia?"; "New World Order: How Deep Does The Cancer Run In World Government?"; "Who Runs America?".

Those in power had a keen desire to crush every living soul on Mount Desert Island. This option was seriously weighed in several darkened boardrooms around the world. They chose, however, to put a sinister smile on this "two steps backward" setback, and let the 'small people' have their day. They had their puppet President, their pioneeringly vile President apologize for the "mistake that was caused by a misunderstanding in the confusion of the moment due to the current physical blows levied against our country by nature, by nature alone". The president ordered all UN personnel, vehicles, weapons, and other materials to return and be returned to their headquarters in Portland, Maine, immediately. This was however, one of the greatest public relation blunders that the marionette formerly in the White House could have made. The press built this up even more than the initial failed coup attempt regarding Jordan Pond and the Virgin Mary. This was headline news for four days in the United States, and for even longer in other parts of the world. In a nutshell a compiled version of the world headlines might have read: "Acadians Tell President, United Nations, and One World Powers To Go To Hell: Will Keep Weapons and Vehicles Used To Launch War Against United States Residents In Maine – UN Troops Granted Asylum and Residency In Maine After Defection". The United Nations Vehicles and weapons were moved into Acadia National Park on the main island on Sunday, to assure their safekeeping. Most of the subsequent television, radio, newspaper, and magazine reporting and interviews of key people were thereafter held at the bridge, or in the field where the UN vehicles and weapons were now under armed guard, or at Jordan Pond, where the Medjugorje Conference was still underway.

Oh and Praise God for his mighty wonderful ways. After the initial first few hours and day of reporting of the historical events on Mount Desert Isle, the world wanted to know what the war was all about in the first place. Yes, they were calling it a war! A war of aggression, but a war all the same! But why were foreign troops sent? Why? An Attack On Religious Freedom? An Attack on Catholicism? Who were the key players? How Did They Get 13,000 people, and later over 20,000 people together on an island in cold Atlantic to pray? Were they armed? Yes, by all means. They were armed with the Rosary!

And so the press came. The world came to Bar Harbor and vicinity. Not the military however. A statement was issued from Hancock County and Bar Harbor that any military aircraft attempting to land at Bar Harbor Airport would be fired upon, no matter what words were written on their side, be they 'Air Force One' or 'Eat At Joe's'. Just how much affect deer rifles would have been on F-14s is debatable, but the point was made. Aggression against Christians getting together to pray or play horseshoes for that matter would not be tolerated Down East. Down Easter's would never, never tolerate these supposed new laws against religious freedom or gatherings. In fact, all laws banning public gatherings, or gatherings by permit only were being stricken from public law up and down the New England Coast. The country was not blind. They had ears to hear, and eyes to see, and hear and see they did and would continue to do. The press loved it. The world saw everything. Most major programming was dropped for the next two weeks in North America. If the media was not covering the earthquake or hurricane or other natural disasters of the period, it was news from Bar Harbor that was in the headlines of the media. Indeed, even when the media was in West Virginia, trying to cover the President and Congress in their makeshift headquarters, the questions of religious freedom and the attack on Maine were the lead stories. Also in the headlines were stories covering foreign troops on American soil, and reports of concentration camps and compounds that had been set up in the United States and Canada

Yes, the press would be able to go on for some days and weeks waving their American Flag and crying 'unfair'. When the country was hungry; when further jobs were threatened; when the President brought the gas lines back; when the country would again bow to Mammon and ask to go back 'into Egypt with Damon' - then the press would grow cold, by order from on high (from the depths, actually), and would shake off any further attempts of playing boy scouts. Those who would not fall in line would have their microphone and/or pen confiscated, or would simply be sent packing, blackballed, and blacklisted. The news anchors would have to choose between feeding their families or picking up their crosses and following Jesus Christ. *Yet, manna was still an option from Heaven.*

In a very short time the world learned of Medjugorje, and Our Lady's messages of prayer, penance, fasting, confession, daily Mass, the Rosary, and endurance. Many in the world fell in love with this Virgin Mary, Her Son Jesus Christ, and this Church He founded, the only church to even care to trace a direct succession of leaders, Popes, in a direct line straight back to Saint Peter. This was the Catholic Church. The world heard about Medjugorje, and Jesus & Mary, through the words of Father Zdenko. They read him for what he was - a saint among us, like a Mother Teresa, unwavering in charity and steadfastness, a promoter of orthodoxy. They heard Father Zdenko, and Boris, and a host of others as far away as Biloxi and Key West, Moscow and Cork, Peking and Seoul, London and Melbourne. They heard them speak of Mary calling the world back to Her Son, Jesus Christ, the only Lord and Savior of us all, while there is yet time. They heard and read the words of the speakers at the 1998 Acadia Medjugorje Conference, via radio, television, newspapers and magazines, and yes, word, sound and even video traveled the world from Acadia National Park to the world through the ineffable Internet. Through this latter means, Our Lady had permeated the strong barriers of hatred for Christianity poised on the borders of the likes of Saudi Arabia, North Korea, Cuba, China, and all places between.

Such news was not welcome by all, to be sure, and they would have none of it. A line had been drawn. Perhaps, from beside a little lake, this Jordan Pond, from the site of a Marian conference, the world had come to understand why America was undergoing chastisements that would reverberate throughout the world, until the end of this era - the time preceding the Reign of the Immaculate Heart of Mary, and The Eucharistic Heart of Jesus. This was hard for some to hear. No, they would have none of it. They would not have their "rights" to abortion ripped from them. They would not surrender their baby killing creams and pills. They would keep their gay rights and wear them on their sleeves. They included the conservatives, the liberals, and many members of the Catholic Church, the Protestant Church, No Church, the New-Agers, and the 'Euthanasers'. They also included those who have at least honestly expressed their hatred for the Catholic Church and what it stands for, the crowd that calls themselves "We Are Church" – the Synagogue of Satan to be sure, referencing Revelations. But again, the Book does say that God wins in the end though. The victory is Christ's.

By 4:30 in the evening, Father Zdenko, Boris Baric, General Renney, four hundred UN Troops, and hundreds of individuals from Mount Desert Island began to seat themselves in the larger grassy area on Thompson Island, the patch of ground in Mount Desert Narrows, just before Mount Desert Island. It was a welcome surprise to the UN troops marching in formation back from Bar Harbor Airport that they were to be the welcomed guests of the town of Bar Harbor and the other communities from Mount Desert Island. The local townspeople had gone to the trouble of preparing enough food for a thousand guests. Locating the lobster was the easy part. Amassing enough greens for salad, breads, and other foods was the challenge. The food was arriving in municipal vehicles as the troops and others were finding a patch of ground to call their own for the next hour. By this time, all of the UN troops, local residents and others arriving on Thompson Island were now aware that they had among them a Saint Francis of sorts. Yes, he was a living saint of God purified by the machinations of communism and other fires, and like the rest of us, still undergoing his trials and purgations. This man of course, was Father Zdenko. Also in their midst was Boris Baric, whom they now knew to be one of the six visionaries of Medjugorje, Bosnia-Herzegovina. If they did not know of the story of Medjugorje, and Our Lady's daily apparitions to the six youthful men and women from this hamlet since June 24, 1981, they now knew. News had spread like wildfire. General Renney had asked his troops to gather around as close to Father and Boris as they could. Father and Boris were about to speak to them while they ate their lobster dinners, which was a first for many of the soldiers. By the grace of God, there was a Muslim from Mostar, Bosnia Herzegovina amongst troops. He was immediately affronted when he was asked to serve as an interpreter for Father, but minutes later, upon meeting Father Zdenko, his heart melted, meeting the saint of God whom looked very much like he could have been his blood brother. And so, Father, through his compatriot interpreter began.

"Dear soldiers of Europe, from Germany and France, Belgium and Holland, England, Spain, Portugal, and yes even my own Bosnia-Herzegovina and Croatia: We might begin by all of us asking ourselves why we are here. Why are you here? I dare to give you in response, the same answer that I give to pilgrims from your very own countries, including millions from the United States, who come to our Medjugorje. It is Our Lady who brought you here. She does not discriminate if you are a Catholic, Protestant, Muslim, or Jew. Her Son Jesus was a Jew. Sometimes he found the most faith amongst those who were not of His faith. She loves you all, and she brought you here. Perhaps you would say, that world leaders sent you here, not a Woman, not God, but Presidents and Prime Ministers. My answer would be the same. A Woman brought you here. Yet since God, through this Woman, used human instruments, it is still fair to ask the question, 'Why did men send you here?' To answer this question we need to examine what has taken place in this country in the last few days, and perhaps in the last fifty years, because the storms and disasters in the United States are not random. They did not just happen. Perhaps they are a wake up call for a nation that has become too puffed up with itself, for a nation that no longer protects the innocent, and the least among the innocent, the unborn. Did the Holy Father not say to this nation just a few years ago that a nation that does not protect the most innocent, the unborn, cannot stand?   Perhaps this nation will learn from this experience.   But let us ask again, why did men send you here?   Why do the world powers want you here?   Why did the United Nations send a small army to attack 15,000 praying people on an island of peace?   What arms did they have but Rosaries and Bibles?   Why did men send you here?   I propose that Satan chose wicked men to send you here, to fight religion, to fight God.   Yet God has used even this for His own purpose.   Here we are now, praising God!"

"It would seem to me that the designs of those men who have sent you here were wicked, and that they have failed.   Defeated by prayer.   Defeated by a Woman.   Most of you have been trained thoroughly in the history of the United States.   You are elite soldiers, chosen from among men.   Freedom.   You all know of American freedom.   The United States is a land that men and women dream of, throughout the world.   So many would give up everything to come here.   Why?   Freedom.   This country was founded on freedom.   You soldiers, I daresay, know of its founders.   You know of George Washington.   You know of the very good man Abraham Lincoln.   What would they think to see you here today?   Men have sent you here to crush liberty.   You are not here to assist the earthquake victims, buried in brick, beams, and metal.   You are not here to assist the victims of flood, fire, and hurricane, for they are not found here.   There was only peace here, and loyalty to a nation founded on goodness and on God, who is all Goodness.   You are the first wave of foreign soldiers sent here to crush a sovereign nation in times of great distress.   You have been defeated, by God, through good people and this lobster fisherman here" said Father with a broad smile on his face.   "You may have seen his boat docked a few hundred feet from the bridge, to the north, as we came on this island."   He heard his nation was under attack by a foreign power.   He came to its aid.   God has raised up a Gideon here, this Mike Kopp.   Come here Mike," said Father.   Mike stoop up and walked over to Father.   "Does he look like your enemy?   Is this fisherman an enemy of peace?   Is this fisherman an enemy of this country?   No?   Then why have men sent you here to attack him and his homeland?   Perhaps you will say 'but no shots were fired'.   I tell you it is enough that you came here armed, prepared to attack religion, to attack a sovereign nation, to attack perhaps the largest Rosary Rally that this nation has seen in decades!   It is enough that you have come with your guns and jeeps."

"A soldier must follow orders you say," said Father.   "True.   Absolutely.   An army without discipline is chaotic and dangerous.   But you must obey God's laws first.   If you do not know God's laws, you must obey the natural laws that God has put into the heart of every man.   Every soldier must obey the natural law, or he will face God's justice.   Your leaders who sent you here - are they obeying the natural law, or are they working to bring about a world of darkness, a subdued world no longer able to respond to great crimes of injustice leveled at people and nations? Ask yourself this, as you are the ones who have been sent here to subdue the people of this sovereign nation. This nation's constitution speaks of one nation under God. Yet, I ask America's lawyers, presidents and governors, congressmen and senators, and you of the secret societies: "Why have you removed the Ten Commandments from your courthouses? Why are you killing the unborn and aged? Why are you proselytizing your children in your schools to the ways of secular humanism, the religion of Satan and unbelief? Why are you allowing that hedonism to take place, which was responsible for the fire falling upon Sodom and Gomorrah? Yes, the United States is a diseased country in a diseased world. You have finally found that you are no longer exempt from pain and suffering, as a nation, despite your riches and bounty. I say to the Americans that are here - God is speaking to you through signs and wonders. I say to the soldiers here, who are you going to believe and follow, God or the Devil? Will you serve the One World Order, or will you serve God? You were the first line of offense for those who think that they are illuminated in the world, the hidden rich in the clubs that rule the world. You will not be the last. Despite this inevitability, you must still ask yourselves whom you as individuals serve."

Father spoke on, about God, about Jesus, the Son of God, and Mary's historic role, and Her role in the world today, like John the Baptist of old, preparing the way for Jesus, who will come again in glory. He then began to speak in detail on Our Lady's messages from Medjugorje. Boris assisted Father with details, history, and anecdotal stories.

An hour later, Father Zdenko and Boris were answering questions and wrapping up their talk to the crowd. General Renney was invited by Father to say a few words. "Men, as you know, eighteen among our ranks have claimed asylum in the United States of America. You all know that regulations call such men traitors and they are subject to death in times of war. Eighteen from among our ranks chose not to risk the possible death of men, women, and children of a sovereign nation who were gathered in peace praying to God. Eighteen. Perhaps there will soon be nineteen. At this time, as prisoners of war, we are being marched further eastward, to our original planned destination. If you get lost, just look for the gentleman with red beard. Do not get in a jeep with him". The crowd broke into an uncontrollable laugh. "We're going on foot. We're leaving now. See you there." As the troops and the many others headed back towards the bridge, now further eastward onto Mount Desert Island, they broke into spontaneous song, singing Amazing Grace. Our Lady has told the visionaries of Medjugorje that this is her favorite song. The

Englishman who a short while ago had held a gun to the head of General Renney, and this same General Renney were singing quietly as they walked along together. They had their arms on each other's shoulders, and tears were coming from their eyes. Father Zdenko and Boris were right behind them.

****

When the troops and attached crowd arrived at Jordan Pond two hours later, about 7:30 PM, they arrived to the sound of the Rosary, echoing throughout the valley. The faithful had foregone talks and music and had continued in prayer in the absence of Father Zdenko, Boris, and the others that had gone to assist them.

As the Rosary finished, Rick Tremont was at the microphone telling the people that they would be hearing from three remaining speakers that evening. First Boris Baric, then a Baptist minister from Alabama, and finally the beloved Father Zdenko.

Boris gave a detailed summary of the events in Medjugorje since June 24th, 1981. He spoke of the faith of the people before this date, historically, and since this date. He covered the heart of Our Lady's messages. Then he entertained a half an hour's worth of questions. The last question came from the Muslim who interpreted for Father Zdenko. "This Mary, the same Virgin Mary mentioned in our Muslim Koran as the Virgin Mother of Jesus, does she ever mention various religious faiths? Perhaps I am the only Muslim here (in fact, there were 16 other Muslims in the group). There does not seem to be anything for my people in these messages. Is that so?"

"Our Lady has never stated to us that everyone should become Catholic. Perhaps she would smile at this, but I do not know. She has told us to respect people of all faiths. The characteristics of how you say in English, Peace, Love, Prayer, Penance, Fasting, and so forth are universal, and should be practiced by people of all faiths. Once we asked, in those early days, if Our Lady would give us an example of a person in our village who was holy, so we would know better, um, how to act. We are a Catholic village, almost everyone. There are just a few Muslims in our village. Everyone gets along great. Our lady told us that the person who was holiest in our village was a Muslim lady. We almost died. We asked her again. We said, 'but she is a Muslim'. Our Lady said she knew that she was a Muslim. She said she was the holiest person in the village. Later, reflecting on this, we could not think of anyone in our village who was more kind than her. It was true. Some Catholics have stopped believing in Our Lady's messages from Medjugorje when they have heard this, or read this. Mary was speaking of an individual, not of a religion, however. We must remember the pagan centurion whose servant Jesus healed. What did he tell him? 'I have not seen such faith in all of Israel'. True, the first story here, about the Muslim lady speaks of holiness, in what you say, in general, and not simply faith in Jesus as in the case of the centurion. Yet, Jesus himself did give us the example of the good Samaritan, where, caritas, that is charity was his quality, not his religion or faith. He was of a different faith than Christ. Charity is very important. It is faith in action. Our Lady comes for all people everywhere, regardless of who we are, or what our faith is. She is the Mother Jesus, the Son of God. She would have us all come to Heaven to be with Her Son...To balance this, she calls us to daily Mass, monthly confession, and so forth. These things can only be found in one place. Yet, she loves us all. Jesus loves us all. Mary's call goes out to us all. It is up to us to respond...

****

At 8:45 PM, the sun was long gone, the stars were out, and sky was as black as the light from the myriad of stars would allow on this warm July evening. Several hundred pilgrims had to leave because of age, or illness, or children who needed to be bedded down for the evening, tucked into warm beds and sleeping bags throughout the island and nearby mainland. An occasional lightning strike somewhere well off in the distance added a beautiful flash in the dark sky every so often. Allison Welday and several other musicians who had joined her were just finishing up the song "As I kneel Before You". Many in the crowd had actually assumed a kneeling position in front of Our Lady's statue that had been brought to the stage. Among them were many of the UN troops who had made their way close to the stage.

Rick Tremont was now about to introduce Rev. John and Paulette Wesley, and their children, who hailed all the way from Schuster Alabama, a forgotten town in the northwest corner of Alabama. John was about to speak of a revival meeting he had just been a part of, a revival that had torn Schuster Alabama asunder.

The introductions were made. John's family made their ways to chairs behind him and to the left of the stage. Father Zdenko was sitting with John's family, next to Paulette Wesley, occasionally sharing a word or two with her and her children while John spoke. Rick Tremont walked off the stage and spent a minute or so with the Bohatch family, and the Pierponts. Then Therese Pierpont and Rick went off to the edge of the balsams, a few hundred feet from the stage, and just a few yards from Jordan Pond. They sat down together to listen to what could have been the climax of this eventful conference of ever climaxing events. John had a story to tell as powerful as any that had been told. The audience was hushed and captured the moment John first started to speak.

"It's a strange thing to find out that the one whom you thought was your greatest enemy, a perilous pitfall for one fifth of the world's population and two thirds of all Christians, is really your friend, your Coredemptrix, Mediatrix, and Advocate. A strange feeling indeed." John paused for a long time, as if his whole life was flashing before his mind, and he was seeking through prayer, the most important aspects of which to convey to the pilgrims. So many things, so many major ideas and events to choose from. "I have had my eyes upon this Jesus of yours all of my life. My faith has never wavered as I have heard, direct from you, as has the faith of so many of you. I thought that you were on a different path than mine, yours on the way to Hell, and I on my born again way to Heaven. I thought that I was a Bible scholar, my degrees said so, but I see now, that I knew nothing. I feel perhaps somewhat like your Thomas Aquinas felt, no - as our Thomas Aquinas felt, when he saw Heaven. He said he would not preach again having been so enraptured by God. The last week of my life has been as if I was at the movies, and even without seeing what was playing, had all knowledge of the events impressed indelibly upon my soul. And the movie was about Jesus, his Eucharist, and His Mother Mary. The knowledge came to me at a revival in Alabama, and in a van on the highway between here and there. It came through the scripture my wife was reading to me as we drove along, and through the conversion stories of Scott Zahn and Tom Rutbensky that I played over and over on the way here. The knowledge came to me when I was awake, and the knowledge came to me in my dreams. I am a different man than the one who left Alabama. And then we arrived here, and my conversion began again. Yes, I have been, until just days ago, a very anti-Catholic Baptist minister with the strange name of John Wesley, strange at least for a Baptist minister. My story is even stranger.

"Jumping through my whole life as a devout Baptist, until just under a week ago, I found myself giving what might have been considered the main sermon at a Christian revival in Schuster, Alabama. In some aspects, the Sacraments aside sadly, it seems that we have been, in Schuster, as the saying goes, 'More Catholic than the Pope'. You see, we never fell for birth control. We never fell for its fruit, abortion. Schuster has the highest birth rate and the lowest divorce rate of any town in the United States. The two go hand in hand. When one says no to life, one says no to marriage. We owe these beliefs to one man, my predecessor Rev. Earl Potter, now deceased. Earl would have burned down the pharmacy himself than to allow the foul stain of this hedonism to be marketed there or anywhere else in town. We are a Baptist town with a fair number of Methodists to boot. Strange, a Catholic would have been welcome in our town, if he checked his faith at the border. Otherwise, us supposedly good Christians might have made things tough for him. What a dichotomy we presented to Jesus. You will find nary a Mason or member of a secret society in Schuster too. Rev. Earl Potter saw to this several decades ago. He personally destroyed a lodge being erected in the town at the time. He used an ax on the stud walls being erected. Strange, the lodge left him alone. Perhaps because he was one of them, to a degree, a White Anglo-Saxon Protestant. The lodge gave the land to the town. Perhaps they felt their brother Earl was demented. Sadly I hear that some of you, supposedly with Rome, have turned to the lodge, this lodge that the Virgin Mary refers to as the Black Beast of Revelations. As I understand it, when a Catholic becomes a Mason he brings automatic excommunication upon himself.

"We are a praying town, and even, it may surprise you a town of fasting and penance. We believe in miracles. When someone in town is sick or injured, or in urgent need of prayer, there are nights when I can assure you that more than half of the adults in town are praying for those special needs, often combining prayer with some form of fasting. So you see, Schuster has been an oddity awash in a sea of sin, and in many ways, as I have said, very akin to things Catholic, and in these respects more devout besides. And you see also, some of my background, and the background of our community. We thought we were so close to God, we thought you were so far from Him. And so I found myself addressing the subject of John 6:48-70 last weekend, at a tent revival in our town. One of our elders had asked me to cover the subject, saying he had never heard a proper explanation preached on it. Strange, I have a considerable portion of the Bible memorized, but when he first told me John 6:48-70, I had no idea what it was about. Yes, I had no idea what these few lines covered, even though the whole of Scriptures hinges on them. I was one of several preachers this day. The whole town turned out, Methodists too. We saw no drastic differences in our faith. The Baptist and Methodist ministers were preaching side by side, as they do in our town.

"I was to give the final sermon Saturday evening. I read the given scriptures to the people: 'I am the bread of life. Your fathers did eat manna in the desert, and they are dead. This is the bread which cometh down from heaven; that if any man eat of it, he may not die. I am the living bread which came down from heaven. If any man eat of this bread, he shall live forever; and the bread that I will give, is my flesh, for the life of the world. The Jews therefore strove among themselves, saying: How can this man give us his flesh to eat? Then Jesus said to them: Amen, amen I say unto you: Except you eat the flesh of the Son of man, and drink his blood, you shall not have life in you. He that eateth my flesh, and drinketh my blood, hath everlasting life: and I will raise him up in the last day. For my flesh is meat indeed: and my blood is drink indeed. He that eateth my flesh, and drinketh my blood, abideth in me, and I in him. As the living Father hath sent me, and I live by the Father; so he that eateth me, the same also shall live by me. This is the bread that came down from heaven. Not as your fathers did eat manna, and are dead. He that eateth this bread, shall live for ever.' And John goes on...

"I thought", continued Rev. Wesley, "I thought that I had given an exquisite discourse on the subject after about 15 minutes of explanation. I had just opened the topic to questions, and the class clown, the class troublemaker, if such a thing could be said of any of our teenagers in Schuster, asked a very pointed question 'Why didn't he call them back?' You see many of Christ's disciples walked away from him – we see this and Christ's response following John 6:59. I gave the brash young man the simple what you might call Protestant response 'They misunderstood him'.

"The young man shot back with question after question, as if he was a Daniel in the audience defending the Susanna in question, or in this case, like Susanna's, defending the truth. He would have no part in the suppression of the truth. He would not have Susanna stoned, nor this truth hidden. He was like a machine gun with his questions. It was as if his whole life had been in preparation for this moment. I daresay the young man was under direct inspiration from the Holy Spirit, because I tell you he was the worst religion student I ever had. I was trying to get away from him, desperately looking for another hand to respond to. He stood up and bluntly asked. 'Rev. Wesley. You know that I am not the best student. I am slow. I have often had to stay after school for help in my classes. I am amazed that I will even be graduating in the coming year. You know this too. If I in my slowness were about to fall into Hell, wouldn't you call me back?'

"I told him I would. He shot back question after question. He said something to the effect 'Then if Christ's disciples, many of them, at least, were about to walk away from Him forever, into Hell, why didn't He call them back?' I responded that Christ surely must have known that they would return at some point in their life.

"The young man said 'No, they never returned'. I responded that surely, in time, they would have returned. Jesus would not let them walk to Hell unawares.

"'No, he responded. They never came back.' I fumbled through the scriptures. There it was, John 6:67: 'After this many of his disciples went back; and walked no more with him'.

"At this point my whole faith was shaken. It was not just the questions from the boy. I too felt the power of the Holy Spirit upon me. Things were being revealed to my soul at this moment, in a way that I cannot explain. I could no longer believe that Jesus would let a large number of his disciples, his best friends walk off from Him, 'no longer to walk with him', because of a misunderstanding. Christ must have meant what he said, 'He that eateth my flesh, and drinketh my blood, abideth in me, and I in him'. The disciples knew what he was saying, as is now very evident to me. We can consider John 6:61: Many therefore of his disciples, hearing it said: This saying is hard, and who can hear it?' *They were not accusing Jesus of a bad joke.* They were accusing Jesus of speaking truth that was hard for them to hear. My discourse with the young man continued, and the audience, miraculously including the many babies in the crowd were hushed. Everyone's ears were tuned to our dialogue. My heart began to long for the Eucharistic Jesus. I was a broken man. I could no longer defend my ways. The young man had defeated me with his pointed questions that opened the doors to truth. They were not stock one-liners memorized for the sole purpose of proselytization, as so often happens. They were the keys to the doors of truth, as is evidenced by scripture in many places; by Christ in John 6 and at the Last Supper, and by Saint Paul himself letting us know that **if we eat and drink the body and blood of Christ unworthily we bring unto ourselves condemnation.** *This does not happen with Pepperidge Farms, or Wonder Bread, white, whole wheat or reduced calorie bread for that matter...*"

John was talking much softer now. The crowd was listening wholeheartedly. The PA system was working perfectly, as if a professional sound crew had been working on it for weeks in advance. Indeed the sound system had received a good deal of attention from Joshua Pauley, who was turning out a mountain of cassettes, and had not missed a single talk or song since setting up on Friday. He had become of tireless hero of preserving the conference for the rest of the world to hear and meditate upon. He, like so many others, was a new man, yes, a 'born-again' Catholic, alive in the ways of Christ and His Church. He was now in the middle of changing tapes, for Paul was on a roll, and continued in his conversion story.

"I do not know what I am going home to – to what we, our family are going home to when we are done here in Maine. I know that I am going home unemployed. How can I complain in the light of the fact that God has still blessed us with life when others are suffering from the effects of earthquakes, hurricanes, flood, and fire. More than that even, God has brought us to true life, and we will, as soon as we can, be entering into the

Faith of old, the Faith of Our Fathers, and your Fathers, before the Reformation – the Roman Catholic Faith, which I so much despised so recent in time.

"I have given you a glimpse of my life in the last few days. I want you to know that the revival was just the beginning. I want to stress the importance of using the tools that God has given us to spread the Catholic Faith. My family's conversion was further clinched by two cassette tapes, scriptures, and a few other Catholic apologetics materials that we have read, studied, and consumed in the last few days. At a rest stop in Alabama some 'idiot' proselytizing for God-knows-what, *I thought*, placed two cassette tapes on our windshield. She escaped with her family in their getaway vehicle before I could yell at her. She must have seen my clergy bumper sticker, as best I can surmise, because the other windshields in the lot were free of her tapes. Or maybe Our Lady told her to put them on our car, I don't know. The tapes were the conversion stories of Professor Scott Zahn and Tom Rutbensky. Though I was determined to become a Catholic after last Saturday night, I see now that I might have fallen into a period of agitation or complacency after the initial shock had worn off, if I had not been allowed by the grace of God to follow up with this blessed Catholic apologetics material. These tapes and other materials, as I said, cinched our desire to become Catholic. We also spent a great deal of time this week listening to a tape on Our Lady by a professor of theology, a well known Mariologist from Franciscan University, but I cannot remember his name. We have been told that there are several holy Mariologists – theologians with a Marian specialty at the College. When a Baptist or a Protestant considers a walk in faith into the Catholic Church, Mary is sometimes the last remaining roadblock. This professor gives such a lucid, biblically and historically based defense for Mary's roll in the Church that I feel he must be the scourge of Hell, speaking so eloquently of such a mother as the Mother of Jesus, and the Mother of us all. I would like to meet this professor some day. God, I wish I could remember his name...

"The materials I have read, or that my wife has read to me in the last few days while we were on the road have answered so many questions that I never even dared to even pose to myself in the past. All of the roadblocks that I have had set in place for Catholicism have come tumbling down - from 'Faith Alone', yes, which James so eloquently puts to rest, to 'Sola Scriptura' - Scripture Only, which is simply not in the Bible, period. I now know what to believe when Catholicism is attacked because of its intimacy with certain questionable persons in history, past or recent. For example, say there was a certain pope that lived in the Middle Ages whom history teaches may not have been particularly known for his chasteness. Well, there is an answer for that, too. And that answer could be - 'Yes, wasn't he a big sinner. And isn't it great that Jesus still works through such people, and sinners like you and me, we who dare to call ourselves Christians. Perhaps a good follow-up would be 'If thou, O Lord, wilt mark iniquities: Lord, who shall stand it?' - Psalm 129. Are we really qualified to cast the first stone? Judas, we must remember too, did not cancel the efficacy of Christ's Church, yet he represented 1/12 of the hierarchy. In the future when I hear the scoffers telling the Papists that Jesus said 'call no man your father but your Father in heaven', I know now to look at the implied context, and to remember that Saint Paul called himself 'Our father in Christ'. When my friends say "But John, the words and phrases such as Pope, Bishop, Archbishop, Queen of Heaven, Immaculate Mary, Eucharist, and on and on and on and on... are not in the Bible, I will remind them that the word 'Bible' is not in the Bible. Neither are the words and phrases such as 'Rapture, Faith Alone, Sola Scriptura, King James Version, altar call, Methodist, Baptist (As in denomination, not John), Presbyterian, and so on.

"My life in the last week, and the life of my family has been an adventure that I am so happy we embarked upon. At first it was a nightmare. Our world had to fall apart first, before God could begin to build us up again, on a new foundation, on the rock, which is Peter. I must begin to end now, my talk that is, and my life as a Baptist Preacher, but I have to tell you that at this moment, in this place..., I feel as if I am almost in heaven now. On this earth there is no place I would rather be at this time, than right here with all of you. It is good to be here."

John paused for a moment, and looked at the stars in the sky. A warm breeze blew, and the distant lightning continued to illuminate the sky every few moments. "It, it is a strange thing, that we have wound up here, in this beautiful state of Maine, on this blessed island that surely must be a glimpse of Paradise. John was looking at the audience now, the sky, and then the crowds again. I thank God and His holy Mother Mary for having brought us here, to such a place, at such a time. Now, I'm not very good at this yet, but would you all join me in saying a Hail Mary for those suffering from the disasters in our nation right now, and for the conversion of our nation. John held a Rosary booklet in one hand, and a flashlight and microphone in the other. He spoke *"Hail Mary, full of Grace, the Lord is with thee. Blessed art thou among women, and blessed is the Fruit of thy womb, Jesus. Holy Mary, Mother of God, pray for us sinners, now and at the hour of our death, amen.* Thank you and God bless you...." Mrs. Wesley and Father Zdenko rose and met John with hugs. The children followed in suit.

****

The Carolinas were taking a pounding from Michael. Evacuations were ongoing. Devastation was complete in many areas. More people were praying in the Carolinas than had ever prayed before. They were joined in their prayers with the people of Florida, Washington D.C., California, and the rest of the nation. Their prayers were brought before the Lamb by the ancients, these intercessors from the book of Revelations who are found in heaven. The prayers were in "golden vials full of odors, which are the prayers of the saints". Many of those who were "going down to sleep" from the power unleashed through nature were reaping the benefits of the prayers of the faithful. A deathbed conversion should not to be gambled upon, as Saint Augustine tells us, but nevertheless it is a pearl of great price, of infinite price.

****

The large waves continued to roll into Mount Desert Island, many of them having arrived with their energy unchallenged after having traveled for thousands of miles. They were pounding the rocks of Mount Desert Island today. They were furious, but their anger ceased at the borders of the island. Only their empty roar continued up the banks and into the balsams.

****

Father Zdenko spoke for merely twenty minutes on Our Lady, as seen through the eyes of that glorious servant of God, Saint Louis Marie Grignon de Montfort. Few in the crowd left during his talk, despite the late hour and the absence of amenities. At the end of his talk he led more than 12,000 people in Saint Louis de Montfort's long consecration to Our Lady. The evening was now complete. He and twenty-seven other priests then lined up in front of the stage and began to pray over the people, one by one, as the crowds began to diminish. They were reminded by Rick Tremont that they would again assemble at the newly scheduled time of 9 AM tomorrow. The crowds would be back. Four hundred UN soldiers began to unfurl their bedrolls on the lawn at Jordan Pond House. Their General was with them. He had just defected to the United States of America. Subsequent to that he had gone to confession with Father Zdenko. He was so thankful that his family had just arrived in the United States, his wife and seven children aged 1 to 14. He had lost his faith long ago, but had been a disciple of Humana Vitae just the same. He was too much of a man to have ever fallen for the filth of artificial birth control.

He stared at the stars with the rest of his former comrades at arms, wondering what he was going to do for a living. At a little known military airstrip, at a barracks in upstate New York, Mrs. Renney and her seven children had just finished praying a Rosary for her husband. She knew that her husband had been sent to Portland, Maine, earlier in the day. She was hoping he would hear of the Medjugorje Conference that was taking place a few hours away on the coast of Maine near Bar Harbor. She read of the conference on a bulletin board at an old Catholic Church, Saint Monica's, nearby the barracks. A young man had just been to the church and put up a flyer on the conference that he had run-off on his computer. He figured that since Bar Harbor *was only nine hours away* some of the parishioners might want to make a run over there. Mrs. Renney prayed that Our Lady would bring the General there. He was a stubborn, proud man that had been away from his Faith for too long. She feared for his soul. But Monica Renney had Faith that could move mountains. She would pray for thirty years if she had to..." After seeing the notice for the conference in the morning, Monica and the children kept themselves busy setting up house in the barracks. There were few others at the base on this day, and the family was left alone. They had not heard the news from Maine...

****

Sunday had come and was now waning. There was Mass, the Rosary, the Chaplet, over 7000 confessions, and several speakers. The world press had come too. There was a Taiwanese contingent, and an Australian crew too. There were several European crews, and journalists and reporters from other diverse parts of North, South, and Central America, and the world as well. The world now knew of the events at Jordan Pond. They knew of the attack on American Sovereignty at the bridge to Mount Desert Island. They knew of Our Lady's messages from a little town in Bosnia-Herzegovina, this Medjugorje. The world heard from a minister from Alabama; a Croatian priest; a Medjugorje visionary; a mechanic from Michigan; and a Catholic evangelist from California. They heard from a Boston lawyer and his lawyer friend from Seattle; a former New-Ager from Purdue and her friend – a formerly fallen away Catholic New Age record producer. They also heard a father from Steubenville who wanted to get a few vacationers together to pray the Rosary; a State Farm agent – the former nemesis of Tom Rutbensky; a couple from Texas; a priest seeking confirmation in his calling to the priesthood; several other priests; two nuns; and a former General with the French military, on loan to the UN, now claiming asylum in the United States of America. They heard too, from a National Park Superintendent. They heard from Mohammed Jackson and his wife Gloria on the subject of God's precious babies. Others spoke briefly, too.

And somehow, by the grace of God, it was told over and over by the national and international press and through the Internet, via the mouths of speakers from Croatia to California that the world was suffering because of sin - that the United States was now suffering from such chastisements due to sin. The greatest among these sins, the greatest affront to God is abortion, and secondarily its related sins of impurity. It was not that the 20,000 or so who had come to pray at Jordan Pond had been exempted from sin – had never seen the inside of an abortion clinic. If only it had been so, for themselves, progeny, and for all mankind. The message from Jordan Pond for the world was that the Mother of Jesus has come to ask us to just try. Just try. That's all. God wants us to get better. He knows we can't go it alone. That's why he sent us his Theotokos, Mary, Mother of God. Before we experience God's justice, God wishes to show us his Mercy. Mary is the Mother of Mercy. She weeps for each of us. God help the enemies of Mary on judgment day. No one likes to hear lies and filth attributed to their mother. There is an infinite bond of love between this Mother and Her Son! Now the world knew, or at least was told such things. For days, videos and sound recordings of this conference were played on television and radio the world over, preempting sitcoms, movies, and other regular programming, in an assortment of languages from Tienenman to Toronto. They were matched with scenes of the armed troops approaching Mount Desert Island, now known affectionately to the world as MDI. The exploits of Mike Kopp, lobsterman and jeep driver were etched indelibly into the minds of the youth of the world, and into the minds of many of the middle-aged and elderly citizens of the world whose minds had stopped questioning, fighting, and praying a long time prior. No, Mike's exploits were not to lead to a series of copycat jeep thefts, but many began to question why Mike Kopp and company and those people who were over at the pond were so upset. The world may still have accepted Visa, but the carte blanche of the New World Order, the United Nations, The Club of Rome, Masonry, The Trilateral Commission, and related organizations had been recalled. The world now knew that the United States was in trouble. With enemies in the White House and Congress, and in political offices nationwide, a battle was sure in the brewing considering the loss of the Capitol and toll of nature in recent days. The world wept and prayed for America, but no relief came, save heavenly. America foundered. The world's governments, the powers that be were part of the plan spoken of in shadows long ago. This was the awaited day. Their time had come. America was being brought down, as they knew she would be.

****

The crowds were slow to leave Jordan Pond in the next few days and weeks. Yes, for days and weeks after the blessed event Rosary rallies were held spontaneously, by the faithful - and not just at Jordan Pond, they were also held on Cadillac Mountain, at Sand Beach, and elsewhere, too. All summer, wherever one would travel in the park, pilgrims and vacationers alike would be seen with Rosary in hand, praying as they were hiking trails, viewing Thunder Hole, or jogging along the shoreline. The captains of several whale-watching boats returned to the Faith of their Fathers. They could be seen sending beads through their fingers counting Hail Mary's when they were not addressing their patrons pointing out to them one of God's marvelous creations, the whales of the Gulf of Maine – the Humpbacks, Fins, Rights, Minkes, and others. Those who took to the sea in the area had a new appreciation for God's gift of the oceans. Every one of the whale watcher and sightseeing captains claimed to be best friends with lobsterman Mike Kopp. Mike Kopp never knew he had so many friends, and could have used them in days gone by. Mike had returned to his fishing. It was a good year for lobster, and the soft-shells were running now. He was quite busy, as a lobsterman must be to pay for his boat, equipment, and mortgage. His boat was often loaded with vacationers who were allowed to travel on his rounds with him. He was happy to have the frequent company, and would take as many as he could safely carry. He would take no fees for their excursions, but his lobsters rarely made it to market, nearly all being purchased by his daily companions. The vacationers also went home with small American Flags and an inexpensive Rosary and Rosary Booklet too that Mike handed out, in care of Our Lady's Rosary Makers, Auburn Branch.

****

On Monday morning, July 6th, 1998, Father Zdenko was on top of Cadillac Mountain meeting with Steve Lebroq, Park Superintendent. On Sunday, the day before, Steve had the sudden inspiration to build a duplicate of the cross on Mount Krizevac, Medjugorje, right on top of their own Cadillac Mountain. Two architects, three civil engineers, and seven builders were also meeting with Father and Steve. They were in attendance at the conference and had been quick to the challenge when Father had mentioned it at Steve's request. There were hundreds of others who had volunteered weeks of effort if needed to help build it. They were to start this very day. They would not waste a single minute on building a cross on this mountain that would cry out to God to bring conversion and peace to a troubled nation. Certainly it was against the Federal Law, as Steve knew. 'Damn the torpedoes' he thought, 'this nation had broken with God'. His job in jeopardy as it was. Steve put everything into God's hands.

Father Zdenko was able to get the exact dimensions of the cross, and its large base from friends, and the architects and engineers were already at work with pen, paper, and notebook computer on the job site. A park service truck was arriving with stakes, shovels, rakes, concrete finishing tools, and even gas and diesel powered equipment. A large park service truck had just left to purchase the steel reinforcements that would be embedded in the base, stem, and arms of the cross. Regis Beach, an engineer who had often been involved in volunteer projects for Our Lady, was given the unofficial title of Project Coordinator. The materials list was completed. Concrete was being ordered for Tuesday morning. Three more days of sunshine were forecast. Rain would come on Friday, but they would be done long before then.

The cross on Krizevac had been built in 1933 by the people of the neighboring hamlets around Medjugorje. Their crops had often been beset with great damage from storms and hail. They had built the cross in honor of the celebration of 2000 years since Christ's crucifixion, death, and resurrection. They pleaded with God to protect their crops in ensuing years, and offered this cross in return. Everything was carried to the top of the mountain by hand. It was a work of tremendous effort, of great love for the Lord. The cross on Krizevac is 33 feet tall.

"Steve, Regis" said Father Zdenko, who had just come back from a short walk while he was praying the Rosary around the peak of Cadillac. He had been talking to God and Our Lady. "Make the cross one foot taller than the cross of Krizevac. America needs all the help it can get", he said, seriously, but with a thoughtful smile.

"Thirty-four feet" said Regis. "You got it".

"When do you think you'll be done Regis?" asked Steve.

"Thursday. We'll be taking off the last forms on Thursday night. We have to be done Thursday; it's going to be raining on Friday. Father, will you come with me to the concrete company later today? I want to try to match the pebbles – the rocks that are in the cross on Krizevac. If I remember, they're roundish and smooth - like they were gathered from a riverbed or something…"

Father nodded.

The cross would be completed on schedule. The cross was donated by Acadia National Park, assisted by one of the island's patriarchal families. It was built by volunteers. In time, Acadia National Park would hire a large cohort of unemployed UN defectors to defend the cross with their lives. Indeed, the cross was threatened on several occasions, not by vandals, but by the powers that be.

****

Many "old friends" from the conference would be staying on for several weeks more at Acadia, at campgrounds, hotels, and at homes of newfound friends on the island. The Bohatch family, Wayne and Betsy Sherman, the Pierponts, Rick Tremont, the Wesley family, and many of the other speakers and pilgrims were included amongst those who lingered on. In fact, most of them had planned their vacation around the island as it was, prior to learning of any conference. Father Zdenko would remain too. His heart was lifted by the cross being erected. He wanted to be there on Friday in what was to be expected as a pouring rain, to bless the cross! How his heart soared. His patron in heaven, Saint Francis saw the cross going up too. Heaven awaited the cross with open arms!

The visionary Boris had gone back to his home and family on Sunday evening. The flow of vacationers and pilgrims to the island continued strong for weeks following the conference. The number of visitors to the park would be double any prior year's visitation.

Rick and Therese had already asked for permission from her parents to marry. They brought Father Zdenko along to her parents in case of 'trouble'. Francis and Anna Pierpont were happy to give their blessing. They too felt like it would be a marriage literally made in heaven. After all, Our Lady had brought them together. They were making plans for a wedding for which they had already set a date, February 11, 1999, the Feast Day of Our Lady of Lourdes.

****

Regis Beach, and the other architects, engineers and volunteers had come through on schedule. They were gathered with thousands of other pilgrims, and even a new round of vacationers turned pilgrims for the cross dedication and blessing on Friday. Several Bishops were on hand as well. They had graciously deferred the blessing of the cross to Father Zdenko. Rick and Therese were adjacent Father Zdenko, holding hands in the pouring rain. Lightning was not far off. Regis had just finished with the lightning rod for the cross just before the rains came. Paul and Barbara

Bohatch were on the other side of Father Zdenko as he prayed. It was just over eight days ago that the Bohatch family left for a quiet vacation on the coast of Maine.

Surrounding Rick and Therese, and the Bohatch family were the many dozens and hundreds of close friends that the aforementioned vacationers had met on their stay in Maine thus far. In the end, the conference had become a volunteer effort of hundreds, and many of them had stayed on to witness the blessing of the Krizevac Cross on Cadillac. Steve Lebroq and most all of the other adults on the mountain who had been near the heart of the past gathering were shedding copious amounts of tears, though one could hardly tell, due to the rain. There was perhaps five thousand on the mountain for the blessing on Friday, at 10 AM. The lightning was all around now. Only a few motioned to leave. The blessing was given. After the prayers were said, Father walked with the Bishops up the stairs of the multi-tiered base of the cross to bless it with holy water. Commerce and pleasure boats were not to be seen on the Atlantic or in Frenchman's Bay on this day. For the rain was now coming in torrents, and only God knew when it would end. Michael, the aftermath of a hurricane, was unleashing a furry of wind and water. At times the rain seemed to be coming down in horizontal runs on top of Cadillac, now resembling Krizevac. The blessing done, bishops, priests, nuns, pilgrims and vacationers alike dashed off to cars and buses that were lining the road that lead to the top of Krizevac. They had planned to say a Rosary after the blessing, but due to the severe rain, Father Zdenko had requested that the pilgrims pray their Rosary as they were heading to the safety of shelters. Steve Lebroq and his family were taking Father Zdenko to the Portland Airport. It was so hard for the core of the speakers, volunteers, and other pilgrims to depart from each other. They felt like they had been woven together by the fabric of heaven, and now it was shear torture for them to be separated. Those who were left as the greater masses departed were the Marian core of this great effort. It was almost like death to have to leave here. It was like death to old ways. Death to old friends, most of who would never see each other again, until Heaven. It was a sacrifice. Yes, God had brought them all together for a few days of prayer, fasting, penance, Mass, the Rosary, and peace, and now it was over. God was asking them to abandon this haven, this tiny shadow of Heaven that they had come to know. God, in his infinite wisdom, would even have these faithful followers of His Son, and His Mother, even offer the sacrifice of not being able to have a proper goodbye, a blessed farewell. They could hardly hear each other on that mountain now, the furry of Michael was pelting all of New England, and they were perched now, high in the midst of the storm. And so it was that as Paul and Barbara Bohatch went around hugging everyone, not all could make out what they were saying.

"We have to go", they said. The wind blew, and the rain beat hard. The noise was near deafening.

"What?" said some of their friends.

"We have to go," said Paul and Barbara Bohatch again.

"What?", they said.

"We have to go", Paul and Barbara shouted again as they were going around hugging all of their friends. Their youngest children were already in the van, awaiting the parents and siblings. A new and sudden wave of wind swept across the mountaintop.

"We have to go," said Paul and Barbara to Rick and Therese, as they embraced each other dearly.

"What?" said Rick and Therese. The wind was howling now. It was a rare day on Cadillac the likes of which had seldom ever before been seen.

"We have to go," said Paul and Barbara, crying their hearts out.

"We'll see you at camp", shouted Rick and Therese, finally understanding what the Paul and Barbara had said.

"No. Home. We're going home", shouted Paul to the wind, his heart ready to break. He thought he was going to have a heart attack the pain was so great. He didn't care. Barbara felt the same. She felt like she was leaving her younger sister behind in Therese. She didn't want to leave any of her newfound friends.

"What?" said Rick.

"Home! We're going home. We love you! God Bless you!" said Paul and Barbara at the top of their lungs, hugging everybody in sight.

"Goodbye Father", shouted Paul. The rain came. Another howl. Another gust. The rain was now actually being swept upward from down in the valleys below at times.

"What?" said Father Zdenko.

"Home", shouted Paul and Barbara again in unison.

"Heaven?", shouted Father, smiling.

"Funny man", shouted Barbara.

"Some Rosary Rally! Keep it up!", shouted Father. Father turned his back to the rain as best he could and blessed the Bohatch family and their children. Tears were flying everywhere as well as the rain. "Gospodin s vama!" (The Lord be with you), he yelled again. "Sveta Marijo, Majko Bozja, moli za nas gresnike sada I na cas smrti nase. Amen! (Holy Mary, Mother of God, pray for us sinners now and at the hour of our death. Amen!) Goodbye", Father shouted in his loudest litany ever.

Paul was now embracing Rick again. Barbara was embracing Therese. Therese and Barbara were almost blown over by the force of the wind. "Telephone", shouted Barbara.

"Yes", shouted Therese. "Steubenville. I'll call you", she shouted again.

"Thanks", shouted Paul with his bloodshot eyes, the rain beating into them as he looked at and tried to communicate to Rick. "Thanks for everything", he shouted.

"Nemo problemo! It was fun. Let's do it again sometime", screamed Rick at the top of his lungs so most of the remaining group of friends could hear. Paul gave Rick and Therese another hug, and he and Barbara dashed off to their car with their older children who were being embraced by Father Zdenko. They waved to all as they made a dash to their van and the now crying younger children.

Father, and Steve and Emily Lebroq gave a last round of hugs and words of love, friendship, and encouragement to the remaining pilgrims and dashed off to the Lebroq's car and waiting children.

Therese's parents and relatives were now heading back to Bar Harbor for shelter and food. They would see the Shermans back at camp. The Wesley family would be around for a while yet, as well as Luke & Alice Miller and their children, Father Green, the Louis Longmire and his newly reclaimed family, the Lebroqs of course, and a host of others. The pain for Rick and Therese, and all parties, some staying, some departing, would decrease in time, and give way to eternal joy in Heaven for those who continue on to run the good race.

All had abandoned the mountain now. All except for the engaged international couple, the Ohio Buckeye and the French Canadian. They sat on the steps on the base of the Cross on Cadillac, hugging each other, and staring out into the tumultuous Atlantic. They stayed there all day in the pouring rain, never seeking shelter. Neither had eaten yet on this glorious, wet Friday. They had offered up their hunger today for Our Lady, and for all of the pilgrims who had come, and those who would yet come to this great island on the Atlantic Coast, to honor the Mother of God. Even the seagulls had been grounded. All day.

As evening came, the young couple made their way, once again, down Cadillac Mountain. It was dark before they reached the base. The rain was ongoing. The island streams were dangerously swollen over. God was speaking. Was the world listening?

****

Later, at Rosalie's Restaurant, Therese was able to phone Bar Harbor Campground and ask the campground personnel if they could let her parents know that she was O.K., and was at Rosalie's Restaurant in town. They were happy to do so. The woman on the other end of the phone was Mrs. Lafayette. She had been to the conference. The campground personnel knew whom Therese and Rick were, and were very happy that they were staying at their campground. The dispatch was sent.

"You know," said Rick, sipping his tap beer at the booth that he and Therese were seated at, "my life would be complete if I only knew what Conteechi, no... Conteeky meant".

"You mean Kon-Tiki," said Therese. She spelled it for him. "That's a no-brainer Rick," said Therese, as she sipped the beer they were sharing while they awaited for the best pizza in the world. Kon-Tiki was a pagan high priest of sorts, and the sun-king of the legendary white skinned race spoken of in the legends of the Incas. Many researchers think that his race may have originally populated the Polynesian islands, long before known white seafarers from Europe arrived. They think that he and his people were driven out of Peru. They called him the sun god; for lack of proper 'Christian upbringing' said Therese, looking deep into Rick's eyes, piercing him with her beautiful smile.

"Oh", she said. "It was a boat too. The Kon-Tiki, a balsa wood log raft that was named after this fellow Kon-Tiki. Several Norwegians and a couple of Swedes I believe, wanted to see if Kon-Tiki could have made his getaway to Polynesia from South America by balsa wood raft. The people in the know said no way. Four months and 4300 miles later the rafters were in Tahiti or thereabouts. They proved it could be done. Now, here's the clincher, I am a distant relative of Thor Heyerdahl, on my mother's side. Thor Heyerdahl was the Norwegian who put this seagoing expedition together in 1947. Now what in the world are you doing asking me about Kon-Tiki?" said Therese.

"Get out of this town! I can't believe it. I'm on a vacation made in heaven. God..." said Rick, about to explain.

"What?" said Therese. "What? Tell me?"

"Somebody up there sure has a sense humor!" said Rick.

"Rick Tremont, get a hold of yourself!" said Therese with a perplexed smile on her face. "What is going through that mind of yours."

"Sun god! Very funny!" said Rick.

"OK, I'm cutting off your beer until you let me in on this!" said Therese, quite enjoying herself in the humor of the moment. She politely grabbed the beer in front of him and took possession of it. She took a sip wondering where the conversation, or lack of it, was going. *My fiancee! He is a funny man. A holy, funny man! Thank you God - I do believe you brought him to me! I believe! You sent him to jail to keep him for me! Thank you! Thank you! Thank you!*

The cat still had Rick's tongue. He was lost in his thoughts from a week ago. *'Oh God, I'm here for God, what am I thinking about marriage for... Wait. He brought me here. Jesus introduced me. I'm going to marry that girl! Jesus, perhaps you don't want me to be a priest after all! You brought me here to meet Therese! How can I know for sure? Jesus! Before this vacation is over, let me know!...'*

Almost The End

****

Epilogue

Frank's wife was yelling at him to put the stupid book down. The kids were screaming, and he'd been neglecting her and the children. Yesterday he had missed a plumbing call and income because he couldn't tear himself away from his book. His wife was seething. She knew that a man should not let his reading interfere with his livelihood. Frank was a plumber.

"Do you know how much that stupid book has cost us?" Frank's wife yelled at him. "You missed two plumbing calls this week. And Father Redlyle has warned the parish about all of these stupid "end of the world" books coming out. All these supposed visionaries. He said it's unhealthy. He said it would be better for the world if all of these supposed visionaries and authors would drop dead and leave us alone. He said the books are poisoning the parish and the diocese. He said everybody's running up to him saying 'Pope John Paul II says do this, Pope John Paul says do that. Why aren't you doing it this way Father? Why aren't you doing it the way the Pope says Father?' He's fed up with the books his parish is reading, and he's going to talk to the Bishop about it! And here you are, keeping the market for that trash going strong. I looked at the last page of that book. Something about a sun god! Stupid books. You're always complaining about the New Age trash in the Church and in the world. Now if that book isn't New Age garbage I don't know what is. Sun god!

Huh! Don't leave that book around for the kids to see. I don't want your strange books putting dangerous thoughts in the their heads…"

"Look honey, I worked 45 hours in the past week. I couldn't take another call. I wanted to, but I couldn't. I'm beat. And look, it's not just this book. Aren't we reading a little of the Bible together everyday with the kids, and the Catechism too? We're praying the daily Rosary together. And Father, Oh God. We're not supposed to talk about priests. Jesus told a bunch of saints that. So I won't use his name. Look, first we pioneered altar girls at our church, then pancakes instead of unleavened bread at Mass. Now, I've heard "Sister You Know Who" has supposedly said a make pretend Mass for twenty parishioners. We're more concerned about how much bingo is making than souls. There's only one other family in our whole parish that we know of that is using Natural Family Planning. The Church is sponsoring a trip to Disney World, an archenemy of the Catholic Church. The catechism that the kids are using at Church, the so called Catholic Catechism for kids that they're using for the younger ones is filthy, full of false teachings and sex indoctrination – they call it education. They try to disguise some of it as so-called chastity education. They should just use the Pope's Catechism across the board. This unnamed priest is calling for women to be allowed into the priesthood, and might just as well be giving out condoms at school and to parishioners because everybody knows what he says about that stuff in the confessional. When Mother Teresa died last year, she was hardly mentioned from the pulpit - and misquoted at that. When John Denver died a few weeks later he was praised from the pulpit in homilies unending for his environmentalism and stewardship for 'Mother Earth' - and my God, he was as pro-death for the unborn babies as they came, even playing music at pro-abort fund raisers. I mean, I loved his music, and I hope he made it 'home', but the babies… Save the whales and seals, kill more babies… My God… The New-Agers never had a greater spokesman than John Denver…

"…And then there's the Church bulletin which could very well have been written by the pro-aborts at the UN and their Mother Earth loving ambassadors. Our parish is allowing 'We Are Church' and 'Common Ground' to use Church facilities. Two of our parish counsel members are Masons, Freemasons. "Father You Know Who" knows it. Now you're telling me the priest is upset with his parish reading about both approved and as of yet unapproved apparitions and messages telling people to pray, fast, go to confession, do penance, pray the Rosary, go to daily Mass, and follow the Pope. Honey, I think we have a problem. I think we need to find a new devout Catholic parish, one that's going to stick it out with the

Pope through everything that is coming at us in the next few years. I think we need to homeschool the children. I..."

"Don't you dare pull the children out of Catholic school or I'll leave you! They're going to get into Notre Dame if it's the last thing they do..."

"Honey, do you know what Notre Dame means?" quipped Frank.

"Yeah, it's Latin. It means, um, ah, some old Catholic type of phrase. Well, I don't know, it's some Catholic religious order or something..."

"Our Lady" said Frank.

"What?" replied Frank's wife.

"Nothing honey. I'm ordering books from Seton Home School tomorrow. I'm going out for a coffee; I've got a headache. I'll get the milk you asked me to get before. I'll be back soon. ...Love you. If the Pope calls, tell him I'll get back with him. No, just tell him I'm with him..."

****

THIS <u>IS</u> THE END

Copyright 1998 Roger C. Thibault